The Break

The Break

MARIAN KEYES

MICHAEL JOSEPH
an imprint of
PENGUIN BOOKS

MICHAEL JOSEPH

UK | USA | Canada | Ireland | Australia
India | New Zealand | South Africa

Michael Joseph is part of the Penguin Random House group of companies
whose addresses can be found at global.penguinrandomhouse.com.

First published 2017

001

Text copyright © Marian Keyes, 2017

The moral right of the author has been asserted

Set in 13/15.5 pt Garamond MT Std
Typeset by Jouve (UK), Milton Keynes
Printed in Great Britain by Clays Ltd, St Ives plc

A CIP catalogue record for this book is available from the British Library

HARDBACK ISBN: 978–0–718–17972–4
TPB ISBN: 978–0–718–17973–1

For Louise Moore, with love and gratitude

Before

I

Friday, 9 September 2016

'Myself and Hugh,' I say. 'We're taking a break.'

'A city-with-fancy-food sort of a break?' Maura narrows her eyes. 'Or a Rihanna sort of a break?'

'Well?' She presses her case. 'Is it the city-with-fancy-food break?'

'No, it's –'

'The Rihanna kind? You've *got* to be joking me, because Rihanna is – what? – twenty-two and you're –'

'Not twenty-two.' It's imperative to shut her down before she utters my age. I don't know how I got to be forty-four. Clearly I'd my eye off the ball but, a bit late to the party, I'm trying to air-brush away all references to it. It's not just the fear-of-dying and, worse, the fear-of-becoming-jowly, it's because I work in PR, a dynamic, youthful sector, which does not value the 'less-young' among us. I've bills to pay, I'm simply being practical here.

So I avoid any stating of my age, like, *ever,* in the hope that if no one says it, no one will know about it and I can stay age-free until the end of time. (My one regret is that I didn't adopt this attitude when I was twenty-seven, but I knew nothing when I was twenty-seven.)

'I'm your sister,' Maura says. 'I'm seven years older than you, so if I'm fifty-one –'

'Of course,' I say very, very quickly, talking over her, to shut her up. 'Of course, of course, of course.' Maura has never worried about getting old. For as long as I can remember she's been ancient, more like Pop's twin sister than his eldest child.

'So it's a "break" where Hugh can go off – where?'

'South East Asia.'

'Seriously? And then . . . what?'

3

'He'll come back.'

'What if he doesn't?'

It was the worst idea ever to admit my news to Maura, but she has a knack for getting the truth out of people. (We call her the Waterboarder.) She can always smell a story. She's known something's been up with me for the past five days – I thought I'd be okay if I kept ducking her calls but clearly I have a strong delusional streak because it was only a matter of time before she showed up at my work and refused to leave until she knew everything.

'Look, nothing is definite,' I try. 'He might not go.' Because he might not.

'You can't let him,' she announces. 'Just tell him he can't and let that be an end to it.'

If only it was that simple. She hadn't read Hugh's letter so she didn't know the torment he was in. Letting him leave was my best chance of saving my marriage. Probably.

'Is it to do with his dad dying?'

I nod. Hugh's dad died eleven months ago, and Hugh had shut down. 'I thought that if enough time passed he'd be okay.'

'But he isn't. He's the opposite of okay.' She's getting worked up. 'This effing family. When will the drama stop? It's like playing Whac-A-Mole.' Maura's rages are familiar and they no longer have the power to utterly terrify me. 'No sooner is one of you toeing the line than another of you blows your life up. Why are you all such disasters?' She means me and my siblings and, actually, we aren't. Well, no more than any other family, which is to say, quite a lot, but so is everyone else's, so we're fairly normal, really.

'It must be my fault,' she declares. 'Was I a bad role model?'

'Yes.'

In actual fact she was the least bad role model that ever lived, but she's upset me. Surely, all things considered, I'm deserving of sympathy.

'You're so cruel!' she says. 'You try being a little girl' (she means herself) 'whose mum is in hospital for months on end with

4

tuberculosis at a time when tuberculosis wasn't even a *thing*, when it was years out of date. A little girl who has four younger brothers and sisters, who won't stop crying, and a big, cold house, which is falling to bits, and a dad who can't cope. Yes, I have an over-developed sense of responsibility but . . .'

I know the speech and could do a word-perfect recitation, but closing her down when she's in full flow is next to impossible. (My siblings and I like to joke that her husband TPB – The Poor Bastard – developed spontaneous mutism shortly after their wedding and that no one has heard him speak for the past twenty-one years. We insist that the last words he'd ever been heard saying – in tones of great doubt – were 'I do . . . ?')

'What's going on?' I ask, baffled by her antipathy. 'I haven't done anything wrong.'

'Yet,' she says. 'Yet!'

'What are you saying?'

She seems surprised. 'If your husband is "on a break" from your marriage' – she does the quotation marks with her fingers – 'then aren't you' – more quotation marks – '"on a break" too?'

It takes a few moments for her words to sink in. Then, to my great surprise, something stirs in me, something hopeful that, after the last five horrible days, feels like the sweetest relief. In a small recess of my soul a tiny pilot light sparks into life.

Slowly, I say, 'Seeing as you put it like that, well, I suppose I am.'

Now that she's got what she came for, Maura gathers up her stuff, a sturdy brown briefcase and a waterproof jacket.

'Please, Maura,' I say fiercely. 'You are *not* to tell the others.'

'But they're your family!' How has she managed to make this sound like a curse? 'And Hugh hasn't been coming for the Friday dinners for ages. They know something's wrong.'

'I'm serious, Maura. The girls don't know yet and they can't find out from Chinese whispers.' I pause. Are we allowed to say 'Chinese whispers', these days? Best not to take chances. 'They can't find out from stray gossip.' Not as colourful, but it would have to do.

'Have you not even told Derry?' Maura sounds surprised.

Derry is our other sister and, at just fifteen months older than me, we're close.

'Look, it may not actually happen. He mightn't go.'

For the first time, compassion appears on her face. 'You're in denial.'

'I'm in something,' I admit. 'Shock, I think.' But there's also shame, fear, sorrow, guilt and, yes, denial, in the mix, everything tangled together in one horrible snarl-up.

'Are you still okay to do the dinner tonight?'

'Yep.' Friday dinner at Mum and Pop's house is a tradition that has endured for at least a decade. Mum isn't hardy enough to cater every week for the numbers who turn up – my siblings, their children, their partners and their ex-partners (oh, yes, very modern, we are) – so the catering rotates week by week. 'Any idea how many are coming tonight?' I ask.

There is such a clatter of O'Connells that it's impossible to ever establish an exact number for catering purposes. Every Friday texts zip to and fro, cancelling and confirming, adding and subtracting, and the one number you can be sure it *won't* be is the number you think it is. But whatever the headcount, it's best to cater for a multitude. God forbid that they run out of food on your watch: you'll never be let forget it.

'Me,' Maura says, listing on her fingers. 'You. Not Hugh, obviously.'

I flinch.

A gentle knock on the door interrupts us. Thamy's head appears. 'Incoming in five,' she says.

'You've to go,' I say to Maura. 'I've a meeting.'

'On a Friday afternoon?' Maura's antennae are quivering. 'Who has a meeting on a Friday afternoon? Someone's in trouble, right?'

'Please,' I say. 'Out.'

Hatch, the tiny agency that I'm one-third of, does all kinds of PR, including Image Management. We rehabilitate politicians, sports-people, actors – public figures of one sort or another who've been publicly shamed. It used to be all about sex scandals but, these days, the opportunities to disgrace yourself have expanded – accusations of racism, that's a big one – which will, quite rightly, lose you your job. Sexism, ageism and size-ism are all dicey, as is bullying, stealing small objects, such as Putin's pen, or parking in a disabled spot when you're not disabled.

Of course, the methods of public shaming have also changed: back in the day, badzers lived in terror of the front page of a Sunday tabloid. But because in today's world everything is caught on phones, the fear is of going viral.

'Any freebies?' Maura asks, as Thamy and I hustle her through the main office and towards the exit.

'Give her some incontinence pants,' I tell Thamy. EverDry is one of our biggest clients and, grim as it sounds, incontinence is a huge growth area.

'Ah, here!' Maura says. 'I'm far from incontinent. Is there no chocolate? Oh, hi, Alastair . . .'

Alastair has just got in from London, so he's looking particularly impressive in his high-end suit and crisp white shirt. He fixes

7

Maura with his silvery eyes, then slowly unleashes The Smile. He is *pathetic*. 'Hi, Maura,' he says, his voice low and intimate.

'Hi,' she squeaks, a flush roaring up from her neck.

'Chocolate?' Alastair says. 'Hold on . . .'

Hatch represent an artisanal chocolate-maker, which is a torment because samples are sent to the office and sometimes it's just too exhausting to resist them.

Alastair grabs a box of chocolates from the cupboard, then a couple of body scrubs made from turf (I *know*). As a small gesture of defiance, I add a pack of incontinence pants to the pile.

Thamy shepherds my sister towards the stairs so she won't bump into Mrs EverDry coming up in the lift. Thamy is a godsend – originally from Brazil, she's our Reception, Invoicing and Goods Inward departments, all in one charming package. She can persuade the most reluctant of debtors to cough up, is never huffy about making coffee and, unlike all of her predecessors, isn't a half-wit. Far from it. (I'm worried now about having used the word 'half-wit' – people have been Twitter-shamed for less. Rehabilitating disgraced people makes you very cognizant of these things.)

Alastair and I make our way to the small conference room, the room in which Maura has just extracted my sad secret from me. (The Hatch premises are tiny because tiny is all we can afford. Mind you, I work from London two days a week, where we can't afford *any* office space.)

There's no time to brush my hair so I ask Alastair, 'Do I look okay?'

When people hear I work in public relations, they can barely hide their surprise. Women PRs are usually tall, bone-thin, blonde and aloof; they wear tight white skirt suits that hug their cellulite-free flanks; their smiles are icy and their auras are positively glacial. Hamstrung as I am with shortness and a tendency to roundness, which I need to watch like a hawk, I certainly don't look the part. It's just as well I'm good at my job.

'Dishevelled can be charming.' Alastair says. 'Makes you seem likeable. But . . .' he begins to straighten my collar '. . . maybe today a little *too* messy?'

I move his hand away. He's far too free and easy when it comes to touching women. Nevertheless my dress is crumpled and my internal unravelling can't start manifesting in my appearance. My mind races through possible ways to upgrade my look. Ironing my work clothes: that would be a good, solid start.

With a stab of wild hope, I wonder about doing something magical with my hair. Maybe cut six inches off it? But that would be tantamount to self-harm – my hair is nothing but good to me. A little needy, perhaps, and, according to magazine articles, far too long for a woman in her forties, but it's the most glamorous thing I possess.

How about the colour? Is it finally time to move on from dark brown and embrace a more age-appropriate lighter hue?

My hairdresser had given me the well-worn lecture about how skin tones fade as a woman ages. 'Keep dyeing your hair this dark,' he'd said, 'and you'll look like you've been embalmed.'

'I know what "they" say,' I'd said, 'I do, Lovatt. But in this instance "they" are wrong. I'm an exception. Or a freak, if you prefer.'

He didn't prefer. His mouth tightened mutinously and he dried my roots matron-bouffy as punishment.

'Doing anything nice for the weekend?' Alastair asks.

I think about Hugh's plans to run away. About the need to tell the girls. About this being the end of my life as I know it. I shrug. 'Nothing much. You?'

'A course.' He looks a little abashed.

'Another of your Learn the Secret to Happiness in Forty-eight Hours things? Alastair,' I say helplessly, 'you're looking for something that doesn't exist.'

He seems to devote a weekend a month to Healing the Wounds of Childhood, or Emptiness in the Age of Plenty, or similar, but so far none of them has worked.

'Here's the secret to happiness,' I say. 'Drink as heavily as you can get away with. Buy stuff. And, if all else fails, spend three days in bed eating doughnuts. How do you think the rest of us manage?'

Before Alastair can defend himself, Tim, the third partner in Hatch, comes in.

All three of us – Tim, Alastair and I – used to work together in a big Irish PR agency, but about five years ago we got laid off. As part of his relentless quest, Alastair went to an ashram in India, which he was asked to leave because he wouldn't stop shagging yoga-bunny acolytes. I spent a few grim years in the freelancing wilderness, and Tim went back to college and qualified as an accountant. This tells you all you need to know about the three different energies that Alastair, Tim and I bring to the table.

We set up our little agency about two and a half years ago and we lurch from month to month, wondering if we'll still be operational in thirty days' time. It's an anxious way to live. So anxious that I have chronic gastritis and one of my main food groups is Zantac. My (twelve-year-old) GP told me to excise all stress and I'd nodded obediently but in my head I was saying, all sarcastic-like, 'You *think*?' Then she told me to lose a couple of pounds and I wanted to weep: that weight was a by-product of giving up cigarettes. It made me consider just doing all the bad stuff and dying an early death but at least I'd have enjoyed my life.

And here comes Mrs EverDry, stout and scary in her tailored dress, and we're all on our feet, warmly welcoming her. Maura had it wrong when she deduced that a Friday-afternoon meeting indicated a crisis: it's when Mrs EverDry likes to receive her monthly progress report. She lives in some rural opposite-of-idyll and it suits her to come to Dublin on a weekend 'for the shops'.

'You.' She points at me.

Shite. What have I done? Or not done?

'I hear you're Neeve Aldin's mother,' she says. 'Neeve Aldin of *Bitch, Please* fame?'

'Oh? Ah. Yes!'

'I watch her make-up vlogs with my fourteen-year-old. She's gas craic, makes us both laugh.'

'Well . . . ah . . . *great*.'

'Mind you, I'm nearly in the poorhouse from having to buy the stuff she pushes. You wouldn't ask her to showcase some cheaper brands?'

'I can try!' There's not an *earthly* that Neeve would listen to me.

'How come she has a different surname to you?'

'She's from my first marriage. Goes by her dad's name.'

'That's that mystery cleared up. Let's get started.'

Off we go and Mrs EverDry is pleased with some of our progress – we got a mention on *Coronation Street*. 'But I've decided that we need an ambassador,' she says.

Her words fall into stunned silence. 'The public face of the brand.'

We know what an ambassador is, we just don't know how to tell her she's totally delusional.

'Interesting . . .' I'm playing for time.

'Don't you "interesting" me,' she says.

Alastair's got to be the one to neutralize this – she *loves* him. 'Mrs Mullen,' he says gently. 'It won't be easy to find someone willing to publicly admit to incontinence.'

'We just need one person,' she says. 'Then everyone will be at it.'

And she's right. It's not so long since having cancer was a secret, or when no one would own up to an Alzheimer's diagnosis.

'Everyone's incontinent!' Mrs EverDry declares. She looks at Alastair, and her tone softens. 'Well, maybe not you. You're perfect.'

'I have more things wrong with me than you could ever imagine.' Alastair thinks he's being charming but I agree with him.

Mrs EverDry studies Tim. 'I'd say you aren't incontinent either.'

'I'm too young,' Tim says.

'And too uptight.'

We all snort with unexpected laughter. Mrs EverDry is our most important client, but you couldn't help liking her.

Now she turns her gaze on me. 'I couldn't claim incontinence,' I say apologetically, 'but my bladder certainly isn't what it was.'

'Maybe not everyone's incontinent *yet*,' Mrs EverDry concedes. 'But soon they will be. Because we're all living too long.'

Which is exactly the point that Hugh had been trying to make when he broke his terrible news to me. The tiny pilot light of hope that Maura's visit had lit is abruptly extinguished and, once again, I'm sad and scared.

3

I'd been well aware that Hugh was suffering – his dad had died, it was only to be expected, and as his mum had been dead for eight years he was now officially an orphan.

None of my family of origin had died yet, but I'd absorbed enough from our *Dr Phil* culture to know that bereavement affects everyone differently and all I could do for Hugh was be there for him. But although I urged him to cry, he didn't shed a tear. And, though permission was tacitly granted for a spell of excessive drinking, he stuck to his usual few bottles of ludicrously named craft beer. I even offered to accompany him snowboarding, in spite of being worried about the state of me in the padded clothing, but he had no interest.

I tried to keep his life as stress-free as possible – which mostly involved defusing tension between him and Neeve – and I'd often ask, 'Would you like to talk?'

But talking was the last thing he wanted to do.

Not much riding either, since we're on the subject. And maybe we weren't, but it has to be said. In fact, in the aftermath of his dad's death, very little of his time was spent in bed. He stayed up late, binge-watching crime things, and was always awake before me in the mornings.

Then one Thursday, maybe four or five months after the funeral, I'd bumped awake around six a.m. Hugh wasn't in bed with me and his spot was cold. Although his car was still outside, he was nowhere in the house. Extremely uneasy, I rang him, and when he didn't pick up, my imagination went to the darkest places. We hear so much about men and suicide, how it happens – seemingly – without warning.

Hugh didn't do anguish. As a rule, he was very steady and, paradoxically, it was this very steadiness that had me convinced he was in the danger zone – too much of a stoic, bottling stuff up.

In a panic, I threw on some clothes and drove around Dundrum, searching for him in the March dawn.

Marley Park seemed like the obvious choice – all those trees – but no one was there so I circled the residential streets in our neighbourhood for probably an hour, a very long one, until my phone rang. It was him. I'd worked myself up into such a state that I could hardly believe his voice. 'Where are you?' he asked.

'Where are *you*?'

'At home.'

'Stay there.'

He claimed he'd gone for a walk. I believed him, but it was deeply unsettling. Running, even middle-of-the-night running, is fairly normal, right? Walking, though, seemed a bit weird.

'I was worried about you,' I said. 'I thought you might have –'

'No. I'd never do that.'

'But I don't know what's going on with you.'

'Yeah.' He'd sighed. 'I don't know what's going on with me either.'

'Sweetie,' I'd said. 'I think it's time you saw someone about anti-depressants.'

After a long silence he'd said, 'Okay.'

Then I was really freaked out. Hugh would do anything to avoid going to the doctor – if his leg fell off he'd dismiss it as a mere flesh wound even as he hopped in place to stop himself toppling over.

But he went and he got a prescription for Seroxat. (Which I knew were 'entry-level' SSRIs – as a middle-class, middle-aged woman, my life was filled with people who had either been on anti-depressants or knew someone who had.)

Even though he took the tablets, Hugh continued to disappear regularly in the middle of the night, and when I told my sister Derry, she said, 'You don't think he's, you know, dropping in on some unaccompanied lady?'

Of *course* the thought had crossed my mind, but instinct told me that whatever internal tussle was taking place in Hugh, it wasn't about extra-curricular riding.

So I sat him down for another chat and suggested he see a grief counsellor.

'What would that achieve?' he asked, his eyes dead.

That stumped me. I knew nothing about the ins and outs of counselling sessions. But ... 'Lots of people who've been bereaved find them helpful.'

'How much would it cost?'

'I could find out.'

'How many times would I have to go?'

'I think it varies.'

'You think it might help me?'

'Well, it helps other people. Why should you be any different?'

'Okay.' He exhaled heavily. 'Maybe I'd better.' Then, 'I can't go on like this.'

That terrified me. 'Sweetie, what do you mean?'

'Just . . . I can't go on like this.'

'Like what?'

'Everything seems pointless.'

'Tell me. Please.'

He shook his head. 'Nothing to tell. Just everything seems pointless.'

I knew better than to say that things weren't pointless. But to witness his pain and be unable to reach him was maddeningly frustrating. We, who'd been so, so close, were light years from each other.

Alastair was my go-to person for all matters related to emotional growth. He gave me the name of a psychotherapist who specialized in bereavement. 'She's spendy,' he warned me.

But I didn't care. Any money was worth it if it coaxed Hugh from his silent, flat-eyed misery.

After the first session I asked Hugh, 'How did it go?'

His face expressionless, he said, 'I don't know.'

'Will you go again?'

'Yeah. Next week. She says I have to commit to ten weeks.'

'Okay. Good. Great, Hugh. Well done.'

He stared at me, as if he didn't know who I was.

So, for several Thursdays in a row, Hugh went to the counsellor. I tried not to quiz him about it, but always managed a breezy, 'How'd it go?'

Usually he shrugged and made noncommittal noises, but towards the end of the course, he said, his tone without inflection, 'I don't think it's working.'

My spirits plummeted, but I forced cheer into my voice and said, 'Give it time.'

What kept me positive was the hope that once we'd got past the first anniversary of his father's death things might ease up for him.

Then the most horrific thing happened: Hugh's friend died, a man he'd known since he was five years old. The nature of the death was particularly dreadful: Gavin had been stung by a wasp and gone into anaphylactic shock. No one had known he was allergic to wasp stings – the entire thing was a bolt from the blue.

I was sorry for Gavin's wife, for his children, for his parents and sibling – but, to my shame, I was more concerned about Hugh. This was bound to impact on him profoundly. Any healing he might have done in the months since his dad had died would surely be negated.

And so it proved. Instantly Hugh abandoned his counselling sessions and left the room whenever I brought up the subject. He began skipping work and spent hour upon hour watching Netflix. He stopped seeing his friends, opted out of all family events and barely spoke.

In July, he, the girls and I went on holiday to Sardinia, me desperate with hope that the sunshine might effect some healing. But all he did was sit in silence and watch the sea with a six-mile stare, while the rest of us tiptoed anxiously around him.

Once we were back home, I realized, with no little despair, that all I could do was wait things out, and that it was likely to be a very long wait.

However, about three weeks ago, we were invited to a drinks thing – someone's birthday – and, to my surprise, he agreed to come. My heart leapt with hope and the ever-present knot in my stomach unwound slightly.

But soon after we got there, my arch-frenemy Genevieve Payne descended on us.

'Hugh! Hello, stranger.' She began stroking his arm. 'The eyes on this man!' she said. 'So blue! So sexy! You know, Amy, if Hugh was my husband, I'd never let him out of bed.'

This was her normal lark with him. My mouth went, 'Ha-ha-ha,' while my eyes went, 'Please can I bury an axe in your head?'

In the past, Hugh had always received her attentions in a strong and silent fashion – not shrugging her off but not leading her on either. You know, *polite*. He knew how her slinky confidence intimidated me.

But this time he turned and smiled at her – I hadn't seen him smile in the last year. Genevieve reddened, she actually looked embarrassed, and something inside me felt very cold and scared.

Driving home I said, 'You can have an affair with anyone in the whole world except for Genevieve Payne.'

Whenever I said that – and I said it every time I saw her – Hugh would reply, 'Babe, I won't have an affair with anyone ever.' But this time he said, 'Okay.' No 'babe'. And just 'Okay.'

I opened my mouth, then thought, No, let it go.

Fast-forward to last Saturday evening, when we were at home, alone. Hugh was at the kitchen table, tapping away on his iPad for hours. A quick look over his shoulder established that he was doing something with figures. I thought nothing of it but on a return visit, ages later, he was still at it.

'What are you doing?'

He hesitated and, whatever way he did it, a thin thread of dread unfurled in my gut. 'Our finances.'

I stared at him for a long, silent beat. This didn't make sense. Only two months earlier, our ropy finances had enjoyed a major facelift because his dad's house had finally sold. The proceeds were divvied up between Hugh and his three brothers, and after we'd ring-fenced Sofie and Kiara's college fees, got braces for Kiara's wonky teeth, repaired our glitchy house-alarm system, fixed the leak in Neeve's bedroom, gone on the holiday to Sardinia and paid off our credit cards, what remained might have bought half a car. (A mid-range car, I don't mean a fancy one.)

As we'd never known financial equilibrium, the unprecedented situation of not worrying if our card would be declined with every transaction we made was joyous.

But to have *an actual fund of actual cash* to play with had nearly toppled me over the edge. I began uttering the phrase 'nest egg', even though heretofore it was the most irritatingly smug thing I'd ever heard.

I had great plans for the 'nest egg' and assembled a lengthy wish list – replacing our unpredictable boiler, getting a much-needed new couch, paying off a tiny amount of our mortgage, or even – this was a secret, desperate hope – sending Hugh and me on a modest mini-break, just the two of us, in the hope that some-how we'd reconnect.

Nothing explained the lengthy calculations Hugh had been doing all evening and I could have pressed the issue but something – fear? – advised me to say nothing.

The very next night, after the girls had gone to bed, he said to me, 'We need to talk.'

That is a sentence no one ever wants to hear. But, as Hugh had barely addressed a syllable to me in the previous year, I was definitely . . . *interested*, I suppose.

He handed me a glass of wine. 'Can we sit at the kitchen table?'

A talk where I had to be softened up with alcohol? A talk where we'd be *facing* each other?

I took a big swig of wine, went to the kitchen, sat at the table and took another swig of wine. 'Off you go.'

Hugh stared downwards, as if the secrets of the universe were written in the limed oak. 'I love you.' He flicked a glance at me and his eyes burnt with sincerity. Then he resumed his study of the table. 'I want to stay married to you.'

Good words, yes, nice words, the *right* words. However, any fool could see that a great big BUT was hanging over us like a block of concrete.

'But?' I prompted.

His hand clenched his beer bottle and it was a moment before he spoke. 'I'd like a break.'

Bad. This was bad, bad, *bad*.

'Could you look at me?' If I could see him, it might be possible to stop this.

'Sorry.' He sat up straight, and the sight of his face, full-on, was kind of a surprise, because when you've been with someone a long time, you rarely bother to study them properly. He looked exhausted.

'I'm not expressing myself well.' He sounded miserable. 'I've written it down in a letter. Can I show it to you?' He slid his iPad across the table.

My angel,

I love you. I will always love you. I want us to be together always.

But I want something else. I need more.

I guess it's because of Dad, then Gavin. All I can think about is the complete futility of life; we get one go, it's very short, and then we die. I feel I haven't done enough with my life. Enough for me. I love Neeve, Sofie and Kiara with everything I've got but I feel I've spent a lot of time putting them ahead of me. I want some time where I put me first.

And as I write this, it sounds so selfish, and I'm aware of all the other people who have terrible lives they can't escape. I know you also feel like your time is constantly colonized and that you're always last on the list. But I feel like I'm being buried alive and that I'll burst if I don't change something. This is destroying me and I can't keep going.

I know it will hurt you and I hate myself for that, but I can't stop my thoughts. I want to stay for you but I need to go for me. It's like being torn in two in a trap.

Yes, it's a mid-life crisis, but I don't want a sports car, I just want some freedom. I really think this will be the best for us in the long run.

I want us to grow old together. I want us to be together till the end.

It's not simply a sex thing. I know you'll worry that it is, but that's not the reason.

This isn't a cowardly way of saying I want us to split up. I love you, I love our life together, I will always love you, and after six months I promise to come back.

Hugh

Jesus Christ. Jesus *Christ*.

Just as well I was sitting down because I was dizzy. He looked at me, his eyes searching, and I stared back, like he was a stranger.

'Amy?'

'I . . . God, I don't know what to . . .'

'It's big, I know,' he said. 'I'm sorry, Amy. I'm so sorry. I hate doing this to you. I don't want to feel this way. I've tried to stop it but it keeps coming back.'

I scanned the words again and they were even more devastating second time round – *torn in two in a trap . . . like I'm being buried alive . . . six months . . . freedom . . .*

Having his internal upheaval laid bare was horrifying – he was in a terrible state. And him wanting six months of freedom wasn't a whim: it was a conclusion he'd reached after painful soul-searching.

He mustn't go – that was clear – but I needed the details so I could manage them.

'Where were you thinking of doing this?' My voice was choked.

'South East Asia, Thailand, Vietnam, those places. Back-packing. I want to learn to scuba-dive.'

The level of detail triggered another wave of dizziness. All that time he'd been going around like a silent ghost, I'd been solicitously enquiring if he'd like to talk, and he'd been plotting his escape.

And *back-packing*? He was forty-six, not nineteen.

Still. Lots of people were giving up their middle-aged, middle-class lives to relive their teenage years. Silver something-or-others. Not that Hugh was a silver anything: his beard and shaggy hair were dark brown, not a hint of grey, he was tall and fit and, when he wasn't in the throes of anguish, he looked younger than his age. He could be a hit on the beach-party-under-a-full-moon circuit.

'But what about your job?'

'I've been talking to Carl.' Carl is his brother and they co-own a sound studio where Hugh is an engineer. 'He says he'll cover with freelancers.'

'You've told Carl?' Before he'd told me. I took another swig of wine. 'So you wouldn't be earning any money for six months?'

What about the mortgage, all the different insurances, the daily drain from the girls, all the small expenses that add up to so much?

Then he looked properly shamefaced. 'I'm so sorry, babe, but the cash left over from Dad's house will cover it.'

I didn't think I could feel any more shocked. No more nest egg. 'When were you thinking of going?' Did I have weeks or months to change his mind?

'Maybe in a week or ten days.'

Jesus *Christ*. 'Have . . . you haven't bought a ticket?'

'I've been looking at flights.'

'Oh, God, Hugh . . .'

'I'm sorry.' Shockingly, his face crumpled and he began to cry, the first tears I'd seen him shed since his dad's death.

'Sweetheart . . .' I scooted round and took him in my arms.

'When I saw Dad lying in that wooden box . . .' he shuddered into my shoulder '. . . all the things he'd wanted to do and now he never would, it just hit me . . .'

I had to wait until he'd cried out his sorrow before my next question. Finally, he swiped the sleeve of his sweatshirt across his wet eyes. 'Sorry,' he mumbled.

'Hugh?' I was breathless with anxiety. 'When you say it's not simply a sex thing? You mean that it *is* a sex thing?'

I was still hoping I might have misunderstood even though I knew, right in the marrow of my bones, that I hadn't.

We exchanged a look and it was as if our entire relationship flashed between us: the promises, the trust, the enmeshed emotions, the rock-solid unity – and now some sort of appalling unravelling where he peeled away on a path of his own.

He shook his head. 'That's not what this is about.'

'But it's not out of the question?'

He studied his hands for a long time. 'Amy, I love you. I'll come back to you. But if it happens . . . then yes.'

Fuuuuuuuck . . .

He grabbed his beer, his knuckles white. 'For the six months, it'd be like . . .' He paused, then blurted, 'Like we wouldn't be married.'

I was plunged into the horrors. Because this had happened to me before – being left by a husband – and it was the worst thing I had ever gone through. It had been so horrible that, to insure myself against a repeat episode, I'd avoided anything serious with any man for half a decade. And when, five years after Richie had legged it, something lovely sparked between me and Hugh, it had scared the daylights out of me.

It was several months before I could talk myself into giving him a chance, and then only because I'd spent the intervening period of chaste denial observing and checking him, the way a horse-buyer inspects a potential purchase, lifting its hoofs and examining its teeth. And the thing I'd been looking for was staying power. I did NOT want a player. I did not want a man who'd change his mind. I did NOT want a man who might leave me. Because it couldn't happen again.

And yet, here it was – happening again.

As if he knew what I was thinking, he said, 'It's only for six months, Amy. Not for ever.'

'Yes, but –'

'I'll come back. I'll definitely come back.'

He couldn't know that. You can't put the toothpaste back in the tube.

But he could have done this the way men usually do it – sneakily, dishonestly, two-mobiles-y. Telling lies that he had to go to some tedious conference when he was actually off to San Sebastián for a weekend of gastro-riding.

At least he was being honest. Did that make it any better? I didn't know.

I reached for my wine and tipped it into me, then said, 'Can you get me a vodka?'

'Sure.' He jumped up, guilt and relief adding extra vigour.

This hurt too much. I needed to get drunk.

Sometime in the ominous pre-dawn I came to. I was in bed, with no memory of getting there. Something catastrophic had happened – I had the feelings before I had the facts. Then I remembered: Hugh wanted to go away for six months of conscious uncoupling.

Half a year. It was a long time. People can change a lot in six months – especially if they're meeting all kinds of new people. A sudden image of Hugh fucking some taut-bodied girl with pretty tattoos and surfy hair made me feel I was awake in a nightmare.

Was this just about sex? He'd said it wasn't but I was suddenly convinced that this was all my fault – I should have made more of an effort on that front. Generally once I'm actually doing the sexing, I like it, but the shameful truth is that in the last couple of years I wouldn't have minded if we'd never done it again.

Because I was afraid of being the cliché I was, I stepped up to the plate every four weeks or so and tried to fool myself that Hugh hadn't noticed my lack of enthusiasm.

However, the very last time it had happened – and it was ages and ages ago – Hugh had said, 'That's your duty done for another month.' A second too late, he'd forced out a laugh. (I'd flailed around searching for the right words as he vamoosed in a passive-aggressive scarper.)

Maybe if we'd had a full-and-frank there and then we might have averted this current situation, but clearly we'd both known there was too much at stake.

In a panic, I nudged his sleeping body. 'Wake up, Hugh, *please*. We could have more sex.' My head was racing through all the ways I could persuade him to stay – I could dress up in saucy rig-outs, send him nudie photos of me, make home videos of us riding . . . I was suddenly aghast that I hadn't done the nudie-photos thing – I suspected he'd like it because whenever nudie photos of celebrities were hacked, a charged atmosphere sprang up between us.

No one could say I hadn't been warned about the perils of stagnation in a long-term relationship – experts were forever writing about it. Recently I'd read a thing by some American couples' counsellor who said that to keep the spark alive you had to – and I quote – 'be each other's whores'. He'd written an entire book on the subject and for half a second I'd contemplated buying it, then thought, No. I won't be anyone's whore.

23

Now I wish I'd bought the fecking thing.

However, alongside these thoughts a loud voice insisted that no woman should have to do anything she didn't want to do just to hold on to her man. But maybe if I'd tried them I'd have liked them . . .

'Wake up!' I shook him, then fumbled for the switch and light flooded the room.

Oh, *why* hadn't I been more adventurous? For the love of God, how hard would it have been to photo my hidey-hole?

But shyness had stopped me. And something else that I was only now seeing properly: an uncomfortable suspicion that our sexual wants were different. In countless ways, Hugh and I were aligned – sometimes it felt as if we actually shared the same brain, and that sense of having an almost-twin was a huge comfort. Except for sex. Buried deep in me was a suspicion that Hugh wanted stuff I didn't. It had never been vocalized – I was afraid that if it was, he'd become like a stranger.

But, instead, this had happened and it was far worse.

'Are you awake?' I asked.

'Yeah . . .' He was blinking and trying to sit up.

'Is this real?' I asked. 'Is this really happening?'

'I'm sorry.' He tried to hold me.

I pushed him off. 'We could have more sex.' I sounded shrill and desperate.

'Babe,' he said gently. 'This isn't about sex.'

Hope flared, then I forced myself to check, 'But you *might* have sex with other people?'

He nodded.

Despair overtook me, followed swiftly by self-revulsion: I was too old, too round, too crap in bed. 'Is it because I'm a porker?' I asked.

He actually laughed – a proper laugh, something that hadn't happened in a while. 'No. And you're not anyway.'

'I am,' I said. 'Well, a bit. It's just, you know, giving up the cigarettes.'

'It's not you, it's me. And I can't even believe I said that.'

'If it's not about sex, what are you looking for?' Maybe I could provide it.

He shut his eyes and opened them again. 'Hope, I think. Something like hope, anyway. Excitement, maybe. Possibility.'

Right. I swallowed. Hope. Excitement. Possibility. I knew about them. 'Newness?' I said. 'Freshness? The chance to be a different person, a better version of yourself?'

He looked a little surprised. 'Yes. Them.'

Well, newness and freshness were things I couldn't provide. 'What about the girls?' I asked.

'I can tell them tomorrow.'

It was already tomorrow. 'No.' Telling the girls would make it real. For as long as only he and I and Carl knew about this, it left the door open for him to change his mind.

'Kiara's barely sixteen,' I said. 'Who's going to mind her when I'm away?' I stayed overnight in London every Tuesday.

'She can mind herself,' Hugh said. 'She's more grounded than you or me. Or Neeve can be in charge.'

I tried again. 'Sixteen's a tricky age for a girl's dad to disappear for half a year.'

'Kiara's an old soul and the most well-adjusted kid you'll meet.'

'The thing is, though . . .' I was going to say that Hugh's disappearance might change all that, then realized it wouldn't make any difference: Hugh was doing this no matter what I said. A wave of anguish rushed up in me. 'Please don't.' I grasped his hand.

'I'm sorry, Amy. I have to.'

'What if I say no?'

He broke eye contact with me and his silence said it all: he'd go anyway.

4

I head for Mum and Pop's in Shankill – when I was growing up, it was practically in the country, but now the south Dublin suburbs have spread out to swallow it and the Friday-evening traffic is heavy. Although it's early September, the weather is shiny and bright, so people are probably heading for the coast, for the last few rays of summer.

As I inch along my phone rings. It's Dominik, Pop's part-time carer. For a long time Maura wouldn't even hear of us getting a carer for Pop. But Mum has a very full schedule of hospital appointments with her own many ailments, and when Pop was left alone in the house, he was liable to flood the bathroom or to give away Mum's jewellery to random callers to the door. One time Mum arrived home to discover three strange men – encouraged loudly by Pop, 'Go on there, lads, now you have her' – wrestling her washing-machine out of the house and into a van.

But dragging Pop along on Mum's hospital visits was no longer working because he'd frequently address the nurse with 'You've the look of a young Rosemary West. How many bodies have you buried in your basement?'

So about five months ago Mum displayed some rare gumption and signed up with Camellia Care.

'Hi, Dominik.' I wonder why he's ringing. Maybe Pop had decided to fling his dinner at the wall again. But that hardly counts as news.

'Amy, your mum is late home and I have next job to get to.' Dominik is very in demand – *very*. In the dementia-carers universe, Dominik is Kate Moss.

The thing is that Pop – carrying on the habit of a lifetime – is a difficult patient and often accuses his carers of being serial killers. Even though these people are used to the bizarre insults of dementia patients, Pop wears them down in no time. In the last five months, we've gone through a long list. Dominik, who'd spent over twenty years in the Czech Army, is the only one robust enough to cope and we can't get on the wrong side of him.

'I'm sure she'll be home in a few minutes.' Mum is very reliable.

'She is already two hours late.'

'Two hours! Have you rung her mobile?'

'Certainly I have rung, but it's on kitchen dresser.'

'But where's she gone?' Mum never goes out except to hospital appointments. 'What time did she leave?' I've horrible visions of her lying on a pavement, surrounded by concerned strangers trying to establish her identity, and of her, with so little sense of self, unable to tell them.

'She go at midday.'

'*Whaaat?* But that's six hours ago!'

'I can tell time, Amy. And your dad say I am worser than Yorkshire Ripper. Six hours I must listen to him.'

'But, Dominik, which hospital did she go to? Where –'

'No hospital today. She go to the fancy lunch –'

'Wait, what, lunch?'

'– in the fancy hotel. She say she is going on the piss.'

'No, Dominik, she'd never say that!'

'Are you calling me liar? She say to me, "Dominik, I am kicking up my heel and going on the piss." Those very words.'

This is *extremely* unlikely, but I need to know more before I draw any conclusions.

'I'll be there in ten minutes.' It'll be more like twenty-five. I'm a chronic liar about my ETA – there's simply never enough time.

'I must leave now,' Dominik says.

'Okay, I'll get someone else over to you ASAP.'

Who should I ring? In the small likelihood that Dominik has his facts straight, I don't want Mum getting into trouble, so Maura can't be involved. Instead Derry gets the call.

'Any chance you could get round to Mum and Pop's in the next ten minutes?' I ask. 'Mum's MIA and Dominik needs to leave.'

'So you ring the unmarried daughter?' Derry says. 'Poor Derry the spinster. No man, no life, all she's good for is taking care of elderly parents. Well, times have changed and –'

'Can you do it or should I ring Joe?'

'I'm going to Cape Town tomorrow. Good job I didn't go today, right? I'll rescue Dominik now, but don't start thinking this is who I really am.' She hangs up.

Half an hour later I turn off the main road to the cold, ramshackle Victorian house I grew up in. Once it had had lots of land, but by the time Dad bought it, it had all been sold off and a council estate built, so our abode loomed like a giant granite gravestone in a sea of three-bed semis.

My childhood had been spent fantasizing about living in a modest, pebble-dashed terrace with an electric cooker, instead of the Aga we had, which engendered untold suspicion from our neighbours.

The trees on either side of the driveway are so heavy that branches bang and slide on the roof of my car – maybe Hugh could come round to do some cutting over the weekend. But no. Hugh has other priorities now. Suddenly I realize that if he goes, all the practical household stuff becomes my responsibility: changing light bulbs, doing the weekly food shop and – yes, it might be a cliché but it's still real – the bins. Even seeing a bin gives me the shudders.

The thoughts of Hugh's extra-curricular riding have been so distressing that I haven't appreciated how his absence is going to impact on my day-to-day life and, actually, I'm almost more upset about the bins.

Is there any handyman who could be commandeered? Neeve and Kiara don't have boyfriends. Sofie's beloved Jackson is a total sweetie, but he's a wispy pixie-boy, who looks too frail to wheel the bins as far as the gate.

I park up tight behind Derry's car, to leave enough space for whoever else is coming today, and by the time I've got a tower of pizzas out of my boot, Derry has opened the front door.

'Is she home?' I'm looking over Derry's shoulder, hoping to see Mum's small, apologetic figure in the gloomy hallway.

'No.'

I step into the house and eye Derry over the stack of food. 'I'm worried. Should we be worried? Listen, was Dominik all right?' I live in terror of him leaving us because then I'd be roped in to babysit Pop and I'm already stretched way too thin.

'He's a narky feck.' Derry closes the door behind me.

'Should we ring the cops about Mum?'

'Seriously, though, I can't be the one who gets the call any time things go wrong with Mum and Pop,' Derry says. 'It's bullshit the way single women are treated, as if we don't have obligations.'

'Derry!' She's always at this lark and usually it's entertaining. Not so much today. I'll have to tell her about Hugh soon – it's weird that I haven't already.

'Our society has a pervasive lack of respect for us.'

That might well be true of other single women, but you'd never make that mistake with Derry.

'Dominik rang me first,' I say, 'and I'm married.' Well, I *am*. Technically.

'I could be married too,' she says.

She probably could. She's quick-witted, charismatic and successful. Also, scrubs up well. In her natural state she looks like all of us O'Connells with our pale skin, light-coloured eyes and tendency to buttiness. (Urzula says we're the most Celtic-looking family she's ever seen.) But via vampire facials, laser resurfacing, silhouette lifts and whatever else you're having, Derry – a vital four inches taller and ten pounds lighter than me – has turbocharged her natural assets into impressive hotness. (Yes, I'm jealous: my funds have never even run to a jab of Botox.)

'You could be married,' I say. 'Except if you go round dumping men because they say "ice and a slice" or call ketchup "catsup" –'

'So I should put up with some gobshite who gets on my nerves just so I won't be treated like a second-class citizen?'

'Yeah,' I say, and we both laugh.

'WHERE'S YOUR MOTHER?' Pop bellows from the front room. 'Give me my stick. I'm going out to look for her.'

'Take these.' I shove my armload of pizzas at Derry, pick up

Pop's stick from the hallstand, race through the kitchen into the scullery and shove the stick into the chest freezer. He's not leaving this house. One missing parent is bad enough. I couldn't cope with two.

I stick my head into the front room and call, 'She'll be home soon, Pop, don't worry.'

'I know you!' His angry expression vanishes. 'Are you my sister?'

'No, Pop, I'm Amy, your daughter.'

'Away to feck! I've no children!'

Car doors are slamming outside.

'It's Joe,' Derry calls, before I start thinking it's Mum.

Our elder brother Joe, his wife Siena, and their three sons, Finn (eight), Pip (six) and Kit (four) pile into the hall. Immediately the boys swarm through the house and into Pop's domain. Against a backdrop of Pop shouting, 'PUT THAT FECKEN' DOWN, YOU LITTLE SCUT!' I explain the crisis to Joe and Siena.

'She said she was going on the *piss*?' Joe can hardly believe it.

'So Dominik said,' Derry says.

'YOU'LL GET FECKEN' ELECTROCUTED AND IT'LL BE GOOD ENOUGH FOR YOU!'

Joe insists on viewing Mum's mobile – which is indeed sitting on the kitchen dresser, just like Dominik had said. 'That's it, all right,' he agrees.

'What should we do?' I ask.

'What do *you* think we should do?' he counters.

This needs to be said: Joe is useless. Charming, well travelled, but useless.

'Look, I'll get the dinner on,' Siena says. 'What do I do?'

If I'm to be frank, Siena is also useless. They are the Useless Family. They get by on their looks.

'Just take the packaging off and sling them into the Aga, as many as you can fit,' I say.

'STOP CHANGING THE STATIONS! STOP CHANGING THE STATIONS!'

The front door opens again and my heart lifts. But as quickly as hope flares, it dies: it isn't Mum. It's Neeve, my eldest daughter, the light of my life and the scourge of my heart.

'What's up?' She stands in the hall and peels off her jacket. She's tiny – barely taller than five foot – and very curvy: buxom, neat waist and round little bum. It's exactly the body-shape I had when *I* was twenty-two but in those days I'd thought I was fat. I wasn't – hindsight is a great thing. And maybe in twenty-two years' time I'll look back at the cut of me now and think I was pretty hot. Frankly, I can't imagine it, but I know that sort of thing happens. And not just regarding the size of my butt. I mean, eight months ago I'd thought my life was nothing special but now I'd give all that I own to return and savour every securely married second of it. As that song tells us, we never know what we've got till it's gone.

'Where's Granny?' Neeve gathers her red-gold hair up into a thick, high ponytail and narrows her glinting eyes around the hallway. She may have got her body-type from me but the rest of her is pure Richie Aldin. 'I've stuff for her.' She indicates a bag crammed to bursting with new make-up.

It is absolute *torture* to watch as envelopes of cosmetics arrive at our house hoping to feature in *Bitch, Please*, Neeve's YouTube channel. If the contents are any good she keeps them, and if they aren't, they're rerouted to the deserving poor. I'm rarely among their number.

'Granny's missing,' I say. 'Dominik says she went on the piss.'

'The *piss*?' Neeve's demeanour, when she's talking to me, is set permanently to scornful, but she truly outdoes herself this time. '*Granny?* Is he *mental*?'

'Lovely, don't say "mental".'

'Why not?'

'Because the mentallers might take offence and –'

'HERE'S KIARA! HERE'S KIARA! HERE'S KIARA!' Finn, Pip and Kit explode into the hall to welcome my other daughter, who has just arrived at the front door. She's in her school uniform. Her shirt has come free from her waistband, her bitten nails are painted with yellow fluorescent pen and she's bent almost double from the weight of books in her backpack.

'Guys!' She shrugs off the backpack, opens her arms wide to the boys and they start clambering up her, as if she's a climbing frame. She's the sweet-tempered *yin* to Neeve's snarky *yang*, proof that it's nature, not nurture. My two girls have very different fathers and very different personalities. Neeve is tricky (at least, she is with Hugh and me: I notice she manages to be nicer to the rest of the world) and Kiara is a sweetie.

'BRING ME MY STICK! I'M GOING OUT TO LOOK FOR MY WIFE!'

'Derry?' I follow the shoal of people into the front room. 'We should ring the police.'

'Oka– Hold on! Car outside! It's Declyn!'

Five years younger than me, Declyn is the baby of the O'Connell family. Everyone – Derry, Neeve, Kiara, Joe, Siena, Finn, Pip and Kit – flows around Pop's chair and surges to the rattly old bay window.

'HAS HE THE CHILD?'

'He's getting out,' someone says. 'It's just him. Awwwww!'

Sixteen months ago Declyn and his husband Hayden had Baby Maisey (via a surrogate, obviously) and we're all wild about her. But it means that Declyn without Baby Maisey has no cachet whatsoever.

'HAS HE THE CHILD? WOULD SOMEONE FECKEN' ANSWER ME!'

'No, Pop, he hasn't,' I say.

'WELL, SHIT ON IT ANYWAY.'

'Pop, we're all here beside you. There's no need to shout.'

'I'M NOT SHOUTING.'

'Wait!' Derry exclaimed. 'He's getting something out of the back seat!'

'Could be his man-bag,' Finn says.

Holding our collective breath, we watch Declyn fiddling around – and a huge cheer goes up when he emerges with Baby Maisey in a car-chair.

Everyone is delighted – everyone except Kit. Quietly he says to me, 'I hate Baby Maisey.'

'What? Why?'

'I used to be the youngest one. I was the favourite.'

I nod. 'Life is hard, little fella.'

'I used to be cute.'

'You're still cute.'

He gives me a very grown-up look. 'Don't,' he says.

We mass towards the door, and as soon as Declyn sets foot into the hall, the car-seat containing Maisey is ferried into the front room where she's rolled on the floor and smothered in kisses by her cousins.

Declyn watches with an indulgent smile, then focuses on me. 'Great dress, Amy. Vintage?'

'Vintage.' Or, to put it another way, second-hand. Some of my clothes are proper, expensive, designers-from-the-seventies vintage. But others are from the wardrobes of recently deceased old ladies that sell for half-nothing in Help the Aged. (You could say that I have a personal shopper – a lovely volunteer called Bronagh Kingston, who rings me if good stuff arrives in.) And really there's no point in being morbid – if the clothes are nice and they're dry-cleaned twice, isn't it heart-warming to think of them continuing to give a person pleasure? (If I sound a little defensive, it's because I have to defend my choices to Neeve who, most mornings, treats me to 'Dead people's clothes – *niiiiiice* . . .')

Not that my vintage stuff can be worn every day – if there's an important meeting, especially a pitch to potential clients, I have to corporate-up, in a suit that isn't cut right for a person of my shortness. But when the client starts to trust me, like Mrs Ever-Dry seems to, my lovely character-filled clothes can be unleashed. (Tim, he doesn't like them either. Tim likes things done by the book. He'd prefer if I toiled in workaday navy tailoring.)

'Edwardian governess meets biker chick.' Declyn spends a few seconds admiring my outfit, then suddenly notices Mum's absence. 'Where is she?'

'No one knows,' I say. 'She went out to lunch.'

'*Lunch?*'

'But that was six and a half hours ago.'

'I think she's home!' Derry says.

We hurry to the window. A taxi has drawn up outside. Through the tangle of branches we see its back door opening and a tiny woman – Mum – wearing a pink leather jacket come tumbling out. Before she lands bodily on the footpath, she manages to right herself and says something to the taxi-driver that makes her double over, laugh a lot and lean on the side of the car.

'Is she all right?' Joe asks.

'Is she *sick*?' This from caring Kiara.

Then Derry articulates what's becoming clear to us all, as we watch Mum weave her way to the door of the house, her face as pink as her jacket. 'Is she . . . scuttered?'

'And *what* is she wearing?'

'My jacket,' Neeve says.

I should have known. Everything is Neeve's.

We swarm towards the front door. Mum erupts into the hall and we fall on her with cries of distress. 'Where were you? We've been so worried.'

'I went OUT!' Mum declares. 'To a lunch! I got drunk and I won a prize!' She waves a box of sweets. 'Turkish Delight! Mint ones!'

'But, Mum, you should have come home earlier.'

'I was *enjoying* myself. I put up with your father all of the time, listening to him talking rubbish about suing the postman for cutting his hair and asking where our dog is when we've no dog and –'

'Granny,' Neeve says. 'That's my jacket! I couldn't find it when I was leaving last week.'

'I know!' Mum beams. 'I borrowed it by hiding it.'

'But why didn't you just ask for it?'

'Because you'd say no. I wanted it.' Mum's eyes are starey and bloodshot. 'And I'm keeping it.' She continues to smile in the most uncharacteristically defiant way at Neeve.

Great, I thought, just great. Now Mum has gone mental too. My husband is leaving me and both my parents are mentally ill.

5

And here's Maura. Cripes!

'Everyone,' I hiss. 'Act normal.' I turn to Mum. 'Especially you.'

Neeve bundles Mum up the stairs and I hurry to greet Maura. Trying not to move my lips, I ask, 'Who have you told about Hugh?'

'No one.'

It's hard to believe that: she's as leaky as Julian Assange.

'Keep it that way because the girls don't even know and, whatever you do, you're not to tell Sofie.'

'I *haven't* told Sofie.'

Seized by fear, I say, 'But you might. And you mustn't.'

Sofie, aged seventeen, is a fragile little creature. She's feckless Joe's eldest child: her mum is the woman who preceded Siena and, for reasons I won't get into now, she's lived with Hugh and me since she was aged three (didn't I *tell* you we were modern?).

Sofie is extremely attached to Hugh and it wouldn't be right for her to hear about his sabbatical from anyone but him.

'I was thinking about Alastair,' Maura says.

Of *course* Maura would fall for him – she's a born interferer and he's the kind of man that most women want to fix. But I see him, week in, week out, cutting a streak through an endless supply of girls and discarding them like old tea-towels.

'Maura, cop on, you're married!'

'Not for me, you fool. For you! *My* husband isn't leaving me.' Of course he wasn't. The silent Poor Bastard had had his spirit broken long ago. 'While Hugh's away, you should, you know, take *your* time out with Alastair.'

Honestly, there is almost nothing I'd enjoy less. Hugh's the only man I want, but if I *could* bring myself to consider another,

Alastair would be close to the bottom of the list. Not at the actual bottom. No. That honour would belong to Richie Aldin.

'He's very . . .' Maura swallows with difficulty and nods '. . . sexy.'

'He's revolting.' I'm fond of Alastair, but thinking of him in that way is distressing. You can just tell that he's a great man for sexual gymnastics. Whenever I imagine him in bed with one of his laydeez (which happens very rarely), the position they're in is reverse cowgirl and they're doing a huge amount of bouncing and whooping – the lucky lady is actually wearing a cowboy hat and swinging a lasso above her head.

A craving for nicotine hits me like a blow. Ten months ago, I gave up cigarettes – not that I was a big smoker, just a precious three a day, but it was lung cancer that Hugh's dad had died from and it had felt disrespectful to continue.

This week has been so tough that there's a real fear I'll start again and, in the hope of heading it off, I've bought an e-cigarette. 'I'm just going to . . .' I head upstairs where, in one of the chilly bedrooms, Neeve is doing Mum's make-up. They're seated at a big old dressing-table that would be an up-cycler's wet dream. Not for me. Too big, too heavy, too gloomy. I sit on the austere old iron bed (no, can't get excited about that either – too high, too rickety, too creaky) and watch them.

Neeve flicks a glance at me and my e-cigarette. 'You look like you're playing a midget's tin-whistle.'

There is so much that's wrong with what she's just said that it's impossible to know where to start. I settle for 'You can't say that word any more.'

'You can't say anything any more,' Mum says. 'Soon it'll be a crime to speak. People are too easily offended. So what are they now?'

I wince. 'Little people. I think.'

'But Little People are leprechauns. Someone should tell them that we're sorry but they'll have to find another word.'

'Mum, *please.*'

36

Mum looks up at Neeve. 'When you said "tin-whistle" there, did you mean something different?'

Neeve laughs softly. 'It's just your dirty mind, Granny.'

'Have I a dirty mind?' Mum is delighted.

'Filthy.'

They collapse into giggles and I watch, ashamed of my jealousy. If Neeve was even a fraction as sweet to me as she is to my mum . . . Mind you, Granny is quite the hit with her granddaughters now. Lately Sofie has been spending the majority of her time here. During the summer just gone, she stopped living with me and Hugh and moved in with Urzula, her mother, in the hope of rebuilding a relationship. Which is in the process of failing. It broke our hearts when Sofie left us and it's breaking them even more to watch her flail around trying to make Urzula act like a mother. But what can you do? Hugh and I are attempting the near-impossible feat of offering Sofie all the benefits and duties of family, while respecting that she has actual biological parents. These days, Sofie ricochets between Urzula and Mum and Pop but I wish she'd come back to me.

Speculatively Neeve watches Mum's made-up face in the mirror. 'You look great, Granny. Maybe I'll do a vlog with you.'

'Would I be on telly?'

'Granny . . .' A note of warning has entered Neeve's voice. 'Don't make me explain the internet to you again.'

'No, no. No. I understand it. It's magic telly for the young people.'

'You'd be on my YouTube channel.'

'I don't want to be on that. The name is mean and – and rude. Imagine me having to tell people I'm on the *Bitch, Please* show. What does it even *mean*? *Bitch, Please*?'

'I'll show you,' Neeve says. 'Mum. Ask me if you can have all of this make-up.' She indicates the dressing-table, scattered with a Tom Ford eye palette, a Charlotte Tilbury foundation, several contouring tools and three different lip colours.

Wearily I say, 'Neeve, can I have all of that make-up?'

Neeve holds up the palm of her hand, side-eyes me and says, in scathing tones, 'Bitch, please. See, Granny?'

'No.'

Neeve smiles. 'Come on, let's go downstairs.'

Off they go to rejoin the raucous mayhem and I sit in the peaceful bedroom, smoke my e-cigarette and meditatively eye the dressing-table. That stuff would be wasted on Mum. Absolutely wasted. I inhale again and consider that it's a very sorry state of affairs when you're reduced to stealing make-up from your seventy-two-year-old mother.

Spurred on by my proximity to cosmetics, I decide to watch the latest on *Bitch, Please*, and see what Neeve's recommending this week. There's the option of asking her in person, I suppose but – and this is a worry – things feel more real if I experience them through my iPad.

This week is an autumn back-to-school special with the *Grange Hill* theme and cute title sequences featuring falling leaves and acorns – *very* pretty. And here's Neeve, her long golden-red hair streaming down over her shoulders, wearing a crocheted hat, scarf and gloves in a dusty blue shade that makes her green eyes pop. In recent times she's expanded to cover clothes and accessories as well as cosmetics and she's caustic about 'the shite' she gets sent.

But these crocheted pieces are far from shite. They're embellished with a scatter of Fendi-inspired leather flowers that are adorable but not over-cutesy and the overall effect is so gorgeous I actually groan. To think she'd got those things for free!

I rarely go into her bedroom because she's an adult woman and entitled to her privacy. *And* I'm afraid I'll lose my shit and start sobbing or trying to eat the lipsticks.

In my more fanciful moments I think sleeping in her bedroom must be akin to sleeping in a giant make-up bag – even though the cramped space is full of her camera, lights and computer, and the walls are lined with stacks of workaday brown boxes, everything as grimly efficient as a mini-warehouse.

Like in a job . . . because it *is* a job.

Not one that makes any money, though. Neeve's rent to me and Hugh is paid using the barter system, by her joining in the house-cleaning we do every Sunday. (This double-jobs as family quality time.)

Her absence of an income is a worry. She has a degree in marketing from UCD, but instead of getting a job in some multi-national, like her fellow graduates, she decided that making vlogs in her bedroom was a viable career path.

And maybe it is.

Because the world is different from when I was her age, right? These days, kids experiment with several irons in the fire, and God knows Neeve works hard. Filming and editing the vlog is the tip of the iceberg. Most of her time is spent badgering advertisers or buttering up publicists. In addition, to keep herself in beer money, she hostesses two nights a week in some 'skeevy-ass club'.

Now, on the vlog, she's talking about new, exciting things in the make-up world, starting off with a primer from Marc Jacobs. She's making it sound so great that my knuckles are clenched white with longing. Next up is a foundation and she's less impressed with that. *Oooooh*. Not impressed at all. She delivers an entertaining rant on its failings, and ends by saying, 'Aw, naw.' She sounds just like a Long Island matron and she makes me laugh. She's a natural comedian and manages to deliver negative reviews without coming across like a bag of bile. There's a twinkle to her, a narky charm, and if only she wasn't so spiky with me . . .

I know it's for reasons she probably doesn't understand but have everything to do with me no longer being married to her dad. And I'm powerless over that and powerless over her and powerless over everything, including Hugh going away, and I don't like all these horrible feelings that I've no control over, and then I discover that the Marc Jacobs primer isn't among the free stuff on the dressing-table, so I click to buy it and I'm *furious* to discover that it's not available in Ireland and they won't post it from abroad and the only place in London that sells it is Harrods and it's impossible for me to go to Harrods because it's like being trapped in an Escher painting.

Terrible memories of previous visits come at me, of going

round and round, from hall to hall, every one of them filled with wired-up crocodile-skin handbags that each cost more than my car. Like in a nightmare, there's exit sign after exit sign but a panicky certainty that the door will never appear –

Cripes, I'd better see how the dinner is doing!

Stealthily I relieve Mum of the Tom Ford eye palette, then go back down to the kitchen where Siena has managed to not burn anything. 'I'll take it from here,' I say.

Vaguely she says, 'Someone needs to bring the garden chairs into the dining room.'

There are so many of us that there are never enough real chairs to go round.

The front door slams again and this time it's Jackson, Sofie's boyfriend – he has his own *key*?

I suppose it's no real surprise: he's very much part of the family. Into the kitchen he wafts – there's a lot of floaty-scarf action, skinny, *skinny* jeans and gorgeous, Versailles-style hair – and gives me a hug. I have to admit I miss him almost as much as I miss Sofie.

'Sofie coming?' I ask him.

'Soon. Need anything done here?'

'Aaah . . .' Siena, drinking wine and gazing into her phone, seems to have no plans to fetch the chairs in. 'Chairs from the garden.'

His look is wry. 'You think I'm strong enough to carry them?'

'Just about.' Jackson's weakling status is an on-going joke. 'They're only plastic.'

6

'Hugh?'

No answer.

The house sings with emptiness, but it doesn't stop me whirling through the living room, then the kitchen, then out into the 'sun-room' (a Plexiglas extension that's Arctic from September onwards and in the summer months magnifies the sun's rays so much that someone will eventually burst into flames).

Upstairs our bedroom is still and silent, the carnage from our busy week – discarded shirts and skirts and towels – frozen in artful crumples. It could be a painting: Life Abandoned Abruptly.

There's no chance he'd be in Kiara's room or in Neeve's mini-warehouse or up in the converted loft where Sofie sleeps, so I check my phone. No text from him. With a sudden infusion of rage, I fire off a speedy **Where r u?** His six months haven't started yet!

What's called for is a trawl through the Outnet and a hefty glass of rioja – I don't like how much I'm drinking but it'll have to be addressed some other time.

To complete this happy tableau, I get my e-cig from my bag.

It's been such a strange week. I've felt sick with shock and unable to separate out all the individual horrors storming around in me – terror, jealousy, sorrow, grief, guilt, incredulity – but the clearest feeling now is of 'wrongness'. Or shame, to give it its correct name. (I learnt that from *Psychologies* magazine. I learn a *lot* from that publication.)

For so much of my life I felt 'wrong'. When I was a kid, Mum was in hospital a lot and our home life was rackety. Dad did his best but his headmaster job took most of his time. Maura tried to be a parent, but she was only a kid like the rest of us, so dinners were sparse, patchy affairs, laundry didn't always get done, or we'd forget to take baths because there was no one to remind us.

Poor Mum suffered the most. Not only was she sick – and she was *very* sick: she spent a full two years in hospital with the tuberculosis, followed by chronic pulmonary disease, which frequently rehospitalized her – but her guilt was colossal. Every time she had to go back into hospital she cried and cried. There's a picture in my head of her tears spilling on to my hands as she choked out, 'I'm sorry, Amy, I'm sorry.' I don't know which of her readmissions I'm remembering – it could have been one of several.

Only when I became a mother myself did I understand her agony. Having to leave us all, knowing we wouldn't get fed properly or simply have her support and affection – the *guilt*, the grief.

We kids handled her absence differently. Joe was the angriest – he often said, 'I wish she'd die. Then Dad could get another mum for us.'

Maura, too, was angry and vocal about it, but the only time I was angry was when Mum produced Declyn. Why would anyone have another baby when they couldn't care for the ones they already had?

I just wanted her to get better, and while she wasn't in hospital for all of my childhood, the uncertainty was ever-present. Even when she was at home, we knew it wouldn't last. There was one occasion she was discharged amid a great deal of 'She's been cured' fanfare – but in just twenty-four hours she was gone again. In the last maybe fifteen years, she's been much better, but we still treat her like she's made of spun sugar. And the residue of shame still lingers. ('I can't play with you because my mum says you've got germs.' And maybe I had – I was grimy, certainly. These days, I'm borderline OCD about personal hygiene.)

When I grew up and left home, that didn't work out so well either – I found myself married, divorced and a single mother by the age of twenty-two. Other girls my age were getting drunk and buying shoes while I was working full-time *and* in sole charge of a child. Even though I'd felt physically and emotionally destroyed most of the time, I can see now that I was a little powerhouse, zipping around the place in Capri pants and snug polka-dot sweaters, baby Neeve under one arm, a vintage briefcase containing a pitch under the other. I could do my hair in a Victory roll in ten seconds and change a nappy in twenty. I was a steady-wristed expert at flicky eyeliner, a dab hand at d'you-wanna-make-something-of-it red lipstick and a super-speedy expresser of breast milk.

By the time I was twenty-seven, so much of my life had been lived feeling out-of-step that I'd accepted it was who I was. Then I met Hugh.

He was burly and handsome, beardy and broad-chested – but it wasn't enough to make me jump into a thing. He persisted with steady, unspoken devotion and was gifted at gauging my needs. Like the night he'd arrived at my front door in London, bearing a giant chocolate muffin and a hot chocolate kit, right down to the mini-marshmallows. He'd even brought a shiny new oversized mug.

It was late, I was knackered, I'd had a hard day – he knew about it because we'd been working together – but I stood aside to let him in. However, he just handed over the goodies and left. Also impressive was that he'd brought nothing for Neeve – I was always a little creeped-out by those men who tried to win me over by being nice to my daughter.

Hugh saw *me*, the woman I was, not a woman who came as a job-lot with another human.

My eventual decision to commit was cautious and cool-headed but I'd never regretted it. Together we built up a life that's been solid and good, and these days I'm part of a community: I feel accepted, I *belong*.

Okay, ideally I'd have the cash and body-shape to wear nothing but MaxMara, but from time to time I think, with pleasure, *Even though it took me longer than most people, I got there in the end.*

Only I didn't, I hadn't. I haven't got anywhere. I'm still a misfit, a woman whose husband wants to do something unprecedented – he doesn't want to leave and neither does he want to stay. Old sensations of shame are back in force.

Maybe Hugh might not actually go.

Several times during the week I've gone to him, white-faced with horror, and said, 'Please don't go.'

Each time he replied, 'I'm sorry, babe, I have to.'

43

But he hasn't told the girls and this gives me hope.

Nevertheless life has been a million miles from normal. I've felt as if I'm lugging rocks in my guts and my sleep has come and gone in peculiar little spurts, like receiving a weak radio signal. Also, and this is downright freakish, I've been instigating sex every morning and every evening. Not in a desperate demonstration that he doesn't need to go halfway around the world – it's been for me. If it was possible, I'd crawl right inside him and zip us both up.

I should really call Derry – there was no chance earlier to pull her aside for a private talk amid the mayhem in Mum and Pop's and I've never waited so long to tell her something this huge.

The impediment – and it takes a while before I've burrowed deep enough to identify it – is that the news will hurt her. My pain becomes her pain, and it cuts both ways.

But we approach life differently. She's proactive, impatient, and if something breaks on her, she replaces it immediately. Nothing ever gets mended and nothing is given time to heal. Her response will be to try to find a new man for me. She belongs to some awful dating agency for rich people and before I know it she'll have bundled me off to an elite club, where I'll have to drink Krug and discuss tax avoidance. No. Extreme no.

Because it's borderline illegal to phone a person 'just for a chat', I consider texting Posh Petra to see if I can ring. But there's no point. Three years ago, at the age of forty-two, she had twin girls, who suffer from what she calls 'Satan Syndrome'. (A condition unique to them.)

They put Joe's three sons to shame: they appear not to sleep. If they're not breaking an object, they're smearing it with something disgusting, and the noise they create – yelling, banging, howling – would fray the hardiest of nerves. Poor Posh Petra . . .

It's hard to know what percentage posh she actually is. Her accent is refined but not bad enough to generate instant dislike; her childhood family holidays were mostly spent in foreign art galleries, but instead of being bored witless like any normal person, she still goes into raptures about Dutch masters. Also, she calls dinner 'supper'.

We'd met more than a decade ago while supervising an outing of five-year-olds – Petra's daughter Anne was in Kiara's class. Petra had surveyed the mass of squealing pinkness, and muttered, 'What fresh hell is this?'

For me, it was like falling in love.

Of all my friends, Petra would most get how I'm feeling about Hugh. But a phone call is impossible because she has to break off every five seconds to shriek at the twins, and visiting her at home is worse because I usually leave with a plateful of baked beans in my hair. Seeing her in the outside world is also difficult because babysitters come once, then leave weeping, swearing never to return – usually with baked beans mashed into their teenage hair. The baked-beans treatment is the girls' thing.

Petra's husband and she cope by divvying up small amounts of time when each goes out alone. Sunday evening is Petra's slot. I'll have to wait until then.

Maybe I could text Steevie. We've been friends since secondary school, but since Lee left her, she won't let a good word be spoken about any man and she'd probably heap spite and rage on Hugh.

Spite and rage that would be coming from a good place – she'd think she was hugely supportive. But she'd simply be channelling my stuff through the prism of her own experience.

If not Steevie, maybe I could try Jana. She's the sweetest person alive but she's also, unaccountably, friends with Genevieve Payne, and even if I beg her not to tell Genevieve, indiscretion is her middle name. I need Hugh to be halfway across the world before Genevieve gets wind of the news.

With each of my friends there's something preventing a full and free vent, and it's a shock that I don't have an actual bestie whom I trust with every last part of me. I'm a pathetic saddo . . . unless it's normal to have a selection of friends who all mean different things. Perhaps that's the grown-up way. A 'portfolio' of friends?

Christ alive, that's *awful*, and I'm never, ever going to think it again. Even if I suspect it may be true.

The reality is that, until now, Hugh has been my best friend.

I've almost no secrets from him and he's always got my back, no matter what goes wrong for me – and, like for everyone, plenty does: regular bust-ups with Neeve, stressful stuff at work, and the downright weird and random (for example, a cold-sore in my *eye*).

Okay, I'm ringing Derry! No, not Derry. Posh Petra, then. No, no point. I go through the same list again, and the thing is, what would I even *say*? This limbo is so novel, there's no language for it. It's not the sort of thing you get in suburban Dublin.

But maybe I'm just the first of many. Maybe soon there will be an epidemic. I'd be an actual trend-setter and people will be saying, 'Hey, aren't you great, with your funny clothes and your modern marriage?'

God, the very *thought*. If Hugh goes, the next six months will be a nightmare. Could I disappear, then reappear when – if? – he comes back?

No. That's impossible. I'll have to spin the news the way I would a tricky work situation and make it sound mutual, positive, even desirable. I construct an imaginary press release.

Amy and Hugh are psyched to share a thrilling new phase of their marriage: a six-month sabbatical where they explore separate timelines in order to reconnect in an even more loving and loyal partnership. Yeah, and all you *suckers*, with your linear, monogamous marriages should feel embarrassed. No need to pity Amy. Instead you should envy her.

Would it fool *anyone*? Who knows? But it might salvage some of my pride. Meanwhile, I'll need a couple of people I can be truly honest with – although they'll be sworn to secrecy because the shame of the real story going viral would turn me into a local landmark. Everywhere I went, people would give me sidelong sympathetic looks and say, 'She gave her husband six months off to go and ride rings around himself. What kind of a cretin *is* she?'

But *am* I a cretin? (And I probably shouldn't say that word.)

The thing is that, in the normal run of things, Cheating Man

46

= Complete Bastard. We're all agreed on that, right? Like my first husband. Richie Aldin = Complete Bastard, no doubt about it: the square-shaped Complete Bastard in the square-shaped hole. Or like Steevie's Lee. He'd fallen for his assistant at work, and we all knew where we stood: Lee = Complete Bastard; Steevie = 'Cry Me A River'. After many months Lee tried to reclaim his old friends but even though some of the menfolk might have met him under cover of darkness, everyone knew: Lee = Complete Bastard. He was shunned.

As more time elapsed, Steevie's equation evolved from 'Cry Me A River' to 'I Will Survive' to 'I'm Gonna Dance On Your Grave One Day, Play Maracas and Sing Olé', but Lee's remained Complete Bastard.

Hugh isn't a Complete Bastard. He loves me, causing me pain is killing him, but having compassion for the person who is hurting me is too weird for words.

A fair dent has been put in the bottle of wine and there's a Ganni box-bag in my basket when the front door opens. I jump up and go to the hall. It's Hugh, in a Joy Division T-shirt that was once black but has been washed so often it's faded to a soft charcoal. It suits him. I've been seeing him through different eyes these last few days and his sexiness is almost shocking – it's easy to understand why Genevieve Payne keeps putting the moves on him.

'Hey.' He pauses, looking awkward.

'Where've you been? Why didn't you text me? You haven't actually left yet so lean the fuck *in*.'

His hands are laden with carrier bags and there's something big and bulky half hidden behind him.

'What's going on?' I ask. 'Were you shopping?'

'Yeah, um . . .'

I twist around him to get a look at whatever he's trying to smuggle in. When I see what it is, it's like being punched in the stomach. It's a massive rucksack.

This is real. This is actually happening. I'd been a total gobshite to have told myself it might not.

'Big rucksack.' My tongue isn't working properly.

'I didn't want you to see this.'

'What's in the bags? Can I look?' Why do this to myself? Wouldn't it be better to know nothing?

'Amy, no, don't –'

'Really, it's grand. I'd like to see.' I want to show that I'm a good sport, that I'm cool with all of this.

'Okay.'

We go into the living room where, reluctantly, Hugh reveals several colourful T-shirts – way too cheery-looking. They'd never have got the green-light from me. It's weird and awful to be excluded from his life like this.

Now he's produced a white linen shirt, the sort you'd wear for an expensive dinner in a hot country. This is close to unbearable but I keep going. 'And this?' I've found a small blue terry-cloth thing.

'One of those towels that dry really quickly.' He unfurls it to reveal a full-sized bath towel. 'You use it, then it's bone-dry in twenty minutes and rolls up tiny again. Takes up nearly no space in the rucksack.'

'That's . . . handy.'

'Come on, Amy, let's stop this.'

'Are you really going?'

'I'm sorry, babe.' He looks sad and shamefaced.

'When are you going to tell the girls?'

'Tomorrow. We're meeting here at ten.'

'Even Sofie?'

'Yeah.'

My heart thumps hard. Here we are with rucksacks and arrangements. 'This is really difficult.' My voice sounds strangled.

'I'm sorry.'

'I know that no person owns another, but I've got into the habit of thinking of you as mine. And now I have to . . . share you.'

He nods awkwardly.

'Even your penis, I've thought of it as mine.'

48

Again he nods.

'I feel you've no right to leave me, that you've no right to have sex with anyone other than me, you know?'

'I know.'

'You've always been nice to me, really nice, like you'd do anything I asked.'

'I love you.'

'I've grown to depend on you and now I hate myself a bit for it. But what was I meant to do, Hugh?' My voice is wobbling. 'We have to trust people. We can't go through life entirely self-contained.' There's something I have to ask. 'Is this my fault? Have I done . . . something?'

He shakes his head. 'It's nothing to do with anyone else. It's all to do with me.'

This is a salve, kind of, and tears of relief flood my eyes.

'I'm sorry,' he says, with fierce sincerity. 'I hate myself for hurting you.'

For a moment my tears threaten to spill over, then I place my fingertips on his chest and push him on to the couch. I clamber on to his lap, straddling him, and cup his face in my hands, my fingertips rasping against his beard, and kiss him passionately. I push up his T-shirt and run the palms of my hands over his chest. These last five days he even smells different – sexy, alien, like I don't know him.

'The girls?' he protests weakly.

'Out.' Well, Kiara is babysitting Finn, Pip and Kit. God knows where Neeve is, and Sofie could arrive at any time, but it doesn't matter. I unbutton his jeans and slide myself down to lick the twitching tip of his erection. Slowly I guide it out, then begin to pull off his jeans.

'You're sure it's safe?' he asks urgently.

'Sure.'

He stands up and whips off the rest of his clothes. I throw the cushions on to the rug and pull him down to me. With fumbling hands we unbutton my dress and take off my pants.

It's been years since we've done it anywhere except a bed, but since Sunday night we've been doing it all over the house – in the shower, in the bath, even on the draining board by the kitchen sink because I keep seeing people doing it there in Danish TV series. (And I have to tell you it's nothing *like* as sexy as it looks on the telly – the aluminium was cold against my bum and it buckled and made a womp-womp noise with each thrust. It was so loud and bouncy that I was actually afraid there would be a permanent dent. It's only three years since we got the kitchen done. It's been such a *pleasure* to have one room in the house that isn't gone to shit that as I womp-womped up and down on the draining board my biggest emotion was anxiety.)

Taking charge, I lay Hugh on the cushions and insist on changing positions every minute or so. It's like a showcase – see all that Amy can offer! I even – clearly with Alastair fresh in my mind – try the reverse cowgirl but can't get the angle right. I practically bend Hugh's erection in half and it still won't go in. 'Stop,' he says gently. 'You're going to break it.'

Grimly I keep trying.

'Come here.' He takes me in his arms and we fall into one of our tried-and-tested routines. We've already had sex today – this morning before work. (And last night. And yesterday morning. And the night before.)

But depression overtakes me. This is joyless. Hugh tries a couple of things that usually work but I speed things up because now I just want it to be over. Eventually he comes, and in the silence that follows, he pushes himself up on his elbow and looks into my eyes. 'I love you,' he says. 'I *will* come back.'

'Will you always love me?'

'Yes.'

'Say it.'

'I'll always love you.'

'Again.'

'I'll always love you.'

But, no matter how often he says it, I can't feel safe.

7
Twenty-two years ago

I pressed my back against the door, to stop him leaving. 'Please!' I was crying so hard I could barely see. 'Don't.'

He took my shoulders, trying to move me from his path. I put my hands on his chest and shoved hard. 'You can't go! You can't. You have to stay.'

He made another attempt to move me. He didn't want to use force, but he was determined, and he managed to shift me a couple of inches. I fought back, determined to keep barricading the door.

'No.' I was hoarse from crying. 'Please.'

He was much stronger than me, but I was much stronger than me too. We grappled for a few horrible seconds, he pushed and I pushed back, but somehow there was a gap, he'd turned the lock and the door was open. 'You'll be okay,' he muttered, and slipped out.

I ran after him into the corridor and to the stairwell. He raced down the stairs and I would have followed him, except back in the flat baby Neeve was wailing. I hesitated for a moment, torn between the two people I loved most in the world, and I made my choice.

Simply remembering it, nearly twenty-two years later, still distresses me. It was the worst night of my life.

It had started at Leeds-Bradford airport. Myself and four-month-old Neeve were flying to Dublin for Christmas. Richie had a party with the club's sponsors; he'd be travelling a day later.

It was 23 December and the airport was, unsurprisingly, utter mayhem. Everything was delayed, including my flight. The time for boarding came and went, and eventually there was an announcement offering a voucher to anyone who'd fly tomorrow morning instead. Clearly the flight was madly overbooked, but because Neeve was so little I'd thought we'd get priority. But Frequent Flyers got first dibs and there were an awful lot of them.

'I have a baby.' I was on the verge of tears.

It did me no good and I was told to come back the following day.

Lugging Neeve in her chair into the flat, I heard noises from the bedroom – Richie must have left the television on before he went out. I put Neeve on the living-room floor and prepared to go back down four flights of stairs to haul up our suitcase, then decided to go to the bedroom instead – because I was naive but not stupid.

She looks really confident. That was my first thought. She was on top, moving up and down. Her hair was long and synthetic-looking – extensions – and there was something weird going on with her boobs: the outside part was bobbing up and down in time with the rest of her but the inside was moving at a slower pace. Implants, I thought. My first time to see them in real life.

Richie's face was caught up in the throes and it's something I wish I'd never seen. It stayed with me for years.

Then he noticed me and he went pale. The girl – I didn't know her – continued her rhythmic bouncing. It took her a few extra seconds to realize something was wrong. She paused mid-move and followed Richie's stare.

'Fuck!' she exclaimed, clambering off him.

Unfamiliar clothes were strewn about the floor – a black bra, a lace thong that wasn't mine, a shiny copper-coloured dress. 'Get dressed.' I gathered them up and flung them at her. 'And get out.'

She was gone in under a minute – in the short shiny dress and platform shoes, she couldn't have looked more different from me if she'd tried – and I waited for Richie to launch into the usual things people say in these situations: 'It was nothing, she was nothing, I was drunk, it was just sex.' Already I was apologizing to myself for forgiving him.

As a teenager, whenever news broke of a famous woman

staying with her cheating husband, Steevie and I were blister-ingly scornful – no way would we hang around! No, we were strong girls with self-respect, we would never be so pathetic. But it's different when it actually happens. When you're young and vulnerable. When you have a baby with the man. And when you love him as much as I loved Richie Aldin.

Richie began to get dressed. Without meeting my eye he said, 'Look, Amy, we should never have got married. We're too young.'

'N-no, we're not,' I stammered.

'You're twenty-two, I'm twenty-three,' he said. 'That's too young. This isn't working. I'm leaving.'

He hauled the soft suitcase out from under the bed and I cried, 'No! You can't.' Adrenalin flooded me and my brain was flicking through all available inducements to make him stay.

'Neeve,' I said. 'Your baby. You can't leave her.'

'I don't want to be a dad.'

'I know it's hard.' I was pleading. 'But it won't always be.'

He dumped three pairs of trainers in the bottom of the suit-case and I flung myself at him, trying to stop him from packing anything else. Effortlessly, he blocked me – he was short but strong and fit – and began pulling stuff from the wardrobe. In the tussle to stop him, something tore and he looked pissed off. His clothes had become more expensive recently, even though we were skint.

'Is it that girl? Do you think you love her?' Maybe I could beg her to back off.

'The one who was here?' Richie was irritated. 'She's nothing.'

'But if she's nothing . . .'

'Amy,' he said, almost gently, 'I do it all the time.'

He was a professional footballer – not Premier League: he played for a club in the Third Division but, even so, football groupies were in plentiful supply.

'But . . .' I was stunned into silence. He'd always sworn he loved me way too much to be tempted and I'd believed him.

'I've been cheating since you were pregnant.'

'No.' I began to choke with tears.

'I wish none of this had happened,' he said. 'You, me, getting married, the baby.'

'But you were the one who wanted a baby.' I was gasping for breath. 'And who wanted to get married.'

We'd been together since our last year in school, and although I was sure we were for ever, I'd worried that it was too soon for a wedding, never mind a baby. Richie (probably under gentle persuasion from his club, I realized, years later) had convinced me otherwise.

He picked up the case and headed for the front door. I got there first and pressed my back against it, determined to keep him from leaving. But, in the end, he went.

I wanted to die but, because of Neeve, I had to endure the longest, coldest, loneliest winter ever. I knew nobody in Leeds – the only reason I was living there was because Richie had been signed by a local club.

Maura tried to get me to move back to Dublin and avail of a network of friends and family, but my friends, all the same age as me, were behaving like normal twenty-two-year-olds, living it up and being irresponsible.

As for my family – they were variously sick (Mum), working all the hours (Pop), living in Australia (Derry), too flaky (Joe), too young (Declyn), and Maura would help far *too* much.

And even though Richie refused to see Neeve or me, it was vital to be nearby in case he changed his mind.

We'd only been married for eight months and Richie disentangled himself super-speedily – the divorce happened in under five months. A terrifying letter arrived from some sharky lawyers employed by his club, saying that Neeve would get a tiny monthly maintenance payment. I couldn't afford a sharky solicitor and had to make do with an unsharky one from Legal Aid, but I pushed back hard and didn't give up until the original offer was tripled.

It was still derisory, though.

But Neeve and I survived that awful winter. I went back to the PR company I'd been an assistant in before I'd gone on maternity leave and worked full-time while being Neeve's sole carer. Life was gruelling – five hours' sleep counted as a good night – and yet in photos from that time, it's astonishing how healthy and sane I look.

There I am in an Audrey Hepburn-esque swingy car-coat in black mohair and black leather gloves to my elbows. Another picture has my hair in a kiss-curl ponytail and – where on earth did I find the time? – some elaborate sort-of-quiffy fringe. Nowadays, the phrase would be 'My inspo is retro,' but back then the only words available were 'Too skint to buy my clothes in real shops.'

Feck alone knows where I got the energy but my weekends were spent haunting the vintage markets of Leeds, Neeve on my hip, and I was *always* in high heels.

There were some great finds – a tulip-skirt in brushed sateen, a vampy, figure-hugging gown in lustrous black satin, several shortie cashmere sweaters and an actual original Givenchy suit: a sheath dress and cute boxy jacket in the pastel blue of a sugared almond.

Most of the clothes are long gone – lost on various house moves or they fell apart from overuse – but even though it's too small for me now, I still have that suit. It's like an emblem: it reminds me of how hard life once was. And, perhaps, how resilient I can be if the need arises.

8

'A break?' Neeve is incredulous. 'Do you think you're Taylor Swift?'

'No.' Hugh rises to the bait. 'I *don't.*'

'Please,' I murmur to Neeve. 'Let's keep things civil. Have a croissant.'

I've set out the kitchen table like a working breakfast – pastries, fruit salad and coffee – but no one has touched the food. It's just like being at work: people regard hunger as a display of weakness. But at the same time they'd be mortally offended if you *didn't* provide buns.

'We know you haven't been very happy,' Kiara says. 'We'll miss you but we'll try to understand.'

'Thanks, hon.'

'So how do we get in touch?' Kiara asks. 'Will you FaceTime us once a week? Like every Saturday morning?'

'No!' Hugh says, way too quickly. The fear on his face shows that the last thing he wants is a routine. 'No, ah . . . no.' He clears his throat. 'But I'll have my mobile, and if any of you girls need me, you can call me any time you like.'

'What about Mum?' Neeve asks snarkily. 'Can *she* call you any time she likes?'

Hugh's look is apologetic. 'If it's an emergency.'

Oh. I hadn't known my contact would be limited to that. God, this hurts so much.

'The important thing to remember,' Hugh says, 'is that I love you all very much. I love you and I'll be back.'

Sofie bursts into noisy tears. 'Everyone always leaves.'

Poor Sofie. She looks frayed and unkempt, her fine white-blonde hair tangled into knots. And she's even thinner than she was a week ago, tiny enough to pass for a twelve-year-old boy. Living with her mother clearly isn't good for her but that's something she needs to work out for herself. I can only stand on the sidelines, with my heart in my mouth.

Before the thought has fully formed, I'm putting half a Danish on her plate and saying, 'Eat something, lovely.'

We all pause, and Sofie is so shocked, her sobs cease. Then Kiara takes the bun off Sofie's plate and disposes of it in two speedy mouthfuls.

Despite my faux-pas, pride warms me – I've high, *high* hopes for Kiara: some kind of ambassadorship at the very least. She's so attuned to the needs of others. For a fierce, bitter moment I wish *she* was the daughter with the vlog – *she*'d share the make-up with me.

Kiara brushes pastry crumbs from her mouth and says to Hugh, 'We can come visit you?'

'No!' Once again he's appalled. 'I mean, no, no, hon, it isn't that sort of break. I'll be moving around and you know . . .'

'We know,' Neeve says meaningfully.

Kiara stares at her. 'Don't. That's not what this is about. He wants to self-actualize – right, Dad?'

'Right!'

Self-actualize. That's a good word. If I can say it without side-eyeing myself, it could be useful.

'But you'll be home for Christmas?' Kiara asks.

'No, hon,' he says gently. 'But I'll call.'

'If you're on a break,' Neeve says, 'it means Mum is too. Right?'

Some unknown expression scuds across his face.

'You hadn't thought of that?' Neeve sounds scornful.

Hugh stares, as if he's assessing how I'd fare on the open market, then he goes blank. 'Amy is on a break too.'

'Boom,' Neeve says to me. 'You can get back with my dad. Everyone knows you never got over him, which must be the only reason you married Taylor Swift here.'

I don't know what to say. Except that I wouldn't touch Richie

57

Aldin if he was the last man on earth – I'd rather have whooping, lasso-waving, reverse-cowgirl-sex with Alastair every day of my life than go down that road again. But I never diss Richie to Neeve – let her discover for herself what a Complete Bastard he is. Unfortunately, however, because he's kept his distance, she's idealized him somewhat.

'I can't believe you're doing this to us.' Sofie sounds like she's going to cry again.

'Honey, Sofie, I'm not leaving for ever.'

'I'm going to Granny's.'

'I'll drive you,' Neeve says. 'In Hugh's car. He won't be needing it for six months. So are we done here?'

'Are we?' Hugh is all big anxious eyes, as he consults the girls.

'Yep,' Neeve decrees.

'But please understand,' Hugh goes for one last burst of sincerity, 'I love you with all my heart and I'll only be gone for six months. I'm coming back.'

Sofie hisses, 'You're destroying everything.' She whirls from the room, leaving Hugh white with distress.

'Sorry to interrupt the disintegration of our family,' Neeve says cheerily, 'but DHL is bringing a delivery from Chanel.'

Instantly I'm wondering how best to steal it – it is *agony* to watch these prestigious cosmetics arrive – but she laughs. 'I know what you're thinking.'

'Can't you give her some?' Hugh asks.

'To ease the pain of you leaving her?'

'I'm not leaving –'

'We'll see.' Neeve closes him down. 'If there's stuff that would suit you, Mum, you can have it.'

'It doesn't have to suit me,' I say. 'I'd be happy with anything.'

She flicks a meaningful look at Hugh. 'That's obvious.'

Before words of protest can leave my mouth, Neeve and Sofie zip from the house. Hugh mutters, 'I'll just . . .' and disappears upstairs, leaving Kiara and me sitting looking at one another.

9

'Wow,' Kiara says. 'Big shock.'

And now I'm raging. Neeve and Sofie had shitty starts to life, but everything had gone smoothly for Kiara. This shouldn't be about me, but Kiara was my clean sheet, my success story, and now Hugh has besmirched that too. 'I'm so sorry, sweetie,' I say. 'Are you okay?'

'I meant, big shock for you.'

'No, no, no –'

'I'm good,' she says. 'I understand that Dad needs to do this. It's you I'm worried for.'

'Kiara . . .' Sometimes Kiara seems more mature than all of us but a lot of that is probably just surface and it would be a mistake to start relying on it.

'Mum, I'm fine. But you're going to need a strategy for the next six months. You should take up rock-climbing.'

'Why?'

'Okay, maybe not rock-climbing. I'm just throwing suggestions out there. But there must be tons of things you wish you'd done with your life and now's your chance!'

God. All I want to do is go to bed for six months and subsist on Sugar Puffs eaten straight from the box. Instead I'm going to have to make new memories, be my best self, do one thing that scares me every day and all that other proactive stuff that pervades Kiara's thinking.

'Like, if you died tomorrow,' she prompts, 'what would you regret not having done?'

This is bullshit. I'm the adult here, she's the child: I'm the one who should be providing comfort and solutions.

'There must be something, Mum.'

Maybe it's the stress but I can think of only one thing. Since

I've given up the cigarettes, I've put on a couple of pounds. And when you're as short as me, every ounce shows. I haven't adjusted to my new weight and I don't want to – this isn't the real me.

'I'd regret not getting thin again,' I say. 'I'd hate to die being the wrong size. I feel that I wouldn't be able to properly enjoy the afterlife – it'd be a bit like going on a hike with a gritty little stone trapped in one of my boots.'

Kiara's smile wobbles. This clearly isn't worthy. Then she recovers. 'Boom,' she says. 'There you go. Eat clean, right?'

'Sweet-potato toast,' I say. 'Unless sweet-potato toast is over already?'

'It's still a thing.'

I wasn't sure it was, but Kiara was kind.

'Maybe you could talk to Urzula,' she suggests.

'Maybe,' I muttered.

'*Aaaaand* maybe not.'

Sofie's mum Urzula is a self-made diet guru, who pops up with increasing regularity on TV, both here in Ireland and in the UK. She has no qualifications, but her icy Baltic thinness and her cruel Latvian-accented judgements are garnering a growing following of people who celebrate her tough-love, sock-it-to-the-fatsos bluntness. She's *obsessed* with fighting lard. In my opinion, she's simply managed to convert her eating disorder into a career.

'Urzula has ice in her soul,' I say.

'No,' Kiara says. 'Urzula has a level teaspoon of millet porridge in her soul.'

We share a laugh and Kiara goes off.

Now that the girls have been told and it's all official, I do what I should have done days ago and ring Derry. 'I've something weird to tell you.' I take a deep breath. 'Hugh is sort of leaving me. For six months,' I add quickly. 'Then he's coming back. But while he's gone, it'll be like he's single.'

For a moment she's silent. Then, 'Where are you? At home? I'll be round in ten.'

It's probably less than eight minutes later that her car hares into our estate, and comes to a sudden halt just outside the gate.

In she sweeps, half of her hair in a bouncy New York blow-dry and the other half still wet.

'Aw, Derry, for the love of God, you didn't have to leave mid-blow-dry.'

'I'm tight on time. Tell me.'

Haltingly, I outline the facts.

'And this happened when?'

'Last Sunday night.'

'And you didn't tell me because . . . it was too weird? You were too humiliated? You were hoping he'd change his mind?'

'All of the above.'

'Jesus Christ, Amy, you poor little baba.' She looks at me with heartfelt sincerity. 'You have shitey luck with husbands.'

'But he swears he's coming back.'

Her expression says it all: even if Hugh comes back, everything will be different. No way can he simply slot back in and take up where he left off.

'Amy, you're a survivor.' She's firm on this and, yes, I appear to be – I survived Richie leaving, I survived all the tricks he played on Neeve, I survived the *Exorcist*-level bile of Neeve's teens, I survived two catastrophic redundancies, one long ago in London, another more recently in Dublin.

But being a survivor is hard bloody work, harder than it looks, and I think I might be running low on survivor juice. Given the choice, I'd far rather a pampered life of indulgence where nothing bad ever happens.

'How can I help?' She's always proactive.

'By letting me vent. And please don't make me go on dates. I want nothing to do with men, not now, not ever.'

'But what about that –'

'Derry, please! That was a moment of lunacy.'

'But you could finish what you st–'

'I'm begging you, Derry, never, ever mention that, like ever. Please.' There's a danger I might cry. 'I just want to bunker down for the six months, keep a low profile and see what things are like when Hugh comes back.'

'When's he going?'

'Soon. In the next week, that sort of soon.'

She's biting her bottom lip. 'Lookit,' she says, 'I'm meant to be flying to Cape Town today.' Derry works in human resources; it involves a lot of travel. 'But I could try and cancel if –'

'Derry, don't be mad. Anyway, he'll be gone for six fecking months. You can't cancel all of your trips.'

'But who's going to mind you if he goes this week? Maura will make it all about her. Jesus, though, she'll go *baloobas* when she hears . . .' She notices my expression. 'Wait, what, she knows?'

'Sorry, Der. She guessed something was up. She came into work yesterday and leant on me till I confessed.'

'The Waterboarder strikes again.'

'To be fair, she wasn't unsympathetic.'

'But, still, she'll be fuck all use if thing go nuclear. What about Steevie? Is she still AMAB?'

I nod. AMAB stands for 'All Men Are Bastards'.

'Could that be a good thing? The pair of you can make little wax men and get out the needles . . . no?'

'No. It sounds mad but Hugh can't help this.'

Derry is incredulous. 'Hugh is a total dick. I love him, you know I do, but he's being a total dick.' She looks confused. 'Why don't you hate him?'

'I do hate him. Sometimes. Well, all the time . . .' Then I explode, 'Why couldn't he have stuck to the promise he made when we got married? Why does he have to be so weak?' Before she can reply, I go on, 'Or am *I* the weak one, letting him go off like this? Would another woman have insisted on the full terms of our marriage contract? "For better, for worse"?'

'Yeah, your words, asshat!'

'But making him stay wouldn't work, Derry. He's been miserable and emotionally unavailable.'

'He's a dick.'

'But, Derry, I still love him. *And* I feel sorry for him. It's a mess.'

'Oh-kay.' It takes a moment. 'I think I get it.' So that wouldn't be *her* response but she's working hard to align her opinions with mine. 'Holding two opposite and opposing thoughts at once. No one ever said this life business would be easy. So who else can help? What about that half-wit Jana Shanahan?'

I snort with unexpected laughter. Derry can't abide Jana: where I see sweetness, she sees profound silliness. She once said about Jana, 'The wheel's still spinning but the hamster's *looong gooooone*.'

'Would she be any good in a crisis?' There's huge doubt in Derry's voice. 'I think she's as useful as Pinterest but you're fond of her.'

'She's friends with Genevieve Payne.'

'And you don't want Genevieve finding out until Hugh's out of her reach? But what about when he's gone?'

'I still don't want her finding out.'

'But she will. Someone will tell her. Fuck it, *everyone* will tell her. Sorry, babes, you're going to be trending, like, for ever.'

'Not if I tell no one. Except you, obviously. And Maura. And the girls. And Jackson will have to know because he's in the house so often. But apart from them, I'm telling no one else.'

Derry's face is a mix of alarm and compassion. 'Amy, honey, you can't – Look, there's no way you can keep this a secret for six months. And you shouldn't have to – you've done nothing wrong.'

'But it's so humiliating,' I whisper.

'It *is* humiliating. But it's going to be really, really tough and you need people who'll be there for you.'

I say nothing. I'm kind of over depending on people. Some of my siblings, grand: our messy childhood united us. But the rest of the world, not for me, not right now.

'It will leak out.' She's pulling no punches. 'You're better off controlling it. Treat it like a work press release.'

What – like that fanciful one I wrote in my head? Not a hope.

'I've to go,' she says. 'I've a flight. I'll FaceTime you. But tell people, Amy, manage it.'

'Okay.' I won't.

She leaves, and I'm sorting the laundry basket when my phone rings. It's Mum. I'm instantly on high alert: what disaster is after happening? 'Is everything okay?' I ask.

'The girls are with me – Neeve and Sofie. They tell me that Hugh is going away?'

'They told you?' You don't tell Mum bad news! We'd learnt at an early age to ring-fence her banjaxed immune system. What were Neeve and Sofie *thinking* of? I'll have to have a stern word with them, Kiara also . . .

But it would be utter madness to make them keep Hugh's absence a secret – they're too young, it would be too much responsibility. Wild with sudden rage, I realize that Derry is right and there's no way this can be contained.

'I'd say you're upset,' Mum says.

'Ah, you know . . .' She really isn't that kind of mum.

'Would you like to hang out with me?'

'Er . . .' *Hang out?*

'We can paint our nails – Neeve gives me lots of polishes.'

Lucky you. I get nothing except anti-dandruff shampoo.

'If you like we can drink wine. It's a great pick-me-up. I wish I'd discovered it years ago.'

She needs to get off the phone because I have an idea. 'Thanks for the offer, Mum.'

We say our goodbyes. Then, in a blind fury, I yell, 'Hugh! HUGH!'

He starts hurrying up the stairs, so I grab my phone and meet him halfway. 'Get that fucking towel!' I say.

'What?'

'The fucking towel that dries in five minutes!'

'What happened?'

'Just. Fucking. Get it.'

He disappears out the back to the shed – clearly his Departure HQ – and reappears with the small blue bundle. 'What's going on?' he asks.

'Unroll it and hold it. Smile.'

'Why?'

'Just fucking do it.'

I take several photos of Hugh holding the towel, a glassy-eyed grimace stapled to his face. 'Fuck's sake, Hugh, SMILE! Lucky you, heading off for a six-month sex holiday!'

I upload the least-miserable-looking photo to Facebook. 'Check this out!' I write. 'Hugh's travel towel. Dries in twenty minutes! Happy travels to him as he heads off for six months. Bring us back some sunshine!' Speedily I bang out about a hundred emojis of planes, suns, ice creams, cocktails and bikinis, and post it to my 1,439 friends.

'Amy, what did you just do?'

I whip the towel from him, scrunch it up into a ball, then fling it hard at his chest. Disappointingly, it's too light to have much impact.

'What did you do?' He grabs my phone and I grab it back.

The story is out in the world now and I'm owning it. I'll probably break the internet, but from here on in the narrative is being controlled by *me*.

10

Eighteen years ago

One clean bright April morning in London, in the late nineties, I was hurrying through Soho, dressed in a pair of dark blue clam-diggers, pointy pink stilettos and a button-through, candy-striped blouse. There were lots of young hip types about, bearing coffee cups or retro briefcases, looking like they were en route to work in advertising or something similarly cool – and I was one of them.

It was one of those rare days that had probably happened four or five times in my life when I felt like a round peg slotted with dazzling snugness into a round hole.

My destination was a sound studio, where I'd be working on a marketing campaign, and my head was already trying to manage any potential pitfalls.

'Hi.' Hugh from the studio had appeared in front of me – and I found I was absolutely delighted to see him.

'Hi!'

We worked together fairly regularly and everyone loved Hugh. He was big and good-looking and quiet and confident. People went on about his 'Irish' eyes – I think they meant they were smiley. If you asked me, they weren't *that* smiley – I'd sensed a slight withholding about him.

People assumed that my affection for Hugh was because we were both Irish, but that was neither here nor there. It was because he was really good at what he did – my life was so riddled with stress that anything that made my job easier was appreciated. Most mornings, facing into my day felt like going to war: I had to get Neeve up, dress her, feed her, drop her to school, get the tube to work, have meetings, manage clients . . . but when I was due to work at Hugh's studio, my spirits always lifted.

When Hugh was manning the decks, things started on time. If a script didn't fit into the thirty-second slot, he'd suggest

66

intelligent edits, even though that wasn't part of his remit. Or when my client started muttering that the actor's delivery didn't embody the brand's core message, Hugh would intercede and tactfully coax more gravitas, or less chirpiness, or whatever was required.

'Good timing,' Hugh said, that sunny morning in Dean Street. 'I was just out getting the coffees.'

'The hardest-working man in ad-making.'

We walked the few steps to the scruffy Soho terraced house where the studio lived.

'Hey, you look amazing this morning,' Hugh said.

'Good amazing or ridiculous amazing?'

'Good amazing.'

I smiled fondly at him. 'Over at Rocket Sounds they call me Timewarp Girl,' I said. 'Or Rockabilly Amy. I much prefer the treatment I get at Hugh's Studio.'

'It's a definite look you've got going.'

By now, we were in the house and climbing the narrow, slopey stairs to the top floor, where the studio was.

'That's because all my clothes are second-hand due to skint-ness. Jesus, these *stairs*.' I paused on a landing and looked out of a narrow window. 'Look at that – the backs of other houses.' I laughed. 'You do know I'm only pretending to admire the view so I can catch my breath. You wouldn't think of getting a lift in here?'

'Listed building,' he said. 'Yeah, you'd never know to look at it.' Then he added, 'But if I could do it for anyone, I'd do it for you.'

The sudden sincerity in his voice made me look at him in surprise, made me look *hard*, and I don't know exactly what happened but the light on him seemed to alter. In an instant he went from being Hugh my fondly regarded colleague to a very different Hugh.

Out of nowhere a powerful attraction had bloomed into life, like one of those super-speedy desert flowers and, with no warning whatsoever, I wanted him. I was *stunned*. What the hell had just happened?

Hoping for enlightenment, I looked up at him. He was a big man, not all of it muscle but, still, yeah, you would . . . He looked as shocked as I felt. I swallowed hard, continued up the stairs and didn't speak again until we were with the others.

After that day on the stairs, things had changed. Over the next three or four months I was giddy and buzzy when we were working together – and quite devastated the time he was on holiday and a freelancer was covering.

Physically, I was hyperaware of him. If he walked near me, the hairs on the back of my neck stood up, and if he left the room, I was irritable and anxious, impatient for his return. Even though our connection was unspoken, when my team needed Hugh to open early, they said, 'Get Amy to ask. He'll do it for her.'

Soho back then was Hook-up Central. Everyone seemed to sleep with everyone else, like they were collecting footballer cards: the Spanish Girl; Maria's boyfriend; the Swedish coke dealer; the kitchen porter at Pollo with the enormous schlong; the bar-girl at the Coach and Horses; the male model from Dundee; the Japanese boy with the Afro. Maybe Hugh was part of that scene and I was just another person to be ticked off a list. 'Rockabilly Amy, with the mad clothes. Yeah, I did her.'

I wouldn't have been the first woman to sleep with a man she thought was wild about her and be ghosted the moment he rolled off her. But my colleague Phoebe offered the intel that Hugh was single and he wasn't a slut, and for a short time relief made me euphoric.

Then a fresh bout of soul-searching engulfed me. Richie's cheating had changed me: the thought of trusting a man scared me witless.

Paradoxically, my life – which had been functioning efficiently – suddenly seemed threadbare and sad. I was only twenty-seven: I should have been sharing a flat with two other girls, drinking our heads off and having one-night stands. My life was empty of fun, spontaneity and connection. Once again, I was the odd-bod.

It was impossible to consider a sex-drenched fling with Hugh. It wasn't just because of Neeve, it was because of me – even before Richie had done what he'd done, casual sex had never held any appeal. If things were to become more serious, Hugh would need to hear my sorry story. But what if I offered myself on a plate, saying, 'These are my wounds,' and he legged it? How was that even survivable?

Then came the night he'd arrived at the front door of my mean flat in Streatham, bearing a giant muffin and a hot chocolate kit.

We'd been together that entire week – me, my assistant, my client, his colleague, the voiceover artist and Hugh, all crowded into the attic studio. It was a challenging campaign and we were on a deadline, living on Haribo and Diet Coke and taking turns to run down to the newsagent to replenish supplies. By then I was openly happy whenever I was around Hugh, even though whatever there was between us remained unspoken.

That evening it was time for me to leave before Hugh had finished the daily edits and I needed to hear them to prep for the following day's work.

'Go,' Hugh said. 'Pick up your daughter. You want me to bike the tapes round when I'm done?'

So I gave him my home address. And could you blame me for wondering if something might happen? A man calling around to a colleague's home is generally considered creepy, but when he appeared at my door, I thought, Here we go, I'm ready. Then he gave me the tapes and the goodies and went away, leaving me mute with disappointment.

Two days later, we finished up that campaign and, because it ended a few hours earlier than expected, we all piled into the pub. For once I was able to stay – I'd booked a childminder, anticipating that I'd be working into the night.

These were all things I took as signs that the planets were in alignment.

Latish in the evening, I encountered Hugh in the corridor. He'd come looking for me. He blocked my path, then backed me against the wall and said, 'So.'

'So?'

'So, Beautiful Amy, what are we going to do?'

A charge zipped through me – this was finally happening. But my terms had to be laid down. 'I'm not in the market for anything casual.'

He took me by the shoulders and fixed me with those eyes, not smiling now, not smiling at all. 'There are three things you need to know. I'm crazy about you. I'm serious about this. I'm loyal as a dog.'

'Okay,' I said.

'Okay?'

'Okay.'

And, oh, that first kiss. Sweet and hot, like tasting a dark chocolate truffle. It lasted and lingered, the kiss that kept on giving, more thrilling and delicious than my most lascivious imaginings.

The first time we went to bed together, he unwrapped me like a present, laid his naked skin next to mine, held me tight and hard, hard enough to hurt a little, and said, 'You've no idea how long I've wanted this.'

In those early days we had kissing sessions that lasted for ever. Wonderful as they were, they were a consequence of Neeve being around – sex happened nothing like as often as I wanted and kissing had to fill the gap. Hugh and I never got the chance, the way other new couples do, to spend our first few months lounging around in bed, enjoying long, lazy weekends of sex and papers and food and more sex.

From the word go, we were corralled by responsibilities, first Neeve, and then, after only four short months, I got pregnant with Kiara. It was an accident: I was on the pill, something must have gone wrong, but Hugh absorbed the news with equanimity. 'Maybe a bit sooner than ideal but kids were always part of the plan, right?'

Then when Kiara was only two years old, we took in Sofie. (Joe had left Urzula when Sofie was still an infant and by the time she was three, neither Joe nor Urzula wanted to take responsibility for her.)

Occasionally, regret bothered me for the carefree part of our relationship we never got to have. My concern was more for Hugh than for myself, but he always dismissed my apologies. 'I love you. I love *you*.'

And I believed him.

11

'So I've booked my flight.'

My heart begins to race. It's Sunday morning, it's gone noon and, surly and sullen, I'm still in bed, making my way through the papers because it counts as work, and as long as I'm working, it's possible to pretend that my life hasn't been entirely derailed. Every few minutes my phone beeps – the photo of Hugh with his magic towel has exploded Facebook – with texts, tweets and missed calls. I've seventy-one unread messages on Facebook Messenger – *seventy-one*!

I'll never read them. There's probably a handful of true friends in there but the majority will be ambulance-chasers. I know this because – and God knows it's not something to be proud of – it's what I'd be like myself if, say, Genevieve Payne posted a thing about her husband going travelling. Agog. Yes. Utterly. And sending frantic texts to see if anyone else had the inside gen.

It's simply human nature – we mistakenly think there are only so many disasters to be allocated, and if it's happening to someone else, we'll be spared.

Hugh has spent the morning cleaning the house. He, Neeve and Kiara have been all industry, banging, clattering, running taps and calling to each other. I suppose he's trying to be nice, as if having an un-dusty lamp will be a great consolation to me during the six months he'll be missing.

I should be with the girls, showing them I can be depended on, but I want to punish Hugh while he's still here to be punished.

At one stage he comes to the bedroom door, looking prim and virtuous in a pair of Marigolds and carrying a basin of cleaning stuff. 'Is it okay if I do our bathroom?'

71

'No.'

'But –'

'No, Stupid Face. Get out.'

And now he's back, with real news. 'Dublin to Dubai to Bangkok.'

As if I give two fecks about his itinerary. 'When?'

'Tuesday.'

'Tuesday, the day after tomorrow?'

'Yeah.'

Oh, God. He really is going – and so soon.

'Amy,' he says quietly, 'am I doing the right thing?'

This is a surprise, a huge, good one. Hastily, I sit up and, trying to muffle any hope in my voice, I say, 'You don't have to go.'

I'm sorry now I posted the thing of him with the towel. I'll have to find some way of defusing it, but that's the least of my worries.

He sits tight and tense, clenched in on himself. For a long, long time he's silent, and it's hard to not jump in with suggestions and reassurances.

Eventually he speaks. 'Sorry. Just having a . . . I'll be okay.'

The disappointment is devastating. 'You're going?' My throat feels swollen.

'Yeah. But I'm scared stiff. Will I get mugged? Will I be lonely? Will people think I'm pathetic? A middle-aged man trying to relive his youth?'

This is the part where I reassure him it'll all be fine. 'Before you've eaten your first banana pancake on the Khoa San Road,' I say, 'your passport will be stolen, your bank account will be cleared out by a prostitute who's spun you a hard-luck story and you'll find that you're an accidental drug mule. You've seen the films.'

He laughs, a little nervously. 'And you'll have to come and bail me out of jail.'

I shrug. 'What if I've met someone else and just decide you can stay there?'

Another nervous laugh. 'Amy, I promise I *will* come back.'

Who knew? Maybe he was just leaving me via the scenic route.

'Tuesday's the thirteenth of September, so you'll be back on the thirteenth of March next year.' Oh, God, it's so far away.

'Or thereabouts.'

'Thereabouts? No, Hugh. Don't fucking "thereabouts" me. Be back on the thirteenth of March.'

'Okay.'

'Hugh, listen to me,' I say urgently. 'Even if you do come back, you'll be different. And I might be different too. "Us" will be gone.'

'Things might be even better,' he says.

In theory. Always assuming I can get past the jealousy. That I can live with the unknown parts of Hugh, the girls he fucked, the laughs he had, those six months that he spent living life to the full without me.

'Don't go,' I say. 'Please, Hugh, we won't survive it. And don't say that must mean we're not strong enough right now. This is real life and this is me you're talking to. Couldn't you just wait it out?'

'I've tried waiting it out.'

'Wait a bit longer.'

He shakes his head. 'I can't go on like this.'

I curse the tears that fill my eyes.

'I can't go on like this,' he repeats. 'I'm so sorry, Amy.'

'Facebook,' I say. 'Are you going to be posting pictures of you wherever you are? With . . . whoever you're with?' I have a vision of him around a beach campfire, looking tanned and young and carefree, surrounded by bikini'd babes wearing bandannas on their heads. 'Because you can't. Think of the girls – you can't have them seeing . . . whatever . . . you know . . .'

'I'll stay off it.'

'Fucking make sure you do.'

'Amy, I'm sorry. For all of this.'

'Oh, Hugh, just fuck off!'

If only there was someone to talk to. There's always Mum's

peculiar offer, to hang out and drink wine, but my world has been upended enough and I can't be dealing with a mother who's behaving wildly out of character.

As if the universe has heard my need for a confidante, my phone rings. But clearly the universe is a little deaf because the person calling is Maura. Again. There are already three missed calls from her. Once the number goes above four, she visits in person, and that would be all kinds of bad. She might give Hugh a severe dressing-down and maybe he deserves it but it wouldn't be helpful.

I sigh and answer, 'Maura?'

'Are you okay? Any news on when he's going?'

'No.' I can't tell her yet. I'm not able for the drama.

'You need to know that you're being quite Scapegoat-y at the moment.'

Maura's done a course that explained the roles assumed in families with absent parents. Apparently there are five: Hero, Scapegoat, Enabler, Lost Child and Mascot. As Maura was so obviously the Hero, she was delighted with this assessment. Declyn, the youngest and cutest O'Connell, was our Mascot. She's had trouble matching Joe, Derry and me to the three remaining roles but basically she thinks we're all Scapegoats. Even Declyn was a Scapegoat for a while, when he came out.

'If Hugh doesn't go,' she says, 'I'll withdraw my allegation. At the moment, we'll call you Scapegoat-in-waiting.'

I might as well just make my peace with being Scapegoat-in-chief. 'Bye, Maura.'

'We'll talk soon.'

Sadly, we undoubtedly will.

I return to my iPad and the Sunday papers. *The Times* has a big, positive profile on my client Bryan Sawyer, the British triathlete who'd been caught on camera earlier this year stealing teaspoons from Marcus Waring's restaurant. Bryan had laughed off the teaspoon theft, claiming he'd done it as a dare. Then his ex-wife sold a story saying Bryan had form as a klepto, and had taken countless gingham napkins from Jamie Oliver's restaurant. (She was photographed, looking sorrowful, at a twelve-seater dining table, with a Jamie napkin beside every place-mat.)

A hotelier came forward: apparently Bryan had stolen two bath towels from him; then another hotelier accused Bryan of thieving seven wooden clothes hangers. A media storm ensued, Bryan's sponsors dropped him, and he'd been in an awful state when he came to see me five months ago.

Mercifully I'd liked him – he's a damaged, vulnerable man who had a tough childhood – because, hard-up though Hatch may be, we don't rehabilitate people who don't deserve it. I'd painstakingly reconstructed his public life – charity work, a delicately curated social-media presence and a public admission of his klepto-quirk – and it's unseemly to brag, but I'm killing it: two of his sponsors have re-signed him and today's glowing article is an indication that my work is nearly complete. Several other papers are running mostly positive pieces in their later editions – some backlash will follow, it always does, but nothing that should impact.

On any other day, my mood would be triumphant and there are probably a few congratulatory messages on my phone, dotted among the pebbledashery of rubbernecking, but it's too risky to look.

It's not just professional pride I'm feeling about Bryan Sawyer, there's also meaningful financial consolation: I'll get a percentage of his sponsorship fees and, frankly, it couldn't have come at a better time. Even without Hugh taking six months off work, money is tight. My income is unpredictable and there's rarely very much left over after I've paid my share of the necessaries.

Of course I'll have access to our fast-reducing 'nest egg' while Hugh is gone . . . Such rage bursts in my chest. It was *lovely* having that money. Knowing that so many of the household problems would be dealt with was an indescribable pleasure, and now Hugh – fucking Hugh – is blowing it on a mid-life crisis.

But is this unreasonable of me? It was *his* parent the money had come from. And Hugh had prioritized funds to put *my* niece through college because her biological parents have perpetual cash-flow problems and we've long given up asking for any. Also, his income is significantly higher than mine so he's always contributed more than I have to our joint account and never once has he groused.

The rights and wrongs of this are terribly confusing.

I skim the rest of the papers, always scouting for business. Any celebrity who's come a cropper and needs to be rehabilitated in the eyes of public opinion might be a potential client.

But my head is melted so I fling down my iPad, lie back on the pillows and probe my tender feelings. It's all too reminiscent of when Richie walked out. Back then, after some recovery time, my promise to myself was that I'd never again be that woman, yet here I am being that woman. Is this what life is all about? To bring us face to face with our worst fears until they no longer scare us?

Could we possibly even be complicit, subconsciously, in their manifestation? Is that what I've done? Because floating in my head is a vague something, maybe a myth or a legend about people meeting their fate on the very road they took to avoid it. Clearly I'd thought that by choosing Hugh I'd escaped my fate of abandonment but – even though it's taken a long time to happen – I'd chosen the exact person to replicate those circumstances.

Well, that's a bit of a sickener.

Perhaps my position should simply be gratitude to have had more than seventeen happy years with Hugh. Lately there's been a plethora of articles that say there's no such thing as 'The One' any more, but a succession of 'Ones'. That every relationship has built-in obsolescence, that sooner or later it'll run out of road and then it's time to move on to the next person.

But contemplating that is just too depressing. Whatever is going to happen is going to happen, but why not defer the worry until it actually has?

And everything might be okay. People get through worse. Far, far worse. Resilience of the human spirit and all that blah.

12

Seventeen years ago

After I got pregnant with Kiara our lives changed with terrifying speed.

'It's time to go back to Ireland,' Hugh said. 'We're a family now. We need to buy a place and we can't afford London prices.'

We couldn't really afford Irish prices either – the boom was still going strong. But if house prices were astronomical, so were wages. Jobs in PR were abundant, as you'd expect in an economy crammed with gleeful people only desperate to spend their new-found wealth. (Which wasn't real, but none of us knew that at the time.)

Testing the waters, still very anxious about the hairpin turn my life was taking, I applied for two PR jobs in Dublin, and even when I 'confessed' to being pregnant, both companies were happy to employ me, let me leave to have Kiara, pay me for six months' maternity leave, then take me back. Like I say, boom-town and that sort of thing *so* wouldn't happen now.

These days, my friends of child-bearing age, who work for any sizeable company, tell me that life is like a dystopian novel, one where women have to swallow their pill in a public cere-mony every morning in the workplace. ('They watch you like a hawk. You can't sneak off to puke from a hangover or put on even an ounce. If they suspect you're pregnant, you're immedi-ately sidelined on to the worst project ever, to make you resign.')

When I asked Hugh what he thought of his chances of getting a job in Dublin, he said, 'Should be no bother.' Then he went a little shifty. 'For a couple of years myself and Carl have been talking about setting up our own studio. Maybe now is the time.'

'How would it happen?'

'We'd get a bank loan.'

'At the same time as taking on a mortgage? Wouldn't that put a lot of pressure on us?'

77

'We can manage it,' he said. 'Just about.'

'Grand, right, okay.'

'And another good thing about moving back to Dublin,' he said, 'is that with us both working, we'll have a network of support from our families.'

'With my family I'm not sure that's a good thing.'

He laughed. 'C'mon, if we were ever stuck, Maura could pick up Neeve from school. If we limit her exposure to short bursts, she'll survive the trauma. And Declyn can babysit, if we ever get to go out again. Then there's my family.'

Oh! Hugh's family! They were *lovely*.

His mum was warm, cuddly and a feeder; his dad was twinkly-eyed, easy-going and handy. He had a giant blue metal toolbox that opened out with accordion springs and within, organized with a logic and order that made my heart happy, was every tool anyone might ever need.

He was the opposite of Pop – all the pictures in our house hung crooked, if they hung at all, gnarly tangles of wire sprouted ominously from broken plug sockets, and his attempts to fix anything invariably ended with him losing his temper, flinging the tool and the incorrectly sized nail or Rawlplug to the floor, shouting, 'You useless hoor of a thing!' and stomping away.

Probably because of its age, things were always going wrong in our house – taps falling off, door hinges rotting, pieces of stucco falling from the ceiling into our dinner – but we learnt to not-see them. One winter, we also developed selective deafness. We'd be watching telly in the living room while the ancient radiator rattled as loudly as a jackhammer drilling into solid rock. The deafening juddering began every evening at five o'clock when the heating came on, but our solution was simply to turn the telly up to bellowing point because the alternative – Pop getting a spanner from the cutlery drawer, hitting the radiator with it until he'd managed to make everything worse, perhaps dislodging it from the wall and sending scalding rusty water spraying around the room (which happened when he 'fixed' the radiator in the hall) – was too much to contemplate.

If Mum was there for any of Pop's handymannery, the sound-track was of stifled laughter, but mostly my memories are of having a knot in my stomach. It's hardly surprising that I have chronic gastritis now – and that I was in love with Hugh's entire family: I used to fantasize about growing up in that kind of home.

In our house we lived on baked potatoes and beans because it was all Maura could make. But Hugh's mum baked cakes and had a different dinner allocated to each day of the week. Sometimes I made Hugh recite it.

'But you know it off by heart,' he'd complain.

'Ah, say it, Hugh!'

'Okay. Sunday, roast chicken. Monday, curry made with the leftovers. Tuesday, stew. Wednesday, shepherd's pie. Thursday, spaghetti. Friday, fish and chips and –'

'On Saturday, cold meats and salad.' I'd sigh with bliss.

'But it was so boring, Amy, and Wednesdays were the pits because shepherd's pie is the worst dinner ever.'

'Can our life be like that?' I asked. 'When we move to Dublin and we're a family and all grown-up?'

'*Mmmaybeeee.* But no shepherd's pie.'

'Grand. No shepherd's pie. But rigid routines, Hugh.' I was gleeful with anticipation.

Carried on a tide of optimism, but woefully unprepared, we arrived in Dublin in 2000 and into the three-bedroom house in Dundrum where we still live now. Immediately I started my new job, where I found myself working with Tim and Alastair.

As well as having gorgeous parents, Hugh had two older brothers and one younger, all deliciously normal. Neeve was lovingly welcomed, even though she took pains to remind them, 'You're not my real granny. You're not my real uncle.'

'You're right,' Fake Granny Sandie or Fake Uncle Carl would say. 'We know we're not the real ones, but is it okay if we love you too?'

'I suppose,' Neeve would concede. 'So long as you remember I'm a chip off the old block.'

(At that time, the only clothes Neeve would let us dress her in were the Rotherham United football kit – a red top, white shorts and red knee socks. Her red-gold hair was cropped and she looked so like Richie that sometimes people recognized him in her. A Rotherham youth in Dublin for a stag weekend declared, 'It's a Richie Aldin mini-me.'

'He's my daddy.'

'I can tell, son. You're a chip off the old block.'

Neeve whispered to me, 'He thought I was a boy.' She was buzzing. 'What does the chip thing mean?'

For years when she was asked what she wanted to be when she grew up, Neeve would reply, 'A professional football player, like my daddy.')

To my heartbreak, Real Granny, Real Grandpa and Real Uncle Aldin resisted my attempts to introduce them to Neeve. Richie, still playing football for one of those up-north teams, had got married again and the Aldins seemed to have decided on collective amnesia regarding his first marriage. On behalf of Neeve, it was like razors across my soul.

Meanwhile, my brothers and sisters overran our lives, with well-intentioned but non-boundaried interference.

They gave practical help – dinners for the freezer, ladders and buckets to wallpaper the house, a loan of a car until we'd found time to buy our own. More importantly, they offered financial help because – who knew? – buying a house in the same month as setting up a recording studio could leave you perilously short of cash.

Maura lent us money and so did Pop. He offered it – I'd never have asked because if you asked Pop for anything, he automatically refused. He wasn't a bad man, just innately contrary.

Trying to get the house sorted in time for the new baby while working long hours was insanely ambitious and I was still unpacking delivery crates when my waters broke. 'It's too soon,' I cried. 'Come on, let's do one more box, while I can!'

'No!' Hugh was wild with panic. 'No more crates. You're going to the fucking hospital.'

Kiara was born after a six-hour labour, which was almost

pain-free – starting as she meant to go on, always such an obli-ging child and nothing like Neeve's entry to the world, which had been a thirty-four-hour torture-fest.

Then I was home from the hospital and, considerate though Kiara was, she was still a tiny baby, and Hugh was setting up the studio, and Neeve was confused and all was chaos. Nothing felt solid – the ground was like sand slipping under our feet, and we never managed the rigid routines of my fantasies.

I'd plan to draw up schedules, I even tried to schedule time to do my schedules, but it was impossible. We were short of everything – time, energy and money, *especially* money, we've never yet achieved financial equilibrium – but we did fine.

Hugh was properly hands-on with Kiara (and with Neeve, when she'd let him). He was obedient and good at following orders. 'I'll do anything you want, but I need instructions.'

He could cook, sort of, if you gave him a recipe, but when it emerged that he could sew it scared the daylights out of me. There had to be a catch, right? (I don't mean sewing like the embroidery that hipster-men do, but he could attach buttons to shirts and name badges to Neeve's school uniform.) 'Mum taught me to sew so I could take care of myself living on my own.' (His mum was 'crafty' and it was how she and I bonded. She was 'a great knitter' and my thing was sewing, but we did a felting course together and for a while every birthday and Christ-mas present from us was a peculiar felt hat or bag.)

It shouldn't be worthy of comment that a man helps in the home, but Hugh fulfilled his duties so diligently that there were times I actually felt sorry for him. I remember stumbling down the stairs one night, it was gone two, and Hugh was in our kit-chen, dolloping homemade puréed carrot into tiny Tupperware pots to be frozen for Kiara's dinners.

'What are you *at*?' I asked.

'You left a note to do them.'

'I didn't mean in the middle of the night, Hugh. They could have waited till tomorrow.'

'But I'll be gone first thing.'

'Cripes. Okay.' I started helping to snap lids on to them and I had to laugh. 'Oh, Hugh, look at you! It's not so long since you were a single man with all of Soho at your sexual disposal. Now you're buried in Dublin suburbia, father to two young girls, one of them not even yours. Aren't you great to "take her on"?'

The 'take her on' was our in-joke because Pop had actually said to Hugh, 'Fair play for taking on another chap's child. You wouldn't catch me doing it.'

And even if no one else articulated it, it was alluded to every time they gave me the full-on heart stare, squeezed my shoulder too hard and said, 'That's a good man you've got there, Amy. A *really* good man.'

'And here you are in the middle of the night, puréeing carrot – where did it all go so wrong?'

He looked up and smiled. 'Babe, you and me, I'm all in. A hundred per cent. Both feet.'

13

'Mum!' Kiara sounds alarmed. 'Get dressed.'

Blearily I look at her. What day is it? Monday? Time for work? No, it's still Sunday – I'd fallen asleep, probably because I haven't slept properly for the past week, but it's always a mistake to sleep in the middle of the afternoon: it takes ages for me to wake up and then I can't sleep that night.

'C'mon,' Kiara says. 'Time for the cinema!'

Oh, God. Oh, God, oh, God, oh, God. I can't go. Several Facebook people will be at the cinema, they'll all have seen my post – I'll be the centre of attention. 'Honey, would you mind –'

'I would,' she says. 'This is our last outing as a family for fuck knows how long so, yes, I would mind.'

I spring from the bed. Kiara never swears and she always puts others first. But her life as she knows it is about to be interrupted, maybe permanently. I lurch towards the bathroom.

'Hop in the shower,' she says. 'I'll make you coffee and choose your clothes.'

'Thanks.' My tongue feels too big for my mouth.

I stand under the hot water, glad Kiara has been straight with me. I've been given a loud and clear message: falling apart is not an option. I'm not the only person affected by Hugh going: my responsibilities to Kiara, Sofie and Neeve come before any responsibility to myself.

She's standing by with coffee and two dresses – a vaguely steampunk midi-length dark blue one, and a vaguely steampunk midi-length dark red one. My 'personal shopper' in Help the Aged is a great woman for sourcing Victorian-style items, which is all good so long as I don't over-accessorize. With a mini top-hat, for example. Or a medicine-bag handbag.

'Which one?' Kiara holds up both dresses.

I'd have been happy in jeans, but Kiara, intuitive as always, sees the power of good clothing.

In fact . . . 'Fuckit, get my Finery dress!'

'Wow. The heavy guns!'

Kiara pulls out an ivy-dark, high-necked, ruffle-bodiced midi, as sexy as a sack. Hugh has never minded me shunning slinky body-con. He's actively steered me towards shin-length dresses with statement sleeves because he knows that's what I'm comfortable in. Men like him are rare.

Yeah, I think, so rare that he actually doesn't exist. After all, he's leaving me to spend time with girlies who'll probably be running around in cut-off shorts and teeny-tiny Lycra sheaths. Quite disconsolate, I pull on some tights.

'Shoes?' Kiara asks. 'Your mary-janes?'

I hesitate. A while ago there had been some article saying that no woman over the age of seventeen should wear mary-janes, and ever since I'd felt apologetic about mine. Another article had said you should find your look and stick to it, which is what I'd been trying to do, but the mary-janes piece haunted me.

'Or your Miu Miu boots?' She has picked up on my hesitation.

'The boots,' I say quickly.

They're the best boots in the whole world – stompy, chunky-heeled black lace-ups, they'd been a gift to myself to celebrate winning the Perry White contract and even then I'd had to wait for the 60 per cent off sale. In theory I'm at least twenty years too old for Miu Miu but these boots work so I ignore any shouts of 'Oi, mutton!'

In fairness, apart from my internal voices, the only person who actually mocks me is Neeve and I can't tell you how fortunate I feel that my feet are two sizes smaller than hers because she steals all my other good stuff. (Then Kiara steals it back and deposits it in my lap like a faithful dog.)

'This bag?' Kiara presents a small pretty clutch.

'Too needy.' Today calls for a bag that can take care of itself. My hands might be required – a sudden unwelcome image of me shoving my way through a throng, all clamouring to know the grisly details of Hugh's holiday, flashes like a horror film.

'This?' She presents my sturdy satchel.

'Perfect.'

We aren't going to a normal cinema, where you sit among a crowd of texting teenage boys chomping their way through giant hot-dogs. This is a cinema *club*, held in our local theatre at five o'clock every Sunday during the school term. It started up again last week after the summer break. The movies are (you may have suspected this) foreign and, between the craft beers and Basque-inspired tapas, the whole business is *mortifyingly* middle-class.

But the girls like it. In fact, honesty compels me to admit that *I* like it. The films themselves are a mixed bag: some are charming and some – particularly the Iranian ones – downright baffling. But the best thing is that Neeve often comes along and observes a ceasefire. After the film, more often than not with Sofie's Jackson also in tow, we go to Wagamama and discuss how mental the film was (if it had been and, happily, it usually had).

In its ordinary way, the whole ritual makes me grateful for everything, and one short week ago, it had summed up my life. Now it's horrifying that I hadn't savoured every wonderful second of it. Like everyone, my focus had been on my worries – Neeve carrying on with 'My Real Dad is the Best Man Ever', poor Sofie and her struggles with food, and my perpetual anxieties about money. Instead I should have been full of gratitude.

'Come on!' Hugh shouts from downstairs. 'The car park will be full!'

You know, I'm even nostalgic about his perpetual irritation from living with a household of tardy women.

'Is Sofie coming today?' I ask Kiara.

'I don't know. She's not answering Dad's texts.'

She was ignoring mine too, and I'm suddenly furious with Hugh all over again because he's not just leaving me he's leaving all of us. I've always found it easier to be angry on someone else's behalf. Poor Sofie, poor little Sofie . . .

14

Fourteen years ago

Hugh, Neeve, Kiara and I were lurching on with our new life in Dublin, perpetually exhausted and focused on some far-off day in the future when everything would be under control. Then, just after Kiara's second birthday, three-year-old Sofie arrived in Ireland.

Joe had left Urzula when Sofie was only a few weeks old. Urzula had done her best to support herself and Sofie in Latvia, but it had proved impossible. After three years of hardship, she'd got a job waitressing on a cruise ship (this was before she'd discovered her true calling as a fatso-botherer). She'd make money but she couldn't take her daughter with her.

So Sofie was despatched to Joe, who had moved back to Dublin.

She arrived semi-feral – she hadn't been potty-trained, she barely spoke, wouldn't make eye contact, and if she ate at all, it was with her hands. It was appalling and shameful: this was my *niece.* I should have known about this and done something to help.

Super-quickly, Joe discovered that he couldn't hold down a full-time job *and* take care of his little girl. Which was utter bull-shit because if he'd been a woman he'd have been expected to make it work. Lots of women did. Lots of men too, in fairness. But not Joe.

He took to foisting Sofie on Maura, Derry or me. Even though we all made fun of Maura, she had a heart of gold – but being in charge of young children distressed her. 'It re-triggers my traumatic childhood. It's why I've had no children of my own.' (Maura has had a lot of therapy. For all the good it has done her. Well, at least she understands her rages. That must count for something.)

As for Derry, she correctly intuited that, as a single woman with no dependants, she was the likeliest candidate to pick up most of the slack – and no way was she having it. Derry's most prized asset was her independence.

Which left me. And Hugh, of course. And from the word go, the only person Sofie seemed to trust was Hugh.

There are some people who have that quality – dogs can usually sense them. Like, if I was with Hugh in a roomful of people and a dog walked in, you'd almost see Champ thinking, Hey, I like *this* one, and heading straight for Hugh.

So, when Joe dropped Sofie off at our house, she'd stand in the corner, staring at the floor and slowly, on stealthy little feet, she'd move closer to Hugh. She'd climb on to the couch and lean against him and, after a while, he'd lift his arm and she'd press her tiny bones against his T-shirted belly. Hugh was the only one who could persuade her to eat, and no one but Hugh was permitted to comb her tangled white-blonde hair.

When Joe returned to pick her up – always late and often very late – she'd put her little hands on Hugh's beardy face and cover it with kisses, then, weeping silent, alarmingly grown-up tears, let herself be led away.

'How is Hugh so good with kids?' Steevie asked me.

'Haven't a notion. He's the second youngest in his family, so it's not like he's learnt by taking care of littlies.'

'Maybe he's just kind.' Steevie sounded doubtful.

'Maybe he is . . .'

A solution for Sofie was a constant worry. She spent so much time in our house that the notion of her officially becoming part of the family was looking inevitable. But Hugh had already 'taken on' another man's child – not that he ever made it seem that way. From the word go, he'd approached Neeve with an open heart (which was far from reciprocated, let me tell you).

But Hugh and I seemed to share the same brain, so it wasn't a huge surprise when, early one Saturday morning, he gently shook me awake. 'Let's go now before it gets too busy,' he said. 'We're buying Sofie a bed. She needs to live with us.'

I thought my heart would burst with love for him.

We decided she could share Kiara's room until we had the cash to convert the attic, then bought a little white bed, which we painted pink because Sofie was very, very girly. A suitable duvet cover was harder to come by: nothing was pretty enough.

'Could you do your Amy magic?' Hugh asked. 'Could you make one with the shiny, sparkly stuff in your sewing box?'

I hoarded offcuts of lustrous fabric and items that could only be called 'haberdashery' – spangly flowers, glittery ribbons and crispy tulle. They'd been gathered at car-boot sales and school fêtes in the hope that they'd come in handy one day. As I created a Wonderland of a duvet cover, it felt good that I'd been finally proved right.

When Sofie saw her winking, twinkling pink bed she stared at it, then stared at us, and whispered, 'Mine?'

'Yours,' we said.

She approached it as if it might bite, then slowly climbed up and started to take in the details of the duvet, cooing and exclaiming as she discovered butterflies, ladybirds and roses. 'Fairy magic!' she announced, with a wide smile.

Hugh's hold on my shoulder tightened so much that it hurt. Both of us were trying not to cry.

So, Sofie moved in and became potty-trained almost overnight. She began speaking fully formed sentences in English. She slept through the night, stopped the incessant sucking of her two middle fingers, started calling Hugh 'Dad' (I was still 'Amy'), never asked about her mum, which was just as well, because phone calls from her were infrequent, and treated Joe with benign indifference.

Unlike poor Neeve, who remained obsessed with her 'bio-dad' (grim phrase) and his new wife and daughters, Sofie blossomed in our care.

15

'If we're going,' Hugh shouts from the kitchen, 'we need to go RIGHT NOW!'

I hurry down the stairs, and he is standing with Neeve, rummaging through the pile of stuff by the draining board. 'Is it this one?' He holds up a lip-glaze.

'No,' she says.

'Is it this one?' Another lip colour.

'No.'

'Is it this one?'

'*Yaaaaassss.*' She snatches a liquid lipstick from him.

'Put it on in the car! We haven't time.'

And, thank God, here's Sofie, coming up the path. But to my enormous shock, she's shaved her hair off.

In a way, she looks adorable, like a duckling, with her white-blonde stubble and huge blue eyes. But you could also say she looks like a medieval penitent, atoning for some obscure sin. She walks straight into Hugh's arms and sobs against him. He holds her tight and lets her cry it out. Eventually she pulls away, pats his arm, gives him a watery smile and they're friends again.

'What d'you do to your *hair*, you mad yoke?' Neeve asks.

Thank God someone addressed it head on.

'Got extensions,' Sofie says.

We all have a laugh.

'Is Jackson coming?' Hugh asks, making a move to the front door.

'We'll meet him there.'

Neeve asks, 'Should I change my jeans?'

'NO!' the rest of us yelp.

Squabbling, talking over each other and finalizing last-minute grooming, the five of us are all finally in the car and Hugh reverses out with a squeal of tyres.

At the theatre, the girls and I usually go into the foyer together while Hugh parks, but today I stick with him because I want us to arrive together and deliver a DOEU (Display of Extreme Unity).

He's been instructed on the matter, so we step through the automatic doors with our arms around each other, then pause momentarily so that anyone who's interested can take a good long look at us. *Check this out. My husband may be leaving me for six months, perhaps even for ever, but we seem really together, right?*

In the foyer the wine o'clock merchants are out in force – hollow-eyed women, who're swilling glasses of Merlot like they've just received word that the grape harvest has failed, and suburban wannabe-hipster dads, downing craft beer and alarmingly expensive Basque ham. ('Hand-reared, acorn-fed, cries easily and enjoys reruns of *Columbo*.')

A couple of heads jerk in our direction but it's not like that scene in *Gone with the Wind* where Scarlett O'Hara brings a ball to a complete standstill because she's been caught up to no good with Ashley Wilkes. (The precise details escape me.)

Hugh starts to move forward but I tighten my hold on his waist. *Not just yet.* A few more seconds to fix the picture in everyone's head. I feel fake and exposed, and I wonder if this is like being the spouse of a disgraced politician, doing a photoshoot as a display of All Grand Here, No Homosexuality or Embezzlement to Worry About.

Okay. That will do. I loosen my hold on Hugh, then someone bangs into us from behind, sending us tumbling apart. 'Sorry!' they cry.

'No, no, we're sorry!'

'No, *we*'re sorry.'

We're *all* sorry, but as they move off I hear one of them say to the other, 'What the hell were they doing just standing there anyway?'

I spot Posh Petra.

'Right,' I say to Hugh. 'There's Petra. You can go to the bar.'

Petra is downing the Merlot good-oh, but when she sees me, she hurtles in my direction. 'Sweetheart.' She's talking like she's trying to not move her mouth. 'I messaged you a billion times.' She pulls me close. 'What's going *on*?'

Once again I'm paranoid. Is every single person here watching me with pity as they eat their costly anchovies? But a quick flick doesn't reveal anything unusual.

'Hugh's going travelling for six months.'

'What do you mean?'

'I mean he's leaving Ireland and going to other countries. He'll be gone six months.'

'Without you? What the actual fuck?'

Usually I love to hear Posh Petra swear.

I shrug. 'He wants to self-actualize.'

'Self-*actualize*?' Petra is so scornful that I think I'd better drop that line.

'Maybe he deserves time off for good behaviour.'

Her face is a mixture of wonder and sympathy. 'But . . . and sorry for probing, is it also time off for bad behaviour?' Posh Petra is clearly appalled. 'Amy, but that's . . . It's awful, isn't it? Are you okay?'

'I don't know yet. I don't think I'll know until he's gone. Which is Tuesday morning.'

'So soon! You know I love you.' Petra looks me in the eyes. 'And it's not just me, you have good friends. Together we'll take care of you.'

Normally I hate being pitied but I'm tired and frightened and so very sad.

'You're welcome at mine any time of the day or night. You can even move in if you like.'

Baked beans, I think. *Baked beans in my hair.*

Petra catches my thought. 'It's those two little bitches, isn't it?' Her eyes are too bright. 'They've ruined my life, Amy. They're ruining my friendships. They're ruining my career.' Petra works in an art gallery. 'Hey,' she says, 'will you come to the opening on Thursday night?'

I consider it. Then, 'No.'

'Oh, Amy, do. They'll have wine.'

'I've wine at home.'

'It'll be good for you. An education.'

This is an ongoing bone of contention between the two of us. I've a thing for simply painted village or rural scenes: they make me feel safe. Petra likes grim, gloomy 'challenging' art. Like, for *why*? Life is challenging enough, why add to our burdens?

'If you come,' she tries to sound tempting, 'I'll ask the dealer if he knows anything about your mystery artist.'

One of my many, many obsessions is with an artist from Serbia, a woman.

You know when you see something phenomenally beautiful – like a Tom Ford eye palette in silvers and greys? Or those embellished Miu Miu handbags? And it has such a powerful impact on you that it's almost like being hit?

Well, this woman's paintings do that to me.

The first time I saw them was on Pinterest and immediately I started googling but I've unearthed feck-all except that she's Serbian. I don't even know if she's still alive. Most frustrating of all, I've found no opportunity to buy her work. God knows if I could afford even a square inch of her paintings, but I'd appreciate an opportunity to find out.

'Maybe,' I say. 'Let's see how the week pans out.'

Petra tries to drink from her empty glass. 'I need more wine. That's what it'll say on my gravestone.'

'I'll walk with you to the bar.' But I'm intercepted by Jana.

'Amy, honey-bun, I've been calling –'

'I know, sorry.'

'What's happening?'

'Hugh's going travelling for six months. Time off for bad behaviour.' I attempt a laugh. It's a fail. 'Then he'll be back.'

She seems confused. 'Are you upset?'

My heart sinks. Maybe Derry is right about Jana. 'What do you think?'

'Sorry. Sorry, Amy. Of course.'

'I know you'll tell Genevieve but could you pretend that I'm not devastated?'

'I won't tell Genevieve anything.'

'Jana . . .'

'Okay,' she admits. 'I'll tell her the facts but I'll say you're cool with it. I *promise*.' Her face is earnest with sincerity and who knows? Maybe she will.

'But, Amy, do you get time off too? For bad behaviour, like? Because that's something, right?'

God, no. This is almost worse than pity.

'Yeah, you go, girl!' She raises her wine glass and gives a small whoop that has heads turning. Loudly, Jana declares, 'Look at us! Drinking wine before six o'clock, eating *pintxos*, about to see a Malaysian film, and now one of us has an open marriage – you've got to hand it to us, we're a sophisticated bunch!'

16

'Morning,' Tim mutters. He barely looks up from his screen.

'Morning.' I don't know which is worse, people wanting to hear every ghoulish detail of Hugh's plans or – as Tim is doing – behaving like nothing is up.

And here comes Alastair, dressed way too casually in faded jeans and a pale blue collarless shirt, which probably means he met some girl on his stupid weekend course and hasn't been home yet. 'Morning.' His teeth glint around the room. 'Good weekends?'

I stare fixedly at my blank screen. Obviously he's been on one of his frequent, short-lived digital detoxes.

'Timothy?' You can always tell that Alastair is in the giddiest of good form, when he starts calling people by their full names. Thamy had probably been given her full name of Thamyres and doubtless I'll be Amelia'd. 'Nice couple of days, Timothy? Let me guess, you cut the grass? Fixed a leaky tap? No, it's all coming back to me – a party, right? A sixth birthday?'

Tim has five children – five! The youngest is twenty months and the oldest is sixteen. His wife is a surgeon who, all credit to her, won't even change a nappy; Tim is very hands-on.

'You made Rice Krispie buns?' Alastair asks.

'I did,' Tim says.

'Any visits to A and E? A child fell out of the tree-house? Or swallowed a battery?'

'The dog got sick and I had to go to the emergency vet with nine six-year-olds.'

'The usual mayhem. Well, I'd a very productive weekend. My course was excellent.'

'You're cured now?' Tim asks.

94

'Cured. Happy. That's me.' It's impossible to tell if he means it, but even if he does, it won't last. It never does. 'So how about you, Amelia? Nice weekend?'

There's a horrible pause.

'What?' Alastair asks. He looks from me to Tim and back again. '*What?*'

'Ehmmmm. Hugh is taking time out for six months.' I listen to myself saying the words. 'Going back-packing. Leaving tomorrow.'

'*Hugh?*' Alastair chokes. 'Your husband Hugh?'

Almost worse than Alastair's shock is Tim's silence – he's totally got the entire situation.

'When you say "time out"?' Alastair asks.

'Yes,' I say. 'Time *out*. Or time off, whatever you want to call it.'

'Even, like, other women? Jesus *Christ*.' Alastair looks scandalized. 'I always thought you guys were rock-solid.'

Yes, well . . . I am *dying* here.

'And what about you?' he asks. 'Are you on time off too?'

'Stop it!' This is Tim's first comment.

'I'm not . . . I don't mean it like that.' Alastair's hurt is genuine. 'I'm only *asking*. Amy's like a sister to me. You are, Amy. Like a sister. I *care*. So, was it a sudden decision? Or coming for a while?'

'Sort of both. It was a shock, a big one. But it probably goes back a while.'

'Since his dad died?'

'Mmm.' Or maybe even longer. Try sixteen months.

'Stop with the interrogation,' Tim says to Alastair. Then, to me, 'Would you like a break from here? A few mental-health days?'

People say that Tim isn't much craic, and even though that's probably true, he can be deeply kind. I shake my head. 'I need to be busy.'

'If Hugh is leaving tomorrow, you want Alastair to take your meetings in London? You can stay in Dublin and say goodbye properly,' Tim says.

No. No way am I going to the airport to wave Hugh off, like

he's going on a gap year, like I *approve*. Nor am I running the risk of having a public meltdown. No, we'll say goodbye the way we do every Tuesday morning at five thirty. He'll be still in bed, barely awake, and I'll give him a quick kiss before I hare out of the door to the airport. For a while I'll let myself pretend that when I get home on Wednesday night he'll be there, like he always is, and not halfway across the world.

'Would you like a hug?' Alastair asks.

'From you?' I ask doubtfully. 'I wouldn't have thought so.' Then I add, 'But thanks anyway.'

'If you change your mind . . .'

I wouldn't. 'Lads, please, I don't want a big deal to be made of this,' I say. 'I'm ashamed and afraid and I just want life to be normal. Come on, let's get to work.'

'Give us a minute.' Alastair goes to 'his' cupboard. Tim and I widen our eyes and exchange a knowing nod as Alastair takes a little volume of Rumi's poetry from a pile of about twenty he keeps in there.

Alastair has *definitely* met someone, a new lady-friend, on his course – we always know he has a new girl on the go when we see him putting one of the books into a Jiffy-bag, along with a handful of dried crocus petals, then trying to slip it into the outgoing office mail. The poor girls are usually gullible enough to think the Rumi means that Alastair is deeply spiritual, but as Tim says, he's so heart-centred he won't even pay the price of the postage. (Although, these days, Alastair makes a big deal of putting a fiver on Thamy's desk and announcing loudly, 'To cover the cost of mailing a personal item,' then giving Tim a baleful stare.)

But Alastair flicks through the pages of the book, finds one that he likes, then puts it in front of me. No! The Rumi poetry is for me! 'Read that.'

Tim looks appalled and sympathetic.

I read the poem.

> *This being human is a Guest House*
> *Every morning a new arrival.*

A joy, a depression, a meanness,
Some momentary awareness comes
As an unexpected visitor.

Welcome and entertain them all!
Even if they're a crowd of sorrows,
Who violently sweep your house
Empty of its furniture.
Still treat each guest honourably,
He may be clearing you out for some new delight.

I don't want any 'new delight' – and by 'new delight' Alastair doubtless means I should sleep with some new man. Not himself, that's not what he's getting at. But *some* man. Honest to God, everyone is *fixated* with sex – last night in the cinema foyer three separate women friends made you-go-girl noises. As if it's a good thing that Hugh is going, when what I feel is nothing but loss, terrible loss.

17

Thamy puts an elaborate arrangement of autumnal branches and berries on my desk.

Unlikely as it is, I get a surge of ridiculous hope that they're from Hugh, saying he's changed his mind. I tear open the card: 'Thank you for giving me back my life. Bryan (Sawyer) xxx.'

Oh.

'Who from?' Alastair asks.

'Bryan Sawyer.'

'The klepto?'

'*Ex*-klepto,' Tim says. 'All shiny and new and respectable again, thanks to Amy.'

Tears of disappointment gather in my eyes, then spill down my face. Discreetly, I swipe them away: I can't be a person who cries at work. Behind me, I hear Tim get up and I try harder to compose myself. Something is put beside my mouse – a small box of tissues. Surprised, I turn to thank him, but he's already back behind his screen. His silent kindness makes my tears flow faster.

I sniff, trying to do it quietly but Alastair hears.

'Y'okay?'

'Hay-fever.' I indicate the bouquet from Bryan.

'Hay-f—? Oh, right, hay-fever.'

'I can see you're hurting.' Alastair corners me later for a pep-talk. 'But you should make the most of this time.'

I know exactly what he's getting at. 'Stop, would you? My confidence is in bits. I'm forty-four and feeling every second of it, and even if I wanted to, there's no way I'd reveal this elderly body to a new man. It'd be like *Game of Thrones* when Melisandra takes off her necklace and ages nine hundred years.'

'You're not that bad,' Alastair says. 'Seriously. *I* would.'

'I thought I was like a sister to you?'

'*Weeeell*, I could probably get past that.'

'Could you?' For a moment I'm genuinely curious.

'Sure!' He sounds way *too* emphatic to be believed.

Nevertheless, I consider him for a long moment – the cheekbones, the jaw, the famous mouth – then think, Reverse cowgirl, and the notion vanishes. It would be AWFUL.

'Ames, are you certain you can't talk Hugh out of this?'

'Certain.'

'But he's so . . . *easy-going.*'

'Only up to a point.' Because when Hugh wanted something, *really* wanted it, he did it.

'Well, look, I'm your friend. If I can help, let me know.'

Off he goes, leaving me alone with a memory of something that happened a couple of years ago.

Hugh is a bit of a muso, always was, and he often says that if Carlsberg did lives, his would be as front man for one of those jangly guitar bands. He loves going to gigs. But for me they're a living hell – being slopped with beer, unable to see anything because of my shortness, having to wear flats because heels sink into the grass . . . misery, all of it.

When we moved back to Dublin, Hugh got in touch with three other lads he'd been in a band with as teenagers (The Janitors) and they decided to start it up again. Hugh played lead guitar and shared the singing with Clancy (they called each other by their surnames, just like they had as kids, Hugh is 'Durrant'), and all four of them took the endeavour semi-seriously. Thursday night was 'band practice', and it didn't matter how inconvenient it was, Hugh staked that time out for himself.

'I need it,' he'd told me. 'I can show up in every other part of my life if I have this.'

So he'd disappear over to Nugent's for several hours, rolling in during the early hours of Friday morning smelling of sweat and weed.

Whatever happened in Nugent's garage, involving amps and plectrums, remained a mystery to me. I'd less than zero interest – and I sort of despised myself for not being a cool muso-girl, with a Chrissie Hynde fringe and winkle-picker shoes, who nurtured ambitions herself to play lead guitar.

But I guess I had my own thing – 'vintage' clothing – and just because Hugh and I were close, we didn't have to be identical twins, right?

Oddly – interestingly? – well, whatever it was, I didn't like being around Hugh when he was hanging out with the other guys from the band. They were nice men, and they were just as ordinary and coupled-up as Hugh. But he was slightly different when he was with them – he'd drink more and his voice would get louder and he'd make in-jokes that I was excluded from. I was so attuned to *my* version of Hugh that any other versions, no matter how minute the difference, jarred. I often got narky and wanted to yell at him, 'Why are you talking shite and shouting?'

About once a year he and the lads went to a foreign city – Copenhagen, Berlin, Manchester – to a gig, and there was an afternoon a couple of years ago when I ended a call from Maura and said to Hugh, 'Big news. Joe's putting a ring on Siena on September the twenty-ninth.'

'September the twenty-ninth?' He shook his head. 'I'll be in Amsterdam at the Smashing Pumpkins.'

'Nuh-uh.' I shook my head. 'No Amsterdam. Sorry, honey. It's my brother's wedding.'

'I've my ticket to the gig. I'm going with the boys. It's all booked.'

There were other issues tied up in this – mostly that Hugh thought Joe was a total arse – and it seemed clear that all that was needed was a little persuasion. 'But –'

'I'm going to the gig, Amy.'

'Hugh . . .' It was inconceivable that he wouldn't do what I wanted.

'I'm not going to Joe's wedding. Not unless he moves the date. Then I'm happy to go.'

It was rare for him to front me out, but the moment I felt the rigour of his resolve, my capitulation was instant. I learnt something that day: you could push Hugh and push Hugh and push Hugh and he'd give in over and over and over, with gracious ease. And then one day you'd hit solid rock and nothing would budge him.

18

'What's for dinner?' Kiara comes into the kitchen.

'Takeaway.'

'On a Monday?' She's delighted.

Monday is my night to cook. Hugh does it Tuesday to Thursday. But . . . 'I'm not fucking cooking tonight.'

Kiara's smile vanishes. 'Yikers.'

Yikers is right. There's no way I'm preparing food to launch Hugh's Big Adventure.

'What can we get?' she asks.

'Whatever you like.'

'Even Eddie Rocket's?'

'Yep.'

Eddie Rocket's is only for special occasions because we all eat far too much – we're incapable of stopping even when we feel sick – but tonight I don't care.

'Oh-*kaaay*,' Kiara says. 'And maybe we'll just get pizzas.'

'Honey, I'm sorry.' It's all kinds of wrong to be taking this out on Kiara. 'Get Eddie Rocket's.'

'No,' she says. 'I mean, it's not like it's a celebration, is it? But pizzas are a good compromise. Oh, here's Dad. Hey, where were you?'

'The tropical-medicine place, getting my jabs!' After all those months where he'd been practically mute, he's chatty and exuberant. I hate him.

'Then I went to Boots,' he indicates his shopping bags, 'and bought a full medicine kit.'

I feel like asking if he'd bought condoms on his chemist run, but manage not to. I mean, he'd better have. If he thinks he can have unprotected sex with countless girls and then come back to me – *Oh, my God, Hugh having sex with other women . . .*

'We're getting pizzas for dinner,' Kiara says.

'Oh? We are?' He gives me an uncertain look and I busy myself making a cup of tea. 'Okay, I'll have my usual.'

'Mum, what would you like?'

'Nothing.'

'Amy . . .' Hugh says.

'I'm not hungry.' I haven't eaten all day.

'Get her some garlic bread,' Hugh tells Kiara.

'*Don't* get me some garlic bread,' I say.

He's scared I'm going to cry – he can never cope with seeing me in tears. But he needn't worry: I'm tense and dry. Every part of me has seized up.

'Sweetie, I'm sorry,' I say to Kiara.

'No need to apologize.' She scoots from the room and calls up to Neeve. 'We're getting pizzas. What do you want?'

Hugh tries to hold me and I wriggle away from him, go into the sitting room and bury my face in my iPad. He follows me in. 'Amy,' he starts. 'I'm sorry.'

'Yeah.' If I had any sense, I'd make sure his last memory is of me being lovely but I'm sick of 'being understanding'. What he's foisted on me is a big, big ask. Another woman would be shouting the odds or mainlining hefty sedation under these circumstances. Probably just point-blank refusing to let him go. I've been extremely well behaved, all things considered. Mind you, it's a pity I couldn't have managed it for a few more hours . . .

'Would you like some wine?'

'Nope.' I'm afraid to start drinking because there's a real chance I'll get scuttered and lose the head.

'Can I get you anything at all?'

'Nope.'

'How about a lie-down?'

'*Yepppp.*' I was doing very brief answers, finishing each word with an excellent smacking noise. It was immensely satisfying. Maybe if I did a Tinder profile I could include it as a hobby.

'Come on, I'll walk you upstairs –'

'*Noppppppe.* Because you'll be in and out of the bedroom all evening, finishing your fucking packing. Anyway!' I say fake-cheerily. 'Soon you'll be gone and I'll have the room all to myself.'

He hangs his head. 'I'll come back.'

I do an elaborate shrug. 'We'll see.'

I lie on the couch and absent myself from all the to-ing and fro-ing and think back to the early days. Yes, we were always tired, yes, we were always short of money, but we were so together.

There was one day, one random day, nothing unusual about it, maybe twelve years ago, when I came home and heard shrieks and screams of delight. I followed the sounds of laughter up the stairs and found Hugh lying on our bedroom floor while Neeve, Kiara and Sofie scribbled on his face with my make-up. This happened a lot and Hugh often went to work wearing glittery nail varnish.

'My spendy lipstick!' I yelped.

'Look at the lady!' Kiara presented Hugh's decorated face – she'd been about four at the time. 'He's a beautiful lady.' And all of them had collapsed into helpless laughter.

'Take it off,' I said. 'We're going out! Taney summer fête!'

'Cleanse, tone, moisturize!' Sofie ordered Hugh, scurrying off to get cotton-wool pads.

'Everyone get ready,' I said. 'Quick! All the good stuff will be gone!'

'What good stuff?'

'Cakes!'

Fifteen minutes later we assembled at the door, Hugh, his face now free of make-up, apart from the occasional hint of glitter in his shaggy hair, wore a Psychedelic Furs T-shirt and black jeans. Neeve was in her footballing kit, while Kiara was dark, sturdy and grave, favouring a 1940s-style look – an embroidered dress, a formal navy coat, ribbed tights, mary-jane shoes and neatly brushed hair secured with a sober black slide. She even carried one of my mum's old handbags, a prim leather affair, in the crook of her elbow.

Sofie, by contrast, looked like she'd been doused in glitter: yellow and black striped bumblebee wellington boots, matching tights, a sparkly pink tutu, a green cardigan covered with shiny embellishments, a pair of twinkly wings attached to her back, fluffy deely-boppers, a plethora of crystalline bracelets on each little arm and a wheely ladybird case. As Pop so often said about her, 'That one's so girly she probably cries glitter.'

'I can carry the cakes in my ladybird,' Sofie confided, in her husky, lispy voice.

'Good thinking, Batgirl.'

I eyed our messy rag-tag bunch and muttered, a little ruefully, to Hugh, 'When I was a kid, all I wanted when I grew up was to live in a family of two-point-four dullness.'

'But, babe, look at us, we're great!'

He was right. In our offbeat way we *were* great and Hugh was the glue that held us together.

I – whisper it – had a happy marriage. This was a truth I had to tiptoe into gradually, so great was my fear of tempting Fate. Not that it was actually a marriage for some years.

Hugh didn't mind whether or not we made it legal. 'I love you,' he said. 'I will love you for ever. But we can do it if you want.'

I shivered. I didn't want. Mad as it sounded, it actually felt safer *not* to be married – if a ring was put on my finger, it might, one day, have to be taken off again.

But the schools thing eventually forced our hand. The state schools in Ireland were controlled by the Catholics so people 'living in sin' had no chance of their kids being admitted. There were some lovely non-denominational schools but they cost money and that was something we remained woefully short of.

So, when Kiara was four, we had a low-key registry-office wedding. Neeve was the ring-bearer, Sofie and Kiara were our flower girls, Derry and Carl the witnesses. I wore a blue satin dress, and afterwards we went to Eddie Rocket's, where every time my wedding ring flashed past me, I felt as if icy water had been flung over my soul.

'It's okay,' Hugh kept whispering. 'It's only a bit of paper. It's not going to alert the Fates. This changes nothing. Remember I love you and I'll always love you.'

19

'I don't want a big tearful scene when I leave in the morning,' I tell Hugh.

'Okay.' He looks relieved.

'I'm just going to get up and go.' My flight to London was leaving Dublin at six forty-five, so I'd be getting up at five as usual.

'Okay.'

'I'll miss you.'

'I'll miss you.'

'Then why are you going?'

He twists away from me.

'If you'd properly left me at least I'd know where I stood.'

'I'm sorry.'

'This is so weird. I don't know how I should feel.'

What is astonishing is how much I've changed – when I'd first met Hugh, self-reliance ran through my core. Somewhere along the line, I'd been reconfigured into someone who was just one half of a marriage, but that fearless woman might still be inside me – there had been a thing in *Psychologies* saying we carry all our earlier selves inside our current self, like those sets of Russian dolls. If I could just reconnect with that version of me, everything would be grand.

'What if I do start to enjoy myself while you're gone?' I ask Hugh. 'What if you come home, all set to slot back into our old life and I don't want to?'

'If that happens, we'll deal with it.'

'If that was meant to make me feel better, it didn't work.'

He laughs, and all of a sudden he's Hugh again, my best friend, my most favourite person in the whole world – and I laugh too.

We both go to bed early, but I'm too sad and angry for sex.

In the darkness I lie on my side and he snuggles up behind me, fitting his body to mine. He puts his arm around my waist, pulls me tight against him and our breathing patterns fall into sync.

This is the last time we'll ever be together like this, I think.

But maybe not. Maybe we'll be together exactly like this at some unspecified time in the future. But there's so much horrible stuff to be endured to get to that point.

My alarm goes off at five a.m., but I'm already awake, curled in silent misery, wishing time would stop. I pull myself out of bed and under the shower, hoping the fall of water might loosen the terrible tightness clamping my chest.

Back in the bedroom, Hugh is also awake.

'Be asleep,' I say. He doesn't reply, just lies, motionless, looking as forlorn as I feel. It's hard to accept that when I get back from London tomorrow night, he'll be gone.

Silently he watches as I do my make-up, then hoick open my underwear drawer and pull out my favourite bra, a bright fuchsia one.

I hesitate. For the first time ever, it feels shaming to be naked in front of him. I don't want him heading off with a memory of my less-than-perky bosoms, which would fare badly in a comparison with any younger ones he might meet on his travels. I pick up all my clothes and finish dressing behind the bathroom door. Then I step into my ankle boots, take the handle of my wheely case and – unexpectedly – in a swift, efficient gesture, snatch up my hairbrush and fire it across the room. It hits him on the temple.

'Amy! Go easy!'

'Did that hurt? Good.' I move towards the door. 'Bye.'

He moves aside the duvet and the sweet male smell of him, warm from the bed, billows out. 'Get in for a second.'

'No.'

'Please.'

So I climb into bed, fully clothed and let him take me in his arms. We hug fiercely, his arms pressing so tightly against my back that it hurts. I bury my face in his neck, trying to capture the smell of his hair, his skin, his breath, knowing that it'll have to last for the next 181 days. And maybe for ever.

His face is wet with tears and my urge is to comfort him. But the only way to help him is to let him leave.

My throat aches and I wrench myself free and hurry down the stairs. I shut my front door behind me, sick at the notion that the next time I open it Hugh will have been swallowed up by some unknowable life on the other side of the world. The early-morning air is cool and smells autumnal, adding to the sense that everything is darkening and dying.

During

It's too dark to see the sea now but I can still hear it, sucking and splashing on Brighton's stony beach.

'We could have our own disco here, stick on some songs. Really! It'll be great!'

He starts fiddling with the hotel sound system and some dancy thing comes on that I half-recognize. Then I hear 'Groove Is In The Heart' and my heart soars. 'Oh, I LOVE this song!' I jump to my feet and kick off my shoes. 'Turn it up!' I'm drunk, maybe a bit drunker than I'd realized, but I love this song and I want to dance. 'Turn it up.'

Instantly the music is ten times louder and pulsing off the walls. The bassline is inside me and the melody is all around me and I feel alive. *I twirl myself around the room and briefly all my worries lift away. There's just me and the music, and I feel happy and free.*

Then I notice him watching me dance, his face tense and still. He's relaxed his body against the sofa, his arms spread along the top. His black tie has disappeared, his shirt collar is open three buttons – I don't remember that happening – and out of nowhere I'm super-aware of undercurrents. It's like I'm giving him a lap-dance. The thought makes me excited, uncomfortable, then a queasy mix of the two.

'Louder!' I say.

Moving only his arm, still watching me avidly, he reaches his hand behind him and, without looking, twists the volume knob.

His silent gaze is too much. 'Come on, get up and dance.' I take his hands and pull him out of the seat.

He's on his feet now but he's still not dancing, just watching me. 'Dance with me,' he says.

'I am.'

'No, you're dancing at *me. I want you to dance* with *me.' He pulls me against him.*

'No!' I don't want to slow down, I don't want to stop. But in a fluid

motion, he sweeps my hair to one side, buries his face in my neck and gives it a small sharp bite. Suddenly he's got my attention.

I'm not dancing any more.

I whisper, 'What was that?'

I want to get away but his arms are hard against my back and, caught in his force-field, all I can do is look at him.

His face is coming closer to mine. He's moved one hand to the back of my head and he's pulling me towards him. Then his mouth is on me, he means business, things aren't going to end at this –

I wrench myself free. 'We can't, I can't!'

I'm panting, he's panting. His shirt is crumpled and his eyes are wild.

He groans and I repeat, 'We can't.' I push myself away, creating distance.

'I'm not sorry.' He steps towards me again. 'I've wanted to do that since for ever.'

'You have?'

'Since the first time I saw you.'

20

Tuesday, 13 September, day one   2016

Irritably I weave through the dithery throngs in Heathrow – I keep hitting little pockets of rage, like emotional turbulence – and finally reach the tube.

Since I left home I've been afraid a full-blown panic attack will grab me, and the way we're squashed into the train makes me feel even more tight-chested and gaspy. This is going to be a tough day.

With no internet to distract me, worry about Hugh starts to gnaw. What if the blow from my hairbrush causes bleeding in his brain? There had been something on *Grey's Anatomy* – he could have an aneurysm. The thought of him collapsing in some foreign city, surrounded only by strangers, makes me cold.

He might die.

Yeah, well, we're all going to die. And he's brought it on himself. If he hadn't decided to take off for six months, he wouldn't have had a hairbrush thrown at his head. I've been with him for more than seventeen years and I've never thrown a hairbrush at him before today. Go figure.

Marble Arch is my stop. I push through the rush-hour crowds, and ten minutes before my first meeting I arrive at my 'office'. It's actually Home House, the private members' club. Both Alastair and I belong to it because the annual fee is a lot less than running a London office.

The next two days will be busy and that's probably good: downtime is no friend to me, not even the occasional second to think, because any hiatus will be like an abyss, and if I tumble in, there might be terrible difficulty in getting back out again.

Over the next forty-eight hours I'll be required to eat and drink a lot, and while the eating might prove a challenge, the drinking bit should be nice.

A good PR firm keeps in with as many influential journos and TV producers as possible so that when the shit hits the fan there are friends to call on for help.

Keeping in with the Irish media is no bother because everyone knows everyone. Then Tim, Alastair and I cover the UK as best we can: Tim goes to Edinburgh every second Thursday; I'm in London every Tuesday and Wednesday and Alastair takes over from me on Thursdays and Fridays.

Unless a crisis blows up – and that happens a fair bit – my work (which doesn't sound like work at all, I know) mostly involves me and my laptop taking up residence in Home House and showing media people some love. I enquire about sick kids, I remember spouses' names and, above all else, I ply them with food and drink.

My day tends to move from breakfast meetings to brunch to lunch to afternoon tea to dinner, and my weekly alcohol unit allowance is nearly always used up by mid-afternoon on Tuesday, thanks to Mimosa at breakfast, Prosecco at brunch, wine at lunch and Champagne at afternoon tea.

I wish I didn't have to drink so much but people take a dim view of me urging them on to get scuttered while restricting my own consumption to sips of fizzy water. However, right now, I'm very grateful to have a job that involves compulsory mid-morning alcohol.

What I do is basically horse-trading – for example, if you kill the story about my client Mr X being cruel to kangaroos, I'll give you an exclusive comeback interview with another of my clients, Ms Y, as soon as she's out of rehab. (Honestly, for every story where a famous person does something idiotic or illegal, there are probably ten that are never published. The stuff that goes *on*, I tell you, you just wouldn't believe it. And it's usually the least powerful and most vulnerable who are publicly shamed. Anyone with any kind of heft gets the bad stories dropped.)

As a teenager my career aspirations involved something

arty – to do with clothes, maybe, or interiors. But I hadn't done art at school – Pop wouldn't let me, insisted it wasn't a real subject – so when I moved to Leeds with Richie, with no qualifications at all, it was just pure chance that my lowly receptionist job happened to be at a PR firm.

I'd known nothing about the publicity game but those people saw something in me, began involving me in campaigns, and I learnt on the job.

So I've been doing this for a long time, first in Leeds, then London, then splitting my time between Dublin and London. Over the years I've got to know a lot of media people, and the long and the short of it is that I'm terrified of causing offence and engendering their enmity.

Hardly comparable to being down the mines, I know, but in its own first-world way, it's scary work. Media types have *so* much power. Also they're usually mad for a bit of banter, and even though I make game efforts to join in, I'm never sure where the line is.

Which means that as soon as the person has left, my brain starts replaying the conversation and my stomach gushes acid. Was it a mistake to laugh at the story of their burglary? Who in their right mind would laugh at a burglary story? But it had been narrated in a funny way and I'd been afraid *not* to laugh. On reflection, should I have found a way that acknowledged (a) the person was a comic genius who'd (b) had a traumatic experience?

My first meeting today is with an eighties pop star who's flirting with bankruptcy and hoping for a rebrand. I should float the EverDry ambassador's job by her, but under the circumstances I simply don't have the emotional energy to finesse something so thorny. All in all, our meet doesn't go so great. And neither does the next one, just a 'catch-up over coffee' with a household-name columnist for the *Guardian*, or the one after that, brunch with a hot-right-now young TV producer.

My head is a long way from being in the game and my lungs won't play ball.

But I'm functioning – saying words, standing, nodding,

breathing occasionally. Frankly, I'm pretty impressed with myself. Perhaps this is one of the benefits of adulthood – you can feel as if you've lost everything that ever mattered and still eat an omelette and enquire after a journalist's pet poodle.

After lunch I have to venture into the actual world. Currently I'm in the process of rehabilitating an ex-politician (expenses scandal) and one of my stratagems is to offer her up as the figure-head for Room, a homelessness charity. It's not a natural fit. My ex-politician, Tabitha Wilton, is posh and brisk. Her voice is a ringing, confident affair that commands instant dislike. Today she will meet with her potential ally face to face and I'm a peculiar mix of nihilistic and profoundly nervous. It's been a battle to get any charity interested in partnering with her – even without the expenses scandal, she doesn't rate highly on the likeability scale.

Yet, if this works, it could do wonders for Tabitha's image, while the charity's profile would definitely rise – with, of course, a commensurate increase in income.

The whole business is as grim as an arranged marriage, with Tabitha as the bride and me as – I don't know – the matchmaker? The bride's down-on-his-luck father? I feel hand-washy and obsequious.

The three representatives from Room are men in suits and I'm not feeling the love.

'What do you know of homelessness?' one asks, somewhat sneerily.

'Very little!' Tabitha announces, as if she's addressing people four counties away. 'But willing to learn.'

'How about you come on a soup run with our volunteers? This evening?'

Tabitha wavers – and recovers. 'Certainly!'

I exhale, a little too audibly.

'You own two homes?'

'Mortgaged to the hilt! Bank talking foreclosure! Bloody terrified, if truth be told!'

This goes down well. One of the suity-men does a small

scribble on his jotter. He could be just reminding himself that he needs to buy tissues, but if he's anything like me, he'll want her to repeat that precise line in a press interview.

'May well be calling on you *myself*, if something doesn't come through for me soon!'

In the wake of this admission, the atmosphere thaws. She's warmer and more humble than the entitled-sounding accent would give you to believe. I like her.

'You come trailing some scandal,' a suit says. 'The press will revisit it, should we choose to work with you. How would you address that?'

My heart is in my mouth. I'm so anxious that I almost want to jump in and answer this myself, but all my coaching has paid off.

'I was an idiot,' Tabitha says. 'Greedy idiot. Stealing from the tax-payer. Inexcusable. Want to make my amends to society.'

More scribbling on a jotter. Remembering he also has to buy sausages? Or is this another good sign?

Now the interrogation moves on to Tabitha's availability.

'Unemployed!' she says. 'Available twenty-four seven!'

Talk of having lunch to meet with trustees ensues – which means that Tabitha has got through to the next round. We gather up our stuff and, with me smiling, smiling, nodding, smiling, bowing my head, twisting an imaginary cap between my hands and basically giving it the Full Unctuous, we say our goodbyes.

As soon as we're outside, Tabitha says, 'Shall we go and get drunk?'

It's a bad idea: client-boundaries have to be observed. Plus I'm shattered, much more tired than I'd normally be. Also, I need to go somewhere private and try to breathe.

'You're going on a soup run later,' I say.

'All the more reason to get blotto.'

But I make my excuses.

The tube is hot, jammers and slow, and it's gone seven when I arrive at Druzie's flat in Shepherds Bush.

Druzie van Zweden has been my friend for more than twenty years. She's originally from Zimbabwe, and our lives intersected in Leeds after Richie left me. She lived in the flat above mine and, despite us having *nothing* in common, we just clicked. For two years, we were up and down the stairs to each other the whole time, and when I got a much better job in London, it was a real wrench to leave her.

But not long after, she moved to London too, and began working for a charity that oversees aid distribution in trouble hotspots. She was promoted and promoted and promoted and, these days, her job entails flitting around the globe but she has a flat in London, to which she gave me (and Alastair) a key. It saves us having to shell out on a hotel once a week, and we get to keep a toothbrush and other bits and pieces here, so it feels like home.

Druzie's easily one of my favourite people on the planet, but I'm guiltily grateful she isn't here tonight: she'd take a dim view of Hugh's shenanigans. She's pragmatic – fascinatingly so – about relationships. In her foreign postings, she finds a boyfriend almost before she's unpacked, and when her employers move her to another country, she leaves without a backward glance.

She'd probably cheerily advise me to shut the door on Hugh for ever, genuinely unable to understand why I can't.

Druzie's garden flat is tidy. There's cheese, there's peace and quiet, there's hash in a little carved box, if you're that way inclined. I'm not myself, but no judgement.

But after yearning to be free from the company of others all day long, I realize there can be such a thing as *too much* peace and quiet. I put on Jeff Buckley – too sad. I try Solange and that's worse. Nile Rodgers is no better.

What next? I'm at a loss, and when my phone rings, I'm grateful. It's Tim. 'What's wrong?' He only rings when something has gone tits-up.

'Nothing. Just checking you're . . .'

Well, that's nice. 'I'm grand, Tim. Really.'

The sitting-room doors open on to the back garden, which catches the mellow evening light. I go out with a cup of tea and my laptop. I'll do some work, then watch *Masterchef*. At times like this, I'm glad of my job: there's always something to be done.

It's only when goosebumps appear on my arms that I see it's almost ten o'clock and the garden is in chilly darkness – I've missed *Masterchef*!

Briefly there's relief that I'm not missing Hugh, then panic seizes me – I should be sadder. Like a cold hand around my heart, I think, We really are over.

I can't breathe! Fuck, I can't breathe! Oh, my God, what if I die here, all alone in Druzie's back garden?

I'm on my feet, leaning on the table and, for some long seconds, I stand with my mouth open, paralysed and desperate to hook on to a breath. Finally my chest grabs one, which goes all the way down and I'm gasping and grateful.

Christ, that was really awful. All of today was awful.

But maybe that was the worst day and everything will get a little easier from here on in.

But I'm *waaaay* too long in the tooth to know that heartbreak doesn't begin at a high watermark of horribleness, then decrease in smooth, steady increments until you land so softly you barely notice.

Emotions – particularly the unpleasant ones – dole themselves out in fits and starts. They play their cards close to their chests, taking pride in their unpredictability. Bad as I feel now, it'll be lots worse when I get home tomorrow night and there's no Hugh. The thought of the house convulsing around his absence generates another round of gasping.

21

Here we go. First night without Hugh. I get into bed in Druzie's spare room, and it's so weird not talking to him on the phone, just before I switch the light out – Wait! Someone's FaceTiming me! For a moment of ferocious hope, I think it's Hugh.

'Hey, babes. Cape Town calling.'

Seeing Derry's face is surprisingly consoling. 'Thanks for this.' It was probably tough for her to find the time.

Derry's role in human resources involves big contracts sourcing the likes of five hundred nurses or three hundred engineers in one country and shifting them to another. The trips are intense – fifteen-hour days spent sifting through sometimes thousands of candidates; interviewing, grading, selecting and making judgement call after judgement call until eventually her critical faculties are eroded to nothing.

'He go?' she asks.

'I suppose. I haven't heard otherwise.'

'How're you doing?'

'Ah, you know. Not too bad.' Now isn't the time. She looks tired and that's rare. 'When you back?'

'Friday. But I've to go to Dubai on Saturday night,' she says.

'Christ, Der, you'll die of exhaustion!'

'I'll be grand. Things have to calm down at some stage, right?' She's paid plenty, but is any amount of money worth this?

'I know you said you wanted nothing to do with any man except Hugh,' she says, 'but us forty-something women are *packed* with sexual energy, our last hurrah before the mentalpause kicks in and we shrivel up and die.'

'Thank you for that happy thought, Derry. You're a gem. Sleep tight. Love you.'

'Love you too.'

I wish people would stop urging me to go sexing because I can't separate the physical from the emotional. Some people are brilliant at it – they fancy a person, throw out a suggestion and in the blink of an eye they're away to the races – and good luck to them. Everyone is different, and living that way could be fun, if you were the right kind of person.

But in my forty-four years I've only slept with six men and had a single one-night-stand. Just one! With a Dutch boy, Elian – I still remember his name, even though I was seventeen at the time, which makes it *twenty-seven* years ago. He was a medical student from Delft, our eyes had met across a crowded bar in Ibiza and next thing we were both weaving through the crowds to reach each other. He was leaving first thing the next morning and we spent the whole night talking and kissing. Together, on the beach, we watched the sun come up, then went to his apartment, where the sex happened about an hour before he had to leave.

Over that one night, I fell in love. Well, some version of love. Our goodbye was tender and sweet – there were no promises to stay in touch, we weren't complete saps, and within days he'd been forgotten about. For that one night, though, we'd connected: I felt I knew him and he knew me.

I was always more about romance than irresistible sexual passion, although sometimes the two overlapped, like with Richie Aldin.

In the post-Richie years, before I met Hugh, I had a paltry two flings. The thing was, there was no time for men: every second of every exhausting day had been earmarked for something more important, like feeding my child or doing my job.

When Neeve was three, there was a divorced dad with a little boy in her crèche whom I bumped into at drop-offs and pick-ups. For about a year we exchanged smiles, and this evolved into a reciprocal arrangement where we'd occasionally pick up the other's kid. Around the time I decided I really liked him, he asked me out. 'Out-out?' I remember asking.

'Out-out,' he confirmed.

But it never fully ignited and didn't last longer than a month.

He was nice but a teeny bit dull, and the ending was as low-key as the entire relationship – one morning he'd smiled a little sadly and said, 'No?'

My strongest emotion was regret that it no longer felt appropriate to ask him to pick up Neeve if I was running late.

My other pre-Hugh thing was entirely different. Max Nicholson was a hugely successful publicist in the big London firm I left Leeds for. Famous as he was for his work, he was more famous for his epic womanizing. He was textbook sexy, fun and flirty, and when he turned the force of his charisma on you, it was irresistible. He slept with whomever he chose and you could always pinpoint his current woman because she practically crackled with flashes of blue electricity. When he began to tire of her – and he *always* tired of her – you could see her power draining away, like a battery running out of energy.

At least two of his discarded women left the company, to find jobs elsewhere, and another poor girl disappeared overnight because she'd had a full-on breakdown.

Then he decided to notice *me*. One morning he tore by my work-station and was already several feet past when he came to a dramatically sudden halt, swivelled a graceful 180 and stared at me, stared hard. 'Hello, gorgeous.'

'Hello, gorgeous, yourself.' I'd wanted to laugh, because he was so over-the-top.

'Irish,' he said thoughtfully.

'English.' I mimicked his tone and kept on looking.

That was the start and he did it *all*. The flowers. The invitations on lavish dates. ('Dinner tonight? In Lisbon?') A pair of Manolo Blahniks in my size arriving by courier.

Daily, Max leant over my desk and murmured, 'You do know you're driving me insane?' Or 'When are you going to sleep with me and put me out of my misery?'

It was fun. Unlike every other poor woman who came under the dazzling spotlight of his attention, I knew exactly what I was getting into – and I. Did. Not. Care. It was like deciding to eat an entire toffee cheesecake – an exercise in self-destruction, but you'd enjoy yourself along the way.

Not even my lack of sexual experience intimidated me, because even if I'd had an actual *degree* in exotic bedroom techniques, he'd still dump me in the end. It was just a question of when.

Except I ended things with him.

One morning, in bed he, very deliberately, traced his finger along a silvery line on my stomach. 'Stretch mark?'

There was so much in those two words: criticism, contempt and a silent exhortation to make more of an effort. Another woman caught in his web would have rushed straight out and bought a gallon of Bio-Oil but I remember thinking, *Here we go. This is the start of the curdling.*

There was no way back from that: he'd already put me into turn-around and all that would follow from there on in would be subtle undermining that became more and more overt.

I rolled from the bed and located my underwear. 'This has been fun, Max.'

'Maybe we'll do it again sometime.'

'Nuh-uh.'

He frowned.

'That was the last time.'

'Excuse me?'

'You knew, Max, this was only . . .' My lines seemed to be coming straight from a Danielle Steele mini-series.

'Only what?'

'Fun?' I'd been going to say 'fucking' but I lost my nerve.

'Fun? But –'

'We're both grown-ups and you're a great guy.' My voice petered away. 'Actually, Max, you're not.'

He went white.

'You're a terrible, *terrible* guy. You play games with human beings. You are astonishingly cruel.'

Even his lips had gone white. 'Are you *quite* all right?'

'I'm fine. But you, Max? I'd worry about you.'

Such a merciless judgement wasn't like me but, looking back, it was clearly some sort of revenge for Richie's caper: one womanizer was being punished for the behaviour of another.

In hindsight, my heart was hard, clenched tight as a fist, and I trusted no one. So it was miraculous that Hugh had managed to nudge me into unfurling, like a tight, bitter bud opening and blossoming.

22

Wednesday, 14 September, day two

At 4.37 a.m., I jerk awake and find myself in Druzie's spare room. I sit up in bed and turn on the light. I know how the dawn horrors work – while I'm awake the artificial chatter of a busy life keeps the terrors tamped down. But in sleep all the layers of meaningless shite gradually lift up and float away until nothing is left but the truth, in its full horror.

Loss, shame, fear of the future – Shit, this is awful. Worst of all, the *sorrow*. I'm suddenly certain I can't survive this. Hugh had loved me, I had loved him. We were each other's happy ending.

I wish I knew how to self-soothe. I should have learnt mindfulness, and it's too late now because it's no good learning it when you're already in crisis: you have to start when things are good. But only the very, very oddest would think, Hey, my life is perfect. I know! I'll sit and waste twenty minutes Observing My Thoughts without Judgement.

I smoke my e-cig and scroll through Facebook – there they all are, with their perfect lives. I've now got ninety-three unread private messages and I can tell without ever opening them that they're just bursting with gossipy hunger. It's horrible being the person in the eye of a scandal, and I'll tell you, it'll make me think twice in the future about jumping on details of another person's drama. Ask not for whom the 'U OK Hun?' tolls. It tolls for thee.

I take a quick look at Hugh's feed. Even though he'd sworn to stay off it, I no longer trust him to keep his promises. There's nothing new: the last thing was three days ago when he was still at home, and he shared one of Kiara's posts about refugees.

I swap to Instagram, hoping for vintage dresses, but it's awash with motivational platitudes. 'Dare To Be Remarkable', 'You Are Stronger Than You Can Ever Imagine.'

Obviously I'm following the wrong people because I've no time for any of that nonsense. Maybe I should start. Maybe I should rethink these six months alone and regard them as an opportunity – to use Kiara's phrase – to self-actualize.

Suddenly, on Instagram, one platitude catches my eye: 'A journey of a thousand miles begins with one foolish decision.' And I laugh, literally out loud – usually I never make noise when I'm alone, not even if, say, I bang my baby toe on the side of the bath. What's the point of saying, 'Christ! My effing TOE!' if no one will come and commiserate with me?

Immediately I heart the Instagram post. I'd treble-heart it if I could. Then I see who's posted it – Josh Rowan – and, abruptly, my laughter stops.

23

Seventeen months ago

So, on a freakishly hot day the April before last, I was in my London 'office', working my way through emails when my phone rang.

It was a client, Premilla Routh, an actor, who'd struggled with an addiction to prescription medication – and a national paper had a recording of her buying drugs on the street.

'The dealer set me up.' She was so overwrought she could hardly speak. 'Amy, please help me. I'll lose my job if this gets out. And I'll probably lose my kids.' She'd already lost her marriage.

'Who contacted you?' I asked.

'Marie Vann.'

This was as bad as it got. Marie Vann was the British *Herald*'s shock-hack, her speciality eviscerating the vulnerable. People with mental illnesses she scorned as self-pitying attention-seekers so she was hardly likely to go easy on Premilla. Asking her to kill the story would only escalate things – like all bullies, Marie Vann had the great gift of manipulating people's attempts at self-defence into own-goals. If I didn't step carefully, Premilla and I would end up being painted as the aggressors in Marie's doubtless vitriolic piece.

My only option – and I'd learnt this from Tim – was to go over Marie Vann's head and throw myself on the mercy of her boss. (Tim, though he seemed colourless and low-key, was a remarkably able publicist.)

But the editor of the *Herald* was a remote figure. It would have been easier to swing an audience with Beyoncé. All I had in my arsenal was a flimsy online link to Marie's immediate superior, the features editor. Josh Rowan was his name and, annoyingly, we hadn't met – I'd extended a few lunch invitations, but he hadn't accepted. We followed each other on Twitter and that was my only in.

'Leave it with me, Premilla,' I said. 'Try not to worry.'

'Thank you, Amy,' she choked. 'Thank you, thank you, thank you.'

Thanks were a bit premature. I'd no idea if I could do this, I rarely did – not unless the journalist was a close personal friend (never) and I had a massive exclusive hidden in my back pocket to use as a bargaining chip (hardly ever).

I gathered up my denim jacket, my satchel, my enormous handbag, headed out into the heat of the streets and straight into a taxi. En route to the *Herald*'s offices in Canary Wharf, I direct-messaged Josh Rowan, asking if he could meet me for a quick coffee. Then I rang the *Herald* switchboard because journalists were among the few people left on the planet who still answered their phones even if they didn't recognize the number. Nothing doing, just his voicemail. So I texted Tim and Alastair, looking for a mobile number.

My stomach started to burn with a familiar mix of adrenalin and anxiety and I rummaged in my bag, found my Gaviscon and took a swig – it was nearly all gone: I got through the stuff as if it was water.

This part of my job, killing a negative story, was like going to war – the strategizing, the anticipation of my opponent's battle-plans, the fear of failure . . . Every time I was plunged into the thick of it, I'd think, I hate having to do this, but funnily enough as soon as a big drama had resolved itself I missed the excitement.

What made this situation all the more important was that Premilla had right on her side – she'd become addicted to benzos when she was given them by a clueless doctor to calm a nervous facial tic. Over the preceding twenty months, she'd been determinedly trying to break free, but the withdrawals were so brutal she kept relapsing. Her livelihood depended on me getting this right.

After twelve tense minutes in the taxi, with me checking my

phone every ten seconds, a direct message popped up: Josh Rowan saying he was available for a phoner. But with a request as delicate as this, only a face-to-facer would swing it. This Josh Rowan had to be made to like me and, by extension, Premilla. I pinged back, saying I'd be in the lobby of his building in half an hour. Seven minutes later came a terse message: he'd be in a pub called the Black Friar at four thirty.

The taxi deposited me at the pub at four thirty-three. It was dim, lined with dark wood and almost empty – there were a couple of small huddles of people in corners but no Josh Rowan.

Worrying, but assuming he did show, I was pulling off a territorial power grab.

A quick scan of the pub revealed the ideal spot for our chat – an upholstered booth, far enough from the huddles that we could speak openly but not so hidden that it looked like we were up to something unsavoury. A few desultory tables were scattered outside the pub, but I didn't want us distracted by the sun bouncing off their zinc tops and half blinding us – one or both of us might have needed sunglasses and eye contact was vital here.

Then I waited.

I didn't order a drink, because it wouldn't look good to be swilling down a large vodka if he ordered a prim cup of tea. Frankly my hopes were high that he'd order a drink-drink, but if he didn't, neither would I. All about the mirroring, in these situations. Saying, I'm just like you. See how alike we are. Yes, you can trust me.

As I waited, I worried, and there was plenty to worry about but, as always, my appearance got the worst of my criticism – perhaps because it was one of the few things under my control.

My clothes were the problem and it was my own fault for not reading the weather forecast. Yesterday morning in Dublin it had been pleasantly mild, but today in London the sun was splitting the stones. And my dress – a 1950s cotton-poplin skater, with elbow-length sleeves and patterned with splashy red and pink roses – looked way too lady-like. It needed my denim jacket to toughen it up. But I would die of heat in it. My blue nail varnish and my shoes – chunky silver sandals – might mitigate somewhat, but there was a strong chance this Josh Rowan would see me as a Doris Day-style sap-lady.

(In its defence, I loved that dress. It was one of the best things Bronagh had ever found me – the cotton was so crisp the dress could almost stand up by itself.)

I didn't dare go to the loo to check my make-up in case I missed him, so I slid my handbag mirror out and took a quick look. Christ, the hair. I was working an ambitious twisty-wavy artful-undone thing that had been achieved that morning with a heated wand and tons of texturizing spray, but during the cross-town dash it had mutated from artful-undone to plain messy.

I rummaged in my giant bag for my comb, and couldn't find it. More systematically I delved a second time, and I was getting nervy because I *needed* it.

On the third go-round, when I'd practically climbed inside the bag, I realized, with rising rage, that my comb was never going to turn up. It had been stolen – probably by Neeve, but it could have been any one of the girls.

'Bitches,' I muttered.

'Who?'

I froze in my hunched searching and looked up to see a man with an intelligent, slightly hangdog face. He looked busy and harassed, his shirt-sleeves pushed up his forearms. I knew it was him, Josh Rowan. And he knew it was me.

'I . . .'

'Who?' he repeated.

There was no choice but to style this out. I sat up straight. 'My daughters. They've stolen my comb.'

'And you need it why?'

'I'm meeting a journalist. I need to look pulled-together so he'll take me seriously.'

He gave me a once-over, then said, 'You look fine. Pulled together. He'll take you seriously.'

And there was a moment. Eye contact. Stillness. Something.

'Okay. Good.' But that tension stayed.

He sounded like he came from Newcastle or thereabouts.

An awful thought hit me. 'You *are* Josh Rowan?'

'No, pet, you've just been telling your secrets to some random man.' At my shock, he relented. 'You're okay. I'm Josh.'

Relief flooded me. 'It *is* you. You look like your Twitter photo. Mind you,' I said, 'experience has taught me that people usually look like older, much more unlucky versions of those photos.'

He made a half-hearted attempt at a smile.

'Now let's get you a drink.' I was working a motherly vibe even though we were around the same age.

'I don't have time –'

'Sure. No bother.' I delivered a warm, confident smile. This was the way to proceed – warm, warm, warm. Then sensible, sensible, sensible. No drama, no heightened emotion, just two grown-ups having a grown-up conversation in a grown-up way.

He took a seat and looked like he wasn't planning on staying long, but I sensed that if I could get him on-side we'd be home and dry. Hard to say what it was about him – his hair was an ordinary mid-brown, his eyes an unremarkable grey – but he had something, perhaps a strong sense of himself coupled with a hint of humanity, that marked him out as special.

'So what is it?'

'Marie Vann,' I said.

Instantly his face shut down. He watched me in silent assessment.

'Premilla Routh is my client,' I said gently.

Still he said nothing, just watched me with his hangdog face and one-way eyes.

'Don't run it,' I said. 'Please.'

'Why not?'

'Because it's mean.'

He barked with laughter.

'She's a decent human,' I said.

'Marie?'

'No,' I spluttered. 'Premilla.'

But I laughed at the idea that Marie could be described as decent. It had bumped me out of my groove. He didn't laugh again but we locked eyes, the tension between us unwound somewhat, and in that moment I felt everything might be okay. 'I know you're in a hurry,' I said. 'And this is confidential but –'

'Maybe I will have a drink. What can I get you?'

'I love your accent,' I blurted. 'Geordie's my favourite.' Blood rushed to my face. 'Sorry.'

There was a tiny exasperated eyeroll. 'So, to drink?'

I reached for my bag. 'Let me.'

He gave a sharp shake of his head. 'I'm buying.'

If he got the drinks I was surrendering all control. But there was no way of insisting without making a thing of it.

'Okay. Thanks. White wine.' I wanted alcohol and was too tired and strung-out to second-guess him. 'Anything. Sauvignon blanc. Whatever they have.'

'We're pretty sophisticated down here in Canary Wharf.' Hard to tell if he was being ironic. Although he probably was.

'Sauvignon blanc is grand.'

He went to the bar and I checked him out properly. He was tallish, but not one of those absurd heights, like six four or six five. Call me old-fashioned – or short – but anything over six one is unnecessary, unless he's Ashley Banjo and, sadly, he never is.

Josh Rowan wore a pale cotton shirt, open at the neck, and it gave the impression that he'd be totally at home in a fast-moving newsroom. All he needed were those funny, elasticated sleeve garters around his guns to complete the picture of classic newspaper man.

He looked fit but some intuition told me he'd scorn the gym. Five-a-side football on a Wednesday night would be more his thing. Or maybe he'd got those guns from shifting furniture around at the weekend to please his wife.

Because there was definitely a wife – he wore a wedding ring and, although my recall was hazy, I'd seen some sort of family-ish pictures on social media.

I was too far away to hear what he was saying to the barman but it was clear he was being pleasant. This shouldn't be worthy of comment but so many people aren't nice, and it gave me hope. Then he was back with my wine and some beer-style drink for himself.

'Canary Wharf's finest.' He drew up a chair to the table.

'Thanks.'

With perfect synchronicity we picked up our drinks and automatically clinked glasses. Then there was a weird pause. We locked eyes and I felt myself colour.

After an awkward moment he said, 'Go on, then. Tell us.'

I gave him a speedy run-through of Premilla's troubles. He listened without comment.

'She's tried very hard,' I said. 'She doesn't deserve the bad stuff she'll get if Marie runs her piece.'

'I'm not promising,' Josh Rowan said, 'and I mean it. But I'll see what I can do. Now I'd better get moving.'

We both got to our feet. I looked up into his face. 'Thank you, Josh Rowan.'

'I mean it, I'm promising nothing.'

'But you'll do your best?'

An exasperated half-laugh. 'Aye.'

We stepped outside the pub into the wall of early-evening heat and I started scanning the streets for a taxi.

'Where you off to now?' he asked.

'Heathrow. Flying home.'

'You live in Ireland?'

'Dublin.'

He raised a hand to flag down a taxi, closed the door once I was installed and stood watching while we drove away.

As soon as we'd turned a corner and he'd disappeared from view, I breathed out, a long, nervy exhalation, then called Premilla and made cautiously optimistic noises. She launched into effusive thanks, which I shut down immediately. It's always best to dampen the expectations of clients, but some instinct told me I'd probably pulled it off.

My flight was long gone but there was a seat available on a later one. Adrenalin was still coursing through me and I wanted to have all the drinks on the departure-lounge menu, but managed to stick to mint tea.

To pass the time I did a deep background on Josh Rowan, which I should have done long ago. Really, it was very remiss: a features editor in a British national and I didn't know his dog's name. (A springer spaniel called Yvonne, I now discovered, via a mutual friend on Facebook.) He had two kids, both boys – perhaps ten and twelve from their photos, but hard for me to know as I didn't really do boys – and a wife, Marcia. I switched over to her feed, which made for more rewarding spying.

I studied her avidly, keen to know how other people managed the tricky, tricky business of being a woman. She looked early forties, attractive but no stunner. Interesting.

Every life event of the Rowans seemed to be documented by Marcia – they'd gone to Portugal, the previous July, to a resort Hugh and I had been to three years earlier. First I marvelled at the coincidence, then slumped into sudden gloom as I understood I was merely a middle-class cliché.

Here came a shot of Marcia in a bikini, then another – Jesus, fair play to her, you wouldn't catch me in a bikini ever again, never mind posting photos on the internet for anyone to see. If I absolutely had to do beachwear, I went for a halter-necked one-piece, preferably with a little skirt. I pretended it was because of my retro-look but really it was just to camouflage my wobbly mid-section. And speaking of wobbly mid-sections – I wasn't being bitchy, merely factual – Marcia could have done with knocking off the bananas. (Or was it only me who had those ads popping up on the internet? They were very effective because I now couldn't even glance at a banana without feeling like I was overspilling my waistband.) But, modest amounts of belly-fat or not, Marcia looked very body-confident.

I kept scrolling down through her feed – then my heart leapt at pictures of Josh with a squad of mud-spattered men. He was at the semi-finals of a five-a-side tournament! I felt wild with joy at my accurate assessment of him. This was a good omen – a great omen!

Automatically, I almost liked it and managed to whip my hand away just in time – couldn't have him knowing he was being stalked.

My attention was split between spying on the Rowans and monitoring the *Herald* site, and by the time my plane was on the runway, nothing about Premilla had appeared online. The steward told me to switch off my phones. Superstitiously, I felt that while I was keeping an eye on things, nothing could go wrong. However, I complied in case the plane crashed. (Even if I was never convinced that mobile phones really do interfere with the plane's instruments, because a few times one of my phones had been left on accidentally for the entire flight and no harm had befallen us. You had to wonder if the airlines only made us turn them off out of spite. Like the way we had to keep the window blinds up for take-off and landing, and all the other random hard-to-take-seriously things they insisted on.)

The second we landed, I switched on my phone. To my alarm, I had several missed calls – and a very bad feeling. Rather than listen to the messages, I went straight to the *Herald*'s site and my heart began to pound as I reached the headline on their landing page: SOAP ACTRESS DRUG SHAME.

With shaking hands, I scrolled through the grubby details of Premilla's drug bust. Remembering how I'd thought Josh Rowan had been won over by Premilla's sad story was humiliating. As if heralding the media storm I was facing into, both my phones started ringing simultaneously. Fuck you, Josh Rowan. Fuck you.

24

On Wednesday night, around eight o'clock, I park my car and eye my little house with something close to dread.

It's not as if my arrival home from London was ever treated with any fanfare – I was mostly only gone for one night and it was a commute that was built into our routine. Hugh would usually hug me, I'd go upstairs and half unpack – a wheely case sat permanently on the bedroom floor with stuff falling out of it – then go back down and he'd make me a cup of tea. Sometimes he'd have dinner waiting and sometimes he wouldn't, and we'd sit and talk. Not *talk* talk, no full-and-franks, but we batted back and forth mundane stuff, like was it the week for the recycling bins and was it worth coughing up the money to send Kiara for extra tutoring in maths, the banality of marriage that gets mocked so frequently, but out of these countless threads of bin-conversations and cash-allocation, a life together is woven.

I gather up my bags and resolve to be strong. Hugh would have had the front door opened by now, but we are where we are.

As soon as my key turns in the lock, Neeve and Kiara flood into the hall. Even Sofie is here. What the hell's up? I'm the head of the household now, and I get to do my worrying alone. 'Hi! Is something wrong?'

'Nothing. No. We just thought we'd . . .'

They flutter around me. One of them takes my wheely bag and another hands me a glass of wine.

'We emptied the dishwasher,' Neeve says. Emptying the dishwasher is – was – Hugh's job.

'And we got you cheese,' Sofie says. 'The worst one on the counter. It smells like death.'

'It's really bad.' Kiara is enthusiastic.

'You won't believe how bad.' Sofie guides me to the kitchen. 'Come and sit down.'

Kiara pulls out a chair for me and Sofie helps me into it, as if I'm an invalid. It's not unpleasant.

Neeve opens the fridge and as the smell of the cheese billows out in a chilly cloud, all three girls exclaim, 'Ouf!'

'Can you smell it?' Neeve is so proud.

I nod. 'It's appalling.' It's really not, but who am I to rain on their parade?

'I know, right? Sofie nearly got sick in the car on the way home with it, didn't you, Sofie?'

'I literally had to roll down the window.'

Gingerly Neeve removes the cheese from the fridge and, holding it away from herself, brings it to the table. 'It's a French one,' she says.

'Toulouse-Lautrec,' Sofie says.

'Camus,' Kiara says. 'That actually sounds like a cheese.' They dissolve into giggles.

'Get her a plate,' Neeve orders. 'And a knife.'

These are produced in short order, followed by a jar of artisanal chutney, a selection of chi-chi crackers and seven pecan nuts, laboriously broken in half. My wine glass is refilled and the girls stand back to admire their handiwork.

'Now!' They beam at me, and they're so very sweet.

'Enjoy your cheese,' Neeve says. 'If such a thing is even possible.'

'That's a good-looking plate of food,' I say, then instantly wish I hadn't because it was one of the many in-jokes Hugh and I shared.

Neeve frowns. 'You what? Oh, what they say on *Masterchef.*' Then she gasps. 'The apple! We forgot the apple!' She flings herself at the fruit bowl. 'You cut it, Sofie.' Sofie's role in the family is to cut things, ever since she did an excellent job on a birthday cake years and years ago. Cutting food makes her highly anxious, but you know what families are like – rules are rules. 'Thin slices,

137

really skinny, like Hugh does.' A few tense minutes follow, as Neeve crowds around Sofie and hisses, 'Fan it. Like a fan. The way Hugh does it.'

The apple appears, cut a little raggedly.

'Okay,' Neeve says. 'Each of us has made a list of things you might like to do while he's away. Kiara, you go first.'

'No,' I protest. 'No! I'm fine, totally.' I'm the adult here, and no matter how bad I feel, they cannot know. They need to trust me to take care of them: their world has been upended enough, they need one parent they can depend on. 'I am *fine*. I'm here for you three. That's my only plan for the next six months.'

'We know you're there for us,' Sofie says. 'But we *have* lives. We're good.'

'Yeah, we're good, Mum.'

In fairness, I have a life too, sort of. 'But I'm the adult.'

'If we find it weird without him, we'll tell you,' Kiara says. 'Communication is key. But you need to know that we're here for you too.'

'Yes, but —'

'Shush now.' Kiara begins with a little speech: 'Most people in a long-term relationship never get an opportunity like this. If both of you use this time wisely, your relationship will be enriched by what you learnt while you were apart. It will be better.'

It seems churlish to mention that it had been fine as it was.

'Here is my list,' Kiara announces. 'Mindfulness. Meditation. Read a classic you've been curious about. Listen to inspirational podcasts while going on long walks alone.' All of Kiara's choices are solo activities because she doesn't want me meeting another man.

She needn't worry. 'Be open to personal growth,' she finishes.

The thing about personal growth, I've discovered, is that you rarely get any choice in it. It only ever happens as a side-effect of some loss or trauma. Judging by how shit all this is making me feel, I'll be a personal Colossus at the end of it.

'Okay, here's my list.' Neeve starts reading from her iPad. 'Get Botox.'

'I'd love to, but I don't think Irish doctors accept payment in pebbles or old lipsticks.'

'Sucks to be you, Mum.' Neeve shakes her head in pretend sympathy. 'Next suggestion, take up running.'

That will *never* happen. I'm the wrong body shape: my Celtic thighs are too short.

'I'll run with you,' Neeve adds.

Even though her thighs are as short as mine, the fact that she's offered to do anything with me is heartening. Perhaps I'll use this time to strengthen the bonds with the people already in my life.

Although the irony is that the one thing I *won't* have is time. I'd almost none when Hugh was around, picking up a lot of the slack, so I'm going to have even less now that he's not here.

'Maybe I should go on Tinder?' I'm aiming for jokey.

'You?' Sofie hoots. 'Tinder?'

All three dissolve into helpless laughter. 'Sorry, Mum,' Kiara tells me. 'You're too old.'

'Anyway,' this from Neeve, 'you'd probably swipe the wrong direction and end up with all the eejits.'

Young people are *so* patronizing.

'Okay, Sofie,' I say. 'Let's hear your list.'

'I could only think of one thing. Get cushions for your bed.'

'Ah?' What the *actual?*

'You love lots of cushions on your bed and Dad doesn't.'

This is true.

'So here's an opportunity to do something you enjoy.'

You know, there might actually be something in this.

'You could, Mum!' Kiara is suddenly enthused. 'Go on your sites and buy those embroidered fairy-tale things you like.'

'Handcrafted by blind peasant girls in the wolf-inhabited forests of Moldova.' Neeve is sneery.

'It gives work to people who desperately need it.' Kiara stares coldly at Neeve. 'Go on, Mum, do it.'

It's not as if I need any encouragement to spend money.

'But when Hugh comes back?' Neeve asks.

'She can move them to the living room.'

'I don't want to be looking at her twee cushion covers.'
This can't be allowed to pass. 'Not twee! They're naive.'
'Twee.' Neeve gives me a side-eyed smile.
'Folksy renderings of idealized peasant life.'
'Twee.'
And I laugh.

25

Neeve's phone beeps. She flicks it a look and says, 'Dad's on his way over.'

I stare at her. What on earth . . . ? Does she mean Richie Aldin? She can't mean Richie Aldin.

'Whose dad?' Kiara sounds as surprised as I feel.

'*My* dad,' Neeve says.

This is *utterly* outlandish.

'What do you mean, he's on his way over?' Sofie asks. 'Over where?'

'Here.' Neeve sounds impatient.

But Richie Aldin doesn't see Neeve more than twice a year. He's flitted in and out of her life, and his absence is a source of chronic pain. And because it cuts her so deep, a source of sorrow for me.

He's a fairly shitty excuse for a man. Three years after he divorced me he got married again and his wife had a daughter, then another, then another, each new arrival tying Neeve up in knots of fear and longing. Over the years she's made several attempts to infiltrate her clan of half-sisters and occasionally they'd admit her some of the way, then the next thing she'd hear they'd gone to EuroDisney or Alton Towers without her and we'd be back to square one, with her sobbing in my arms, saying all she wanted was to be part of 'a real family'.

On two separate occasions, I got on a plane and flew to Leeds just to beg Richie to include Neeve in his family holidays. I'd cover all costs, if they'd just let her come. Both times he said he'd see, but ultimately he let her down. Again and again, he's hurt her.

And yet I can't ever be mean about him to her. He's her dad and any relationship is better than none.

'He's doing a vlog for me,' Neeve says. 'On male grooming.'

'Why tonight, honey?'

'Only time he can do it.'

Whatever she says, it's no accident that he's here on this night of all nights. Any fool knows that Richie and I will never be together again, but she still holds out hope. And that could break my heart, if I let it.

'He's a busy man.' She's acting defiant, like I might try to stop Richie coming into the house. Which would never happen. Mind you, I'd *like* to.

He's never apologized to me, he never will, and while I don't hold a grudge, I heartily dislike him. Things always go his way – a lengthy and moderately successful spell as a soccer player in the UK, where he kept his head down and accumulated plenty of money. When that career came to its natural conclusion, he didn't buy a pub and drink it dry, the way lots of ex-footballers allegedly do (according to an article I read somewhere). Instead he returned to Ireland and set up a football academy, which functions as a well-respected feeder for English clubs and, from what the press says, makes bucketloads of money.

Nor does his personal life cause him any angst. A few years ago, he upped and left his second wife; according to Neeve, he was 'bored'. I don't know the details but it wasn't a decision that seemed to generate soul-searching or guilt.

He has never seemed to have a crisis of confidence or conscience. He does exactly what he wants and gets away with it.

These days he has a succession of pretty, charming girlfriends but I don't see him often enough to keep track.

Does he know that Hugh is gone?

Actually, I don't care.

'When's he coming?' Kiara is grave. She disapproves of him.

'He's on his way.'

'I wonder what car he'll have,' Sofie says. 'Something flashy, I guess.' She's none too keen on him either. 'Maybe an Aston Martin.'

'Or a Lamborghini,' I say.

'Definitely expensive?' Kiara asks.

'Yes!'

'If I had to have a car,' Kiara says wistfully, 'I'd love a Citroën Dyane.'

'Until it broke down for the seventeenth time in a mile,' Neeve says. 'Then you'd be begging for a Beemer.'

'It'll be a Ferrari,' Sofie says.

'Not a Ferrari.' Neeve defends her sorry excuse for a father.

The doorbell rings.

'Here already?'

All four of us go, keen to see what Richie is driving . . . and on the step stands Genevieve Payne. Holding what looks like a casserole. 'Hi!' She beams. 'Just dropping this over.'

'What is it?' Neeve demands.

'A casserole.'

'Why?' Neeve asks. 'No one has died.'

'But –'

'My step-dad has gone away to self-actualize. He totally rocks. Keep your casserole.'

Genevieve attempts panicky eye-contact with me. 'Amy, I –'

But Neeve is shutting the door.

And then the door is actually closed and I'm backing away down the hall, shocked and giddy and afraid of repercussions.

'What a dick!' Neeve says.

'Neevey!' Sofie exclaims. 'Slay! All day! Total badass!'

She *is* a total badass. When she's on your side, there's no one more loyal and fierce.

'"Keep your casserole",' Kiara exclaims, in admiring tones. 'Bow *down*.'

'But, *daaaaamn*, casseroles are for when people be dead!'

'We ain't playin'!'

'We *ain't* playin'.'

'Drag that bitch's ass!'

I can glean the meaning of the words but I'd never be able to use them with confidence myself.

'"Keep your casserole",' Sofie says, and unexpectedly, we're all convulsing. I laugh until my face is wet and finally the spasm calms.

Then Kiara says, '"Keep your casserole",' and we're all off again.

An Audi with flashy headlights pulls up outside.

'Damn,' Kiara says. 'None of us wins.'

'Hi, Amy.' Richie Aldin is standing in the hall and gives me a polite kiss on the cheek. He smells of some expensive man-perfume. He never smells of just himself. Maybe it's a footballer thing, them and their incessant showers. 'You look good,' he says.

He looks good too, again in a footballery sort of way. His red-gold hair is 'tended', cut modern and tufty, and he's compact and muscular, not tall but powerful. He probably still trains, what with running his lucrative academy and all.

'Hi, hun.' He hugs Neeve.

'Hi, Daddy.'

It hurts to see how happy she is. Could he not have been kinder to her these past twenty-two years? What makes it even more painful is that they look *so* alike – those scornful glinty eyes, the scattering of freckles across their noses, their shining rare-hued hair.

'Hugh not around?'

I freeze. 'Um, no.'

'What?' He looks from me to Neeve. Nosy feck.

'C'mon, Dad,' Neeve says. 'Let's get started.'

'But –'

'I'll explain,' she says.

26

Thursday, 15 September, day three

Thursday is late-night shopping and my plan is to go on a looking-at-lovely-things outing when I finish up at work. But my phone rings. It's Mum and my heartrate rockets.

'Amy, I need you to come over tonight. Dominik's let me down and I'm going out.'

'Oh! But . . . where are you going?'

'Out.' She sounds almost huffy. 'For a drink.'

'With whom?'

'Friends.'

'Mum, *what* friends?'

'Friends of mine,' she all but hisses. 'And Dominik is getting too big for his boots.'

This is extremely worrying: Dominik keeps the show on the road. 'What happened? He cancelled?'

'He didn't cancel. But he wouldn't make himself available. Says he has another job.'

'But –'

'Be here at seven.' She hangs up.

This – Mum's assertiveness, her unreasonableness – is unprecedented. I'll ask Hugh what I should do and – Oh! I can't.

It's literally unbelievable that he has gone away. How did everything go so bad so quickly?

I call Mum back, but it goes straight to message. Next I try the landline and it's the same story so I've no choice but to drive all the way out there.

Mum is in Neeve's leather jacket, waiting by the front door. 'Thanks for this,' she says. 'If I don't get out and away from him,' she nods in Pop's direction, 'I'll go fucking insane.'

145

'Um . . . okay.' I'm certain I've never before heard her use the F-word. 'Who are you going with?'

She answers by taking one of my hands between both of hers and asking, 'How're you managing, love? Since Hugh went?'

'Oh. Ah. It's weird. But early days.'

'Well, I'm here for you. Come over any time.'

'So where are you off to now?'

'Who's doing the dinner tomorrow night?'

'Maura.'

'Oh.'

Maura's is the lowest point in the five-week cycle because all she can cook is baked potatoes and grated cheese, which generates aggrieved griping that she could at least order in pizzas, seeing as she has plenty of money.

I *do* get pizzas on my week, but they're only supermarket ones, which I suspect also generates aggrieved griping. But, feck them, I don't have the resources that Maura does.

Joe and Declyn are both good cooks, so their weeks are happy ones. But Derry's week is the jewel in the crown, the Met Ball, the event that no one misses. Derry is a great woman for flinging money around and always sends out to Rasam for a small mountain of fabulous Indian food.

Something beeps outside.

'Here's my taxi,' Mum says. 'I'll be home by eleven.'

'Have you your phone?' I ask.

'Yes.' She scampers away.

'Is it switched on?'

'Yes.' Her voice floats back to me. I'm certain she's lying.

Feeling confused and hard-done-by, I go in to Pop, who greets me by bellowing, 'Who are you?'

'Amy.'

'Amy who?'

'Amy O'Connell.'

'I'm an O'Connell, could we be related?'

'I'm your daughter.'

'Away to feck, I've no children. Who are you?'

146

'Amy.'

'Amy who?'

'Amy O'Connell.'

After about ten minutes of this lark, I really want to hit him with a hammer. I can actually visualize the whole thing, picking up a hammer, clonking Pop on the skull with it, then watching him lapse into the silence of the comatose. No wonder elder abuse is so prevalent.

It's suddenly a lot easier to sympathize with Mum needing to go out with these mysterious friends of hers.

I can't even go on the internet and escape into looking at cushion covers or fantasy holidays because in this house you can only get Wi-Fi in an upstairs bedroom and I'd better not leave Pop on his own.

The thing with the Wi-Fi is that we're actually stealing it from the neighbours, the Floods. I'm ashamed of this but the story of how Derry and I tried and failed to get broadband installed is too long and too boring. However, living internet-free is hard and sometimes the temptation to jump aboard the Floods' Wi-Fi is irresistible. As compensation, we bought them a case of Argentinian wine, but Joe went around with it and, for reasons we never got to the bottom of, neglected to explain what it was actually for. So the moment to 'fess up has passed and we live in fear that the Floods will start using a password.

At eight o'clock things get worse: Pop wants to watch a documentary about serial killers but I want – *need* – to watch *Masterchef*. Pop seems much tougher going tonight than ever before. Then I remember that the few evenings I've minded him in the past, Hugh was with me. It's a lot easier when there's two of you. 'You'll like this,' I say to him, keeping a tight hold of the remote.

But Pop heaps such loud, lavish insults on Marcus Waring and the misfortunate contestants that I quickly admit defeat and switch over to *Jeffrey Dahmer: The Milwaukee Cannibal*.

'The lad with the kettle!' Pop says. 'This is a great one.'

27

Friday, 16 September, day four

Alastair breezes in from London around two p.m., like he does every Friday. 'Plans for the weekend, Amy?'

'Neeve and Kiara are talking about us going bowling.'

'Bowling!'

I have to laugh. 'Apart from anything else, the *shoes*. No, just the cinema on Sunday, all part of the routine.'

'Routines are good. So, anything social? What about your girlfriends?'

'Lunch with Steevie tomorrow, after I do battle with my hair-dresser. Then, tomorrow night it's Vivi Cooper's birthday.'

'Who?'

'Wife of Hugh's friend Frankie. Hugh said yes before he decided to skip the country so I've inherited the obligation. It's in Ananda, six couples and me. I'm not going. Vivi says I can decide at the last minute but I already know it's a no-way.'

'You don't think it might be good for y–'

'I'd be mortified. Having to pretend to be okay but – Oh, God!' Suddenly I'm struggling to catch my breath.

'Easy,' Alastair soothes. Gently he rubs my back until I can get some air in. 'Sorry,' he says.

'It's grand. You were only trying to help. It's just, what if I got the panic in a situation like that? When I'd be trapped with all those people?'

He nods. 'Maybe just see people one on one?'

I'm not sure. Apart from the girls, there's no one I feel entirely safe with.

'But tomorrow night,' he says, picking up my thoughts, 'just stay in, eat and look at runway shows on vogue.com. You're in shock. Your world changed too quickly. You're still processing it.'

'Is that what it is?' I'm desperate for an explanation.

'The transition will take time,' Alastair says. 'You've to metabolize all these new factors.'

'And then I'll be okay?'

He laughs, a little sadly.

'Okay,' Tim announces to me and Alastair. 'Quick meeting.'

'Feck off,' Alastair cries. 'It's ten to five. It's nearly the weekend.'

'Media Awards?' Tim continues as if Alastair hasn't spoken. 'On Friday, November the eleventh, in Brighton. Do we go? And, if so, which of us?'

Because the British media has to pretend it isn't entirely London-centric, these awards – 'the Oscars of the News World' – take place outside the capital. About seven hundred presenters, producers, researchers, directors and journalists descend on a seaside resort, where approximately a gazillion prizes are doled out for every imaginable version of current affairs.

Something about being away from home encourages late nights and bad behaviour. Accolades are dished out to the great and the good over a rowdy dinner. Then there's an old-school disco, featuring lots of dad dancing and multiple after-parties in various hotel rooms. In some you drink whisky and play poker until sun-up and in others you dance around a trouser-press, drunkenly convinced you're talented enough to be on a podium in Pacha.

Pity the unlucky person whose bedroom is right below an after-party – they won't get a moment's sleep. And there's no point complaining: the staff are too scared to intervene, and if the sleepless guest goes upstairs to demand the racket quietens down, there's a good chance they'll be hoicked into the room and force-fed rum.

All kinds of unlikely alliances are forged on such a night – holding back the hair of your mortal enemy as she pukes, after one B52 too many. Or walking hand in hand on the shingle beach as the sun rises with a man you'd never previously had down as doable.

If you were prone to infidelity, it's the perfect setting.

'D'you want to go, Amy?' Tim asks.

'Yes.' It's always a fun night and I hadn't gone last year because Hugh's dad had just died.

'We should all go, really,' Tim says. 'Having nearly every journalist in Britain in one room is too good an opportunity.'

'Can we afford for the three of us to go?' Between airfares, hotel costs and ticket prices, these things are expensive.

Alastair and I look at Tim expectantly, awaiting his verdict. We're equal partners in our business, but in all financial matters we treat Tim like he's our dad.

'Thamy?' Tim calls. 'Costings for flights to Gatwick on November the eleventh? And the cheapest rooms at the Gresham Hotel in Brighton?'

We drift back into our work, and when Thamy shows her findings to Tim he obviously likes what he sees because he says, 'Book them.' Then, 'Okay. We're all going.'

Out of nowhere I wonder if Josh Rowan will be there.

28

Seventeen months ago

The terrible evening when Premilla's drug shame had appeared online, I stood on the plane, waiting impatiently to exit, scrolling down through the grisly details and strategizing.

I had to change the conversation fast from Premilla-who-bought-drugs-on-the-street to Premilla-the-respectable-woman-who'd-been-badly-served-by-the-medical-community. An interview with a journalist I trusted? A slot on *This Morning*?

Both my phones were ringing. I answered one at random. 'Amy O'Connell.'

'It's Josh Rowan.'

I said nothing. I was silent. Furious.

'Are you there?'

'What do you want?' No publicist could afford an enemy in the press but I was very sore about this.

'I'm sorry,' he said. 'About Marie Vann.' That lovely Geordie accent. 'Most trusted accent,' some survey had said. 'I did my best. She went over my head. But I can offer something else. A damage-limitation interview with Chrissy Heathers. Big spread. Two pages on Friday. Sympathetic.'

Silently I considered this. Chrissy Heathers was a different proposition from Marie Vann. Chrissy's pieces were probing but they were generally balanced and fair. And now that Premilla's dirty laundry was being washed in public, the only option left was a mop-up operation. But even if I decided to trust the *Herald*, there was no knowing if Premilla would talk to the paper that had shafted her.

'Copy approval?' I asked.

He sighed. 'No.'

It had been a long shot. Journalists almost never ceded it because it meant anything negative could – and would – be removed by the interviewee until nothing remained but a sanitized fluff-job.

'Look, I'll see what I can do.'

'But you can't promise anything,' I echoed.

Sounding a little weary he said, 'Aye.'

My first call was to Hugh to tell him I wouldn't be home. Then as soon as we were let off the plane I went straight upstairs to Departures and bought a flight back to London, the last of the evening.

Running through the airport, I rang Premilla and promised her that wheels were in motion, then called her sister to tell her to take care of her. Then I rang Josh Rowan back.

'Why should I trust you?' I asked.

'Because you can.'

'You've just demonstrated that I can't.'

'I didn't promise anything. I couldn't. Marie wasn't my hire, I've no sway with her, but everyone else in Features is mine.'

I was thinking fast, fast, fast. True, Marie Vann had been hired by the remote-as-Beyoncé editor in a wrong-headed attempt to halt declining sales. Speedily, I flicked through a mental index card of all my fluffier journalists – plenty who'd do me a tame piece but because they wrote for weekend supplements we'd be looking at a lead time of two weeks. This story needed turning around immediately, before the public perception of Premilla the street junkie crystallized.

'Friday?' I asked. 'This Friday? The day after tomorrow? Two pages?'

'This Friday. Two pages. Sympathetic. I'll try for copy approval and either way I'll personally oversee the subs.'

An important factor. A sympathetic piece could be rendered worthless if the sub-editors shoved in a trashy tabloid headline, like 'My Druggie Shame'.

My indecision was agonizing; there was a lot to lose here with the wrong call.

'Or you can go to another outlet,' he said. 'Who could blame you?'

Paradoxically, that was what decided it. A defence of Premilla in the *Guardian* or *The Times* could look like one newspaper point-scoring against another. But if it was in the *Herald*, it might almost neutralize the original story.

'Okay. Chrissy Heathers interviews Premilla tomorrow in a hotel.' No journalist was getting anywhere near Premilla's home to go through her bathroom cabinet and report on the contents.

'And it's an exclusive. Wait. Are you *running*?' he asked.

'Yep. Catching the last flight back to London.'

'In the shoes you were wearing earlier?'

'When you're as short as I am, you get used to doing every-thing in high – Oh, my God!' My wrist was suddenly vibrating.

'What is it?'

'Oh. I see.' I didn't break pace. 'It's my Fitbit. I must have hit my ten thousand steps for today. It happens so rarely I didn't know what was happening.'

'Yet the perky encouragement never stops. Apparently I've walked the length of Britain but it's taken me about three years. Right. So we're clear that this is an exclusive?'

'Clear.'

More than clear. It was vital that Premilla didn't speak to any other media outlet. Deafening silence was the only sensible response, until we had a game-changing piece on Friday.

My stomach was burning up with acid. I didn't know how far to trust Josh Rowan.

He'd already shafted me once.

It was close to midnight when I arrived at Premilla's flat in Lad-broke Grove to spend the night. A clamouring scrum of media waited outside, the lenses of the photographers trained on her first-floor windows.

The crowd was even bigger the following morning when two big Lithuanian security men and I shepherded Premilla to the waiting car. 'Ignore them.' I spoke softly into her ear as the journos yelled insults and accusations, anything to trigger a response from her. Premilla's nails were bitten so far down that blood was visible, and her beautiful face was flaky and red from stress-psoriasis.

A hotel suite in central London was booked for the interview. Standing outside its door, Premilla was trembling.

'It'll be okay,' I said fiercely. 'It will.' Well, I'd do everything in my power to make it so. I led her in by the hand.

Chrissy Heathers was there, her plump face and curly, messy hair giving the false impression of someone perfectly benign. Also milling about were a photographer, a stylist, a make-up artist and – leaning against a wall, watching them – Josh Rowan. My heart thumped hard at the sight of him and a messy mix of feelings flooded through me: mistrust, rancour and some variant of shame.

His arms were folded across his chest and he was perfectly still in the midst of all the activity. We locked eyes for a moment longer than necessary and my skin flamed with heat. Why was he even here? Editors didn't usually show up at interviews, no matter how big a splash.

A choking noise from Premilla distracted me – she was so distressed by the scale of this operation that she was crying. 'Sssh,' I said softly. 'It's okay.'

Chrissy had noticed our arrival so I plastered on a big smile for her – but she shut me down. 'You've full copy appro.'

I *had*? This was great news. 'Thank you.'

'Not my call.' God, she was pissed off. 'Thank him.' She jerked her head in Josh Rowan's direction – he had suddenly appeared at my side.

'Premilla? Josh Rowan, I edit the section you'll run in. I'm sorry you have to go through this. But we'll do all we can to make today bearable.' There he went, with his 'most trusted' accent, trying to charm her.

Premilla swallowed and nodded.

'We just want to make you look good,' Josh Rowan said. 'And you and Amy have full copy approval. That means –'

'Premilla knows what that means,' I said. Patronizing arse.

'Let's get going, shall we?' Chrissy really wasn't happy.

'Just a moment.' This didn't start until Premilla was comfortable. I guided her to an armchair. 'What would you like to drink, lovely? Water? Camomile tea?'

'Tea.'

'I'll make it,' Josh Rowan said.

Was that why he was here? As a tea-boy? Like, *hardly*.

While he was gone to whatever part of the suite the camomile tea happened in, Chrissy started firing questions – clearly the interview was under way without any of the soft-soaping that usually precedes them.

Shaky and scared, Premilla stumbled over her first answer, and fury filled me.

'Just a moment.' My face was smiley but my voice was sharp. 'Chrissy, a quick word? In private?' I was on my feet, walking away with purpose.

In the corridor that connected the living room and the bedroom, I said, 'I get that giving copy appro is a bummer. But Premilla is genuinely fragile. Can't you be kind?'

She gave me the death-glare, then her expression wavered. 'Okay.' She sighed. 'Okay.'

She turned and went back in, me behind her, just as Josh Rowan appeared in the corridor and blocked my path. 'Everything okay?'

Suddenly the rage had a hold of me again. 'Did you orchestrate this?' I asked. 'Letting Marie run that shitty piece so your paper gets a juicy exclusive?'

'No.' His voice was polite, his face like stone.

He sounded convincing but he was hard to get a read on.

'What are you even doing here?' I asked.

He went to say something, then stopped, and in that hiatus, those unuttered words, I felt the . . . something, the whatever-there-was between us.

He shrugged. 'I want to make things right.'

I nodded, but that wasn't the truth. Or, at least, not the whole truth.

Out we went, and the interview recommenced, but now Chrissy was pleasant and Premilla visibly relaxed.

Josh Rowan resumed his original position, propped against the wall, watching us, and again I wondered why he was there.

'Excuse me.' My tone was cold. 'Would you mind leaving?'

'He needs to stay,' Chrissy said. 'He'll be finalizing copy.'

Suddenly all was clear: her name would be on the by-line but Josh Rowan would control the content. Okay, so he stayed.

After an hour Chrissy disappeared to write her copy and it was time for the photoshoot, which was at least as important as the interview. The stylist had set up three racks of clothes in the bedroom and, with a gimlet eye, I flicked through them. 'No. No. No jeans. No denim.'

'How about this?' She held up an amazing Roksanda shift, but it was red and red was too celebratory.

'It's beautiful.' There was real longing in my voice. 'But no red, yellow, pink or orange. No bright colours. Think atonement.'

'The movie? I've got a green bias-cut –'

'Not the movie.' I couldn't help a laugh. 'The emotion, the noun, whatever it is.'

Something made me look up. Josh Rowan was in the room. He'd overheard and, without him smiling or making any kind of noise, I knew he was amused.

No. No in-jokes. We couldn't be complicit in anything. I wasn't having it.

After several false starts, Premilla's look eventually met my approval – tailored black trousers, a floaty Chloé blouse, and the dullest shoes you've ever seen (black leather, rounded toe, two-inch heels). She looked like a slightly stylish headmistress.

Next I stuck like glue to the make-up artist as she did Premilla's face, making sure the red patches of psoriasis were covered, nixing too-bright lip-glosses and insisting that her hair be tidied away into a neat bun. Throughout this the photographer was giving me hard looks and he was correct to be worried: as soon as the shoot started, I was right in there.

'Don't put her behind a desk,' I said. 'She stands, she's got nothing to hide. Okay, smile, Premilla, but no teeth.' It was a fine line, she couldn't look like she was delighted to be a drug addict but the 'tragic Premilla' poses had also to be avoided. 'Think "tentatively hopeful".'

The photographer handed me a camera. 'Great idea – why don't you take the shots?'

'I know.' I held up my hands and shrugged in a what-can-you-do manner. 'I'm a nightmare.' Yes, he hated me but it was my job to protect Premilla.

And all the time this was happening I could feel Josh Rowan's eyes on me. It made me feel . . . self-conscious. Resentful. Confused. Excited.

By the time the photos were done, it was gone seven. I put Premilla into a cab to her sister's.

Josh Rowan said, 'Chrissy's filed. Emailing it to you.'

'Thanks – yeah, okay, bye-bye, thank you, bye.' The stylist and the rest of them were leaving.

I clicked on the attachment and my heart sank at the first sentence: 'Curled up in the tasteful upholstery of a luxurious London hotel . . .'

Josh was reading it too, sitting opposite me in the living room, which was suddenly very quiet now that everyone was gone.

'No,' I said.

'I know.'

I looked around. 'It *is* luxurious . . .'

'But hardly relevant.'

'There can be no hint that she's profited in any way from this.'

'On it.' He quickly typed something.

'A disclaimer she wasn't paid for this?'

'Done.'

'So let's strike that opener and –'

'Describe how upset she was when she arrived?'

'Don't overdo it. Make clear it was emotional distress, not physical withdrawals.'

'Okay.' He started typing again. Little flurries of words, followed by deletions, and long stretches of him just staring at the screen before the flurries started again. 'How about this?' He read out, ' "This wasn't what Premilla Routh had planned for her life. All her years of hard work, playing draughty theatres in provincial towns, followed by the bootcamp ethic of *Misery Street* shooting four shows a week, only to be catapulted into the headlines for buying prescription medication on the streets. She's devastated." '

'A bit tabloid-y,' I said. 'But good. Excise "on the streets" and keep going.'

Over the next few hours Josh and I back-and-forthed over copy and entirely rewrote the profile. Chrissy's original piece hadn't been mean – she'd got the brief – but this new one was much more insightful, focusing on the horrors of accidental addiction. The actual drug purchase was barely mentioned. Josh had obviously listened intently to everything that Premilla had said. It had been worth letting him stay in the room.

As the piece took shape it became clear that this was much, much better than a mere mop-up operation – it could even act as the pivot for Premilla's new future. A benzo addiction group would probably snap her up as their spokesperson and she'd be considered for darker, more serious acting roles, seeing as she'd endured and survived her own mini-hell.

'Premilla will come out of this looking good,' I acknowledged.

'Best thing that ever happened to her,' Josh said.

My head snapped up.

Then I saw that he was joking.

'Our greatest crisis is also our greatest opportunity.' His tone was mockingly solemn.

I replied, 'Everything happens for a reason.'

'Sometimes it takes a wrong turn to get you to the right place.'

'My personal hate,' I said, 'is "Life isn't about waiting for the storm to pass, it's about learning to dance in the rain." '

'Mine is "Don't run from your bad feelings. Instead –'

'– dance with them",' I finished.

The mood had lightened. We were both smiling, his a one-sided, reluctant-looking affair.

'Instagram is the worst for that inspirational crap,' I said.

'Yep. Nothing is too banal or too obvious that it can't be posted.'

'Pinterest is bad too. I hate-follow loads of asshats just to see the platitudes they post.'

'I've never really got on with Pinterest. Too much tapestry.' He looked at his screen. 'So.'

So. Back to work.

'To finish this up,' he said. 'For the shoutline, how about "My GP Prescribed It"?'

'Great.' It was making the piece about the drug, not the person.

'Read it through one more time and, if you're happy, I'll send it in.'

I scanned it again. Perfect. I gave him the nod and the moment he pressed Send, the exhaustion hit me.

'What time is it?' I checked my phone. 'Christ. Quarter past eleven. Missed the last flight home.' And too late to arrive round to Druzie's. 'I'd better get a hotel.'

'You're *in* a hotel.'

'Are you delusional? No normal person could spring for a joint like this.'

'But the *Herald* have already paid. You should stay. In this *luxurious* suite.'

That made me smile. 'Well, it *is* luxurious . . . but me staying here would be all kinds of wrong. You should stay.' Suddenly giddy, because a tougher-than-tough day had finally ended, I exclaimed, 'Hey, why don't we both stay?'

At his expression my face flared with heat. 'I just meant . . .' What *had* I meant? 'I was only . . . joking.'

He stared at me for a long, long moment. 'That's a shame.'

29

Saturday, 17 September, day five

Saturday morning . . . the gorgeous, dreamy realization that today is the day I can stay in bed for as long as I like . . .

Then I remember.

Down in my half-sleep, I've run full-tilt into a steel door. Struggling for breath, pawing for the light-switch, I sit up, hoping it's a bad dream but knowing it isn't.

Now I'm wide awake and the room is bright. I stare at his side of the bed. Empty.

I stare and stare, then lift the duvet and touch the sheet that he had once lain on. *Where are you now? Who are you with?*

And why haven't you called me?

He'd said he wouldn't but I nurse a hope that he won't stick to it.

Missing him is exhausting, the urge to ring him almost unendurable. Just to hear his unmistakable voice – it would pierce my pain and fill the need in my chest. Hugh has the perfect voice – the right depth, the right volume, properly warm and comforting. Even the words he speaks are the right ones. He chooses them carefully. He won't say something if he doesn't mean it. I'm only fully appreciating all of this now.

I reach for my phone, look at his contact details and hover on the edge of pressing Call for second after second after second. He'd pick up because he'd think it was an emergency. Then he'd probably be pissed off with me and maybe I need to keep my powder dry for some real emergency.

But doesn't he miss me? I've missed him for almost every single second since Tuesday.

Sobs force themselves out of me and, barely knowing what I'm at, I punch his stack of pillows and cry-shout, 'Why haven't you called me?' I hit the pillows a second whack. 'You fucker!' Another blow lands. 'You complete bastard!' And another. 'You fucking disloyal pr–'

'Mum?'

Shite! Which one is it?

It's okay. It's Neeve who's standing at my bedroom door, staring in shock. Neeve can handle seeing this. Kiara couldn't.

'Are you okay?' She sounds tentative.

'Completely fucking fabulous!' My face is roasting and the salty tears sting my skin. I clout the pillows again. 'I just can't believe he hasn't called me.'

'Mum, he said he wouldn't.'

'But he SHOULD HAVE!' I screech – into my hands so Kiara won't hear.

'That's just how Hugh is.'

'So fucking cold!'

'Not cold. Just . . . linear. Is that the word? If he says he'll do something, he sticks to it.'

'Well, he said he'd love me for ever!'

'He's coming back.'

'It'll be all fucked up. It'll never be the same.'

'I'll make you a cup of tea.'

She bolts from the room while sobs are wrenched from me. After a while I'm dimly aware that she's returned.

'What are you doing today?' she asks.

My answer is punctuated by sobbing. 'The weekly. Fucking. Shop.'

'No, Mum. Don't do that to yourself.'

'I have to. We need STUFF!'

'Do it online.'

'But they're such useless fuckers online,' I sob. 'I order Pink Ladies and they bring Gala apples instead, and that's the least worst thing they do, and I know they're first-world problems, I know, but please don't judge me.'

'I'll do the shop,' she offers.

'You're a useless fucker too.' Now I'm cry-laughing.

'Seriously, Mum, I'll do it.'

'Okay.' I wipe my face on the duvet cover. Like, what's the worst thing that can happen? Fear seizes my heart and I clutch her arm. 'Don't forget the wine.'

'So what are we doing today?' Lovatt lifts and lets fall a lock of my hair. 'Taking it down a couple of shades?'

In the mirror I stare at him. I'm in a peculiar mood: all the crying has emptied me out. Eventually my numb lips form a word. 'No.'

He sighs heavily. 'Well, what are we doing with these ends?'

That's another thing he's always at – bullying me into getting it cut before I'm ready. I could just leave. I could stand up, take off the gown and leave. There's the door, right there. I gaze at it, then meet his eye once more. He swallows and says, 'I'll just mix up the colour.'

'I'm going to sack my hairdresser.' This is how I greet Steevie.

She rolls her eyes. We've played this game frequently over the past thirty years. 'No,' she says. 'Amy, this is the worst time to be making important life decisions. It'll be just as bad with the new one. Sooner or later you'll run out of hairdressers.'

'There are billions of hairdressers in the world.'

'Not good ones, there aren't. They're like good men, only a very small supply.'

How have we already fallen into an All Men Are Bastards conversation?

'You don't want to end up like me,' she says, 'having to cut your own hair.'

'But you don't.' Steevie has a stunning cut, an out-there spiky crop that hugs the shape of her pretty head. She goes to Jim Hatton.

'It's a euphemism.'

It's really quite depressing how quickly she brings everything back to her being abandoned by Lee.

Suitable conversation subjects: velvet boots; verve or swerve?; Syrian refugees; is another fundraising piss-up in order?; Dads with Alzheimer's – can hitting them with an iPad ever be justified? (Just a small tap, not intended to hurt, simply to reprove.)

'Have you ordered yet?' I ask.

'Course not. Waited for you.' She passes me a menu.

God, there are so many options. And each dish has so many *parts* – halibut with samphire and Champagne sauce, autumn vegetable crumble and duchesse potatoes. That sounds, well . . . revolting.

'What starter are you having?' she asks.

Starter? God. I can't eat one, never mind *two* complicated courses.

'No starter for me.'

'Oh? Okay. No harm, I suppose. I'll skip it too.'

Wearily I choose the least disgusting-sounding lunch. Then Steevie says, 'So how're you doing?'

This is where the discussion of velvet boots should start but I waver, then admit, 'A bit shit.'

She nods. 'That's what happens when your *loving husband* shows his true colours. When Lee left, I felt like my heart had been ripped from my chest and stomped on.'

She's waiting for my agreement, but that's not how it is for me. 'I feel . . . like I'm living under a dark shadow. As if every light bulb in the world has been changed to those low-energy eco ones that start off dim as fuck, then get brighter. Except, these days, they never get brighter. Everything seems ominous, as if a terrible thing is about to happen. Then I realize it already has.'

'Oh, it *has*.'

'Most of the time I can't believe he's gone. I still think that when I go home later he'll be there.'

Meeting Steevie was meant to be a good thing, cheery – okay, maybe cheery was going too far, but comforting. Instead my spirits are sinking to the centre of the earth, at the same time as panic is rising.

'He hasn't called me. He's heartless.'

'I always knew that about him.'

'You did?'

'Oh, yeah. Heartless. And a cheater.'

'*Hugh?*'

'Amy.' She looks concerned. 'Why are you so surprised?'

'Are you saying that Hugh's been cheating? Here? In Dublin?'

'Love of God, no, Amy! Not that I know of anyway. I'm just saying they're all cheaters. Hugh's made it trickier for himself than most. He had to manufacture some mad crisis and travel to the other side of the world to do his cheating, so he could feel okay about it. But he's still a cheater.'

Right. AMAB. All Men Are Bastards. Well, she's right, of course. Except *is* Hugh a bastard?

'So you're going to Vivi Cooper's thing tonight?' Steevie asks.

I start to explain, then abruptly decide against it – my fear is that Steevie will suggest we go out together instead and, for reasons I don't understand, I want to get away from her. 'Yep. Vivi's birthday thing.'

'You and all the couples.'

Steevie and Vivi aren't friends, but since Lee left her, Steevie regularly implies she's omitted from events because she no longer has a husband.

In softer tones, she says, 'It's tougher than it looks, Amy. Being the only single person at a table of couples.'

Our food arrives and I'm hoping she'll abandon the subject, but no.

'It's fucking horrible, Amy.' Her voice cracks. 'And I'm not sure you're up to it.'

God. I stare at my plate, at all the mysterious blobs and smears. There's no way any of that can go into my mouth.

'You'll never recover,' she adds. 'You'll never go back to the person you were. But in time you'll come to terms with it.'

Trying to keep the wobble from my voice, I say, 'Knowing me, I'll probably come to terms with it just around the time he arrives home.'

It was supposed to be funny, but Steevie looks appalled. 'Amy, that's just when it'll be kicking off. Once they've, you know . . .' she winces '. . . excuse my language, *fucked* another woman, they can never settle again.'

This is pretty much what Derry said to me, and it's what I'd implied to Neeve only a few hours ago: that when – if – Hugh comes back, life won't slot neatly back into place, as if nothing had ever happened.

But the way Steevie is saying it is scaring me sideways.

'That's assuming he doesn't come back with STDs and herpes and genital warts and . . .'

Oh, God, I'm looking at the blobs and smears again and remembering that Lee gave her genital herpes, so she knows what she's talking about, and my stomach bucks and I hear myself say, 'You know, Steevie, I don't feel well. I'm so sorry, but I'm just going to . . .' I swipe my bag from the floor and I'm tearing through my wallet, looking for cash, because I need to leave right now – there's no time to do the card thing.

A fiver appears. That won't be enough. Panic tightens my chest. I need to leave! There's a twenty, thank God. And maybe some coins. Yes, coins, couple of two-euros in there. I dump a load of change on top of the notes and say, my voice breathless, 'If I owe more, I'll pay you back. So sorry.'

'Amy.' She's standing up, making an attempt to grab my arm. 'I was just trying to –'

'All fine, sweetie.' I twist my body free. 'Just my stomach giving me gyp. Gotta go.'

30

Sunday, 18 September, day six

My mouth goes dry. Jesus Christ! I mean Jesus, like, *Christ.* I'm looking at an exact copy of a navy velvet Dolce & Gabbana dress, like *exact*, right down to the sequin embellishments. Except instead of it costing eight trillion euro, it's sixty-five dollars!

I click to enlarge it as much as possible and maybe the velvet looks just *slightly* flammable but, you know, sixty-five dollars! It would be criminal to pass this up. It's hard to say exactly when I'd wear it, but who cares? A dress like that, you could wear it anywhere, right? Well, maybe not to work. Or to the supermarket. But everywhere else.

This site is *amazing.* I should buy dresses for all the girls, really, seeing as everything's so beautiful and cheap. I could even throw one in for Thamy to thank her for telling me about it.

So what size am I, in this strange Chinese knock-off universe? What does 42 mean? Is it Italian 42? French 42? Chinese 42?

I click for details. There's a picture of a woman with a tape measure, and the sizes are demonstrated in centimetres. There's probably a tape measure in the house somewhere but it would mean getting out of bed and I'm happy here, clicking on clothes in faraway lands.

Why must it be centimetres? I know my measurements – which I'm guessing at – in inches. Feck it, I'll go for a size 40, and if it's too big, I can return it. Can't I? Maybe a dodgy site like this wouldn't make returns easy. Or maybe they would. Don't they say the Chinese are great business people? Ah, what the hell, it's only sixty-five dollars, which isn't much. I'm not sure of the exchange rate but dollars are worth less than euros.

I'm doing it! I input my details, relieved they'll deliver to

Ireland, pay with PayPal, which isn't declined, thank Christ – and then up flashes, 'Delivered within sixty working days'. *Sixty?* That's two months!

My bubble bursts. I can't wait two months for this dress. I want it tomorrow. Today, even. I need the happiness now!

I'm cancelling the order, I am, but I click and click and can't find that option. I'd better contact PayPal. Well, *I* won't but I'll ask Hugh to – Oh! He's not here.

My disappointment is multi-layered – not only is he perhaps having sex with other women, but he's not here to help me reverse a rash online purchase. For a moment I'm not sure which I resent more.

Suddenly I feel very low. I've just wasted nearly an hour looking at dresses I don't need, can't afford, and won't get for two months. Or is it time wasted? Like, what else would I have done with that hour? At least while I was looking at knock-off dresses I was enjoying myself.

It's wrong, though, to be lying in bed alone on a Sunday afternoon: I should be engaging with other humans. But I just want to be online, looking at things to buy.

Neeve and Kiara are at home – well, they had been when we'd cleaned the house earlier, so I get up and go down to them.

In the living room, something very loud and crashy is on the TV and sitting on the couch is Baby Maisey. Declyn must have dropped her over. She's squashed between Sofie – who I'm delighted to see – and Kiara, who are both buried in their phones and totally ignoring her. But Maisey, who adores her girl cousins, is wearing a 'BEST! DAY! EVER!' gleam on her pudgy little face.

Kiara spots me. 'Hi, Mum, y'okay?'

'What's that racket?' I can't believe I've just said that.

Kiara squints at the TV. '*Planet of the Apes*?'

'Is that the right thing for a toddler?' I try squeezing Maisey but she shoves me off.

'Declyn isn't paying us.' Neeve appears from behind me. 'So we can mind her whatever way we like.'

'Right. Why don't we all do something?'

'More cleaning?' Neeve asks suspiciously.

'Something nice. Is Maisey's buggy here? It is? Why don't we go shopping?'

After a startled silence, Kiara asks, 'For what?'

'Clothes! Shoes! Nice things! Come on, we're in walking distance of the biggest shopping centre in Ireland.'

'Ah, Mum.' Neeve slings her arm around my shoulders. 'Get a grip.'

'It wouldn't be a happy thing,' Sofie says.

'You'd be doing it out of sadness,' Kiara says. 'Overcompensating, trying to be two parents instead of one.'

It's too weird when your sixteen-year-old daughter seems wiser than yourself. But if the girls don't want to go out, that frees up a couple of guilt-free hours to go back online. This time I'll look at household stuff, rugs, embroidered cushion covers and affordable paintings.

'Dude!' Sofie leaps off the couch. 'You've done a smelly thing!'

Maisey is wearing a dangerous smile.

'A fart?' Kiara asks. 'Or an actual poo?'

'I don't know!' Sofie is at the door. 'And I can't look.'

Kiara tentatively sniffs Maiscy's bum. 'Oh, man! You need a new nappy!'

'I can't change her,' Sofie calls from the kitchen.

'Neither can I,' Neeve says.

'I *could* do it . . .' Kiara looks at me with big, sad eyes.

Oh, for the love of God. 'Gimme the nappy-bag.'

'If we don't go, everyone will notice,' Sofie says.

'Are we that important?' Kiara asks.

'Bitch doing a drive-by with her casserole threw serious shade.' Neeve is insistent. 'Mum's gone viral – so what do we do?'

Obediently Sofie and Kiara intone, 'We twirl on them haters.'

'Mum?' Neeve frowns at me.

'Um, yes, sorry, Neevey, we twirl on them haters.'

'We will *draaaag* that bitch's ass,' Neeve promises.

We're locked in a four-way discussion about going to the cinema club. My responsibility is to keep life as normal as possible but have I the bandwidth to seem happyhappyhappy? *Yep, my husband is on a six-month sex holiday but I'm cool about it.*

Also, none of my true friends are going tonight. Steevie is still pissed off because of me running out on yesterday's lunch. Even after I sent an apology, she replied with a pass-agg *Grand.* Then I texted, to see if she was coming to the cinema and she replied, *Busy.* I feel a mixture of aggrieved and guilty, but the energy just isn't there to fully exploit.

Jana isn't going either, a family thing, and nor is Posh Petra, some disaster caused by the twins.

'None of us wants to go,' Kiara says. 'Which is more important? Taking care of ourselves? Or the opinion of others?'

Such wisdom!

'Dude, you can wear my hat,' Neeve says.

Kiara bites back a squeak. 'The one in the vlog? With the flowers?'

'That one.'

Kiara wavers. Then, abruptly, her resolve collapses. 'And maybe the scarf?'

'I'll even throw in the gloves.'

'*Yaaaaaaaaas!*'

'Come on now, ladies.' Neeve claps her hands. 'Let's all get in formation!'

They flutter around, grooming each other, swapping coats and fixing hair-dos until Neeve decrees we slay: Kiara is in knee-high Doc Martens, skinny combats, a huge boxy black mohair sweater and the beautiful hat, scarf and gloves on loan from Neeve. 'If anyone asks you about them,' Neeve says, 'you say they're mine.'

Because Sofie's clothes are at Urzula's or my mum's, Neeve styles her in a denim parka with a bright blue fake-fur hood. Neeve herself wears an oversized boyfriend coat, black jaguar-print leggings and silver brogues, and I'm in one of my prize pieces – possibly the prize-iest of all my pieces: the tightly waisted, swingy-skirted red coat from Dior, which I'd found on the floor in TK Maxx for a price so low I'd thought I was having a psychotic break. I'm wearing it with shiny black knee boots, and Neeve decks me out with berry-coloured lips.

'Selfie! Selfie!'

The photo is all hair and lips and cheeks and smiles – Neeve looks adorably wicked, Kiara a little solemn and Sofie as cute as a kitten. My heart nearly bursts with love for them.

The four of us stand in the hall, furiously uploading the picture to our preferred social media, then out we go into the cold September evening. We decide we'll walk and the four of us hold hands and I feel okay.

31

Seventeen months ago

So I said, 'I'm joking,' and Josh Rowan looked like he wanted to shove me on to the bed and start unbuckling his belt. Then he said, 'That's a shame.' And what he meant was, It's a shame because I think you're the hottest woman I've met in the longest time and –

'Mum?' Kiara's voice made me jump. 'What are you doing up here?'

My fuzzy-edged reverie was broken. 'Lying on my bed,' I said snippily. 'What the feck does it look like?'

'But, like, *why*?'

To keep reliving the moment when Josh Rowan said, 'That's a shame.'

'I'd a really tough week at work and I'm tired.'

'*Still* tired?'

God above, I've been lying down for less than an hour and they're all behaving like I've been bed-bound for a month.

'Yes, still tired. I'm going to have a snooze now. Don't come back up.'

'Why are you so mean?'

'Because I'm tired.'

. . . and he said, 'That's a shame.'

He'd thought it was a shame! That I was only joking about staying in the hotel with him! Which meant he wanted to stay in the hotel with me! In the bedroom! In the bed!

And the thought of me and him naked and him pulling my hair and pressing his hardness against me . . . It was both thrilling and terrifying.

'*What does he look like, Amy?*'

'*Like he's nursing a secret sorrow.*'

'*Oh! That's so romantic.*'

Okay, so I had a crush on Josh Rowan, the sort of thing that could happen to anyone, right? But it was a first in all my years with Hugh.

Like, I fancied Jamie Dornan and Aidan Turner and most of the men in the Scandinavian TV series (Hugh called them my 'Scandi-lusts') but this was the first time I'd got properly giddy about an actual real-life man. Some coupled-up women I knew had flings, affairs, one-night stands. Sometimes they even jumped ship from a long-term thing to a man they'd been overlapping with and embarked on a new relationship. It happened. Derry had done it.

But I'd literally never even snogged another man since Hugh and I had got together. The thought was alien. I loved Hugh, the very bones of him. Plus I *liked* him – which I'd come to realize happened less often in long-term relationships than you'd think. I respected him, appreciated him and felt huge fondness for him. He was a million times my favourite person.

So it was far from normal to find myself alone late at night in a hotel room with a man who was probably a creepy player but who, at that moment, seemed really hot.

Not textbook handsome, nothing like that, but confident and just-macho-enough. It was hard to say what was suddenly so wantable about Josh Rowan. You couldn't single out his eyes or his cheekbones, none of the usual, but something in the combination of his hangdog features worked.

Also, there was more than a hint of the unreconstructed about him. Definitely *not* a vegetarian. That was a description I liked and I was using it a lot in my many imaginary conversations.

'What's he like, Amy?'

'Not a vegetarian. That's what he's like.'

And the conversations were rapidly becoming more elaborate.

'What's he like, Amy, this man who's in love with you?'

'A journalist. English. Hot. Not a vegetarian.'

'Ooooh!'

Every time I thought about Josh Rowan, it felt like stars were sparking under my skin and coursing through my blood. Suddenly a part of my life had exploded into glorious technicolour.

Would we get to see each other again, Josh and I?

He'd called me the morning Premilla's piece had run. I'd spent the night in one of those hotels at the airport where, if you breathed too close to a bottle of water in the mini-bar, your credit card instantly got charged a king's ransom.

'You've seen the spread?'

'It's great. Thank you . . .' I paused, then tentatively said his name '. . . Josh.' Hearing myself say it felt oddly daring. 'It's great.'

'You off to Ireland now? Have a good weekend.'

'You too . . . Josh.' This time saying his name fizzed me with a powerful little thrill.

'Bye, Amy.'

'Bye.' I didn't say his name a third time – vaguely anxious about what could happen. I might combust or something.

Maybe we could have a working lunch. I'd suggested that in the past and been rebuffed. Things were different now, we definitely had a working relationship, but then I'd be making the running and those feels weren't lovely ones: those feels were a little pathetic.

Perhaps it would be best simply to let things lapse.

But no! That drained me of every drop of joy. Quick! Before the joyous feels slithered away completely! . . . *and he said, 'That's a shame.'* I savoured the memory of how he'd looked at me before he'd spoken – like he meant it, like he'd fucking *meant* it!

But he was probably a player . . . Wait, of *course* he was a player! How naive was I? The man was married!

Then again, so was I. Did that make me a player too?

No. No, no, no, no, no. In my heart of hearts there was no intention of actually *doing* anything with Josh Rowan – if there was, wouldn't I just have had sex with him there and then? After all, there had been a hotel room, a bed, the two of us – there had been nothing at all to stop us – but we'd refrained.

Neither of us were players. Yes: that was the conclusion that suited me best. God, it was only a little flirtation. What was the harm?

He said, 'That's a shame . . .' He was a loyal man who'd never strayed from feisty Marcia, but was so drawn to me that he couldn't help himself. He saw things in me that bypassed most people. He didn't mind that I was short and not-young. He liked my peculiar clothes – he saw them as evidence of a rare, uncommon person.

Reality crashed in. He was a man. With a dick. In a hotel room with a woman. Who had – let's not forget – suggested they both spend the night there. Yes. *I* had. Not him – me.

What the *hell* had I been thinking?

Mixing work and flirting – worst idea ever. But in retrospect I'd had an off-the-scale stressy thirty-six hours: my intense focus on saving Premilla had cauterized all my links with the outside world and I'd temporarily forgotten who I was.

It had just been a stupid giddy thing blurted out in the giddy heat of the giddy moment.

But Freud said there were no accidents, giddy or otherwise. Clearly this had been my subconscious speaking up, articulating what the more polite part of my brain wouldn't dare admit.

I grabbed my iPad and opened Facebook: time for a little light spying.

Feeling thrilled and ashamed I scrolled down his feed, being extremely careful not to like anything of his.

Then, right before my astonished eyes, Josh Rowan liked something of mine. Yes! It said it! Josh Rowan liked your post! I stared at it, hungry with joy, my knuckles white with concentration. Clearly he was stalking me, just like I was stalking him! Almost immediately it got unliked – just like me, he was trying to cover his tracks. Christ alive! *'That's a shame . . .'*

'You okay?' Hugh's voice set my heart thudding.

For the love of God! How hard is it to have some time to myself in my own head, playing with my own happy thoughts? Just for once!

'Yeah. Grand.' My voice carried a hint of my resentment. 'Just on Facebook.'

'You need anything?'

Some uninterrupted time to think my own thoughts would be nice.

'No. Thanks. I'll be down in a while.'

. . . and he said, 'That's a shame.'

32

'If he was going to lose his nerve and come home,' Druzie says, 'it would have happened by now.' It's Tuesday evening and we're sitting in her garden, eating cheese. She's back from Syria for a few days and, in her dusty sand-coloured clothes, she looks like a soldier or a foreign correspondent. Everything about her seems to be the same colour: her short hair is dirty-blonde and her skin is tanned and freckled.

'He's been living his new life for a week,' she says. 'Getting the hang of it, meeting other travellers, starting to enjoy himself. Too harsh?'

Despite everything, I laugh. 'Of *course*. But you're right.' In the first few days after Hugh had left I'd thought he really might not be able for the loneliness, for the enormity of what he'd done. But now? He's gone for the duration.

'So what are you going to do?' Druzie asks. 'You've six months, minus a week. You can achieve a lot in that time.'

'Ah, stop, I'm not you.'

Druzie is never afraid. A Zimbabwean who doesn't watch television and knows how to fire a rifle, she doesn't give a shite about societal rules. She's the first person I'd call if I found myself arrested in a dodgy foreign country.

'C'mon, what do you want from life, Amy?'

'Nothing,' I admit. 'Apart from Hugh to come home. But the other stuff, bucket list, unfulfilled ambition – not really.'

'Huh.'

'Embarrassing, right? I mean, I'd like the girls to be okay. A mother is only ever as happy as her least happy child, and I worry about Neeve because of Richie –'

'Idiot.'

'Idiot is right. I worry she won't ever make an income. It's rough on her still living at home – she's twenty-two, she should be out having fun, swiping right. And Sofie, I just want her to be happy.'

'Sounds so simple, but –'

'– it's the hardest thing ever. As for Kiara, she should be President of the World. Then I worry that everyone's expectations might send her off the rails.' I lapse into silent thought, while the wind gets up a bit. I'd like to go inside but Druzie is outdoorsy and doesn't feel the cold. 'Now I feel pitiful that my only goals are around my children. That's nearly as bad as simply wanting Hugh to come back. I'm living through other people.'

'You don't want to be that woman. C'mon, Amy, put some thought into this.'

I go down a couple of exploratory avenues and the best I can come up with is 'I'd like to feel safe.'

'And be thin?' Druzie thinks wanting to be thin is utterly pathetic.

'Says the woman who forgets to eat!'

'Says the woman who works in war zones with starving people. But go for it, honey, indulge yourself.'

I know it's shallow, but . . . 'Yeah, okay, and be thin. And have nice clothes and go on fabulous holidays with Hugh and live in an extremely beautiful house with a squad of invisible cleaners and gardeners and a man whose sole job is to fix small annoying problems, like loose light-switches and broken panes of glass, and I wouldn't even have to ask him to do anything – he'd magically spirit himself around the house, making things right without me even knowing anything was wrong instead of standing before me and telling me all the reasons why he *couldn't* fix it.'

Druzie smiles. She can do all those things herself. But I'm on a roll now.

'We'd have so many rooms in the house that I'd have my own to decorate exactly in my taste and I'd commission special wallpaper from artisans in Hungary or places like that – it would be an actual painting but on wallpaper, you know? And hand-embroidered curtains. And hand-embroidered cushions, not the same as the curtains because matchy-matchy is twee, but they'd be *similar*. Or maybe they'd actually clash, but in a strangely harmonious way.'

'Strangely harmonious? Huh.'

'And paintings. I'd buy every one of Dušanka Petrović's paintings.'

'Who?'

'The mystery Serbian artist I'm obsessed by. We'd have a gym and a movie room and maybe a swimming pool . . . but what if we didn't use it? I'm worried that after the initial thrill we wouldn't, and then I'd feel guilty about the water being heated every day, and it would be like Elton John spending a fortune on flowers in all his homes, even when he's not there, and this is a fantasy and it's supposed to be enjoyable, but now it's just making me anxious.'

'What if Hugh doesn't come back? Do you still want to be rich?'

I swallow hard. 'I might as well.'

'But what use would all that money be, if you didn't have Hugh?'

'I know, right!'

This long-running in-joke started when I was in post-Richie bitterness and she was in permanent pragmatic Druzie-ness. We used to scorn our sexist society for telling women they counted for nothing if they didn't have a man on their arm.

'Sad and all as your life is now, Amy,' her tone is tragi-mocking, 'it would be worse to be rich and single.'

'Too right. Gold-digger men would prey upon me, young men who'd rain compliments down on my head.'

'And because you'd had stuff injected into your face –'

'– and could afford Simone Rocha dresses –'

'– you'd believe them.'

'But they wouldn't love me at all! They'd have a *real* girlfriend –'

'– or boyfriend.'

'*Or* boyfriend. They'd propose marriage, but they'd only do it if we had a pre-nup giving them nothing.'

'And because of you being a total idiot, you'd think this meant true love and you'd say, "No, no, we won't have a pre-nup."'

'Then I'd happily get spliced even though everyone – Derry, Neeve, even *Kiara* – was telling me that your man was a shyster.'

'So your new husband fancies himself as a film director –'

'Oh, yes! Love it. I'd finance a couple of vanity films, which starred his secret girlfriend –'

'– or boyfriend.'

'The films would be car-crashes and all the critics would mock me.'

'Then you'd die in suspicious circumstances and they'd do a big piece about you in *Vanity Fair*.'

'Which would be mortifying. *And* I'd be dead. And, bad as things are, I don't want to be dead. I'm curious about how things will turn out. This is good, right?'

33

'Hello, hello!' Friday lunchtime, and Alastair struts in from London with his usual fanfare.

Tim ends a call and says, 'Give us a debrief and make it quick. I'm leaving at three.'

'What's up?'

'My wife is taking me to Paris for the weekend.'

Both Alastair and I are stunned into silence.

'That's wonderful.' I'm nearly *sick* with envy.

Then Tim says, 'Mrs Staunton's just landed tickets for the rugby.'

Aaaaah. My vision of a sexy, romantic weekend of rumpled sheets and luxury-macarooning, adorable little boutiques and flea-markets-full-of-vintage-Chanel vanishes. The *rugby*. Wouldn't be for me.

'Mrs Staunton loves rugby,' Tim says. 'Loves France. Nothing she likes better than sitting in a café on the Champs-Élysées sipping absinthe and smoking a cheroot.'

You never know if Tim is joking or not.

'Okay, maybe not a cheroot,' he says. 'Just a cigarette. Or twenty.'

'Who's minding your many children?' Alastair asks.

'Mrs Staunton's parents. They command terror.'

If they're anything like their daughter, I can well believe it. Alastair and I have known Tim for donkey's years but we've never bonded with Mrs Staunton. She's always really, really busy and arrives late to everything, even the party we threw to launch Hatch. She doesn't bother with niceties and she tends to the abrupt. When Alastair flirts with her she does perplexed frowns, as if he's speaking Swahili (I must admit I admire that). And she doesn't do that thing women usually do, where I show her handbag lots of love, then she does the same to mine, then I tell her she has great hair and she says it's usually a disaster, but it's not so bad since she got the sixteen-week blow-dry and so on.

But she and Tim seem to knock along very nicely. Each to their own.

'Would you get me some stuff in Sephora?' I ask.

'No.'

'You don't even know what Sephora is.'

'Do you mind? I've a teenage daughter.'

'I'll do an email. You'd just have to show your phone to the lady – you wouldn't even have to speak.'

'No.'

'Ah, Tim,' Alastair says. 'Have a heart. Poor Amy.'

'I'm sorry, Amy, but Mrs Staunton has informed me she wants my undivided.'

At three on the dot, Tim switches off his screen. 'I'm away. Have nice weekends. See you Monday.'

'*Au revoir!*'

'*Bonne chance!*'

'It's the Marc Jacobs primer,' I call after him. 'Just in case.'

Tim shakes his head in exasperation, then goes.

'Lucky Tim,' Alastair says.

I check he's properly gone before I say, 'But he has to go to the rugby. I think I'd actually cry.'

'And he has to go with Rosanna.'

'She's . . . God, she's an odd one.' We have this conversation regularly. 'Definitely the alpha in that marriage.' Then I add, 'Fair play to her.' Because, yeah, fair play to her. Woman. Surgeon. Five children. Taking her husband away for the weekend.

'Mind you,' says Alastair. 'Tim is so cut-and-dried about everything, not everyone would put up with him.'

'Ah, no!' I'm not having it. 'Tim is great. He's *so* reliable, and hard-working, and a good father and kind – he's *kind*, Alastair. We're lucky to have him. Him and Rosanna, okay, she's not the most likeable, but it works for them.'

'Is it the rule that the alpha doesn't have to be nice to the beta's colleagues?'

'I wouldn't know. Neither Hugh nor I is an alpha, neither of us earns enough . . .'

'Amy? Hello? Amy?'

Should I still be thinking of Hugh and me in the present tense?

'Amy? Talk to me. Are you okay?'

'Sorry.'

'Seriously, are you okay?'

'Yep.'

34

Sixteen months ago

'. . . which brings us to our next award of the evening . . .' Up on the stage the MC droned on. During the prize giving and the humble-brag acceptance speeches, these media award events were so *bone-crushingly* boring.

If only they'd finish up so I could loiter in the general area of Josh Rowan's table. But that was still a long way off, and if something nice didn't happen inside my head soon, there was a real fear I'd go mental – a quick ten minutes in the powder-room on Asos might save me.

'I'm going to the loo,' I whispered to Alastair.

My browsing would have been done right at the table if I wasn't so afraid of giving offence to our hosts, the multi-media group who'd invited me, Tim and Alastair to this, the Press Awards.

Alastair gripped my arm tight. 'Make bloody sure you come back. Do *not* abandon me. No man left behind, right?'

'Grand.' With my head down, desperate to not make eye-contact and risk being shamed for leaving during someone's proud moment, I scurried around the circular tables, heading for the Ladies, which was at the back of the ballroom, about half a mile away.

The trick was to move speedily in a running crouch so as not to break people's view of the stage. I'd just passed the invisible line where the rows of tables ended, feeling like a person who'd escaped from a cruel regime, when my head butted against someone's chest. 'Sorry,' I muttered, already moving away.

'Hey, Amy.' My forearm was grabbed and I looked up. Christ alive, it was Josh.

'Hi!' I was suddenly breathless.

It was almost four weeks, twenty-five days, to be precise,

since the Premilla Routh interview, and in those twenty-five days I'd thought of him. Quite a bit. To be honest, it was bordering on mild obsession.

A few days after I'd last seen him, he'd Instagrammed me a motivational platitude of exquisite awfulness. This had plunged me into a *yin-yang* state of thrilled shame and, after spending far too long deleting dozens of possible responses, I'd eventually replied with a smiling emoji and a single 'x'. Immediately I followed him on Instagram and Twitter and, minutes later, he followed me.

Another platitude arrived two days later. Then, after wasting far too long trying to find something special, I sent him one. Things ramped up, when I retweeted a video of a dog dancing to Wham! He retweeted it, then – obviously thinking this was my sort of thing, which it was – he sent me a GIF of cocker spaniels dressed up as penguins. Since then we'd been bouncing funny stuff across the Irish Sea, the jokiness undercut by the number of Xs we signed off with. We were now up to three.

In the meantime we'd become Facebook friends. My digital stalking was under control during daylight hours, but late at night, when I'd had maybe a bit too much to drink, I'd sneak on to Facebook, both his and Marcia's pages, just to see what was going on.

They'd recently got a new puppy, a Labrador cross, that was proving a nightmare to train, but it was upbeat stuff: chewed shoes – hilaire! The legs of the chairs gnawed to bits – all the lolz!

About two weeks ago, Marcia had installed a black wood-burning stove in their living room and, even though it was beyond me as to why anyone would want something so needy, she was ecstatic about it.

Shortly after that, the whole family went skiing in Utah – I'd have thought Utah would be *way* too warm for skiing, but clearly I hadn't a clue. There were tons of photos of the four of them kitted out in reflective sunglasses and padded snowsuits against a background of blinding snow; they'd seemed to be having a great time.

That plunged me into lip-gnawing worry because you could

never call me outdoorsy. But maybe Josh could do that with his male friends. Or, indeed, his sons. But, oh, God, I'd have broken up their happy home . . .

And their home *did* look happy. Josh's marriage seemed like a good one, and I'd find myself puzzling over the flirtiness, attraction, whatever it was, that had crackled between us.

In my less insane moments I admitted he was probably just a shagger who was good at compartmentalizing. But thinking that way didn't generate the sparky feels I'd become too fond of, and it felt far nicer to reconfigure the whole business into a wild, romantic fantasy.

We had been certain to bump into each other tonight – we'd made a studiedly light and casual arrangement to find each other after the speeches. As a consequence, I'd gone to too much trouble with my hair and clothes. Indeed, earlier, before we'd entered the ballroom, Alastair had narrowed his eyes at me and said, 'What's with the knockers?'

'I'm a woman,' I'd said, a little haughtily. 'I have breasts.'

'Yeah, but . . .'

I also had an arse and a stomach. 'Let me look.' I stood in front of the full-length mirror in the lobby and studied myself in the slippery bias-cut sheath. God, I was a bit bursty and not just in the chest region.

'Seriously,' Alastair said, 'don't you have a shawl thing?'

There was a wrap back in my room but I didn't want to be a woman who wore wraps. Or, worse still, a shrug. I wanted to be a defiant warrior woman, who strode about with bare arms and a straight back and an out-and-proud embonpoint.

Tim had arrived, looking eleven years of age, in his neat black tux and black dickie-bow. 'Tim, is this too much?' I gestured in the general direction of my bosom and he gave an I'm-sorry-to-be-the-bearer-of-bad-news smile. Well, if Tim thought it . . .

I'd returned to my room and the spirit-dampening wrap had accompanied me to the ballroom – but now Josh Rowan was standing looking at me, still holding on to my arm, and my wrap was miles away, slithering around on the back of my chair.

'You look great.'

'So do you! Very James Bond in your tux. *Very* Daniel Craig. Sorry, sorry.' Apologetically I flapped a hand in front of my face. He didn't look like Daniel Craig . . . well, not in his colouring, maybe a little in the uncompromising expression. I pulled him close and said into his ear, 'I'm a bit pissed.'

'That's okay.' He moved back enough, just so I could see his face. 'So am I.'

Together we said, 'Only way to get through these things.' Then we both laughed, quite long and quite hard.

When the laughter had stopped and we were standing, smiling broadly at each other, I said, 'You know something?'

'What?'

'I have a room upstairs.'

'And?'

'You like to come up and join me there?'

35

Saturday, 24 September, day twelve

'Hiiii!' Bronagh Kingston greets me with a bright smile. 'How *are* you?'

'Yes, good!' I exclaim. Is that positive enough? Maybe not. 'Great!' I say. 'Top form! Yourself?'

'Wow, you're in a good mood.' She laughs. 'Have you had good news or something?'

'Er . . .' Oddly, I'm finding my downtime more challenging than work – especially having conversations with those who don't know what's going on between myself and Hugh.

Bronagh had texted on Tuesday that she'd put aside tons of clothes for me. So, during the week, whenever the horror hit, I'd calm myself with the promise of gorgeous affordable clothes on Saturday. There seems, however, to be a gap between anticipated events and their reality. Bronagh is lovely but we've never crossed the line into the personal full-and-franks, so talking to her is a surprising effort.

'I've loads of great stuff to show you.' With pride, she displays a heap of dead people's clothes and, because my instinctive-response centre seems to have shut down, I'm having to manufacture my reactions. I'm aiming for positive but clearly my pitch is off because at one stage Bronagh says, with concern, 'Are you okay, Amy? You seem a bit . . . manic?'

Manic? Right. I'd better tone down the chirpiness. It's hard to get the balance right – it'll take trial and error, I guess. Well, I've six months (minus twelve days) to get it down. No doubt I'll be pitch perfect by March.

To apologize for my weirdness I buy too much, stuff I wouldn't have shelled out for if my mind hadn't been unhinged, and when

I leave, whether it's due to the waste of money or the loneliness of faking a bond with someone when it used to come naturally, I feel extremely low.

From there I go to meet Steevie for a coffee. We made up during the week – a flurry of 'Sorry' and 'No, *I'm* sorry' and 'No, I'm *more* sorry!' But as I hurry across town, it's clear that my bond with everyone is fragile. If Steevie mocks my bag of dead people's clothes or if she tries to make me wish gonorrhoea on Hugh, I don't think I can deal.

There she is, at a window table in Il Valentino. She wanted us to have lunch but I'd asked if it could be something shorter, then had to speak at high speed to ameliorate her resentful silence with the admission that I've become prone to panic.

'Even with *me*?' She'd been hurt.

'With everyone,' I'd replied, which wasn't entirely true.

'Just since Hugh went?'

'Yes.'

'Poor Amy. Fucking Hugh.' She added, in a grim tone, 'I hope he gets rabies of the dick.'

But we get on fine, lovely even. I tell her about Genevieve Payne showing up with the casserole, and even though she'd already heard it from numerous sources, she wants my version. She laughs and laughs at Neeve saying, 'Keep your casserole.' Although the report that reached her ears was 'You can stick your fucking casserole, lid and all, up your skinny arse, you piece of trash.'

Then I wonder if I should worry about Neeve being slandered.

'Look, Jana and me are going to a party tonight and we want you to come –'

'No, Steevie. Please, no.'

'But it's so wrong, you hiding under a rock, while Hugh is riding girls left, right and centre.'

I wish she wouldn't say stuff like that. He may be. I just don't want to think about it and I don't want it spoken about so casually. But if I say anything to her, it might make things weird again.

It's a relief to go home to an empty house, climb into bed with my iPad and look at the new arrivals on net-a-porter. All the beautiful things . . . It's uplifting to examine them. Statement coats, witty clutch bags – and then, making me actually gasp out loud, *the* most indescribable pair of shoes. Super-high, super-magical, with all kinds of sparkly embellishments on the heels; I know, without having to check, that they're by Gucci. Not because I'm a regular purchaser of Gucci – I couldn't afford even a keyring – but I have a gift for identifying spendy brands.

I see women on *The Graham Norton Show* and, right away, I can tell you who their dress and shoes are by. Or Claudia's clothes on *Strictly*. Or whatever the female judges on *X Factor* are wearing. 'Ask Amy,' people say. 'Amy will know.'

We all have our gifts and admittedly, yes, mine is fairly niche, but if there was a career in it, I'd be extremely highly regarded.

Kiara disapproves. She says that being *au fait* with so much designer stuff isn't something to be proud of. But, feck it, what harm does it do?

Transfixed, I stare at the enchanting Gucci shoes. They've such a cute shape – they remind me of My Little Pony – that, even though I could never afford them, they make me happy.

Asos might have copies! Six points of difference: that's all a knock-off needs to be allowed to exist. But Asos has nothing, so I move on to Kurt Geiger, then Zara, TopShop, Russell & Bromley . . .

I click on site after site and somehow get sidetracked by a pair of knee boots from Dune, lovely lace-up Edwardian-looking things, and even though I don't need them, and don't have the money, I click enough times that they become mine.

36

Monday morning is being very Monday-y.

'Kiara, get up!'

'Oh, Mu-um! Bring me orange juice.'

'Sofie,' I yell up into the attic room. 'Get up!' She'd stayed here last night but her school uniform is at Urzula's and I've to drive her there before going to work. 'Kiara, it's ten to eight, get up!'

'Orange juice!'

'Get the feck up!' Neeve howls, from her bedroom. 'I'm trying to sleep.'

I race down the stairs to get Kiara's glass of juice. Sofie still hasn't appeared and I let a roar up at her. 'Sofie! I'll be late for work if you don't come right now!'

'Shut the FUCK up!' Neeve shrieks.

'Mum, where's my school shirts?'

'In your wardrobe!'

'I can't see them.'

I thunder into Kiara's room, go straight to her wardrobe and yank one out.

'It wasn't there two minutes ago,' she says sulkily. Kiara, normally lovely, isn't so good in the mornings.

Sofie stumbles down the steps and, really, this situation, where she's living between three different homes, can't go on. Urzula and she do nothing but clash, and I've felt I've no choice but to let it play out. But maybe it's finally time to have a conversation about it.

Automatically I open my mouth to ask Hugh's opinion – and, oh, of course, he's not here to ask, and the loss is still raw and shocking, and it's going to take a long, long time to unlearn the impulse to run every thought by him.

But it *is* possible: people who lose a hand or a leg eventually manage to edit it from their list of available limbs.

'Amy,' Sofie says, 'can I have money for charcoal? For art class. Mum's away for a few days.'

'Well, stay here. Unless you want to stay at Granny's,' I add hurriedly.

'I'll stay here.'

'Grand. But come on, we've got to get your uniform.'

'Mum, can you pick me up from swimming at seven p.m.?' Kiara asks.

'And I need a lift to my history tutor at seven,' Sofie says.

They're in opposite directions and I can't do both. I tap on Neeve's door.

'WHAT?'

'Can you take Sofie to her history tutor at seven?'

'No! I've a work thing! Now could you all shut up?'

For the love of God! 'Okay, Sofie, I'll take you.'

'What about me?' Kiara demands.

'Cycle home.'

'With wet hair? Cycle home in the cold with wet hair? Well, if I get the flu and die, it'll be on you.'

'You don't get the flu from wet hair,' Neeve yells from her room. 'More's the fucking pity!'

After all this drama, I'm about twenty minutes late for work – Tim and Alastair are already there when I slink in. In theory, there are no bosses in our partnership, but it's poor form to be late. None of us wants to look like we're not pulling our weight. 'Hello,' I mumble. 'Sorry.'

I'm brought up short by the sight of a black and white bag on my desk. It's from Sephora. Stunned, I look hard at it, then whirl around on Tim. 'You got me the primer!'

'I did.' He looks like he's about to burst with pride *and* die of embarrassment.

'Oh, God!' I start ripping off the fancy black Sellotape and my hands are shaking. I open the bag and peer inside. There's more than one thing nestling within! 'Tim!' I close the bag and stare at him. I'm laughing, amazed and delighted, my Monday misery forgotten. I peep in again – there are at least three things – then whip my head up to him. I can feel my eyes bulge. 'Tim! What's going on?'

'They had a launch. For a new mascara. I know you like it when things are just out.'

'"New and exciting".' I'm shrill with glee. 'I *do*.' I've located the primer and the mascara and I'm turning them over in my hands.

'Then I got you a –'

'Lipstick!' I've just found the box.

'Because it meant I'd spent enough to qualify for a free eyeliner. So I got a black one. Is that okay?'

'Course! Can't go wrong with a black eyeliner.'

Then the lipstick, which I'm resigned to being awful, maybe a coral or an orangy red, which make my teeth look jaundiced. But, still, whatever the colour, it doesn't matter because Tim is so grea– Oh! My! God! It's beautiful. It's a dark red, seasonally suitable, but in blue tones that are perfect for my pale skin. I breathe at him, 'How did you *know*?'

'I described you to *la femme*.'

'What did you *say*?' I'm speaking in a near whisper.

'Ah, you know, said you're typically Celtic.'

'Oh, God.' I've got my mirror out and I'm applying it – the texture! And the finish! 'Jesus, I fucking *love* it!'

'I did good?' Tim asks shyly.

'Oh, Tim, you did *so* good!'

He looks ridiculously pleased with himself, standing there in his little suit, pink patches of pride in his cheeks.

I launch myself at him and he steps back. 'I'm sorry, Tim,' I say. 'But I *have* to hug you.'

'No good deed goes unpunished,' he murmurs, as I clasp him.

'Ha-ha-ha-ha-ha-ha!' I can't stop laughing. I'm really giddy. 'You're too funny.' I plant a big red smacker on his cheek. 'Thanks, Tim. Seriously. Thanks, Tim, thanks a million, trillion times.'

'Welcome. And we'll say no more about it.'

'Money! How much do I owe you?'

He shakes his head. 'It's a present. Now, calm down, it's time for work. Boardroom, Alastair and Amy.'

Oh, noes! It's the last Monday of the month, so it's our financial review. Where's my Nexium? Oh, my poor anxious stomach. I hate these meetings. We look at work generated, and by whom, because our income is allocated in a complex manner: the highest percentage goes to whichever of us actually brought in the work, but another percentage goes to the other two partners, then more is sliced off the top to pay Thamy, rent, airfares and all our other expenses. But, however we break it down, it's never really enough.

'Well?' Anxiously Alastair and I look at Tim. 'How bad is it?'

'The figures are all there on your laptops,' Tim says.

'Just tell us.'

Tim reads accountancy reports like I read *Grazia*.

'We're doing better. Turnover is up eight per cent on last month and twenty-two per cent on this time last year, while our expenses have remained steady.'

'What does that mean?' I ask. 'In actual money in my bank?'

'You're confusing turnover with cash flow,' Tim says. 'Turnover means nothing until people pay.'

'Well, how do we make them pay?'

'That's why we have Thamy.'

Okay. I relax a little. Thamy takes shite from no one.

I return to my desk, just in time for Mum to ring. 'I need you to mind that gomaloon tonight.'

'Mum, I can't. I've got to drop Sofie to her history tutor and collect her an hour later.'

'So what am I meant to do?'

'You've four other children. Ask Maura.'

'Pop can't stick Maura.'

'Derry?'

'She's met a fella.'

'*Has* she?'

'Don't get too excited. The poor schmuck will probably mispronounce "scone" and that'll be the end of him.'

When did Mum start using words like 'schmuck'?

'How about Joe?'

Mum starts singing, 'Oh, the fairy-tales of Ireland . . .' This is to imply that Joe invents elaborate, transparent excuses whenever he's asked to do something he doesn't want to do, which is always.

'Declyn?' My voice is tentative.

'But we couldn't ask Declyn. He's only young.'

'He's thirty-nine.'

'That's no age. Amy, it has to be you.'

Despair swamps me.

'Amy, I'll kill him if I don't get out.'

I understand, I do. But I might kill him too. 'Mum, seriously, I can't, not tonight. If you gave me more notice . . . Look, try Declyn. Bye!'

37

Sixteen months ago

Josh Rowan dropped my arm like it was radioactive. 'Join you? In your hotel room?'

'Um, yes.'

'For what?'

Christ, kill me now. Please. Just drop one of those giant chandeliers on my head. 'Nothing,' I said. 'Sorry, no, nothing, just . . .' What the hell was I *at*? I was drunk, but drunk enough to proposition someone? 'Forget I said anything.' Jesus, let me die.

Too much time had been spent in my head, fantasizing and being mental. But fantasy had just crashed into reality, with mortifying results. I turned to move away and Josh grabbed my wrist, pulling me back to face him. 'Amy, if you say something like that, you've got to mean it.'

Mutely I looked up at him.

'So do you?' he asked softly. 'Mean it?'

I thought of Hugh and how lovely he was to me, of Marcia and her wood-burning stove, of going up in the lift with Josh Rowan, of the awkwardness of us arriving into the hotel room, of writhing around on the bed that so many others had writhed around on before us, of revealing my forty-three-year-old body to him . . . The entire montage was appalling.

'No.' I bowed my head.

Still holding my wrist he led me out of the ballroom and into the blazing light of the giant lobby. I went along obediently because I felt as contrite as a child.

Shame was my strongest emotion, deep shame. The fantasy man I'd been playing games with hadn't been real, but this man *was*. It wasn't right to throw out sexy invitations if I'd had no intention of going through with them.

'What's this all about?' Josh asked.

What should I say? Should I tell him about the mild obsessing I'd been doing?

'Let's sit down a minute.' We crossed the vast marble floor to a couch. I parked myself in a corner and Josh also sat, keeping a big distance between us.

When a waiter showed up with a tray, Josh said, 'No thanks, mate.' And only when the man had entirely gone did he focus on me and say, 'So? What's going on?'

'I . . . ah . . . look.' The only decent thing was to tell him the truth. 'I got a . . . crush on you. That day, the day of Premilla's interview.'

He looked at me for a long time. 'You're married.'

I covered my face with my hands. 'I know. Please. I know. I love Hugh. I don't know what I'm at.'

'What would you have done if I'd said yes just now?'

I groaned again. 'Probably bottled it before we'd even got as far as the lift.' Fresh shame washed over me. 'Maybe I just wanted some attention – I wanted to know what you'd say. Could we pretend this never happened?' Because now my worry was about how this would impact on me professionally as well as personally. What if Josh Rowan told every journalist in London about it? It would destroy a lot of the respect that I – and Tim and Alastair – had worked so hard to build up. 'Please,' I said. 'It's way out of character for me. Probably some sort of mid-life thing. Peri-menopause, maybe – apparently it sends people a bit insane.'

'It's okay, Amy, pet,' he said. 'We're all only human.' Oh, that *accent*.

'Thanks.' I breathed out, a long, shuddery exhalation. Then: 'Would you have said yes?'

His eyes met mine. 'Yes.'

It was like receiving a jolt of electricity. I swallowed. 'Right.'

'It wasn't an accident that I bumped into you.' He nodded in the direction of the ballroom. 'I've been counting the days.'

Fuck! It was the sort of thing he said in my fantasies. But now that it was being said in real life, it was scaring me witless.

'I've been stalking you all evening.'

After some mute moments, I managed to say, 'I've literally never played away.'

He smiled. A proper smile, not his usual lopsided, withholding one. 'It's sort of obvious.'

'How about you? Have you . . . ?'

Without speaking, he nodded.

'A lot?'

'No . . . But sometimes.'

I felt sick – offended, jealous, ashamed. I wanted him to be faithful to Marcia. And I wanted him to want me. But he couldn't do both. 'Josh. I'm going outside now for a cigarette. Alone.'

'I could have lied,' he said.

'It's not that.' Well, it wasn't *just* that. It was me as much as him. I couldn't handle this version of myself. 'But, really, I need a cigarette.'

'Okay. But when you get home to your husband,' he said, 'make sure he knows what a hot wife he has. Right, I'd better get back inside. I might have won something.'

'Oh, Christ, sorry!'

'That was a joke. Unless there's a prize for most undermined editor in Britain.'

My smile wobbled off my face and he was gone.

Right, where were my smokes? My sparkly clutch bag was ridiculously tinchy, but my little nicotine sticks were proving elusive . . . As I rummaged, something made me look up. It was Tim, he'd emerged from the ballroom and was standing with his back to the door, watching me.

My heart banged. How long had he been there? Long enough, if the hard stare he gave Josh as he scooted by was any indication.

All thoughts of cigarettes vanished, and my heels clattered on the marble as I hurried across to Tim.

'What was that about?' he asked.

'Nothing.'

He looked sceptical.

'Really, honestly, nothing.' I was choosing to trust that Josh would keep a lid on this.

'That was Josh Rowan from the *Herald*, right?'

'Right. But there's nothing going on.'

He still looked suspicious but there was no way I was telling Tim: we didn't have that sort of relationship. Also he might be furious with me for potentially damaging Hatch's reputation. What an omnishambles . . .

38

Friday, 30 September, day eighteen

Once again it's Friday. Hugh has been gone over two weeks now and this last week has felt like an assault course: laundry, cooking, supervising homework, airport, London, meetings, airport, staggering in exhausted on Wednesday night to find Neeve and Kiara almost incoherent with horror because the Wi-Fi wasn't working and they thought I – me! – would know how to fix it. That was the point where I thought the week couldn't get any worse, but then Mum nabbed me for unexpected Pop-sitting on Thursday night.

Professionally, the week hasn't been a total bust: finally, after sending her on a series of soup runs designed to humble her, Room has decided to take on Tabitha Wilson as their new ambassador and tasked me with grooming her for a big, glitzy press launch in six weeks' time.

But infusing every single event and encounter with a type of sepia dread is Hugh's absence. And now Alastair wants to know what delights the weekend holds for me.

'Oh, you know, going to Tesco's, doing the finances, cleaning the house, being the prize attraction at the cinema club on Sunday – fun times all the way.'

'Anything nice at *all*? What about Derry?'

'Busy. Riding. She's got a new man.'

'*Has* she? It won't last, though, it never does. She and I are very similar . . .'

'No, you totally aren't. You're never without a girl.'

'I've none at the moment, if you don't mind. I'm holding out for someone special. My therapist says –'

I snigger. Then, 'Sorry, Alastair.'

'What's wrong with having a therapist? I'm committed to changing for the better!'

'I *am* sorry. I don't know why it made me laugh. It's not as funny as the time you had your colours done. I'm not myself, Al. Please forgive me.'

'Okay.' Never holds a grudge, Alastair, you can say that about him. 'So how about Posh Petra? Or Steevie? Could you do something nice with them?'

It's a while before I answer. 'You know, Alastair, things are weird with Steevie.' There, I've said it. My oldest friend, our connection has survived decades and I don't know what exactly it is, but we're not on the same page right now. 'When I'm with her I get the fear.'

'What? Why?'

'She's so angry with Hugh, she says these terrible things. But it's actually not about Hugh at all.'

'About the husband who left her?'

'Yeah. She wants to go for lunch tomorrow, but I *have* to, *really* have to, sit down with my finances. I'd rather look my out-of-control spending in the face than see her. That's bad, isn't it?'

'It is what it is. So what'll you do tomorrow night?'

'If Mum doesn't try and nab me for some impromptu Pop-sitting –'

'What's the story there? Is she going out a lot more than she used to, or does it just seem that way?'

'No, yeah, you're right, she is. Not that I blame her. Except I wish she'd ask one of the others instead of me. So anyway! Assuming I'm not Pop-sitting, I'll bunker down with a load of savoury snacks and watch whatever foreign yoke is on BBC4, then hopefully I'll sleep. I can't sleep, Alastair. I haven't slept properly in weeks.'

He looks at me thoughtfully. 'I know what you need.'

'Why does this fill me with dread?'

'It's a – a thing . . . You go and have a story read to you. Not for kids, adults, we're adults, but a man with a deep voice, his name is Grigori, reads a fable. In the Kingsley Hotel in town. There are beanbags and hot chocolate and dim lights. Lots of people go. Every Saturday night. It's . . . comforting. It'll help you sleep. It costs a tenner.'

'And who goes? What sort of people?'

'All ages. Some come alone, some with mates. The vibe is friendly, the way yoga classes are friendly.'

Yoga classes are *not* friendly. Yoga classes – in my admittedly limited experience – are peopled with snooty body-Fascists who live on green powder.

'Friendly, but not sleazy, is that what you mean? Would I be too old?'

'All ages,' he says firmly. 'Saturday nights, nine o'clock. Very good for the central nervous system.'

'What would I have to do?'

'Listen to the story. Drink hot chocolate.'

'And that's all. You're certain?'

'I'm certain.'

Okay.

Thamy races into the office. 'Look professional, she's on her way up!'

It's the day for Mrs EverDry's monthly progress report, and even though we've got her so much favourable coverage, an incontinence ambassador continues to elude us. She's going to give us hell.

But it's *impossible*. No one, no matter how down on their luck, is willing to publicly admit they've difficulty in holding on to their wees.

39

It's Derry's week to do the dinner.

A Peshwari naan is always ordered for my exclusive use – low-carbing be damned – but the traffic is bad this evening, I'm late and I'm afraid it'll have been eaten on me.

Loads of cars are crammed in front of the house – on Derry's Fridays, a massive crowd of O'Connells turns out, even Maura's husband, The Poor Bastard, whom we never otherwise clap eyes on.

Sometimes actual Urzula shows up, looking literally like the spectre at the feast. She never orders food for herself, but asks for teaspoons of other people's, then mocks us for eating so much.

I'm really afraid someone will have had my naan.

I can't find my key and Jackson lets me in.

'Has the food arrived yet?' I'm feeling almost panicky.

He puts a finger to his lips. 'Shush. Neeve's doing a make-up vlog with Sofie's granny. She's just starting.' He tiptoes up the stairs, to a cluster of people around a bedroom door. I see Derry, Sofie, Kiara, Maura, The Poor Bastard, Joe, Siena – even Pop's carer, Dominik, is here.

With silent purpose I shoulder my way to the front to see what's happening.

Mum is on a chair, under the white glare of Neeve's lights. She's facing the camera, her hair and make-up looking really 'done', and she's wearing a cobalt-blue suede skirt and a T-shirt with a fashionably torn neck. She looks … nothing like my mother. She's cool and hip and like a groovy granny.

I'm dumbfounded.

'We're starting now,' Neeve announces. 'If anyone makes any noise, I will kill them! Okay, Granny. Just look into the camera and answer the questions.'

'What if I get it wrong?'

'If you get it wrong we can do it again. But you won't get it wrong.' This sounds like an order. 'Okay, Lilian, tell us a little bit about yourself.'

'I'm Lilian O'Connell,' Mum says. 'I'm seventy-two years old, I'm a mother of five and I believe leopard-print is a neutral.' She flicks a nervous little look at Neeve to see if she'd said the leopard-print line correctly.

'You've great skin, Lilian. How do you take care of it?'

'I drink plenty of tea and once a week I exfoliate with a cotton pad soaked in nail-varnish remover.'

Neeve lets a beat pass. They've obviously rehearsed this. 'Nail-varnish remover?'

'That's right.'

'That's going to shock people, Lilian.'

'It does sting but it makes my skin look clear. I first used it by accident – I thought it was toner. The bottles looked the same. And the thing is, even if people say you shouldn't, if it feels right for you, then do it.'

'What are your desert-island products?'

'I couldn't leave the house without my foundation.' She throws a haunted look Neeve's way. 'I mean my base. I like good coverage – I don't understand "veils" and "sheers" and that.' She holds up a bottle of foundation. 'This one is good and thick. And I like this bronzer. I like things that make me look brown.' She freezes. 'Am I allowed to say that? That I like to look brown? Or should I check my privilege?'

Neeve snorts with laughter. 'You're okay.'

'And I like this eyeshadow set because none of the colours are mad.' She displays a quartet of browns and beiges.

'What are your thoughts on Botox and other injectables?' Neeve asks.

'I'd never say never.' Mum gives a cute little smile. 'Who knows? Maybe when I'm older.'

She's . . . well, I'd have to see it on screen to know for sure, but she's . . . *adorable.*

'Thank you for your wisdom, Lilian.'

'Can I say something else?' Mum asks.

I don't think this bit has been rehearsed but Neeve says, 'Go for it.'

'If you find your lipstick shade, and it might take most of your life but when you find it, buy at least three of them because they'll stop making it as soon as they hear you like it.'

'Great advice.'

'And the lady in the shop will try to make you buy a found—base that's the same colour as your face. But get a darker one if that's the one you like. It's your money, it's your face.'

'Thank you, Lilian. Okay, that's a wrap.'

Naturally enough, we all clap. We clap and whoop and whistle, because we're a rowdy bunch. There's a lot that's wrong with my family but, all credit to us, we know when to clap.

Downstairs we go, just in time to greet Declyn, his husband Hayden and Baby Maisey, who is instantly ferried off by a selection of her cousins.

In the kitchen, people mill about, waiting for the food to arrive. Mum is in the thick of everyone, still looking unnervingly like Hot Granny.

And here's the food!

Everyone crowds into the dining room, except Pop, who insists on having his dinner in the living room in front of *The One Show*, Sofie, who can't eat if anyone other than Jackson is watching, Finn, Pip and Kit, who live life in constant motion, and Neeve, who needs Snapchat to keep her company so must lie on the landing for the Wi-Fi.

Derry goes to the head of the table, unwraps the first bag and shouts, 'Murgh makhani?'

'Me!' says Joe and, immediately, it's passed from hand to hand till it reaches him.

It's like one of those heart-warming scenes when ordinary people form a human chain to put out a blazing fire.

'Lal maas?'

'Me,' Dominik says.

Derry included him to show our appreciation as a family/bribe him with Indian food never to leave us. He was touchingly surprised but hung back in the race for seats at the dining table, so has joined both The Poor Bastard and Joe, who also missed out. They will eat their dinner standing up, their plates on the windowsill.

'Beetroot chicken?'

This is what The Poor Bastard always orders – will he speak?

'His!' Maura yelps, pointing at her husband.

'Rice for everyone,' Derry says, passing down several cartons. 'And here's a garlic naan. No, it's a Peshwari. Hands off, it's Amy's.'

Mutterings of 'We *know* it's Amy's' reaches me.

Oh, sweet Jesus, here's Urzula. She looks like a biscuit-coloured skeleton with cold blue marbles for eyes. Urzula's brand of skinny is a world away from 'wellness'. She's just bones with skin shrink-wrapped around them. Even her hair is thin.

'Urzula,' Derry says levelly. Derry isn't scared of Urzula. 'You should have said you were coming. I haven't ordered you a dinner.'

'Not an issue. I could not *possibly* eat an entire carton.'

Around the table, heads bow in shame. All of us could eat an entire carton, no bother.

'But perhaps someone will spare me a spoonful of theirs.'

The only good thing is that she literally means a spoonful. Even so, no one offers.

'Where's Sofie?' she asks.

'Upstairs.'

'What is she eating?'

No one answers. We're not shopping poor Sofie who, anyway, only ordered a starter and will probably persuade Jackson to eat most of it.

'Help yourself to mine.' I need to stay on good terms with Urzula because I love Sofie. 'And would you like some naan?'

'Let me see it.' She picks apart a quarter of my naan before thrusting it away like it's infectious. 'Marzipan? Raisins? Amy, this is cake!'

She eats her spoonful of curry, then inspects the rest of us as we tuck in. 'You eat too quickly,' she says. 'Slow down! It takes twenty minutes for the brain to receive fullness messages from the stomach.'

Our heads bow lower and lower.

'You should drink a big glass of water between each mouthful,' she says.

Suddenly, from the living room, Pop yells, 'Fuck off with yourself! Fuck away off, you miserable yoke!'

40

Saturday, 1 October, day nineteen

What the hell do I wear to a story-telling thing? Something comfortable, probably. But I need the protection of nice clothes.

There's a skirt in my wardrobe I've never worn, a flared navy crêpe with – very best things ever – pockets in the sides. It's another of Bronagh's finds, and it's genuinely from the fifties, you can tell from the cut, which works well on a woman of my shortness.

I try the skirt with a black blouse patterned with cartoony cats and decide that I'll do. But the blouse fastens at the back and I can't reach to get my zip all the way up. I'm not even going to think about Hugh, so I step on to the landing and call, 'Zip!'

Neeve emerges from her bedroom. 'Where are you off to in your dead person's threads?'

'Out. To a story-telling thing. In town.'

'*You* are?' She does the zip.

'You know about it?'

'Yeah. The Google kids and those types like it. They're all overworked and stressed and, unlike Irish people, they haven't embraced the relaxing effect of heavy drinking.' Something terrible seems to occur to her. She clutches my arm. 'You're not going on your own?'

'No, with Alastair.'

'Work Alastair? Ah, he's cool.'

I remember now that when the girls had waitressed at the party to launch Hatch, Alastair had tipped them lavishly.

'Seeing as it's him you're going with,' Neeve says, 'you're allowed to enjoy yourself.'

In the lobby of the Kingsley Hotel, in faded jeans and a soft, loose, collarless shirt, Alastair looks younger and hipper, scruffier than his work persona. Yesterday he was clean-shaven but today he has enough chin-hair to almost qualify as a beard. How? Miracle-Gro?

Up the stairs we go and over to a door-girl, who's wearing the biggest denim jacket I've ever seen – it's easily the size of a shed.

While I'm still fumbling at my bag, Alastair has paid for us both and is hustling me into the room.

'Stop rushing me!' I locate a tenner. 'Here.'

'My shout.'

'I don't want it to be your shout. Take the money.'

'Calm down, Amy. Really.'

'Okay. I'll buy the hot chocolate.'

'The hot chocolate is included.'

It's a big, cosy room, the floor scattered with beanbags, hammocks and low couches. The lighting is dim and rosy, and there are snuggly throws strewn about. Lots of people are here already – nearly every man has a beard and a man-bun, and the women are the height of millennial fashion, which is to say they look like they'd got dressed this morning in the first things they found on someone else's bedroom floor: too-big jackets over dayglo crop-tops and high-waisted acid-wash jeans or shapeless jumpers almost as long as the shiny pleated mini-skirts they purport to cover.

I watch them with envy – I was there for grunge the first time round: the look didn't work for me then and it wouldn't work for me now.

Everyone seems to be moving about, stepping over bodies and administering enthusiastic hugs.

Alastair scans the room, says, 'Over there.' We pick our way through soft furnishings to an island made from floor cushions, a beanbag, a low table and a nightlight. A girl flaps towards us, wearing what seems to be an entire convent's worth of black pinafore, and dispenses hot chocolate.

Alastair sits cross-legged on one of the floor cushions and carefully I lower myself to the beanbag. My skirt is too short for this lark – yes, I'm wearing tights, but anyone on gusset-watch would be quids in. Then I realize I'll have to stand up again to go to the bar. 'What do you want to drink?'

'There's no bar.'

'What? No alcohol?' I want to go home. This isn't for me at all. I'm too old, too set in my ways, too sober . . .

'Try your hot chocolate.'

I take a sip. And now my tongue is burnt. 'So, come here, about Mrs EverDry, I was thinking –'

'We're not talking about work.'

'Well, then, what will we talk about?'

'Non-work stuff.'

'You mean personal stuff? I'll need a drink.'

'Okay. I'll go downstairs to the bar.' He gets to his feet with such lithe grace that a girl standing nearby stares hard at him. 'What do you want?'

'Vodka and tonic.'

Left on my own, sprawled on the beanbag, I feel like a bit of an eejit. I try to let a little smile play around my lips, so that I don't look as uncomfortable as I feel, but it's no good so I get out my phone and look at emails.

'Hi.' A man is staring down at me. He looks slightly messianic – long hair, beard, intense eyes. His age? Impossible to tell, these days, with young men and their beards, right? But somewhere between nineteen and thirty-seven.

'Can I join you?'

I freeze. What's the etiquette here? 'You can, I guess. But –' And, thank God, here comes Alastair, carrying two glasses.

Messiah Boy follows my stare. 'You're with someone? That's cool. Great top.'

'Which? Oh, mine? Thank you.'

'Are they cats?'

'Yes.'

His clothes are very weird – acid-washed skinnies, sheepskin slippers, sports socks and a shrunken fisherman-style sweater, pilled and bally and the funny thing is that it might have come from a charity shop or it could just as easily have cost seven hundred euro from Dries van Noten.

He retreats to a nearby hammock, where he swings back and forth and eyes me a little insolently.

'What's going on?' Alastair gives me my vodka. 'Did you get hit on?'

'I don't know.' I take a swig of my drink, which is pleasingly strong, and say, 'Maybe he was just being friendly. Is this a double?'

'I thought I'd save myself a second trip downstairs.'

I look around. The room has filled up a lot, and people are lying everywhere. 'This looks like the setting for an orgy.'

'It doesn't,' says Alastair.

'How do you know?'

He gives a little smile.

'Have you really been to an orgy?' I ask.

'Why? Would you like to come to one?'

'I would fecking not,' I say hotly.

'You sure?' He finds this funny. 'How can you know until you've tried it?'

'Because,' I take another swig of my drink, 'to be honest, it's not sex, *per se*, that floats my boat. I like romance, I like passion, I like the feels you get when a man says, "I can't stop thinking about you." Or "You're in my head the whole time." You know?'

'I'm listening.'

'See, I'd never be bothered with a lesbian thing. I don't want sex to be equal – *Jesus*, this vodka is making me chatty. I like to be dominated in bed, not like spanked dominated, just ordinary dominated. I like to be flung on a bed and for a man to say, "I've waited so long to do this," and I *love* the weight of a man pressing down on me.'

Alastair's gone very still. 'Vanilla.'

'Totally. I'm ashamed, Alastair, that I've no interest in multiples or anal or bondage. What I like is waiting. I like sexual tension. I like being desired. But I'm shy in bed. I'd never do . . .' I watch closely for his reaction '. . . reverse cowgirl.'

'Hmm, yeah.' He's thoughtful. 'I can't really see it.'

And now I'm offended.

A young woman has parked herself on the end of Alastair's couch. I lower my voice and lean in to him. 'Is she on her own?'

'Stop projecting.'

'I've been married for a long time,' I hiss. 'I'm transitioning as fast as I can.'

'And even if someone arrives here on their own,' he says, 'they may not leave on their own. And whatever happens, they'll hear a nice story and get hot chocolate. Here's Grigori.'

A huge man, tall and heavy-set, is crossing the room. He's got a curly beard and wears a linen tunic, a tapestry waistcoat and baggy linen trousers, tucked into leather boots.

'Oh! He looks just like a story-teller!' I'm delighted.

Grigori sits on a big carved wooden chair and produces a book. A thrill seems to move through the room, then silence falls. Grigori sounds like a Slavic Stephen Fry, which is entirely right for the story, a fable that concerns a woodcutter, a forest, orphans, Simnel cake, a reflecting pool, evil people, good people, mysterious people . . .

A blanket of calm floats on to me, easing the tightness in my chest. My breathing is slow and steady and strong, and I swear I can feel the actual insides of my stomach unclench. The beanbag takes my weight as I drift in the most delicious way. My eyes close, merciful sleep is coming for me – and I have a question. I pull Alastair's sleeve. 'Is Grigori an actor? Or is he real?'

'He's real.'

He's real. I'm glad. I tuck that comforting thought into me and surrender again. I'm floating on a boat on a gentle sea. Sleep steals towards me, doing all the work. It doesn't matter that I'm not in my own bed. I'll stay the night here on this beanbag . . . I'll pay whatever they want for the room. No amount of money is too much for this bliss . . .

*

'Wha'?!' I'm dreaming that small, furry creatures called coots have attached themselves to the sides of my face so I look like I've sideburns. I'm pulling and tearing, trying to get them off me . . .

'Amy . . . Amy . . .'

I don't want to be a woman with sideburns. 'I'm no hipster!' I call out – and, abruptly, I'm awake. Alastair's face is looming over me.

'Amy,' he says tenderly. 'Story's over. It's time to wake up.'

41

The weirdest thing has just happened. A text in from Richie Aldin: **Amy, can we meet? Quick conversation x**

I'm *flooded* with alarm. What the hell is this about? Money? That's all it can be. But what money? He'd stopped Neeve's maintenance when she was eighteen.

My Thursday has just taken a turn for the worst.

The whole week has been a route march: a blur of early mornings, trying to get Kiara – and Sofie when she stays over – up for school, helping find the countless things they've mislaid, feeding the lot of us in the evenings, keeping on top of laundry and all the rest of the household shite, including countless random glitches and breakages, stuff that was usually Hugh's remit.

On Monday night Mum nabbed me for Pop-sitting – more drinks with these mysterious friends of hers, whatever the hell she's up to.

My two days in London almost felt like respite, because the only person I was responsible for was me.

Also, I've landed two new clients. My successful rehabilitation of Bryan Sawyer seems to have raised me above the radar, and to know that more money will be coming in is one worry eased.

Nevertheless, Hugh is perpetually in my thoughts. I'm moving through my life where everything is the same as it always was but poisoned by profound dread. Keeping myself from ringing him is utterly exhausting.

The urge to start smoking again has abated, which would be good news except that I've swapped it for another addiction: my online shopping has hit code red. My current obsession is with finding the perfect dress for the awards thing in Brighton. It needs to be sexy, formal, age-appropriate, funky, long, short and flattering. As a result of this demanding brief, every dress that arrives is wrong so has to be returned and three or four more ordered. I suppose I'm giving welcome employment to the DPD men, the UPS men, the Parcelforce men and the rest. All part of the trickle-down economy, right?

Buzzing with anxiety, I text Richie: **What's up?**

Nothing bad. I can come to you x

I'd been planning to get my nails done after work, but I'm so panicky that I decide to cancel. Then I decide not to. Whatever he's got on me, it can wait one more hour. I spent too many years dancing to his tune and it's not about to start again. It's hard, though.

I text: **Meet me 7.30 the Bailey**

Seconds later he replies: **Too crowded. The Marker 7.45 x**

No. The Marker is too far away and it's in the wrong direction. Already weary from his bullshit, my next text says: **I'll be in the Bailey 7.30**

Immediately **K x** pings back.

Sitting through the manicure and having to act normal is a challenge. It would have been tricky anyway, the way everything is tricky right now, but Richie has really put the wind up me. The beautician is chatty but speedy so we finish early and I duck into Brown Thomas to kill time by looking at lovely things. It's madly busy. You can already sense Christmas, even though it's only 6 October. It's all too shovey and pushy, so at twenty past seven I give up and go to the pub.

It's crowded but not full and, proving Richie's objections wrong, I get a seat straight away. He's so territorial: everything always has to be on his terms.

Oh, here he is, also early. Decked out in an expensive-looking herringbone tweed coat and some soft scarf in a shade of khaki. He spots me and nods, then someone – a woman – intercepts him. Watching the conversation, I see that she's some sort of admirer. He speaks, he smiles – and she melts. Now he's making his excuses and she's looking downcast.

Finally he reaches me. 'Sorry about that.' He kisses my cheek, then straddles a nearby stool and peels off his scarf and coat. Underneath his coat he's wearing a heather-coloured V-neck jumper in some lightweight wool. The purplish shade makes his hair look more golden and his eyes greener.

A scornful phrase from my teenage years speaks in my head: *If he was chocolate, he'd eat himself.*

He picks up my hand. 'Nice *nails*. Pretty.'

'Thanks,' I mutter, too polite not to.

'Just get them done?'

'Yep. So,' I ask, 'what's up?'

'Drink?'

'Got one.' I indicate my vodka because this is definitely a vodka kind of conversation.

'I'll just get a . . .' He goes to the bar and obviously gets served immediately because he's back almost as soon as he leaves, with what looks like water, then rearranges his seat position so that he's directly opposite me.

'So?' I ask.

'Okay.' He spreads his fingers on his thighs, takes a deep breath and looks me in the eye. 'I want to tell you that I'm sorry.'

Surprise and suspicion silence me. Eventually I manage, 'For what?'

Another deep breath. Another sincere gaze. 'For leaving you. For you finding out the way you did. For not giving you enough money. For not seeing Neeve.'

I'm dumbfounded. I open and shut my mouth, then say, 'Why now?'

'I –'

'Have you cancer? Found God? In recovery and doing your steps?'

'No, none of them. Just . . . I owe you an apology.'

'But . . .' I'm really struggling. 'Like, twenty years later?'

'Twenty-two.'

Whatever.

'Amy, I'm sorry to say that I didn't see it for a long time, how selfish I was. It must have devastated you.'

'It didn't.'

'I wasn't suggesting . . .' He's Mr Sincerity. 'Sorry, Amy, I didn't mean to imply . . . Just you were young. And you had to bring up a baby on your own. It must have been hard.'

'But it all worked out.'

'I don't know why it took me so long to see how selfish I was. I don't know why I was so mean. When Neeve told me that Hugh had left you —'

'Hold on a minute there. Hugh hasn't left me. He's taking time out. And it's okay.' No way am I getting into the complexities with Richie Aldin.

'But Neeve said —'

'She was wrong. Mistaken. Whatever. Wrong. Okay?'

He nods. 'Okay. But when I — mistakenly — thought he'd left you, it made me think of how it must have been when *I* left.' He looks as if he's in anguish. 'Do you think . . . I mean, can you ever forgive me?'

In that moment I realize that I forgave him a long time ago. The rancour must have just vaporized while I wasn't looking. 'I forgive you for leaving me the way you did. But I can never forgive you for all the ways you hurt Neeve.'

'I know, I get it, and I'm going to make it up to her.'

Surprised, I say, 'You can't. I'm not being mean, Richie, these are just the facts. You can never give her back those years when she wanted a dad.'

'I can. I will.'

There he sits, so calm and so certain, his glinty green eyes limpid with good intentions. 'I don't understand,' I stammer. 'How can you think . . . What I mean is, the only way you can fix Neeve's childhood is with time travel.'

He laughs, but I'm not being funny.

'There are other ways,' he says.

'Like what?'

'I'm going to spend more time with her. I'll make her happy in the now.'

'Yes, but . . .' That's not going to alter what's happened. 'Hey, don't mess with Neeve.' I'm afraid now that he's going to burst in and build up her hopes, then disappear again as soon as he loses interest.

'I'm not going to mess with her.' He sounds astonished. 'I'm going to make everything right, and I really want you and me to be friends.'

'Why would we be friends?' I pause. 'I don't mean that the way it sounds. But, seriously, why would we be friends?'

'Because we were everything to each other once. Weren't we?'

To my surprise, a memory flashes. Being with Richie was the first time I'd had a sense of home. After a perpetually uncertain childhood, it was thrilling to step away from the substandard family Fate had foisted on me and simply create a new one. I'd thought I'd found the secret to life. But I was wrong. My original family weren't as substandard as I'd once thought when my new one imploded. 'None of that feeling is left,' I say.

'So let's start over. As friends.'

'But, Richie –' I'm struggling to say what I mean – 'I've a policy of liking my friends and I don't think I can make an exception for you.'

He laughs again, and again it's not meant to be funny.

'I'm going to make things right.' He's full of fierce conviction. There was a time when this would have made me die with joy. 'I'm going to make everything up to you.'

'No. Please don't. Please, Richie, don't.'

As soon as I arrive home, Neeve calls, 'Mum, you owe me a hundred and twelve euro.'

'For what?'

'You bought a load of stuff from Korea?'

'Oh, ah, one or two things. Essentials.'

'There were Customs charges.'

There were? 'They never said that on the site!' I feel foolish and stung. I'd thought it was a nice site. Run by nice people.

'He's a laugh, George, the DPD man,' Neeve says.

'You know his name!' Sofie says.

'He's here so often with Mum's stuff, we're practically engaged. Anyway, let's have a look at what she bought.'

There are two boxes on the coffee table. Kiara, Sofie and Neeve crowd around as I open them. I can hardly remember what was in this consignment – it had been late at night and I might have been a bit drunk and I'm ordering so much stuff that it's all merging into one and – Oh, it's coming back to me now. Dresses, wasn't it? I unfold one, a maxi in black lace, with an elasticated neckline. Or is it an elasticated hem? It's hard to know which end of the dress is which because, well, it's enormous.

'What *size* did you get?' Neeve asks.

'Ten.' My voice is faint.

'It looks like a size *thirty*.'

'Check the label.'

'Yep, it says ten. But it's totally not.'

'Two of us could fit in it,' Kiara says.

'We could!' Neeve is pulling it on, then Kiara is shimmying underneath it, before her head pops out next to Neeve's. The elasticated neckline stretches around both sets of shoulders and they're in convulsions. 'Come on, Sofie, come on, Mum, there's room for all of us in here!'

42

Sixteen months ago

'Hugh, have you ever cheated on me?'

'Wait! What?' He twisted to look at me. 'You even have to ask?'

'Sorry.' I shook my head. 'I'm an eejit. Don't mind me.'

It was the evening after the awards dinner in London where I'd propositioned Josh Rowan. From the moment I'd woken up that morning I was awash with shame.

How could I have done that to Hugh? Hugh, whom I loved with such fierce tenderness. Hugh, who was so good to me and so good to everyone. It wasn't just the previous night I was ashamed about but the entire almost-month I'd been narky, barely present and spending as much time as possible in my head, thinking dreamy thoughts about another man. It was all so *wrong*.

I loathed myself. I was despicable. And, like, *mad*. Because I hadn't even been *that* drunk when the invitation to Josh Rowan had tumbled from my mouth.

If I'd been Jekyll-and-Hyde, borderline-psychotic scuttered, it might be understandable that I'd propositioned him. You hear of people doing the maddest things when they're that stotious – stealing JCB diggers and driving them along Oxford Street, offering lifts. But no way had I been that drunk.

What had it been about? I'd been playing a game, that's what. Wondering if someone would fancy me. And that was contemptible because Josh Rowan was a person. He had feelings. And he had a wife.

By the time I'd got back to Dublin my shame had evolved into ecstatic gratitude that nothing had happened.

When Hugh had opened our front door, I'd walked straight into his arms and pressed myself against his comforting bigness, hugging him so hard and for so long that eventually he had to peel me off him. 'What's up?' He was half laughing.

I stared up into his beloved face, his honest blue eyes, and gently touched the prickles of his beard with my fingers. 'Hugh Durrant, you're the best man on earth, do you know that?'

'You're scaring me now.'

'I missed you. Am I not allowed to miss you?'

'Yeah, but . . .'

In the kitchen, an atavistic urge to touch all my stuff came over me, to feel the solidity of my life.

I'd gone away and I'd come back and nothing was different – *nothing*. There was no tear in the fabric of my marriage and no shameful betrayal burning holes in my soul. I had the same elation you'd have walking away without a scratch from a crash that destroyed your car.

'Something to eat?' Hugh asked.

'No . . . Okay, maybe.' For the first time all day food was a possibility. 'What have you?'

'Your cheese. I picked it up from the sorting office. The poor bastards said they'd been breathing through their mouths for the past week.'

God, what a man! He'd gone out of his way to collect my cheese, the cheese that arrived every month, thanks to him buying me membership of a cheese club. 'Okay, then, yes, please.'

'Wine?'

I almost shuddered. 'No wine.'

'Last night was *that* bad?'

Then I did actually shudder. 'Awful.'

While Hugh moved around the kitchen, gathering a plate, a knife, some crackers, bursts of panic started attacking me.

Me and Josh Rowan naked.

It didn't happen.

Josh rearing over me, unrolling a condom along the length of his erection.

It didn't happen.

Josh sliding himself into me.

219

It didn't happen.

But what if things had gone differently? If I was sitting here now, in my kitchen, having had sex with another man?

Hugh would know, wouldn't he? We were so in sync that he'd intuit something bad had happened, and the thought of having a secret from him, a secret that would destroy him, made me feel sick all over again.

But it didn't happen. I didn't do it. Thank you, God.

Mind you, who knew that being a cheater was almost as bad as being cheated on?

Then a little thought wormed in: maybe at some stage *Hugh* had cheated?

So I asked him and his response – 'You even have to ask?' – let me know how way off course I was.

'But wouldn't it be so hard . . . ?' I was thinking aloud.

'What would?'

'The guilt. You know, having to keep the secret from the one person you tell everything to.'

Hugh put down the knife he'd been using and he went very still. All that moved were his eyes, questions in them, as his gaze roamed over my face. 'Is there something you want to tell me?'

'No.' Once again I was soaring with relief. So gloriously grateful that nothing had happened with Josh Rowan. I felt clean and ecstatic. 'No, sweetie. No. Nothing. Hey, listen,' I said. 'Leave the cheese. Come upstairs with me.'

He gave me a hard look to see if he understood my meaning.

'I'm lighting the candles.' An in-joke: it was how I signalled to Hugh that I was in the mood.

He looked unimpressed but he followed me upstairs, where I performed wildly enthusiastic non-cheater's sex and didn't spend a single second fantasizing about Josh. Not that I'd ever done that – at least, not during sex with Hugh. Once or twice, on my own, I had – those nights in London, sleeping by myself.

But never again.

43

Saturday morning, I'm awake in the darkness, and even though I'd drunk no alcohol last night, my head is pounding. Probably a sugar hangover.

Sugar isn't my usual thing. I'm more of a savoury person. I get frenzied around sausage rolls – but, anyway, last night I started in on the Haribo Starmix, then moved on to chocolate and, by close of business, I was tearing the cupboards apart, looking for biscuits.

And there had been no one there to stop me because Neeve, Sofie and Kiara were out – babysitting Posh Petra's pair of horrors.

To my shock, I hear another person breathing – someone's in bed with me! Who? My hand shoots out and lands on an arm, a slender one, too slender to belong to Hugh – so he hadn't arrived home in the dead of night and sneaked into bed to surprise me. I know it's unlikely but, God, that painful dart of dashed hope . . .

'Oh, my good Christ,' Neeve intones into the darkness. 'Those fucking twins.'

Despite everything, I giggle.

'You might have warned us,' she says.

'I did warn you.'

'Sofie is traumatized.'

'They didn't do the –'

'The baked-beans thing on her head? They did.'

'Oh, no.'

I'd thought that Neeve's toughness and Kiara's sweetness would be a match for the twins of Satan. I wasn't sure about exposing Sofie to them, but because she's here so much, it's natural to include her in all family activities.

'You should have seen Posh Petra when she got home,' Neeve says.

'How?'

'*Scuttered*. So drunk she couldn't walk and had to be carried into the house between Posh Peter and the taxi-driver. Like a wounded soldier! And, hey, no judgement, if those kids were mine, I'd be doing time for a double homicide. Are you awake now? Okay, I'm going to my own room. I need more sleep.'

She leaves. I'm not sure what she was doing here in the first place, but we often play musical beds, and I check the time: 4.37 a.m. On a Saturday. I'd get up but what would I do?

I remember the days when I'd have joyfully gone back to sleep. Oh, how I loved my bed. I used to tumble so gratefully into its welcoming arms, but since Hugh went, it's the place I miss him the most. Late at night and first thing in the morning are the worst. I guess they're the times when there aren't enough other thoughts rushing around to mask the truth. And weekends are the worst mornings of all. All the other days, I'm getting the girls to school or else I'm haring to the airport or across London.

But on Saturday and Sunday mornings, I'm allowed a lie-in and, right now, time on my hands is just something to kill and I'm finding the social stuff almost impossible. I keep trying, showing up with fake versions of myself, then having to retreat, exhausted, into solitude and online shopping.

I despise myself for not 'doing' more with this unexpected hiatus. But I can only do what I can do and, in my defence, I'm showing up for the important stuff, like work.

I get my iPad and, once again, I check Hugh's Facebook page – no posts, no activity, nothing. Everything's frozen. It's what I'd asked for, but it's still incredibly strange, almost as if he's dead.

I'd nearly prefer to see a picture of him sitting on a tropical beach, drinking a beer, surrounded by fresh young friends, just to know that he's okay. Missing him is getting worse, not easier. It's like torture. For what feels like the millionth time, I get my phone and fantasize about calling him. I stare and stare at his name. I could just touch the screen and listen to the ringing noise, then the click as he picked up, and the *thought* – oh, the *thought*! – of hearing his voice, of hearing him say, 'Amy?'

The astonishing wonder, the aching longing, of how close he is. Just one press of my finger would make it happen. 'Come home,' I'd say, and he'd say, 'Okay.' Then everything would be fixed.

44

Okay, Monday mornings are never a reason to have a parade but, today, no sooner have I arrived at my desk than an email arrives from Richie Aldin. What now? A quick read establishes the facts. The cheeky bastard! He's invited me to a charity ball!

I make an outraged little sound and Alastair looks up. 'What?'

'Richie Aldin has invited me to a do next month.'

Alastair looks confused. 'Who? Oh! The Richie Aldin you were married to when you were eleven? What's brought this on?'

I cast a furtive glance over both shoulders. 'Where's Tim?'

Alastair assumes a matching conspiratorial air and mutters, 'Out.'

Good. I don't like talking about personal stuff in front of Tim. 'Richie wants me and him to be friends. Because of Hugh leaving, he says he realizes how I must have felt when he left me.'

'But Hugh hasn't *left*-left.'

Unless he has. 'You know, Alastair,' I exclaim, 'I think there's something wrong with Richie. For whatever reason, guilt has finally caught up with him and he doesn't like it, so he thinks he can magic it away by bulldozing me into friendship. But he can't just *decide* that we're going to be friends, can he?'

'Not if you don't want it.'

'He's so used to life going his way that he thinks the force of his will is enough to make anything happen. But I don't have to oblige, do I? It's like he's telling me, "I hurt you and now I feel guilty, so I'm going to make you be friends with me. I know you don't want to, but my wishes will prevail."'

But now Alastair is wondering why I'd married such a man and, unexpectedly, I say, 'I was *crazy* about him. I don't think I've ever loved anyone the way I loved him. Not even Hugh.'

'First love.' Alastair is unimpressed.

I get a sudden flashback to how sexually combustible I was with Richie – aged seventeen and insatiable, I was constantly borderline orgasmic.

'What?' Alastair asks.

'Before we got married –'

'What age were you?'

'Nineteen. Madness.'

'And your parents let you?'

'Mum was in hospital again and Dad's eye was off the ball. I took advantage of that. They went bananas when they found out. But before that Richie and I were both living with our parents and the opportunities for sex were limited, so one time I literally pulled him into a cupboard so we could, you know, do it. And another time I made us steal a little boat from Greystones harbour and row it out a few hundred yards just so we could fuck in it.'

Alastair is eyeing me in a speculative fashion.

'I've never had sex with anyone like the sex I had with him.'

'Nobody ends up with their best-sex person. It always happens with the wrong person because there's an element of hate-sex in it.'

'I didn't hate him,' I say. 'I've never been so crazy about anyone.'

We'd fallen in love during our last year in school, and while everyone else's future was unknown, we mapped out ours with precision: he would be a First Division footballer and I'd be a dress designer, and we'd be together for ever.

I was only nineteen when I ran away to Leeds and married him in a registry office, but I didn't feel young: I felt in the right place, in the right life.

'So what are you going to do?' Alastair asks. 'About his charity ball?'

'Ignore the email.'

'He might take it as a yes.'

Alastair was right: he might. So I bang out, 'No, thanks,' hit the Send key a clatter, and hope my resentment comes across.

*

'Can you babysit Pop tonight?'

'Mum, I've to oversee the girls' homework, and tomorrow morning I've to be up at five to go to London.'

'I'll be home by eleven.'

She won't. The last time it was closer to midnight and then I had a half-hour's drive home.

'Why can't Dominik do it?'

'Dominik –' her tone is almost bitter – 'has a regular "gig" – that's the word he says, like he's Bruno Mars – on a Monday night, minding some cracked oul' hag in Ballybrack so her son can go to Zumba. And if you'd believe that, you'd believe anything.'

'Mum, it sounds plausible.'

'A man? Doing Zumba? Oh, please! Anyway, everyone knows Zumba is over.'

I'm worried about her. The stress is obviously too much. 'Mum, where do you go to on your nights out?'

'I go *out*, Amy, that's where I go when I go out. Out!'

'Who with?'

'Friends.'

'*What* friends?'

After a long pause, she says, choosing her words carefully, 'On a Thursday morning, me and Pop, we go to a thing with other old people who are gone in the head. We sit in a circle and sing songs from our youth. It's desperate. The living end, as you'd say. Well, me and some of the other carers, the ones who *aren't* gone in the head, we've palled up. We go for gin-and-tonics and talk about wanting to kill our person. It's marvellous, Amy. It gives me life.'

What can I say? 'I'll be over at seven.'

45

Friday, 14 October, day thirty-two

We can talk of nothing else but the latest twist in the divorce of Ruthie Billingham and Matthew Carlisle. She's a British National Treasure actress while he's a narky-arse serious journalist who grills lying politicians. ('The thinking woman's Jamie Dornan.')

Until a couple of months ago they'd lived a shiny, happy life with their two adorable-looking children when, out of a clear blue sky, they announced they were getting divorced. No reason was given but murky rumours circulated that Matthew had been riding rings around himself. A few weeks back Ruthie seemed to confirm the speculation by saying in a radio interview, 'One day my perfect life just blew up in my face.'

But on Tuesday this week, Ruthie popped up on the sidebar of shame having a furtive snog with a new man – Ozzie Brown, from *Game of Thrones*. (If you ask me, he seems like a lightweight compared to her narky-arse husband but maybe lightweight is all she's able for right now.)

The grainy photo of the snog prompted outraged opinion pieces, the gist being that it was too soon for Ruthie to be jumping into bed with someone else – people tend to treat her like their little sister. Ruthie made it's-very-early-days noises, but the mood music remained judgy. Now she's trying the would-you-begrudge-me-a-chance-at-happiness card and still the snarky stuff continues. (Headlines such as 'Ruthie, Think of Your Kids'.)

But today – Friday – thrillingly terrible allegations have surfaced that Matthew has been having an affair with the family nanny, a South African beauty called Sharmaine King, who looks like a younger version of Ruthie. There's no actual proof – it's all 'sources close to Ruthie' stuff. And, even though both Matthew and Sharmaine muttered panicked denials as they battled their way through the throngs of journalists outside their respective homes, the world is up in arms.

Apparently Sharmaine has been sacked and both she and Matthew are in (separate) hiding and getting death threats on Twitter.

Matthew is well able to look after himself but Sharmaine King will be needing some image management down the line, and past experience is telling me that Tim will suggest that Hatch 'reach out' to her.

I very much do not want to 'reach out' to her. I want nothing to do with this story. Cheating husbands do not gladden my heart.

And, on that subject, Richie Aldin emailed me again yesterday, trying to persuade me to go to his wretched ball. What is *wrong* with him?

46

Fifteen months ago

'So where would it happen?' I asked Derry.

'Druzie's?' She sounded doubtful.

The idea of bringing Josh Rowan to Druzie's spare room for illicit sex felt all kinds of wrong. 'No.'

'His house?'

Marcia's home? Be in her space? Possibly see her wood-burning stove? 'No way.'

'Then it has to be a hotel.'

'That feels tacky. Sordid.'

Derry stayed silent for a moment and let my words settle. *Tacky. Sordid.* 'That's the reality of getting into a thing with someone else's husband when you're married yourself.' Quickly, she added. 'I'm not being judgy. Just . . . '

My resolution to stay the hell away from Josh Rowan hadn't lasted. In fact, no later than two days after the awards ceremony I'd clumsily introduced his name into a working breakfast, trying to solicit information.

Since then, at every meeting with a member of the British press, the conversation was soon steered – sometimes awkwardly enough to induce whiplash – to Josh.

'. . . so, he's a good boss, is he?'

And *'You've met the wife. What's she like?'*

And *'Up to? Me? No, nothing. Just, might have a client considering working for him and I like to know who I'm getting into bed with. Not that I'd be getting into bed with him. Only a figure of speech, right?'*

A few suspicions were aroused but I'd gleaned plenty. Marcia, apparently, 'gave as good as she got'. Which chimed with my online stalking – she seemed ballsy and confident. From admittedly scanty information, I constructed a picture of their marriage: they were one of those couples who clashed a lot, who had shouty disagreements and ping-ponged between conflict and passion.

More distressing was when, under my clumsy questioning, a female journalist confided that she knew Josh had had a thing with a twenty-eight-year-old from a rival newspaper. It wasn't just the confirmation that he was a cheater – which had upset me plenty when *he*'d told me – but how could I compete with a woman in her twenties?

However, he'd ended it because – and my confidante said, 'This is a direct quote – "You're a great girl but you're too optimistic for me." '

A bark of astonished laughter issued from me. 'What does that even mean?'

'You've met him, Amy. He's not exactly Mr Sunshine.'

In fairness, he *did* look like he was nursing a secret sorrow. But that was just fanciful talk, the sort of thing a woman who was spending too long in her own head, running romantic scenarios, would think. I mean, most of the human race probably look like they've stuff on their mind. We can't all be the Dalai Lama.

Then Josh invited me to lunch.

I liked the idea of lunch. It was safe. Un-date-like. Nothing to feel guilty about. And yet it was a chance to show up as the very best version of myself and see if I had any power left – power as a woman. I got to flex that muscle, perhaps for the last time.

We met in a small, cosy place in Charlotte Street, where Josh asked question after question about *me*, and I spilt out all kinds of random opinions, like how I disliked the modern world's insistence that we have dinner a certain way.

'First we have to sit upright at a table and that usually feels like a punishment. Then the food arrives and I'm obliged to stare at the plate for at least eleven seconds. Then my sense of smell gets involved. And when it's eventually okay to eat, only tiny forkfuls are permitted, which must be chewed super-slowly . . .'

He was smiling slightly at this – just the right side of his mouth quirked upwards.

'I like to eat my dinner curled up on the couch, looking at the new arrivals on net-a-porter and shovelling food into me like they've just declared a famine. That's what makes me happy. And yet I'm perpetually dogged by the sense that I'm failing life.'

'Aye.' He'd managed to speak volumes with one word and his smile had vanished.

But he thawed again when I told him about the one-day mindfulness course that Alastair had persuaded me to go on. 'We had to spend half an hour eating a single raisin. Then an hour appreciating a flower. The thing that these live-in-the-moment merchants don't seem to get is that I can appreciate things speedily. I can see a flower and think, Ooh, that's pretty. Right, moving on. I don't have to stop in my tracks and, like, *lick* every individual petal.'

That drew a proper smile from him, a full, symmetrical, white-teeth dazzler, and it felt like winning a prize. 'What's your favourite movie?' he asked.

I put my head in my hands and groaned. 'Stop. Don't. We're not kids. Next you'll be making me a mix-tape.' I peeped through my fingers. He looked hurt.

'I'm just trying to get to know you.'

Quickly I'd said, 'I love Wes Anderson's films.' Slightly defensively I added, 'I know they're more style than substance, but I love their atmosphere.'

'At least you didn't say something starring Jennifer Aniston.'

'I like Jennifer Aniston too.'

When he gave me a you're-joking look, I said, 'I *do*.'

'Oh-*kay*.'

'So what about you? What's your favourite movie? No! Let me guess.' I ran through the usual suspects – *The Godfather, Raging Bull, Citizen Kane* . . . Suddenly I was utterly certain. '*The Lives of Others*.'

His face went quite blank. A beat passed, then another. 'How did you know?'

It wasn't that hard. Most of the men I knew would have that

on their list. (Mind you, Hugh's favourite was *It's a Wonderful Life*.) 'Just,' I said. 'You know . . .'

'Wow.' He shook his head. 'It's a great movie, isn't it?'

'Um, I haven't seen it.'

'Jesus.' He's appalled. 'That's a *crime*.'

'Movies are your passion?'

'My *passion*?' He lingers on the word while looking me in the eye. 'One of them. Script-writing, yeah, I'd have loved . . .' He changes the subject. 'What about art? Your favourite artist?'

'Everyone probably says Picasso or Van Gogh, and I *do* like them . . .' I hesitate before saying any more.

'What?'

'I didn't go to third-level education. I'm a bit touchy about it – people act as if you were brought up by feral dogs – and I'm worried you'll judge me.'

'I didn't judge you for the Aniston thing.'

'Ah, you did, a bit.' I smile at him. 'But you definitely won't have heard of my favourite artist. A Serbian woman called Dušanka Petrović.'

Regretfully he shook his head.

'She paints in the naive style. I've only seen her work on Pinterest but I love it.'

'Does she do exhibitions?'

'The only ones I've found are in a Serbian town called Jagodina. I've emailed to see about buying prints but they probably don't understand English, and I've tried ringing but no one answers the phone.'

'Maybe it's closed.'

'Things happen on their Facebook page. I can't understand the language but the dates are current.'

'But your artist must have a website?'

'Swear to God, she doesn't. She mightn't even be still alive. But one day I'm going on a road trip to the Jagodina place.'

A flash of resentment sparked in me. All my holidays were picked to please the girls and Hugh – mostly the girls, to be fair – and everything got prioritized over what I wanted.

There was never enough money for Hugh and me to go on weekend jaunts to European cities. Very occasionally one of us would be sent to an appealing work spot and the other would tag along for a day and a half at the end.

But the one time we found ourselves with some spare money, due to an unexpected tax rebate, and I'd asked Hugh straight out if we could visit the museum in Jagodina, he'd said, 'I'm sorry, babe, I just can't get excited about Serbia. The thought of spending money on going there when we could spend it instead on Marrakech or Porto . . .'

'You okay?' Josh was watching my face.

'Yes.' No way would I ever complain to him about Hugh.

Josh changed the subject by enquiring about my clothes, so I told him about Bronagh, and as I spoke, he watched me avidly, the admiration in his eyes contrasting with the granite set of his face.

All of that attention was seductive and, call me pathetic, it was pretty cool to see myself as an interesting woman dressed in one-off vintage and whose favourite artist wasn't a predictable pick but some low-key Serbian. The reality, of course, was that I was hard-up and badly educated, but everything is about presentation.

At the end of the lunch I said, 'So we've managed to get through an encounter without me propositioning you. Progress.'

Another proper smile. Then, 'Proposition me any time you like.'

'Ha-ha-ha-ha.' I blushed – and he noticed.

'Amy . . .' He touched his knuckles to my hot face.

'Gotta go.' I scarpered.

Since then we'd had lunch three more times, always on a Tuesday, always in the same place, always with me doing most of the talking and him watching me as if I was the most interesting woman alive. His questions were about things that nobody else usually asked me.

I tried turning the tables and grilling him, but he offered up a lot less than I did. All the same, he admitted a few things: that he loved the sea, that his most favourite place in the world was the Northumbrian coast; that he suffered from early-waking insomnia; that he rarely cried but when he did it was usually triggered by a news story about wounded children – 'That little boy in the ambulance in Aleppo did my head in. When you've kids of your own, you personalize everything.'

Things went a bit awkward with that remark, reminding us both of our other lives, where we had children and spouses.

Derry was the only person I told about the lunches and she wasn't impressed. 'How would you feel if Hugh was meeting a woman the way you're meeting Josh Rowan?' she asked.

I squirmed. I'd be deeply wounded, *deeply*, and worried sick. 'Nothing has happened,' I said. 'Nothing is *going* to happen. It's just harmless flirting.'

Except there was nothing harmless about it. I wanted to stick my fingers in my ears and la-la-la-la-la-la away the truth that emotional infidelity was a thing. Maybe not as bad as actual *carnal-knowledge* infidelity, but still bad.

'I'll tell you what you're doing,' Derry said. 'You're easing yourself into a thing with him by Normalizing the Abnormal.'

I knew that phrase, which had originated in addiction circles; it meant that a person didn't go to bed one night perfectly healthy and wake up the following morning a full-blown addict. Instead it was something that happened in stealthy increments. A person took a single daring step away from the correct course, and only when that no longer felt aberrant did they take another. Once again, they waited for the shame and fear to settle, and when it did, they were emboldened to take one more step, all the while moving further and further off the righteous path.

'Nothing is going to happen,' I repeated. 'Hey! Would you like to see pictures of him?' I was already reaching for my iPad.

'No. Amy. Get a hold of yourself. Listen to me, this isn't Josh Rowan's first rodeo. Soon you're going to have to move this forward. I don't know the man, but I can tell you one thing. He's not in this for the hand-holding.'

'We haven't held hands. We don't hold hands. We don't even air-kiss hello.'

'Men like to fuck things.'

'Ah, Derry!'

'You and him aren't any different from anyone else considering an extra-marital fuck-fest.' She was being deliberately brutal. 'Seriously, Amy, don't try dressing this up with talk of special connections or irresistible attractions.'

That plunged me into despondency because, yes, it's what I *had* been doing.

'Can I ask why?' she said. 'Is it Hugh? Is he being . . . I don't know, not there for you?'

'It's not Hugh.' I was adamant. 'Whatever this is, it's all on me. Could I be bored of monogamy?'

'It'd be entirely out of character if you were. But *all* of this is out of character. Could it be your age? Maybe your body knows the decline has started and is urging you to have one last hurrah.'

'I don't know . . . The best I can tell you, Derry, is that I just want something for me. I want one part of my life that no one else can have.'

I felt as if I couldn't call my soul my own. The girls blithely took my possessions without asking – even my shoes were lent to a friend of Neeve's – and my time was colonized with careless disregard: the girls issued orders to be dropped here and picked up there without anyone ever asking if it suited me.

With Hugh, our chronic sex-deficit dogged me so badly that my favourite way of unwinding – which was to lie in bed with my iPad – just made me feel guilty. Well, guilty, then resentful, when he arrived and made vaguely lecherous noises about joining me. I'd be thinking, *For the love of God, I'm so burdened, can't you just let me lie here and monkey-brain online from article to article and be unfettered for a short while?*

Derry looked thoughtful. 'You work really hard.'

'I'm always tired. And I'm always worried. I've a near-constant pain in my stomach – it's there so much I almost don't notice it. There's never enough money. There's never enough time. And nothing I do is ever enough. My house is always manky. I never reach my ten thousand steps on my Fitbit. If I pull off a success in work, it counts for nothing because we still don't have enough business. I worry about Neeve, I worry about Sofie, and I despise myself for whining when I've enough to eat and we're not at war, but . . .'

'Mmm.'

'And anything I do as a treat – drink, smoke, have a popcorn binge at the cinema – just makes me feel guilty. Listen, will you tell me how it was for you?'

Derry had been in an eight-year relationship with a man called Mark when she started a covert thing with someone else. The new man – Steven – was married.

'It was shit,' she said. 'Lying to Mark, well, the guilt was exhausting, and being Steven's sordid secret felt super-shame-y. And I felt even more shame-y about poor Hannah.' Hannah had been Steven's wife. 'I never wanted to be that woman, the home-wrecker, the husband-stealer, and you're a lot more sappy than me, so you'd find it much tougher.'

'But there must have been good bits because you wouldn't have done it otherwise?'

'Yeah, but, it wasn't real. Like, I'd wait and wait and he'd finally text and then I'd be high with happiness. It was like a drug. You know, it *is* an actual chemical – dopamine.'

I knew about dopamine. Again, *Psychologies*. The simple explanation is it's a chemical the brain produces in response to certain stimuli and it makes you feel nice. And, yes, whenever Josh emailed me a dancing dog or a painting of a Slavic village scene, my mood soared.

'Whenever Steven texted, I'd get a hit of dopamine,' Derry said. 'Or the anticipation of our next meeting could keep me buzzing for days.'

Yes. Looking forward to those Tuesday lunches was thrilling, nervy stuff.

She sighed. 'I think I was simply addicted to relief. And look at how it played out for me.'

She'd left Mark; Steven had left Hannah; Derry and Steven went public. They'd lasted less than a year.

'Is that what you want?' Derry asked. 'To tell Hugh? To leave him? To set up home with Josh Rowan?'

Jesus. The thought seized me with hair-standing terror. I didn't want that at all. No. Josh Rowan was just a fantasy thing. 'All I want is to feel that a hot man is mad about me. What's so wrong with that?'

'Be careful, Amy,' Derry said. 'You've a lot to lose.'

'Derry, how do relationships survive when one person has a fling? Even if they don't get found out. Is something lost? It has to be, surely?'

'Of course. Innocence. Trust.'

'But is it naive to expect unsullied records? Should people just accept that, in any long-term thing, ruptures will happen and you just have to live with them? Like scars on a body, or flaws in a hand-woven rug. Like, one in three women in middle age have an affair.'

'I think you should stop seeing him.'

'I can't stay away from him.'

'Dopamine.' She was dismissive.

'We only have lunch.'

'So stop it.'

'I don't want to.'

'Dopamine.'

I stammered, 'All I want is some harmless fun.'

'Harmless fun?' Derry shook her head wearily. 'Buy yourself a trampoline.'

47

'Will there be drink at this party?' I ask, and Kiara, Neeve, Sofie and Jackson promptly dissolve into howls of laughter.

'Will there be drink at this party?' Neeve repeats, in a trembly old-lady parody of my voice.

'Oh, Mum!' Kiara is in convulsions.

Primly, I carry on scrubbing the hob. What's so funny?

'Of *course* there'll be drink at it!' Kiara sings.

It's every parent's wish that their children be independent. But I'm not sure I like them acting as if I'm some dithery dinosaur, who needs to be shepherded through the modern world.

While we clean the house, we've been discussing a Hallowe'en 'social' that Kiara is going to. It's two weeks away but already she's planning her outfit. It was just after she said, 'Derry probably has a dress I can borrow,' that I uttered my hilarious line about drink.

'You know there's always drink at "these things",' Kiara says. 'You've gone so *strict*.'

'When you're not showering us with cash,' Sofie adds.

That's as may be but I'll tell you something, it's *hard* suddenly being a lone parent. It's almost like having to relearn everything from scratch. It isn't enough simply to carry on as I always have, because Hugh and I shared the role. Between the two of us, we applied the rules and rewards in a smooth two-hander, and now that his presence has been wrenched abruptly away, the responses that once felt intuitive no longer do.

'There'll be boys too.' Kiara is teasing me but now I'm worried. Is she sexually active? *How* sexually active? Should she go on the pill? Sofie is on the pill, she has been for a year, and that conversation – instigated by me, about how sex is an expression of tenderness and love – was so hard I took to my bed afterwards. A similar conversation with Kiara should be easier because she's so much more open.

But is it too soon? She's never had a boyfriend, not one that Hugh and I know about anyway, plenty of friends who are boys, but maybe this is the time for that talk and what does Hugh think?

'That's my fifteen minutes done!' Neeve steps away from the ironing board.

'You only did twelve.' Jackson looks at the stop-watch.

I stop scrubbing the hob – these rings of burnt-in food are more resistant than hardened lava – and look at the clock. 'It was only twelve.'

'Yeah!' Kiara says.

'Twelve,' Sofie says. 'But you go. I don't mind ironing.'

'Freak,' Neeve says, with affection.

Everyone has preferred household tasks – I'll happily do the oven, Jackson does the bathrooms when he's here, and Neeve enjoys mopping the floor – but as ironing is so unpopular, we each have to take a fifteen-minute slot.

I still don't know if Sofie is officially living with us again. She's here several mornings a week and shows up most evenings to do her homework, but she disappears for two or three days at a time, sometimes to Urzula's, sometimes to my mum's. It's messy, it can't be good for her, but I'm just her aunt.

If only there was someone I could unburden myself to, but being with people is difficult. Even though Posh Petra is stressed and miserable, she's one of the few people I can relax with. Yesterday we went for a walk, just the two of us. I didn't want to go and neither did she, but she said it would be a good thing – 'Nature, oxygen, all of that. Make a change from me drinking myself into a stupor.'

'And me.' Actually, I haven't been drinking myself into a stupor. I mean, I've been drinking a *bit*, just not too much because it makes me feel even lower the day after. But I was demonstrating

Emotional Contagion, something that's been observed in the animal world – they do it to strengthen bonds. (Yes, *Psychologies* again.)

We went to some forest or other where Petra stared into the fast-running river, like she was considering throwing herself in, then said bleakly, 'I wish I'd had an abortion.'

'No, Petra, please don't!'

'I do, Amy. I wish I'd had it. I nearly did.'

I knew. We'd back-and-forthed on it for a couple of weeks, before she'd decided her unexpected late-in-life pregnancy and children might be a blessing.

'Women are allowed to regret abortions,' she said. 'What about those of us who regret *not* having an abortion?'

'Petra, maybe you should go to the doctor. Maybe get some tablets.'

'Cyanide? For me or for them?' She'd produced a mini-bottle of red wine from her bag. 'Want some? Please say no.'

'You okay, Amy?' Sofie asks.

I've frozen, like a mannequin. 'Oh . . . ah, yes, grand.' My hair is damp with sweat from scrubbing the hob.

'Where's the rubber gloves?' Jackson asks. 'I'll do the down-stairs loo now.'

The rest of us shudder and he laughs at us.

'Tie up your hair, boo,' Sofie says. She produces a hair-bobble and tenderly twists Jackson's super-lustrous locks into a top-knot. They rub their noses together and giggle.

'Oi!' Neeve says. 'No PDAs.'

'There they are.' Kiara finds the Marigolds for him, flings them into the basin of cleaning stuff, then pauses in the act of handing it over. Suddenly wistful, she says, 'I wonder if Dad's thinking about us. I wonder if he's missing us.'

My heart contracts.

'Yeah, right,' Neeve says. 'Missing this.' She indicates the five of us, attired in sweatpants and T-shirts, sporting red faces and limp hair. 'Who'd want a tropical paradise when you could be cleaning a fridge?'

They all laugh, even Kiara.

The doorbell rings and we pause in our tasks to look at each other with mild alarm. Who the hell calls around to people's homes on a Sunday morning?

'Probably Maura,' I say.

'Why?'

'Just . . . because . . .'

'Yeah, Maura be like,' Neeve says, and the three of them squeal with laughter.

I try hard to keep up with their speak, but the precise meaning of that sentence eludes me. And I'm not asking, not so soon after they'd mocked me for the drink question.

Walking down the hall, I'm praying that if it isn't Maura, it won't be some 'concerned' neighbour.

To my great surprise, standing in the chilly mid-October morning is Sofie's skeletal mother. 'Urzula, hi,' I say. 'Er . . . come in!'

She passes me a bin-liner. 'Is Sofie's stuff. And the stuff of that Jackson boy.'

'Oh? Ah . . .' What the hell? Is she kicking Sofie out?

'Urzula, come in, do!' We'd better talk about this.

'She is difficult girl.'

I don't want Sofie hearing any of this so I pull the door closed behind me, and step outside. 'No, she's not.'

'She is very difficult girl.'

'No, Urzula, she's a sweetheart.'

Urzula switches focus by giving me a once-over, her expression a mixture of scorn and distress. 'Amy. I am dietician. Believe me when I say mini-Magnums are as satisfying as big Magnums.'

I don't know how to respond. Insults aside, this is patently untrue.

And I realize something: I used to think that the line dividing sane people from insane people was entirely black or white – sane or not-sane – with no grey area. But suddenly I see now that the grey area is enormous. It spreads far and wide and into every part of life. Mad people aren't just those poor souls confined to locked wards. Mad people are everywhere, living among us, masquerading as non-mads. Mad people are in positions of power and influence and sometimes get their own TV show on UK Living, shaming fat people into being less fat. (At least temporarily: one article I read said as soon as those people escaped from Urzula, most of them ate more than ever.)

'I love Sofie,' I say. 'I'm delighted she'll be living with me again.'

'And your Hugh?' The sly eyes on her! 'He is not here to be delighted, is he?'

'Hugh will be back.'

'Hugh will leave again when he sees you and your Magnum-fat.'

If I *am* fat, and I'm not sure that I am – in fact, I don't know *what* I am because I've entirely lost contact with my body – it's mostly down to cheese and crisps, not ice cream.

'Why don't you come in and talk things out with Sofie?' I say. 'I'm not trying to persuade you into anything but you should at least talk face to face.'

'No.'

'Can I give her a message from you?'

'You can tell her she is difficult girl.' She turns to leave.

'Urzula, please, wait, hang on . . .' But she's gone.

48

Monday, 17 October, day thirty-five

Monday morning, and it's actually a relief that the weekend is over.

After Urzula's dramatic visit, I diplomatically broke the news to Sofie and, although Jackson seemed quietly furious, she was sanguine. 'I tried my best with her,' she said.

'More than your best.' Jackson, for all that he looks slight and fey, is strong and supportive of Sofie.

'Nothing more you can do than your best,' I told her. 'Not everyone's cut out to be a mother.' I wasn't sure if this was over-stepping boundaries but, feck it, Sofie is a sweetie and I didn't want her feeling this was on her.

The whole thing was so emotionally exhausting that I went to bed and priced a seventeen-day holiday to Argentina and Chile, for all of us including Jackson, sometime next July. I'd picked July because it seemed like a reasonable amount of time for us all to have recovered from Hugh's return home.

Of course, I know in my heart that we may never recover, but all that's keeping me going is hope. I guess I was doing the life equivalent of a wish board, and I did it in minute detail – looking up *everything*: the flights, the hotels, the transfers, everything.

I flew us business class (not first: even in my fantasy, I had some grasp of reality). Instead of selecting the poshest hotel in each city (Buenos Aires, Córdoba, Santiago) I chose the third fanciest. The girls would stay in regular rooms – and, yes, Jackson could bunk in with Sofie. Hugh and myself would be put up in suites, in the 'old' part of the hotels.

All totalled up, it was shockingly expensive. Even when I amended some details – Jackson's parents paying for his flight,

Neeve and Kiara sharing a room, no hotel cars from the airport – it was still extortionate. Nevertheless, it kept me occupied.

In the office my coat is barely off when Tim says, 'Sharmaine King. I've talked with her management. They've invited us to pitch.'

I love Tim's ambition. Usually.

'Which of us should go after it?' he asks Alastair. 'You or me? She's South African but UK-based, so it'll be UK-centric.'

Alastair glances my way. 'Well, Amy's in London as much as I . . . Ah, right! Yeah, I'll take it. Ping me over whatever you've got.'

I'm grateful for Tim's protection but ashamed to be considered a sad sack so I disappear into my work.

Just before lunch, my phone rings. It's a London number, unknown. I clear my throat, sit up straighter. 'Amy O'Connell speaking.'

'Dan Gordon. Representing a party interested in working with you.'

'O-*kaaaay*.' New business is always good. Well, nearly always. 'May I ask who it is?'

'Not at liberty. Client wants to meet today. Central London.'

'I'm afraid I'm in Dublin.'

'Catch a plane?'

I consider it for a moment. But, no, by the time I got there and had the meeting it would be too late to fly back this evening. Kiara and Sofie need me – it's bad enough that I'm gone every Tuesday night.

'How about one of my colleagues?' I offer. 'They're both exceptional publicists.'

'You handled Bryan Sawyer? Client insists on you.'

Well, it's nice to be wanted. Unless the mysterious client is Robert Mugabe.

'I'll be in London tomorrow,' I say.

'Must be today.'

I brace myself for some more persuading, but there's a click – he's hung up on me! I stare at the phone, then yell, 'Manners cost nothing!'

I look up and find Tim, Alastair, even Thamy watching me. They seem shocked.

'What?' I demand. 'He'd hung up, he didn't hear me.'

Three pairs of eyes are trained on me.

'He was rude,' I say. 'He was really rude.'

On my way back from lunch, I exit the lift to the sound of Alastair laughing, the full-on ha-ha-ha-ha-ha. This is followed by an eruption of multiple people's laughter and I hurry into the office because I'm in the market for something cheery.

Tim and Thamy are crowded around Alastair's screen. 'Amy!' they cry. 'Come here, you have to see this!'

Over I go and, to my utter astonishment, it's Mum! It's her vlog!

I gasp. 'How do you know about it?'

'Someone tweeted it to me.'

'On what?'

I push nearer the screen and see that the vlog has been retweeted more than three hundred times! It's *impossible* to overstate how difficult it is to make that happen. I've tried so hard with various clients to raise their profile with tweets and vlogs and they nearly all just died in the water.

'She's so *cute*,' Alastair says. 'And so funny. She might get Botox when she's older! That's absolute gas.'

I'm so proud of her. And of Neeve – that was a flash of inspiration, doing a session with Mum.

'She's a looker, isn't she?' Thamy says. 'I can see where you get it, Amy.'

'Get what?' I don't like being patronized.

'Ah, now!' they chorus. They're in wild high spirits from it all. 'Shur, you're fabulous.'

'Imagine having Lilian O'Connell, mother of five, as your mother-in-law!' Alastair looks at me. 'How's that hot sister of yours?'

I side-eye him and go back to my desk. Then I ring Neeve and we shriek with excitement at each other.

'It only went live this morning!' Neeve says. 'It's been like, wow!'

'You slay, sweetie.'

'Oh, Mum . . .'

'Ha-ha-ha!' I'm quite giddy. 'How about "Well done, darling daughter, I'm most *terrifically* proud of you"?'

Alastair proceeds to spend the best part of the afternoon watching Neeve's vlogs and providing running commentaries. 'Ha! I never knew that!'

'What?'

'The difference between dry skin and dehydrated skin. They're not the same! Who knew?'

I say, 'Dry is lacking oil and dehydrated is lacking water.' I've watched that vlog too.

'I wonder which mine is. I'm going down to Space NK to find out.' He's halfway out of his chair. 'I'll just watch one more before I go.'

Forty minutes later he's still sitting there.

At one stage I get up and go to the loo, and when I come back Alastair calls across the office, 'You know she's done one with Mr Best Sex Ever?'

Tim jerks his head up, Thamy twists her head around from her desk for a better look, and I blanch. 'Who? Richie Aldin? I know but, Jesus, Alastair, don't call him that!'

'How about the Prick You Used To Be Married To?'

'Better.'

'Let's hate-watch it.'

Tim and Thamy have hopped out of their places and, once again, we gather around Alastair's desk.

And there's Richie, telling Neeve about what shampoo he uses.

'He loves himself.' Alastair is so scathing. 'So pleased with himself, the pompous arse. Oh, here's a good bit, listen to this, Amy.'

Richie says, 'My skin never gives me any bother.'

'Can you *believe* that?' Alastair says. In a comedy voice he repeats, '"My skin never gives me any bother." As if it's all down to him, the prick.'

'I think he's hot,' Thamy says.

Off-camera Neeve asks Richie what his thoughts are on Botox. With a smirk, Richie says, 'I don't need it.'

'But what about when you're older?'

'I'll never need it.'

Alastair splutters, 'So he can predict the future now, can he? Stay away from him, Amy, because the kind of man he is, he'll just push and shove till you say yes.'

I don't know how he can make this assessment on three minutes forty seconds of a chat about SPF.

'He wants you back?' Thamy is agog.

'Well, no, not like that –'

'Wow. Go for it, he is a FOX!'

Out of curiosity, I say to Tim, 'What do you think of him?'

Tim's answer is simple. 'He won't stop until he gets what he wants.'

And I laugh and think, Richie Aldin can go fuck himself.

49

Fourteen months ago

Ouch! A spatter of bacon fat had jumped out of the frying pan and fizzed on my arm. The pain dimmed immediately but I couldn't run the risk of the hot fat speckling my top: it was only just on and the laundry basket was already full.

I pulled off my T-shirt, threw it on to a chair, but the apron wasn't in its spot, hanging from the radiator. God knows who had done what with it, but there wasn't time to find another. I'd have to finish cooking the dinner in my jeans and bra, but I barely noticed: my head was full of Josh Rowan.

On our regular lunch last Tuesday – the sixth week in a row that we'd met – he'd suddenly thrown into the conversation, 'I miss you propositioning me.'

'Do you! Ah, okay. Ha-ha-ha.'

'Have you any plans to do it again?'

'I don't know.'

'So should I do it instead? Proposition you?'

Right. Well, I'd known this would happen.

And, oh, the thoughts of sex with him. Both of us naked. Him pressing me by my hips on to the bed. Sitting astride me with a giant erection. Playing with me . . .

Druzie's flat was empty tonight. I could bring him back there and no one would know.

But this was so dangerous. I was going down a path there might be no way back from.

'I love Hugh.'

He nodded. It was his turn to say he loved Marcia, but he stayed silent.

And the way he was looking at me . . . his mouth in a grim line, his eyes ablaze with want, oh-so-serious about this.

He turned his palms upwards, revealing the pale skin of his

inner arms and the blue tracery beneath the surface, like a map of a river. The twitching of his pulse was visible and all that vulnerability crushed something tender and painful in me.

'Don't take this the wrong way,' he said, 'but I wish I'd never met you that day in the Black Friar.' He stared at the table as he spoke. 'I was doing okay. But when I saw you, searching for your comb and you looked up, and your sweet face and your clothes, it was a shock, Amy, *weird*, because you're a one-off but I felt like I already knew you.'

He could be feeding me a line.

'Then the fierce way you fought Premilla's case. So many publicists, they say the nice words but their hearts are cold. You, I knew you were kind. I tried harder than I usually would to get the Marie Vann piece pulled. I didn't like failing but it gave me another chance to see you. I'd have stayed with you that night. I'd have gone to your room the night of the awards. I want you.'

Hearing all this sent thrill after thrill through me. 'But, look, Josh. If we started a . . . thing, what would happen?' Quickly, I added, 'I don't mean what kind of sex or . . .' I swallowed. I froze, thinking about him naked, sliding himself into me . . . and from the still, intense way he held my gaze, I was sure that was what he, too, was imagining.

'Jesus.' He pressed his hand over his eyes and made a small, strange sound, a cross between a groan and a whimper. Then he looked at me again. 'You mean, what would happen ultimately? Would you leave your husband? Would I leave my wife? I don't know, Amy.' He shrugged helplessly. 'There's no script here.'

I wanted a script. I needed to know the ending before I could start anything. 'What about you and your wife? Do you love her?'

'Sometimes.' He sighed. 'But now isn't one of them.'

'Does love work like that?'

'I don't know about other people, but it's how Marcia and I seem to do it.'

'Your other times, did you feel guilty? Did your wife ever suspect?'

'Yes and yes.'

'And what happened? Did you tell her?'

'No. But Marcia's had her own things.'

'Things? You mean affairs? She told you?'

'I guessed. I asked her. Like me, she lied.'

'And?'

'I waited for them to run their course.'

'Josh, I'm out of my depth. I'm . . .' I searched for the right words. 'I'm not like you. Or like your wife. You're tough. Tougher than me.'

'I'm not tough. But, Amy, you love your husband, right? Why are you even here?' Josh leant forward with intent. 'Here's what I think you want. You'd like me to say I don't love my wife, that we've already split up and we're about to tell the kids. You want to magic away all the mess, the other people, the ones we'd hurt. You want Hugh to still be there for you long-term but for a cosmic hall pass to be given, so he'd never know and you'd not feel any guilt. But, Amy, this is real life and real life is messy.'

His words fell into silence. His assessment was spot-on.

I'd wanted a romance, a love affair, and for any sordidness to be conveniently swept away by the force of our passion.

I might as well admit it. 'I want to feel . . . desired, like you're crazy with want for me.'

'As it happens, I am.'

My mouth went dry. 'I want you not to have done it before. I know. I'm pathetic. And hypocritical.'

'I could have lied and you'd think I was a better man than you do.'

'I want to be all cool about you and your other . . . others. But I'm not. I feel like a . . . hick. Unsophisticated. I want to know details but I despise myself for it.'

'Okay, I'll tell you. One lasted about six months, then she met someone else. Another was with a twenty-something and it finished up because I couldn't take her . . .' He fell into thought. 'Her chirpiness.'

That fitted with the facts I'd gleaned.

'But this, with you, Amy?' he said. 'I can't take another lunch. I want more.'

So did I. But was I able?

'Can I think about it?' I asked.

'Don't take too long.'

Was that a threat? Should I get huffy? I decided no. 'What if I decide to not . . . go ahead?' I asked. 'Will we still see each other?'

'No.'

Oh.

'I mean it, Amy. I can't handle any more of this.'

Maybe I should have been offended – True Love Waits and all that – but I appreciated his grown-up honesty.

Since then, indecision was eating me from the inside out. I'd been waking in the early hours, flip-flopping from one stance to another. I'd decide I'd definitely go to a hotel with him and see what happened. Then a load of guilt would avalanche on top of me because I truly loved Hugh and had always seen us growing old together.

But the draw to Josh was powerful and I'd quickly find myself, once again, planning to sleep with him.

What if I got caught? The thought scared me witless. I didn't want to hurt Hugh and I didn't want my marriage to end. Also, what did I *really* know about Josh? We'd spent a good deal of time together but I'd done most of the talking.

I knew he was hot.

Yeah, I knew he was hot all right!

And over and back I wavered.

What I'd really love would be some sort of disaster where Josh and I got abandoned in a remote place – help would eventually come, that was always on the cards, but while we were waiting, we could behave as badly as we liked.

Meanwhile my sleepless nights had me dragging myself through my days, exhausted and worried-worried-worried, the lining of my stomach worn away by the acid of anxiety.

As Tuesday rolled around, I still hadn't decided, so I didn't meet him. But now, eleven days since I'd seen him, as I stood at my hob, frying rashers, I knew I needed a resolution. Today. Right now. Because if this to-ing and fro-ing kept on in my head, I'd go insane.

So I made my choice: no more Josh.

I'd send him an email on Monday. It was a bad idea to see him in person: it would only kick everything off all over again.

Ending it was the right thing to do. Eventually I'd be grateful. But right then I felt how the Little Match Girl must have felt when her last match went out. *Pop* went all the colour and joy and thrill, and suddenly everything was grey and cold and sad.

'What's going on?' Hugh's voice came from behind me.

'Rasher sandwiches for dinner.' I didn't turn around. 'They need to be used up today.'

'No, I meant . . .' He appeared at my side. 'What's happened to your clothes?'

'Oh. I thought my top might get spattered.' I clattered the fish slice around the pan.

'But look at you.' He slid himself between me and the hob. His hands were on my waist and his voice was filled with wonder. 'Cooking rashers in your foxy bra. You're like some fantasy woman.'

I glanced down. My bra was red satin. I'd only worn it because all the others were in the overflowing laundry basket.

'You probably know the football scores as well.' He swept my hair over one shoulder and buried his face in my neck.

'It's July, the season hasn't started yet.' I shook him off me.

'See what I mean? Which other woman would know that?' He groaned and slid his hands up over my ribcage and under my breasts. 'Oh, Amy.'

'Hugh.' I twisted sideways out of his hold. 'I'm trying to cook.'

'Oh, yeah?' Holding my gaze, he reached behind himself and, without looking, found the switch for the cooker. His hand lingered on it for a second or two, then still looking into my eyes, he slowly and deliberately flicked it from on to off. Instantly the red light of the hob disappeared. 'Whoops,' he said, widening his eyes with mock surprise. 'Power cut.'

'Turn it back on, Hugh.'

'Come on, babe, the girls are out and you're so –'

'Not now, Hugh.'

I stepped away from him and switched the cooker back on. Without meeting his eyes I said, 'Dinner will be ready in ten minutes.'

It was almost as if Josh had intuited that I'd decided against him because later that same day he sent a text: **So the timing on this couldn't be worse, but I'm about to send a work-related email. It's genuine. Josh xxx**

Hi, Amy. Hope you're having a good weekend. An idea came up at a meeting yesterday – would Premilla Routh be interested in doing a weekly column for us? Can be ghost-written, if that makes it more attractive to her. Let me know?

Thanks
Josh

A weekly column? Paid or unpaid? About her recovery from addiction or a more general thing? Time specific or open-ended? There was plenty to discuss but, in principle, it was a welcome proposal – decent money and very little work for Premilla.

She was dyslexic, Josh knew that, which was why he'd suggested a ghost-writer. And that sort of set-up needed a lot of on-going babysitting: instead of Premilla simply writing and filing copy, a week-by-week meet would have to be set up for her to tell her thoughts to the journalist, who would then construct the column. This would be sent to me for approval: very often in these relationships, the journalist either deliberately or accidentally misrepresents something, in the hope of turning it into a more sensational article. Which would mean me having to lock horns with the commissioning editor – Josh.

I couldn't do it. Extricating myself from him hurt. The last thing I could do was commit to on-going professional contact.

I mulled it over and my options were stark: turning down Josh's offer without speaking to Premilla, in the hope that she never found out.

But that would be unfair on Premilla.

My other option was to pass Premilla on to Alastair as his client. And say goodbye to a steady stream of income: as Premilla's publicist, the monthly retainer would go to Alastair instead of me. A sickener but my only real choice.

So I rang her and, with passionate talk of keeping her publicity fresh, sold her the idea of Alastair. She was initally bemused but, by the end of the call, enthusiastic.

Next I rang Alastair and said, 'Don't ask me why, because I won't give you an answer, but Premilla Routh is now your client.' Just like Premilla, he was bemused but enthusiastic.

Then it was time to deal with Josh.

There was the brutal option – I could unfriend him on Facebook, unfollow him on Twitter and Instagram, block his emails . . .

But that felt like overkill. Also, professionally we were obliged to remain cordial. So I replied to his email, telling him that if he had any future work queries to refer them to Alastair.

Almost immediately he texted: **Does this mean what I think it does?**

I waited a few minutes, wondering what exactly to say until, with a heavy heart, I clicked out: **Josh, I'm sorry.**

Moments later my phone rang: it was him and I didn't pick up.

He left a message, which I deleted without listening to it. Then I quietly unfollowed him on Instagram and muted him on Twitter. Not as brutal as blocking and unfriending but it meant I didn't stumble across reminders of what I'd been considering.

Even so, from time to time, I'd come across a re-shared post or a memory would flare, always followed by excruciating guilt.

50

Tuesday, 18 October, day thirty-six

Tuesday morning, 7.48 a.m. in a crowded, chaotic Heathrow, my phone rings. It's not even eight o'clock, what the actual! The number is withheld but, half looking for a scrap, I answer anyway. 'Amy O'Connell.'

'Dan Gordon.'

Who? Oh! The rude man who hung up on me yesterday.

'You in London?' he asks.

'What's this in —'

'You free to take a meeting with my client in the next hour?'

'I'm free today at three fifteen.'

'Needs to be earlier.'

'I'm in meetings until then.'

Your man does an irritated tsk. 'Okay. Where are you?'

'Home House.' Well, it's where I'll be in an hour's time.

'Sort out a private meeting room. Very private, right? See you at three fifteen. Prompt.'

Prompt? Who says *prompt*?

My day is busy. There's a stream of disgraced or forgotten 'celebrities' looking for a relaunch, and I size up every single one of them as a potential EverDry ambassador because Mrs Mullen simply will not be talked down.

But it's proving difficult.

Obviously, it would have to be someone well liked. But *poor.* Because no one is going to become an incontinence ambassador for the prestige, right?

So, well liked but poor, preferably desperate. And attractive, because no one wants to identify with a horror-show. In addition, they must be the right age, which means no older than fifty because people don't like seeing themselves in the same boat as crocks. But realistically they can't be much younger than fifty because no one would believe they were incontinent. God, it's difficult.

Not a single one of today's potential clients fits the bill and all my hopes are hanging on my mysterious three-fifteen appointment.

Dan Gordon looks like an accountant crossed with a hungry greyhound, or perhaps a lanky-limbed Harry Potter who's just heard that Voldemort has won a Ferrari – bespectacled, besuited and aggressive. In our *very private* meeting room (which is exactly the same as all the other private meeting rooms), I stand up to shake hands. In reply, he opens a cardboard folder, whips out a non-disclosure agreement and slides it in front of me. 'Sign it.'

'I'll read it first, if you don't mind.' I smile sweetly. Christ, what a knob. God only knows how awful the actual client will be. But I don't have to take the job. Yes, business is always appreciated but with some gigs no money is worth it.

The contract is standard – basically the meeting with the mystery person never happened and if I monetized anything I learnt, I'd be sued into the poorhouse.

'Okay.' With a flourish, I sign as Minnie O'Mouse, and barely bother to disguise the words. 'There you go. So, what happens now?'

Dan Gordon snatches up the contract and clicks out a text. Such *rudeness*.

'This better be good,' I say.

He ignores me, as his phone beeps with a message. 'He'll be here in fifteen minutes.'

'So it's a he?'

Dan Gordon clamps his mouth tight.

'It doesn't matter now,' I said. 'I'll be meeting *him* in a few minutes. Is it Wayne Rooney?'

He snorts. 'No.'

'The leader of North Korea?'

He goes quiet.

'It *is* the leader of North Korea?'

'It's not the leader of North Korea.'

'Aw, come on.' I poke his leg with the toe of my boot. 'Play with me. Is it Emma Stone?'

'You know it's a man.'

'That was a trick question. Is it Terry Wogan?'

'Terry Wogan is dead.'

Dan Gordon won't say another word and I don't like the silence: there's too much time for thinking. Out of nowhere I wonder if Hugh is dead. But if he'd died, wouldn't an embassy have contacted me? Unless he'd fallen into a river in Thailand and no one has found him. But why would he fall into a river? People don't just fall into rivers . . . unless the crack on his head from the hairbrush I threw at him really had given him an aneurysm. Unlikely as this is, my spine goes cold with fear and I can't keep my anxiety to myself. 'Mr Gordon, can a person die from getting hit on the head with a hairbrush?'

He gives me a look. 'Are you going to hit me on the head with a hairbrush?'

'No.' Suddenly I'm scornful. 'Not everything's about you. So, can they?'

'I'm not a doctor. Google it.'

I need to stop this mad catastrophizing. Except obviously it's about my genuine fears. It's almost easier to accept that Hugh is dead in the Mekong, being eaten by vicious Asian fish, than that he hasn't wanted to call me.

Dan Gordon's phone beeps. He leaves the room and returns moments later with another man. Whom I recognize. In fact, I almost pass out. It's Matthew Carlisle, Ruthie Billingham's husband, who's been cheating with their nanny, Sharmaine King! And he's fucking gorgeous! Tall, like really tall, *imposing* tall. He's got black hair, in a shortish buzz-cut, glasses with stylish black frames and deep brown eyes. Some famouses are far less impressive in real life but Matthew Carlisle is more, *much* more.

'Thank you for seeing me at short notice,' he says, with a tired smile.

'Of course,' I murmur. 'Won't you sit down?'

He takes an armchair opposite me and Dan Gordon sits beside him, like a guard dog who hasn't been fed in some days.

'Can I get you coffee?' I ask. 'Water?'

He shakes his beautifully shaped head. 'No, thanks, I'm fine.'

'Something stronger, maybe?'

Interest flares in his eyes. 'No. I can't start drinking in the afternoons.'

'So how can I help?' Two short days ago I'd wanted nothing to do with this painful story, but that was before Matthew Carlisle had treated me to a short burst of his industrial-grade charisma. Only fair to hear the man out, right?

'Ruthie Billingham,' Matthew says. 'The actress? She's my wife. Ex-wife. Well, not yet, we're getting divorced.'

Gently I say, 'I know who you are.' Before he gets paranoid, I say, 'Because it's my job to know. You don't have to fill me in.'

'Oh, okay. She's been having an affair with Ozzie Brown for two and a half years.'

Two and a half *years*? The story she'd given the press was that she and Ozzie had only been stepping out for a couple of weeks.

'Ruthie can't be seen as the bad guy, not in the eyes of the public.'

Of course. Ruthie gets all her work on her girl-next-door persona.

'So she – well, her publicists – planted the stories about me and our nanny. So people will look the other way.'

But the question has to be asked. 'Are the stories true? For me to do my job properly, I need to know everything. Without all the facts I can't help you.'

'Sharmaine's a sweet girl,' Matthew says. 'She's a great nanny. But nothing ever happened.'

My mind is racing, Ruthie's publicists work at the most powerful agency in the UK – they could probably rehabilitate Jimmy Savile if they put their mind to it. 'Why have you come to me?' I ask.

'Because no one knows who you are,' Dan says. 'We need to keep this quiet.'

'*Some* people know who I –'

'You did a great job with Bryan Sawyer.' Matthew's smile derails my ire. I am *pathetic*. 'And Tabitha Wilton says you're effective.'

'What do you want from this process?' I ask.

'I don't want an image as the bad guy. I'm *not* the bad guy.'

'You're a serious broadcaster, why does it even matter?'

'Because it's not true.'

Right. He's an idealist.

'Can you fix it?' he asks.

It would be tough. The public *adore* Ruthie. They were really sad they had to be cross with her for moving on so quickly. They appreciated having Matthew to blame for their sweetheart being a little slutty. The public mood is now firmly behind Ruthie, as far as I can tell, and it'll be hard to switch their allegiance again.

In addition, you can't prove a negative: Matthew and the nanny can deny until they're blue in the face, but it will never be beyond doubt.

'Can you get something into a broadsheet by this weekend?' Dan asks. 'A big, huge interview with Matthew, where he gives his side of the story?'

'That would be a mistake.' A *terrible* mistake. 'That would turn this into a "he says/she says" slanging match, Matthew. You'd be "tabloided" and that's a toxin harder to shake off than napalm.'

He looks stricken.

'But issuing an official press release is vital,' I say. 'Denying everything and asking for privacy, especially for your children. Simple and dignified.'

'That's *all* you'd do?' Dan is furious.

'No, but previous experience, of which I have plenty, is telling me to play a much longer game.'

'So what *would* you do?' Matthew asks.

That's a huge question and, to be blunt, it depends on how many of my hours he's prepared to buy. 'I'd have to look at everything – the current coverage, which journalists Ruthie owns, what precisely you want your outcome to be – but I can definitely change the conversation. Medium-term, I can work to alter your public profile.'

'People will still think I'm a cheater.'

'If they do, it won't matter.'

'Oh! I get it. It's not binary,' Matthew says.

'Exactly!' I could kiss him. 'A quiet, steady denial that you cheated with Sharmaine, if the subject ever comes up. And eventually it won't.'

'Give us an example of what you'd do to alter his public profile,' Dan demands.

God, I've only known Matthew Carlisle ten minutes, how am I meant to come up with a plan of campaign? And then inspiration hits. '*Children in Need*!'

Matthew Carlisle covered in custard, standing in a bucket, a glass bowl at a jaunty angle on his head, trifle dripping down his beautiful face – 'Serious Political Journalist Shows He Can Take a Little Humiliation'. People *love* that stuff.

'*Children in Need*?' Dan Gordon's scorn is epic. Matthew places a restraining hand on him.

'Give me a few days, I'll put together a comprehensive plan,' I say. 'Send out feelers, see who's interested in working with you.' Hastily I add, 'Which is everyone, of course.' Never forget how fragile famous egos are!

There's a small conspiratorial smile behind Matthew's black-framed spectacles. Clearly he's not as narcissistic as most.

'What can I do?' he asks, then takes off his glasses, rubs his beautiful, tired eyes and says, 'For you.'

He really shouldn't go round phrasing questions in that manner when he's as ridey as he is. It's not decent.

'I mean, you know, to help you do your job?' But there's a hint of a twinkle, almost an apology, as if he realized, too late, how his question had sounded.

I smile to convey silently that I understand. This is good, we're communicating. 'First of all, I'd need you to trust me.'

'Why should we trust you?' Dan Gordon says.

Irritably I turn on him, 'What's *your* role in all this?'

'I'm his brother.'

'Whose brother?'

'His.' With a jerk of his head, he indicates Matthew.

In amazement my eyes flash from God-like Matthew to angry-but-dull Dan. Then I have to clamp my lips together to stop the laugh escaping.

'What sort of brothers?' Perhaps he means close-friends-style brothers.

'Full siblings,' Matthew says, with a glint of warning in his voice. 'Children from the same parents. Those sort of brothers.'

What comes to mind is that film where Arnold Schwarzenegger and Danny DeVito are twins and, once again, I'm afraid the laughter will rush out of my mouth and blow this gig. 'But you have different surnames?' That's the best I can produce to explain my far-too-evident astonishment.

'My name's not Dan Gordon,' Dan Gordon says, 'Needed a fake name until you'd signed the non-disclosure. Name's Dan Carlisle.'

'Actually Dante Carlisle,' Matthew says. 'Italian mother.'

'But I don't look like a Dante,' Dan says.

You can say that again. Dante sounds dark and dramatic, like he should be striding about, swirling a long, black cape.

Now is as good a time as any to produce Hatch's basic contract, for ten hours of my time.

Matthew reads through it, with Dan breathing down his neck, then Matthew signs it, and it's all too much, and I want to quietly bite my knuckle with the thrill of it. Matthew Carlisle! My client! Matthew actual Carlisle!

I'm star-struck – star-struck as *fuck*!

'I'll compose a press release and send it to you later. Once we've made any amendments you might want, it'll go to all the news outlets.'

'It can't be a secret he has a publicist?' Dan asks.

'No!' Cheeky bastard. What am I? A prostitute?

'You know I'm in London only on Tuesday and Wednesday,' I remind Matthew. 'My colleague Alastair is here every Thursday and half of Friday. You should meet, he can work with me.'

261

'Happy to,' Matthew says. 'But I want my primary contact to be with you.'

Well, I mean – how *EFFING BRILLIANT* is that! 'Certainly,' I murmur, trying to hide my red-with-pleasure face in my iPad. 'So, shall we meet next Tuesday? I'll have a raft of ideas for you.'

'Come to my house,' Dan says, 'where Matthew's hiding right now. I'll email the address.'

It takes a lot of work to compose myself for my four o'clock.

51

Out in the bar, who do I come face-to-face with? Only Alastair!
'What are you doing here?'

'Meeting a maybe client,' he says.

Suddenly a very bad feeling creeps over me. 'It's not Sharmaine
King, is it?'

'Yep.'

'No, Alastair, you can't. I've just signed Matthew Carlisle.'

He stares. 'I thought you didn't want to touch this story.'

'It was Tim's decision. Trying to protect me,' I add quickly.
'But I'm fine. It's all fine.'

'Oh-*kaaay*. Nice work, though. Matthew Carlisle – that's
impressive! Is he as much of a babe in real life?'

'Oh, Alastair, he's a *total* babe. Look, sorry you've had a wasted
journey.'

'Ah, shur, what harm? Heathrow is always charming at this
time of year. Hey, maybe I'll stay in London tonight and we can
get dinner. Are you staying in Druzie's? Can I bunk in with you?'

'No. No to everything. I *am* staying in Druzie's but I'll be doing
a crash-course in Matthew Carlisle, so no dinner, no bunking.'

'Grand so. Christ, here she is. Talk to you later.'

The arrival of Sharmaine King is causing a right frisson even
among the Home House media types, who're well used to
famouses. She's lovely – blonde, vibrant and not-skinny, just all-
round beautiful, the way healthy young people are always
beautiful. She's in rolled-up jeans, brogues and an oversized
tweed boyfriend coat, which she removes to display a boxy
raggedy-edged jumper.

The press is wrong: she doesn't look like Ruthie at all. Yes,
they're both blonde and they're both wholesome but I've always
found Ruthie a bit watery and this Sharmaine is radiant.

There's a moment of genuine sorrow that we won't be signing her – she looks very promotable – followed by relief that we won't have any part in ruining her. Another agency will snap her up and it's obvious how things will play out – she'll end up on *Love Island* or *Celebrity Big Brother* and for a couple of years she'll be subject to daily snarking from the sidebar of shame. Eventually she'll crash and burn – they all do. They think a scandal like this is an *entrée* to a world of riches and fame, but ultimately it's just a one-way ticket to misery and oblivion.

Alastair takes Sharmaine off to a secluded couch at the far end of the room and my four o'clock arrives, a profile-writer from *The Times*. At about five, she takes her leave, and when we stand to say our goodbyes, Alastair and Sharmaine King are still in a cosy huddle at the far end of the room. For the love of *God*. He was simply meant to be shutting things down.

All my meetings have finished but I decide to hang around, work on Matthew Carlisle's press release, then scold Alastair when he finally releases Sharmaine . . . Shite, three missed calls. Tim. I call him back.

'You certain about this Matthew Carlisle thing?' he asks.

'Oh, I am, Tim. I'm glad to have a big new project.'

'Alastair can do him.'

'Um, no, he wants me specifically.' Pleasure leaks out in my tone.

'If you're sure. He's shortlisted for a prize at the Brighton Media Awards, but that's a secret. He doesn't know yet.'

'How do *you* know?'

'Ah, someone mentioned it . . . But Paxman is also up.'

'Guess this isn't Matthew's year.'

Tim says goodbye and I write Matthew's press release.

Recent rumours in the press imply I had an inappropriate relationship with my children's nanny. I emphatically and unreservedly deny all of these unsubstantiated rumours. There was no impropriety. This is a very difficult time for our family and I respectfully ask for our children's privacy to be respected. There will be no further comment from me on this matter.

I email it to Matthew and his wretched brother for their approval . . . And what the *hell* is keeping Alastair? I stretch tall like a meerkat – they're still in a head-to-head huddle.

I feel oddly protective of Sharmaine King, and if they haven't finished in ten minutes' time, I'm breaking things up.

Finally, Alastair stands. With narrowed eyes I watch him help Sharmaine into her coat – God, I wish I was tall: that coat is amazing. Zara, I recognize it from my online adventures, but it would swamp me. He places his hands on her forearms and – get this – slides his hands along, pushing the coat and jumper upwards, so he's touching her bare skin. Everyone in the place is looking. He shifts her a few inches so that they're facing right into each other, drops his knees slightly so that his hips are angled towards hers, kisses her fresh young cheek, lets his lips linger a moment too long . . . She blushes. I sigh. I'll fucking kill him.

'Bye,' she breathes, then stumbles over her brogues. She's gone and from the loud exhalation it's clear the entire room has been holding their breath. Everyone seems to wake up from a reverie, looking at their companions quizzically, as if to say, 'Who on God's earth are *you*?'

I snatch up my stuff and meet Alastair at the door. 'Come on.' I'm walking at speed. 'You're catching a taxi to Heathrow – you need to get out of this country.'

'What have I done?'

'You tell me.' We're walking down the stairs and out into the street. 'That poor girl! You were meant to be giving her the kiss-off. It should have taken ten minutes tops.'

I see a taxi and stick my hand up. It stops before me, its engine ticking. 'Get in.' I prod Alastair.

'Heathrow via Shepherd's Bush,' I tell the cabbie.

As soon as we're settled, Alastair says, 'I'm lonely.'

'But you're going about things the wrong way.' The amount of times he's already been told this stuff probably runs into the hundreds, but I'm going to tell him again. 'You think The One is going to appear and the giddy feeling that everyone gets at the start of a relationship will last for ever. Okay, you fancy them and do the sexing, at least in the early days. But we're all just flawed human beings, lurching along together as best we can. Eventually The One will annoy you, the way your friends sometimes annoy you – they'll disappoint you, or when they're eating apple crumble and custard, the sound of their spoon banging against their teeth will fill you with rage. But you can't bail . . .' My voice meanders to nothing. Because, of course, Hugh bailed.

It hits me like a blow in the chest. Again. Groundhog break-up.

Alastair prompts me. 'You haven't finished. Say the stuff about a relationship being like a small country. It's for my good.'

I carry on my well-worn lecture on auto-pilot. 'Creating a healthy relationship is like creating a small, land-locked country. The borders are always under threat and every day you have to shore them up. So when something in the country implodes, the shockwaves move outwards and the borders push back until eventually the crisis subsides . . .'

What right have I to say any of this to Alastair? None. Not now. Hugh and I have ruptured, our borders haven't endured . . .

Alastair gives me a sharp nudge. 'Amy, we're not finished! Tell me I'm too good-looking, et cetera, et cetera. Come on!'

He's like a child insisting on his bedtime story. Wearily, I gear up for the final part of my scolding. 'People think it's great to be good-looking but, Alastair, it's the worst thing that could have happened to you. You're irresponsible with it.'

'It's like?' he prompted.

'It's like putting a child in charge of a gun.'

He nods. He looks simultaneously happy and hangdog. We sit in silence and, after about eight seconds, he gets out his phone, then so do I.

We don't speak until we get to the flat in Shepherd's Bush.

'Tell Druzie I said hey.' He lifts my wheely case out of the cab and places it on the pavement.

We hug. I'm fond of him and I feel bad for having lectured him. Pot, kettle and all that.

52

I'm running down a dusty grey street, tall broken buildings on either side of me. Far ahead in the distance is Hugh, and I try to call to him, but my voice won't work. This is a dangerous place, a ruined city, snipers above me, enemies all around. In my arms are several kittens, wriggling and trying to escape, but when I look down, they're not kittens, they're baby girls. There's Sofie. And Kiara. And Neeve. And one, two, no, three more Sofies, their baby faces looking up at me with weird blue eyes.

Through the smoke Hugh is still visible but he's moving away fast so I try to speed up too. Then a tiny Sofie, much smaller than the others, slips from my hold and there's no time to stop so I scoop her up by her ear and she's wailing in pain but Hugh has disappeared now and I must run faster, but my legs are too heavy. The sky is darkening with my terror – if I don't catch him, our family is broken for ever, but he's gone, he's gone, he's gone.

He didn't know I was there. He didn't know how hard I was trying to catch him. I don't matter to him, not at all, and that loss is like a blow to my chest. It crackles with green electricity, painful enough to kill but I'm not allowed to die.

Then I wake up.

Lying in the darkness, my heart is pounding and it takes a few moments for the crackling sensation in my chest to disperse. I fumble for the light-switch and the instant brightness erases the horror of the nightmare.

53

'How about "Star in the Reasonably Priced Car"?' I call across the office to Alastair. 'Too laddish?'

'Maybe. Fine line – you need him normal and likeable, but not so blokey he could be a nanny-shagger.'

'Mmm.'

I'm working flat out on Matthew Carlisle and the greatest source of inspiration is the *Guardian* questionnaire he did two years ago.

Matthew Carlisle (39), the son of an electrician and an Italian immigrant, was brought up in Sheffield. For three years, he's presented BBC political flagship *This Week*. He's married to actor Ruthie Billingham, they have two children and live in London.

- *When were you happiest?* Last Tuesday: wife, kids, couch, movie, pizza.
- *What is your greatest fear?* No pizza.
- *Which living person do you most admire and why?* My mum. Came from Naples to the UK in 1968 with two pounds and worked three jobs after our dad left us.
- *What is the trait you most deplore in yourself?* Impatience. Queues, microwaves, online orders, everything could happen faster.
- *What is the trait you most deplore in others?* Lying by omission. (I spend a lot of my life around politicians.)
- *What makes you unhappy?* Single socks.
- *What did you want to be when you were growing up?* A Premier League footballer.

- *Who or what is the greatest love of your life?* RB.
- *What does love feel like?* Home.
- *If you could bring something extinct back to life, what would you choose?* Pink Panther bars. Happy memories of spending my pocket money.
- *What would your super-power be?* Redistribution of wealth.
- *What was your most embarrassing moment?* Stroking a stationary Maserati without noticing both the (slightly terrified) owners were sat in it.
- *What makes you cry?* Ikea.
- *What do you most dislike about your appearance?* My eyes are too close together.
- *Who would play you in the film of your life?* Someone boss-eyed.
- *What do you consider your greatest achievement?* Getting Ruthie to say yes.
- *To whom would you like to say sorry and why?* My first wife. I was a crap husband.
- *How often do you have sex?* Not often enough.
- *What single thing would improve the quality of your life?* A dog.
- *What's your favourite smell?* My wife.
- *How do you relax?* I like to cook.
- *What lesson has life taught you?* We're all faking it.
- *Tell us a secret about you?* I'm really just a big softy.
- *Tell us a joke.* What do you call a sheep with no legs? A cloud. (Sorry, my daughter told it to me.)

Matthew's eyes are *not* too close together – they're intelligent and warm and *perfectly* proportioned. I'm delighted to discover that he likes to cook – I've already talked to someone from *Celebrity Masterchef*. And he's a dog-lover, so I'm planning to partner him with Dogs Trust. Nothing like a segment on *The One Show* of a grown man playing with abandoned puppies to melt hearts . . .

Then there's the Maserati story, so he's obviously a petrol-head. And maybe we could do some sort of comedy segment called 'The Man Who Learnt to Love Ikea' . . .

Most of Matthew's profiles lazily trot out the same facts – mum an Italian cleaning lady; dad an electrician, who deserted the family when Matthew was a baby; ferociously intelligent even as a child; won a scholarship to Oxford; got a double-first in PPE, blah-dee-blah. An ill-judged, short-lived early marriage to a posho addict, followed by high-profile wedding to Ruthie.

There are two tones to the interviews: either breathless and giddy (the journalist was invariably female) or a sense that the writer admired him but felt he could do with lightening up. He fails the Howard Hunter Pint Test. ('Would I want to go for a pint with this man? The answer is no.')

Until recently all his coverage was uncontroversial – loves his wife and kids, lives and breathes politics and is zero-tolerant of double-dealing. If he's guilty of anything, it's a slight lack of a sense of humour. That, coupled with rumours of infidelity, does not play well.

Cheating + sense of humour = Lovable Rogue.

Cheating – sense of humour = Sleazy McSleaze.

He needs warming up and any excess pomposity excised so that he'd effortlessly pass the Howard Hunter Pint Test – every man in the country should want to go for a pint with him. And every woman should fancy him, while also being certain that he still loves Ruthie – What the hell?

It's hard to believe but Richie has just sent another email, this time a screenshot of the actual invitation and underneath, 'Think of the poor blind children.' His behaviour is so pushy that I'm confused – surely he can't seriously think he's being persuasive.

'Alastair, come and look at this.'

He reads it. 'He's gone insane,' he says. 'No other explanation. Now go home. Plans for the weekend?'

'Tomorrow Steevie's having a brunch and I know it's going to be a Why Can't They Keep Their Lads in Their Pants special.'

'Sounds fun.'

'She means well, but she'll want me to get drunk and bitch about Hugh and I don't want to.'

'No?'

'I wish none of this was happening, but if he comes back and wants to make everything right, I don't want to be full of hate and resentment.'

'It takes all sorts, I suppose. How's Derry? Still riding?'

'I believe so.'

'Tell her I say hey.'

'I won't.'

At Mum and Pop's all the talk is of Mum's vlogging debut and spirits are very high.

'They'd seen it at work,' Joe says. 'Everyone says she's a hoot, talking about checking her privilege.'

It's already the most-watched vlog Neeve has ever done.

'Can we do another one?' Mum asks Neeve. 'Can you sort me out with new hair? I was thinking I'd like to go blonde.'

Neeve swallows. 'Um, sure. Probably. Leave it with me.'

'Now, don't shout at me,' Mum says, 'because this is my moment. But where exactly is it?'

'Where's what?'

'The internet? Where do they keep all the stuff? Like the shoes you got for me and the picky-up thing for Pop. And now my videos. Is it in a big warehouse? Like, out beyond the M50?'

Poor Neeve. It's almost visible how she shoves down her rage. 'Granny, it's not in a place. It hangs in the air, like, like electricity. Or God!'

Mum gives Neeve a look. 'God is dead.'

'Is he?' Pop says. 'Well, he had a good innings.'

54

Saturday, 22 October, day forty

Steevie comes to her front door, towel-drying her hair. She looks startled and well she might: I'm twenty minutes early. 'Amy! What time is it?'

'You're okay, it's only twenty to.' I step into the hall and pass over a bottle. 'Listen, Steevie, before the others arrive, can I ask a favour?'

'Course.'

'Today, do you mind if we don't have any toasts to bad things happening to Hugh?'

'Like what?'

I'm striving for a jokey tone. 'Well, like him getting the clap and his dick going green and dropping off.'

Her face falls. 'Why not?'

She was meant to laugh. Laugh and agree to go along with my wishes. I take a second to gather my resolve. 'Because I don't feel that way.'

'But you should! The nerve of him, taking off for six months, leaving you here to face the humiliation. It's a disgrace what he's done and he's a total fucker! I hope his dick *does* go green and drop off!'

'See, I don't think Hugh's a total fucker.' I keep my tone mild.

'But he *is*. He *is* a total fucker.'

She's confused – and hurt. Not only has she gone to the trouble of having a brunch for me, of getting up early and making her famous vegetarian moussaka, then doing her chocolate pavlova, then going to Donnybrook Fair and buying four different types of salad and a selection of expensive cheese but I have the outrageous cheek to throw it all back in her face by not thinking my husband is a total fucker.

My spirits slide: this is going to be a long brunch.

'Have some wine,' Steevie says. 'And don't worry about Hugh. He'll eventually get what's coming to him.'

And here comes Jana 'Loose Lips Sink Ships' Shanahan, in some ditsy-looking dress, her hair in a falling-down updo. Her juvenile look has always charmed me, but I think I might be going off it.

I'm still wondering what the fallout from Casserole-gate is going to be. It's a weird thing, being bound by middle-class mores, where even if someone uses a casserole as a pretext for shameless rubbernecking, you're obliged to pretend that their intentions were noble. For a moment I wonder what would happen if I stopped with the fakery and calmly said, 'Genevieve Payne is a bitch.'

God, no. I'm not brave enough.

Mind you, even now, weeks later, whenever I think of Neeve saying, 'Keep your casserole,' I convulse with silent laughter.

Shortly after Jana's arrival, we greet Tasha Ingersoll, dolled up to the nines in – eek! – a blue Hervé Leger bandage dress. I haven't seen her in at least a year and I've never liked her. Next, in skinny jeans and a floaty shirt, is Mo Edgeworth. She's nice enough but I barely know her, and it's only then that the common denominator is revealed: every woman here has been shafted by a man.

Steevie's Lee left her for his assistant. Four days before Jana was due to get married, her fella called it off. Tasha Ingersoll 'stole' Neil O'Hegarty from Siobhan O'Hegarty, then Neil escaped and went back to Siobhan. Mo Edgeworth's boyfriend was married and she didn't know. Then there's me . . .

I should have checked who'd be here. I thought I'd done well by insisting to Steevie that Genevieve Payne couldn't come. But in the relief of that victory my eye was off the ball and it's too late now. Everyone greets me with the 'Full Heart Stare' where they take my hands, gaze into my eyes and flex a compassion muscle. It's the look I give people when they've had a bereavement or a cancer diagnosis, and it's only now that I see how humiliating it is to be on the receiving end. I'll be more careful in future.

'The moussaka is ready.' Steevie sounds wounded and snippy.

We sit at the table and I swig my wine, aware that there's a danger of overdoing it.

'So!' Tasha says. 'How have you been *coping*?'

'Honestly, I'm fine.'

My answer is received in rancorous silence.

'What have you been *doing*?'

'Busy, you know, work is all go. Took on a new client on Tuesday. Guess who he is. Hint, he's a bit fabulous!'

'Hugh Jackman?'

'Not that fabulous. Works for the BBC.'

'Bruce Forsyth.'

'Ah, come on.'

'Who is it, Amy?'

'Matthew Carlisle.'

'The nanny-shagger!'

'He's not –'

Then Tasha says, 'I think he looks like Tom Ford,' like it's a bad thing!

'Anything else?' Mo prompts.

'Spending quality time with my girls. Sofie has moved back in, which I'm delighted about!'

But tales of my daughters don't cut the mustard in this particular milieu. At the very least I should confide that I've just joined Whiskr, or whatever the name of the site is, that matches beard-loving ladies with beardy men. In the ensuing silence I eat too much moussaka to offer a blatantly dishonest display of gratitude for this grim get-together.

'So? Any men?' Steevie asks Tasha, and I want to stand up and leave. Only the promise of the fancy cheese restrains me.

Tasha launches into a grisly tale of some dreadful man who had a ninety-degree bend in his penis and that was the least bad thing about him. I'm drinking steadily but heavily. Tasha ends her epic with snarky side-eyes and, 'All ahead of you, Amy.'

It's *not* all ahead of me. I say, 'We're failing the Bechdel Test in spectacular fashion.'

Steevie glares, actually glares, then jerkily clears away the plates, and I realize I've eaten about seven times as much as any-one else. And here comes the pavlova. Just this course to get through, then the cheese, and then I can go.

I'm never coming to another of these gatherings. I can't. Then Steevie will take umbrage. So I'm looking an unpleasant choice straight in the face: either I please Steevie or I protect myself – and in the process damage an important friendship. I don't want this to happen. But that's personal growth for you. The circumstances that beget it are always unpleasant and so is the actual process. Some day down the road I might feel smug and wise but it'll be a while coming.

I accept a plate of chocolate pavlova and horse in, barely tast-ing it.

'Wooh! Watch that girl eat her feelings!' Tasha says.

I'm appalled by her bitchiness but my riposte is a great phrase that Neeve taught me: 'Ouch. Rush me to the burns unit.'

'Wait till you see her when the cheese arrives,' Steevie says – oh, no! We've just jumped from pass-agg snarkiness to open mean-girlery.

For a second I contemplate throwing my napkin on the table and leaving, but I'm too scared. Instead I tip half a glass of wine down my gullet.

'So, hey, Amy, while Hugh is away, have you a bucket list?' Jana is trying desperately to resuscitate things.

'Aaaaah, travel?' I blag. 'Macchu Pichu?'

'Do the three-day trek?' Jana asks.

'Isn't there a train? Not hiking for three days, don't wanna see it that much.' You know, I'm a bit pissed.

'Dolphins?' Jana again. 'Swimming with them?'

'I worry about the whole dolphin thing. They've been tolerant of us until now, but I sense they might turn.' I really am *quite* pissed. 'The only thing I really love is clothes.' I'm slurring – 'clothes' is one long slide of a word. 'If I could, I'd spend my days scouting second-hand shops.' God, *waaaay* too many Ss in that sentence. 'Tracking down beautiful vintage pieces. I'd have my own shop.' I'm making a big effort to enunciate clearly.

'You should do that, Amy.' Jana is encouraging. Tasha is actually checking her phone.

'Ah, no!' I wave away Jana's enthusiasm. 'No illusions. Isn't a career. You might look at two hundred dresses, all of them just cheap old rags. Cheap. Old. Rags.' I focus on Tasha as I say those words and a desire to laugh bubbles up in me. 'People would get cross because a dress costs a fiver, when the dry-cleaning cost me a tenner. And I could sit there for three days and no one would buy anything and I couldn't pay the shop rent. Then I'd be evicted.'

On this cheery note, Tasha stands. 'I have to go.'

'So do I,' I say.

'You haven't had your cheese,' Steevie says.

I look her in the eye. 'I don't want any.' It's bad. Bad, bad, bad. Hard to know how this happened but we're at war. It's terrible and I'm afraid.

'One thing you should know,' Tasha cuts across us. 'When Genevieve brought that casserole over to you, she was only being nice.'

'Bullshit.'

'Please don't swear at me.' Tasha has gone super-prim.

'My apologies.' Sarcasm. Blistering. *Most* abject. 'Genevieve was just being a disaster-tourist.'

'Why would she do that?' Steevie asks coldly – the same Steevie who knows exactly what Genevieve is like.

'You think Genevieve fancies Hugh.' Tasha is scathing.

I'm saying nothing.

I *could* tell the story of when Hugh got his new car, a second-hand Volkswagen, and Genevieve cooed, 'Cool wheels,' then asked if he'd take her for a drive in it, like it was a Porsche.

I could.

But I don't.

'She does fancy him,' Mo interjects. 'Genevieve told me.'

So Mo is friends with Genevieve as well? They're all her friends! I'm in a snake-pit of Genevieve Payne lovers!

'Well . . .' Poor Jana is flailing around, trying to reconfigure this into something blameless. 'Well, maybe she does fancy him because, yeah, Hugh is pretty hot!'

55

I can't drive home, I've had far too much to drink, so I set off on foot in my too-high shoes. When I'm safely away from my Bechdel-Test-failing lunch companions, tears start streaming down my face.

I handled that really badly. I'm ashamed but I'm also resentful. I'm defensive but I'm also sad. Steevie and I have been friends for a long time and suddenly it's gone to shit. Is everything going to fall apart? Is Hugh's leaving the start of a major life unravelling?

I hate confrontation, I hate ill-feeling, and I'm shaky and nauseous.

I hobble on in my wrong shoes and, passing Marley Park, I decide to give my poor feet a break, maybe even sober up.

There's a bench near a huge big tree – it might be an oak – and I sit down for a few minutes. Before my eyes, a leaf detaches from its branch and eddies to the ground. Game over for that one. And here's another, already dark and crisping. And another. And another. All of them dying, like it's raining leaves, raining death, and I miss Hugh, I miss him so much. I'd give all that I own just to go home and find him there, just knocking about the house, reading the paper, listening to music.

Hugh would provide an antidote to the snarly mess with Steevie. He'd pull me on to his lap and hug me, offering the warmth of his body to counteract the coldness in my gut. He'd let me rant, and he might even offer a calm counter-argument. But he's not here.

And it's a lot longer than six weeks that he's been unavailable to me. It's suddenly obvious that when he got the news his dad was dying, in August of last year, he checked out.

I'd found him in our bedroom, sitting stiffly on the bed, and the look on his face – strange and cold – made me think, *He's found out about Josh.* Even though it was over a month since I'd ended things with him, my guilt was never far from the surface.

'What's wrong?'

'Dad. He's sick.' Hugh's expression wasn't coldness, but shock, terrible shock – my guilt was distorting reality.

'What kind of sick?'

Cancer. I knew before he even said it.

'His lungs. It's bad, Amy.'

'But chemo –'

'No. He's . . . dying. He's going to die.'

This wasn't a time for platitudes. 'Tell me.'

'Three months.'

'It could be longer – doctors often get it wrong.'

'In three months my dad will be dead.' Hugh frowned and muttered, 'Twelve weeks' time. That's weird.'

When his mum, Sandie, had died eight years earlier, it had been a bitter, bitter thing. She'd been sixty-two, which was shockingly young, and she'd been such a wonderful person – warm, sensible, solid. She'd really been the heart of their home.

But within a year or so, the Durrants had rearranged themselves around her appalling absence, forming themselves into a new unit, possibly even tighter than before, always acknowledging their loss, but a family once again.

It might be odd to say but Hugh grieved his mum perfectly: he cried often; he had outbursts of inexplicable rage, which, aghast, he immediately apologized for; he looked at old photos and related fond memories of her. We grieved together, because I'd loved her too. In fact, the death of Sandie seemed to affect *me* more than it affected him. It felt like a small earthquake at my core, as if tectonic plates were shifting and collapsing, stopping me sleeping, propelling me to overeat and plunging me into a spell where everything seemed meaningless. It passed, but the aftershocks continued for a couple of years, and every now and then I'd have three sleepless nights in a row.

However, a powerful instinct was warning me that it would be different for Hugh this time. Maybe because this was his sole surviving parent. Whatever the reason, this time would be darker, uglier, scarier. And I needed to be there for Hugh. *Fully* present. Not frying rashers in my bra, daydreaming about Josh Rowan. That I'd ended things with him felt like a clean relief. 'We have to make those three months wonderful,' I said.

But there was no opportunity to fill Robert's final days with pleasure, no chance to tick off a few items on his modest bucket list. Right from the start he was grotesquely sick. He survived for two months and his suffering was shocking. Every morning I sent out a silent invocation to the universe: Please let him die today. Witnessing another person in excruciating pain, standing helplessly at their bedside, hearing them plead for morphine, was gruelling and surreal.

Hugh's brother Carl articulated what we were all thinking: 'Can't they do something? To . . . end this? Take him to that place in Switzerland? What do you think, Hugh?'

Stiffly, Hugh shook his head.

'No,' Carl admitted tearfully. 'I only said it out of . . .'

'Desperation,' I supplied.

'Yeah.' He gave me a grateful look but Hugh was no longer engaged. He'd closed up tight. He barely spoke to his brothers – and, to my surprise, he rebuffed my attempts to persuade him to talk. 'Don't, Amy. Let's just get through this.'

Finally, on a squally day in October, Robert was allowed to leave his body and my relief was so great that it took me a while to realize that he was dead. Then I cried and cried, because he'd been so nice, with his toolbox and his bad puns.

Just as Robert's death had released Robert, I thought it would release Hugh too: he'd shut down to endure his dad's suffering and now we'd move into a new phase of grief, a healthier, more cathartic one. But he remained shrink-wrapped and unreachable in unuttered thoughts and feelings, far, far away from me.

Sometimes it seemed there might be an opening – like the evening he announced, in the middle of *Game of Thrones*, 'He was seventy-three. No age.'

'It's far too young.' I grabbed the remote, all set for a heart-to-heart, but Hugh stood up and left the room.

Then there was the night in bed when he voiced, into the darkness, 'I'm next.'

'For what?' But I knew. His silent preoccupation with death was saturating everything.

'Sweetie . . .' I tried wrapping my body around his, but he lay tense and unresponsive.

I switched on the light and he switched it off again immediately. 'Night, Amy.'

'Hugh . . .' But he'd turned his back on me.

The time since Robert had got his diagnosis has been . . . lonely, I suppose is the word. But I hadn't fully faced it because Hugh and I still had the infrastructure of a shared life. He was still here in body and we had our routine and were civil to each other.

And all relationships go through good spells and bad spells – I get that, I really do. Not just marriages, but me and Derry, me and Alastair, me and everyone. There are times when your heart is bursting with love for them and there are spells when you tense up at the sound of them entering the room. That Hugh and I were going through a disconnected patch had been flickering in my subconscious. It had happened a couple of times in the past: when Hugh turned forty, he disappeared deep inside himself for a couple of months. Five years ago, when I was made redundant, there was a bleak three-month period when I felt detached from everyone, even Hugh. Eventually, though, we'd always bonded again. But this time we didn't.

56

The key to getting people to do something they don't want to do, is first to offer them options that are far, far worse.

'So!' My smile is bright, as I look at dreamy Matthew Carlisle, then at his considerably less dreamy brother. 'I've had calls from the producers of *I'm a Celebrity* and *Celebrity Big Brother.*'

I *have* had calls from them. Not in relation to Matthew. And not recently. But technically I'm not lying . . .

It's Tuesday morning and I'm in Dan Carlisle's kitchen.

'*I'm a Celebrity?*' His voice is sharp and he actually stands up to show his displeasure. 'Making him eat emu toes? *This* is your masterplan?'

I radiate control and seek the special voice that makes people do what I want. 'Not for a second. It's simply to illustrate that there's a lot of interest in Matthew.'

Matthew barely reacts. He's staring at his big, sexy hands, which are resting on his brother's kitchen table; his handsome face is pale and sad.

The *nerve* of those bitches on Sunday not being impressed that he's my client. Oh, shite, I shouldn't have remembered that lunch – the memory makes my stomach lurch. On Monday morning, I'd had to sneak over to Steevie's before work, to retrieve my abandoned car. Steevie's Mini was still in her drive: there was a good chance she'd open her front door, come marching out in her suit, and spot me. Crouching low, I scurried furtively car-wards but part of me was hoping to see her. Face to face, we'd stand a better chance of getting past whatever weird shit had gone down. We'd probably hug and both apologize and laugh a little and cry a little and then we'd be grand. We've had scraps in the past, of course – we've been friends a long time – but this felt more rancorous than any of our other bust-ups.

I drag myself back to the present, where Dan Carlisle is giving me the full sarcasm. 'Let me guess,' he says. 'You've signed him up for *Strictly Come Dancing*?'

Frankly, that would be bloody fantastic. Something tells me that Matthew can't dance but would try very hard to learn – the combination of leading man looks, clodhopper feet and earnest, furrowed diligence would get him as far as Hallowe'en, maybe even to Blackpool. I could see Bruno in convulsions at Matthew's salsa, saying, 'My darling, you are truly terrible, but you gave it your all!' Then collapsing into more paroxysms and awarding him a six out of pity.

He'd be the darling of the nation by the end of week two.

'It's nearly the end of October,' I say to Dan. 'Way too late for *Strictly*. Now, please sit down.'

Dan Carlisle's kitchen, a super-sleek white lacquer and steel affair, is my worst nightmare. It's cold and hard and repellent. Just like Dan himself, in fact.

Gently I say to Matthew, 'You don't have to do anything you don't want to. It's not my plan to dumb you down.'

He looks at me gratefully.

'You enjoy cooking,' I say. 'In your comfort zone? How about *Celebrity Masterchef*?'

He nods. 'That might be all right.'

'Great.' I smile broadly. 'So you'd be okay if I contacted the producer?' No need to tell him I've already been on to her.

'I'd better start practising.' Matthew is suddenly energized.

'No need, you don't want to be too good – people don't like that. Being okay, then improving, that plays a lot better.'

'This is all so cynical,' Matthew says, once again mournful.

'Coming from the man who spends his time with politicians.' I smile.

'Yeah.' He grins back with unexpected cheer. 'This is far worse.'

'What else have you got?' Dan interjects.

Addressing Matthew, I say, 'You love dogs.'

'But Ruthie's allergic.'

I fight the urge to sigh. 'A dog might be a comfort to you now.' I've already made contact with a production company to gauge their interest in making a half-hour documentary about Matthew Carlisle and his new puppy.

'If I get a dog, won't it look like a sign to Ruthie that we really are over?'

Matthew may as well treat himself to a pack of full-grown huskies – from the way Ruthie has thrown him to the media vultures: she obviously wants nothing to do with him ever again.

Unless I'm wrong. Isn't every relationship a mystery, which reveals itself only to the two people who are in it? 'Think about it,' I say lightly. 'It would be heart-warming.'

'Heart-warming? He's the cleverest man in Britain!' Dan sneers.

Why was this asshat even here? 'Shouldn't you be at work?' Attached by a long rattly chain outside a remote warehouse, tensed to bark at intruders?

'You know what, I should. But taking care of my brother is more important.'

'*I* can take care of him.'

'Can you?'

'What other ideas have you?' Matthew asks. I'm guessing this happens a lot, him having to pour oil on waters that have been troubled by his brother.

'Okay, hear me out.' This is going to be a harder sell. 'Have you heard of a show called *Deadly Intentions*?'

It's a late-night comedy on BBC2, a dark subversive thing, which features a character called Matthew Carlisle, who says stuff like 'I'm Matthew Carlisle and under my suit I'm wearing Angela Merkel's knickers.'

Matthew says, 'I'm Matthew Carlisle and when I come I shout out, "Bernie Sanders!"'

Right. So he knows the show. That, at least, saves me the very awkward task of explaining it to him.

'You want him to go on that?' Dan almost combusts. 'It's offensive!'

'Just light-hearted silliness.' More confident smiling from me. 'But if Matthew could out-Matthew the Matthew character, people would love it. Showing you can laugh at yourself is very endearing.'

'Okay,' Matthew says. 'I'll do it.'

'Well, great!' I hadn't expected this to be so easy.

'"I'm Matthew Carlisle and I'm prepared to humiliate myself on national telly if it means clearing my name."'

'Ha-ha-ha, good one, funny.' Actually it *was* quite funny.

'So what do I have to do?'

'They start filming the new series in November.'

'November?' Dan pounces. 'So when will it be on telly?'

'Early next year. Remember what I said to you when we met last week? This is a long-term project, a slow, careful recalibration of how the public perceive Matthew.'

'But what's going on *now*, people thinking he's a nanny-shagger, is killing him. We insist you do something *today*.'

'Matthew,' I say. 'We can end this here. I'll refund you for the unused hours and you can find another publicist.'

'Oh.' Matthew seems startled. 'Are we that bad?'

'This relationship needs to work for both of us.' I'm pleasant but firm.

'Oh. Well. Yes, but . . .' Matthew turns to his brother. 'I want to stay with her.'

Dan closes his eyes. He looks a little sick. And I feel – because I'm only human – triumphant.

'Dan is just looking out for me.' Matthew is earnest. 'We've only ever had each other.'

'I sympathize.' Which isn't true. I neither sympathize nor not-sympathize, I just want to do my job. 'But all this aggro isn't helpful.'

'Sorry,' Matthew says. 'We'll be more cooperative.'

'Thank you.' I'm gracious in victory. Apart from the side-eyes I flash at Dan, but it happens so quickly, you'd barely notice. 'A few more things. You should ally yourself with a charity, so think of one you're passionate about. And you support Fulham, right? Start showing up at matches. Eat pies. Look approachable. Now, Twitter. I need access to your account to supplement your content.'

'Videos of cats dancing.' Once again Dan is sneery. But, to give him his due, he immediately mutters, 'Sorry.'

'Puppies,' I say. '*Puppies* dancing. Matthew is a dog person.' I engage Matthew in intense eye contact. 'I cannot emphasize this enough – no romance. Not a one-night stand. *Nothing.*'

And, you know, there's the tiniest flicker, a barely visible blink-and-flick, that I can't decipher.

'It's *vital,*' I say.

'Okay,' he says.

'We're clear?'

'Clear.'

'One final thing, the Media Awards on Friday week – congratulations on being shortlisted. But no plus one allowed.'

'Ruthie always came with me to these things.'

'I know.' I make consolatory noises. 'But you can't bring a female companion this time.'

'Not even Mara Nordstrom? She's a colleague.'

'Matthew, *no.*' Mara Nordstrom is one of the most lusted-after presenters on telly.

'You've got to think how an ill-timed photo of you and Mara would look to the Great British Public. If you really want an ally, bring Dante.'

Matthew throws him an aggrieved look, and Dan says, 'Charming.'

'I'll be there,' I say. 'You'll have lots of support.'

'Oh. Oh-*kay.* That's all right, then.'

'Good.' I gather my stuff.

'I'll see you out.' Dan follows me down the hall and says, over my shoulder, 'Nice move back there. Offering to jump ship. Now he *really* trusts you.'

'Because he can!' Out of Matthew's earshot, I vent some frustration. 'What is your problem with me?'

'Just trying to take care of my big brother.'

'He already told me that.'

He looks appalled. I'm pretty appalled myself. This is unprofessional. 'You know what?' His face is furrowed with shock. 'You're like one of those snappy little dogs.'

'Actually, *you*'re like one of those snappy little dogs!' I step out into the street and feel the door slam shut behind me.

'Nice kitchen, *Dante*,' I say out loud. Then, much louder, 'Not!'

57

'Mum,' Neeve says, when I get home from work on Thursday, 'is your phone off?'

'No. Why?'

'Because Dad rang.'

My heart jumps almost out of my mouth – Hugh rang?

'About a charity ball,' Neeve says.

I'm frozen. I'm right on the edge where unbearable relief falls away into unbearable disappointment: Richie Aldin. Yeah, I'd seen his call come in and, no, I hadn't answered it because I've already declined his wretched effing charity ball about a hundred billion times and his caper is bordering on harassment.

'He said the three of us should go together!'

Her happy, hopeful face strikes the fear of God into me and this is something that needs to be handled right now. 'Neevey, I'm not going to the ball thing.' My tone is gentle. 'But let me talk to your dad about it.'

I find his number and ring him. He answers too quickly. 'Amy?' All eager.

'Can we meet for a chat?'

'I can come to yours.'

'Starbucks in Dundrum.' I'm not prepared to travel any distance. 'How soon can you get there?'

'Oh, you mean right now? But I'm at home in Clontarf. It'll take a while.'

'Get driving so. Text me when you arrive.'

'Wouldn't it be easier if I just came to you?'

'Text me from Starbucks.'

*

287

My phone beeps.

I'm here. What you like to drink?

Mint tea.

Okay, on it! xx

Richie looks smiley and happy, delighted to see me. 'Amy.' He leans in for a kiss and goes for the mouth, something I'd half expected so I turn away in time. This surprises him, but not for long.

'You look great,' he declares. '*Cute* coat.' He makes some signal to the lad behind the counter, who materializes with a pot of boiling water, for my mint tea.

'Didn't want your tea getting cold on you,' Richie explains, with yet another smile. I hadn't noticed this before but at some stage he'd obviously got veneers: his teeth are unnaturally square and even. Can teeth be described as smug?

'I got you a muffin.' He slides a plate across the table to me. 'Cinnamon okay?'

He pours my tea. 'So what's up? Couldn't wait until Saturday week to see me?' A flash of the smug veneers.

'Richie, I'm really not going to that ball with you.'

The expectant expression on his face doesn't change. 'You don't like that sort of thing? I guess you do a lot of them in your job. Well, how about dinner? Anywhere you like! The Greenhouse? Guilbaud's? Or we –'

'Richie, I don't want to go to anything with you.'

'Why not? You're on a break.'

'Hugh's on a break, but I'm not. And even if I was, I don't have those sorts of feelings for you.'

'You just need to try. C'mon, Amy, remember the way we were? *I* do.'

There must be a name for this, the utter absence of empathy. It's obviously some sort of personality disorder. Would it be narcissism? I must google the exact symptoms.

'You deserve to have things made right,' he says.

'But it no longer matters.'

'It does to me. I feel guilty. Amy, I'm . . . troubled. I wake up at night and I'm thinking about you and Neeve, and you were so young, the age Neeve is now, and on your own and I screwed you on the money and –'

'I forgive you. You already know that.'

'But the remorse won't go away.'

I shrug helplessly. 'I don't know what to suggest. Maybe you could walk the Camino.'

'But it's more than just guilt,' he says. 'I'm still attracted to you.'

Oh, for the love of God.

'Yes,' he says. 'I mean sexually.'

How can I not laugh? *Yes. I mean sexually.* This will make a fabulous anecdote. Wait till I tell Hugh – oh, God, Hugh is gone. But other people. Derry. It already has the makings of a great catchphrase. *Yes. I mean sexually.*

May I have that leg of lamb? Yes. I mean sexually.

I LOVE your hair. Yes. I mean sexually.

He must think my hoot of mirth is an expression of pleasure because he continues, earnestly, 'It doesn't matter that you're in your forties. So am I. When I look at you, seventeen-year-old Amy is the Amy I see.'

'Stop, Richie.' He's making a show of himself. I'm actually embarrassed for him.

But could someone please tell me what's going on? Is this some sort of cosmic consolation prize? The universe takes away one husband, a great one, and as a salve, re-gifts you the gobshite you'd loved twenty years ago?

How strange that, once upon a time, a Richie pleading for forgiveness would have had me delirious with joy. Suddenly I wonder if Hugh and I will sit together like this one day on opposite sides of a table in a busy Starbucks, when we're all done and dusted and consigned to The Past? The thought elicits a stab of unbearable grief.

Where does love go when it dies? Into flowers and other beautiful things? Back out into the universe to be recycled? Because

Richie was right: he and I had loved each other passionately and now nothing remains, except his self-indulgent, long-overdue guilt.

'Trust me, Amy,' Richie says. 'We can go back to the way we were.'

'We absolutely can't.'

'You're not trying. *Try*. You have to because I can't take feeling this way.'

'Richie, maybe you should see a doctor. Get yourself checked out, it'd do no harm.'

'You're punishing me!'

It's not my intention. But I can't give him what he wants, not now, it's years too late, and with that I see that everything passes. Everything passes in the end, good and bad, love and pain. It's a bittersweet truth to hold on to. *Everything passes in the end.* 'Go into therapy,' I suggest. 'Or volunteer in a soup kitchen. One way or another, Richie, just learn to live with the guilt.'

'Okay.' Unexpectedly he's all bluster. 'If you won't see me, I won't see Neeve.'

Now I'm scared. But only for half a second. Because just say I was mad enough to go along with his bullshit request, he'd tire of me super-fast and Neeve would be kicked to the kerb once more. 'Seriously, Richie, threats? This is how you make things right? Maybe treating your daughter with kindness might help dampen down your guilt. Why don't you take her to the poor blind children's ball?'

'I only wanted –'

'Richie, you need to hear this. I don't want to spend time with you. I don't want to see you.' I stand up. 'I don't want to hear from you unless it's about Neeve.'

'Ah, no, Amy –'

The knife rattling on the plate, I slide the muffin back to him. 'One last thing, I hate cinnamon. I've always hated cinnamon. Everyone knows.'

Neeve is hovering by the front door. 'How'd it go?'

'Neeve.' I swallow. 'Let's sit down.'

She knows. I can see it in her. She knows what I'm going to say and already her tears are falling, my poor Neevey, who almost never cries.

We sit knee to knee on the sofa, her hands in mine.

'Neeve, I love Hugh,' I speak softly, because I'm speaking to a little girl. 'You'd like your daddy and me to be together, and that's easy to understand. But it was a long time ago and I love somebody else now.'

'But Hugh is so mean.' The tears are gushing. 'He's gone away and left you, and Daddy is here and he's sorry. He told me, Mum, how sorry he is, how he wishes he could change everything. He'll fix it all, he told me. He'll fix it for both of us, for the three of us.'

'But I love Hugh.'

She cries short, hard howls, as if they're being stabbed out of her.

It is excruciating.

I let her cry because there is nothing – *nothing* – else I can do.

58

Saturday, 29 October, day forty-seven

Saturday morning, it's not even ten o'clock, and already I've ordered a satin skirt from Asos, done the weekly shop, made a frittata, read the papers and wondered if Steevie will ever talk to me again. There's a lot to be said for insomnia.

And here's Kiara.

'Morning,' I say. 'Will we put up the Hallowe'en stuff today?'

'Is there any point doing Hallowe'en without Dad?' She sounds mournful.

Thanks to Hugh's skill with electronics, we always have the best house on our road at Hallowe'en, maybe even the best house in the whole estate – thunder and lightning boom and flash in the garden while screechy cackles and hollow laughs ring out. Every single year since we moved here, he's dressed up as an executioner to give out sweets. But even with his chainmail helmet and mask, all the kids know who he is. I love watching him doling out mini-Haribos to little ghostlings and tiny skeletons, all of them saying, 'Thanks, Hugh, thanks, Hugh.' And sometimes 'Deadly costume, Hugh.'

'There's every point in us doing it!' I say stoutly. 'We're still here, we count too!'

'Mum,' Kiara says, 'I feel, you know, resentful of Dad. For going away. At the start I kinda admired it but now I'm, like, angry.'

'Kiara.' It's good she's told me, but the burden of saying the right words is onerous. 'He loves you with every bit of his being. Going away like this, it wasn't a – a . . . you know, a jaunt, a jolly. It was something he had no choice about.'

'Do *you* believe that, Mum? And don't lie just to make me feel better.'

'Hand on heart, Kiara, I truly believe he had no choice. He hated having to hurt us but if he didn't go, his mental health was really going to suffer. He was already on anti-depressants.'

'He was? Oh, poor Dad.'

'Granddad Robert dying did something to him that he couldn't manage.'

'So weird,' she says. 'I thought when you were Dad's age that things like people dying didn't upset you.'

'Well, there you go.'

'Wow. So! We'll Hallowe'en the house.' Kiara never stays down for long. 'I'll wake Neeve and Sofie.'

She thunders up the stairs and I hear Neeve grousing about being woken early on a Saturday morning for 'some Hallowe'en bullshit'. But by the time I've arrived on the landing, she's out of bed. For no reason at all she hugs me. Something has shifted since Thursday night: we're suddenly closer.

Sofie sticks her head out of her trapdoor. 'Hallowe'en! Cool!'

'Where's the decorations?' Kiara asks.

'Up in the roof space.' One of us will have to crawl in there to get the boxes. It's usually Hugh. So now it's me. I don't even sigh.

Neeve hands me the torch and I carefully climb the foldaway ladder that Hugh had installed. In the beam of torchlight the boxes are easy to spot: Hugh has drawn a skull and crossbones on them to distinguish them from the Christmas decorations, which are marked with green trees. Shite, there's a spider, a black, thick-legged horror, sitting on the top box. I give it a hard glare and it scurries away.

'Go, me,' I say – quictly, though, because it's not good to be talking to myself even if it's simply a device to make me brave.

The girls cluster at the foot of the ladder as I descend with the boxes. Then they start dragging stuff out. 'Pumpkin lights! Grave-stones! Cobwebs! This is sick!'

'What's this?' Neeve pulls out a length of black fabric. 'Oh! Hugh's costume!' She balls up the executioner outfit and lobs it in my direction.

'Why am I getting it?'

'You've to be both parents now,' Neeve says. 'G'wan! Put it on!'

She's joking – apart from anything else it would be swimming on me – and we all manage to laugh.

'Oh, well,' Kiara says. 'Next year we'll be back to normal.'

But when they've hurried away to plant gravestones by the front door, I put the costume to my face and take a cautious sniff. It's nearly a year since he's worn it so it's unlikely that any trace of him still lingers, but it does and a wave of memory makes me dizzy. The exact Hugh smell: it's impossible to describe, warm, sweet, earthy, just *him*. The nostalgia, the terrible sense of loss, momentarily feels unbearable.

But it *is* bearable, I remind myself. I've survived worse.

Just after four o'clock Derry appears, with three dresses – it's Kiara's Hallowe'en social tonight.

'Any word from Steevie?' she asks quietly.

Since the disastrous brunch a week ago, I haven't contacted Steevie and she hasn't contacted me. Worse, neither of us has liked any of the other's Facebook posts, the modern equivalent of pistols at dawn.

I hate being on the outs with anyone but, right now, Steevie and I can't be what the other needs. It's shit, but what can you do?

'Show us the lovely dresses!' Beautiful things might take my mind off it.

'I thought this was seasonal-looking.' Derry waves a black, floor-length velvet sheath, with a thigh-high slit, at Kiara.

'Give me that.' I go straight to the label. It's Givenchy. 'Aaargh! I knew it! God, Derry, you're good to yourself. *Why* can't we be the same height?'

'Because life is shite.'

This strikes me as so funny that I hoot.

Kiara tries on the dress. She's so tall and slender and beautiful that I have to swallow convulsively. 'I dunno.' She's trying to hold the thigh slit closed. 'I don't think it's me.'

'Stand up straight,' Derry orders. 'Go on, you're a stunner.'

'Ah, no, give me another one to try.'

The second, a double-layer of navy silk jersey from Preen, also fits. But the back is cut all the way down to the waist and, as Derry points out, 'You can't wear a bra.'

Kiara colours and says, 'I can't not wear a bra.'

'You're not exactly Emily Ratajkowski.'

'I'm wearing my bra.'

God, she didn't get her strong will from me!

The third dress is a slender column of heavy creamy-white satin – long-sleeved, high-necked, very modest – very Kiara.

'It's like a wedding dress,' Neeve exclaims. 'Is there something you want to tell us, Derry?'

Derry gives her a scathing look.

'You're my hero, Der!'

'I like this one best,' Kiara says.

'Corpse bride,' I exclaim.

'Totally!'

'You'll need a head thing.' Neeve is googling. 'Black flowers. A veil. Mum, look in your sewing box!'

There are definitely black fabric roses in there. I remember the day I bought them, less than two years ago, at the Taney Christmas fair. Every summer and Christmas, the fair was a family tradition but one by one the girls became too grown-up to come. Two years ago was the first time that all three of them bailed on me. I still wanted to go – there would be cakes and cheap books and the possibility of stumbling over something wonderful – so when Hugh saw my gloom, he said, 'Feck the rest of them, you and me will go up.'

We held hands and we had fun. There was a stall strewn with sewing accessories and, encouraged by Hugh, I loaded up with ribbons and fabric appliqués, which cost half-nothing.

Hugh also hit pay-dirt when he found a red fibreglass sled. 'Look!' he cried. 'It's in perfect condition. Neevy would love this, right?'

I wasn't so sure. Neevy was a bit grown-up for sledding. All of them were.

'Ah, no.' Realization hit him at the same time. 'Why can't they be little girls for ever?'

'I know.' I was mournful.

'Let's have another baby,' he said.

I laughed a soft, wifely, you-total-lunatic laugh. Now I wished we'd come straight home and had sex. Not in the hope of having another child but because it was a moment of connection we should have jumped on.

Well, it's too late now so I return to the task at hand. I'm certain there's a length of white toile in the box that would do for Kiara's veil. 'I'll need a hairband.'

'On it!' Sofie is all business. 'Leave the hair stuff to me.'

Neeve sits Kiara on a kitchen chair in the middle of the living room, applying corpse-bride make-up, while I sew black roses on to a black velvet hairband. Derry presses the white dress, then carries on down the laundry pile. 'As I've the iron on, I might as well.'

At some stage we open one of the boxes of Celebrations I'd bought for the Hallowe'en kids. A while later, Derry, Neeve and I have a glass of Baileys. It might be the alcohol or the sugar, but as I lounge on the sofa, watching Neeve apply false lashes to Kiara, Sofie leaning against me, Derry sitting on the floor, her head on my knees, I realize I feel okay. My life is so far from perfect and in five minutes' time I might be in so much sorrow that I'll want to tear my heart out, but in this moment I feel content and I'm so bloody glad for the respite.

'Can I look yet?' Kiara asks.

'Nope.' Neeve has painted her face white and created thick purple circles around her eyes. Now she gives her black lipstick, and when that's done, Sofie jumps in, backcombing Kiara's hair, clipping in dark blue hair extensions, twisting locks into Medusa-like ropes, then blasting the whole confection with salt-spray.

'Okay, Amy,' Sofie says. 'Now do her veil.'

Carefully I attach the black-rose hairband and veil to Kiara's elaborate nest of hair, then step back.

'That looks great,' Derry says. 'Really great.'

'*Now* you can look!' Neeve decrees, sticking a mirror under Kiara's nose.

'Oh! Oh!' Kiara squeals. 'I look good, right?' Her gleeful face is still there under all the make-up.

'You look *amazing*.'

'Now, you'd better have something to eat,' I say.

'Oh, Mu-um,' Kiara complains. Then, 'Okay.'

'Pasta all right? I'll do you the butterflies.'

I throw some red stuff from a jar over Kiara's pasta and she says, echoing what Hugh and I – *Masterchef* fans – say, 'That's a good-looking plate of food.'

She really is the sweetest creature.

At five past seven her date arrives.

'Ten minutes early?' Derry is suspicious.

'Good manners,' I say.

'Super-neurotic, more like.'

I hiss a sharp 'Shush!' at her.

Neeve opens the door to him. 'Are you Reilly? Kiara will be down in a minute.'

'Come in, till we have a look at you,' Derry calls.

'Ah, no, I'll just –'

'Come in!'

'I think you'd better,' Neeve says.

So in the poor lad shuffles.

It's hard to tell what he's actually like because he's made up as a vampire – white foundation, black guy-liner and a lot of red drool around his mouth. But he's tall, which is nice, because Kiara is also tall and self-conscious about it.

And here she is, tripping down the stairs. They squeal at the sight of each other. 'Dude!'

'*Duuuuude!*'

'You're totally Hallowe'en-tastic!'

'You're *more* Hallowe'en-tastic!'

Kiara leaves in a flurry of 'Bye, Mum. Bye, everyone!'

'Um, bye,' I bleat. 'Have a good time. Have you your phone?' I've to fight the urge to call, 'Don't have sex.'

The door slams shut behind them. Then the four of us stare at each other, our eyes popping.

'Our baby girl is all grown-up!' Neeve exclaims. Then, 'Oh, Mum! You're not fecking crying *again*?'

It's late on Saturday night and I've just realized that Jana is ghosting me.

I'd texted her twice during the week, once to thank her for being nice to me at the toxic brunch, then a second time to make sure she'd got my first text. Both times deafening silence was what I got in response but I was so busy angsting about Steevie blanking me that I neglected to realize that so was Jana.

Five minutes ago, paranoia hit me, like a slab of concrete, and when I checked my Facebook timeline, Jana hadn't liked any of my posts since last Saturday.

She's picked a side. Until now I hadn't known there were sides to be picked. I'd thought Steevie and I would sort this out and soon. But apparently it's bigger than just me and Steevie.

Now I'm afraid: who else is Steevie going to recruit? Because I'm certain that Jana didn't unilaterally decide to take agin me. Is Steevie going to turn everyone against me?

I'm also terribly hurt. I'm so fond of Jana – I feel very tenderly about her. I don't like when people mock her for being silly and I've stood up for her against several people including – yes! – Steevie. If Jana is being allocated, *I'm* the one who deserves her.

But haven't I learnt that that's not the way life works?

59

Wednesday, 2 November, day fifty-one

Caroline Snowden, the journalist sitting opposite me, has something to get off her chest. I wait it out.

'Amy,' she says eventually. 'Ruthie Billingham's done a big interview for this week's *Sunday Times* magazine.'

Shite. This is the first print interview Ruthie has done. Until now, everything has been 'sources close to'.

'Look, you're going to have to put out this fire.' Caroline brings our lunch to a premature finish.

'I'm so sorry, Caroline.'

'It's time I got back, anyway.' She's really nice. 'We'll see each other soon.'

I give her the full-body hug in gratitude, and I have twenty-one minutes before my next meeting. Think, think, think . . .

Right. A photo op with the kids. Where? In a playground? Hmm, something more meaningful would be better. Okay, got it, the football!

I reach for my phone. 'Matthew?'

'Amy?' He sounds distracted.

'Can you talk? Couple of questions. When are Fulham next playing a home match?'

'This Saturday.'

'Can you take the kids?'

'It's my weekend with them and we have season tickets.'

'Even Beata?'

He half laughs. 'Gender stereotyping, Amy!'

'Ha-ha, my bad.' Come on, I don't have time for this. 'Okay. I need to see you ASAP.'

'Why? What?'

'To set up a paparazzi op at the match.'

'I'm not having my kids in a paper.'

They've already been in several. 'They'll pixellate out their faces.'

'It's wrong. Can't I just be at the match on my own? Or with Dan?'

For a clever man, he can be astonishingly clueless. 'Matthew.' I'm gentle. 'Two blokes. At a football match? Forgive me for being crass but it's nothing *like* tragic single dad on a rare afternoon out with his two beloved children.'

I actually hear him swallow. 'Today is crazy.'

Right. It's Wednesday, when he does his shaming-the-politicians show.

'All I can spare,' he says, 'is fifteen minutes around five thirty.'

I'd miss my flight home, but so be it. 'You're at the BBC? I'll meet you there.'

'So something's finally happening. Dan will be happy.'

I doubt that very much.

Seconds before I arrive at the BBC, there's a strange twang on my right shoulder, followed by a swift droop of my right breast. What the . . . Oh, God, one of my bra straps has just given up the ghost.

Desperately I look along Oxford Street – there's a Marks & Spencer so near I can almost see it, but I can't chance being late for Matthew. I need every available second with him. Maybe I could nip to the Ladies, pin the strap back to the main body of the bra and hoist my knocker upwards once more? But that assumes I've a pin on my person and I don't . . .

My frontage is lopsided, I can tell just by looking down at it. I could take off the bra entirely and then my low-slung shelf would be at least symmetrical. But, no, decency insists that the bra stays on.

Shite. This is terrible timing, and unfortunately I'm wearing the wrong clothes – some days I'm in strict tailoring, which assists in keeping everything corralled. But today it's a high-collared

Victorian-style dress, which provides no support. There is nothing to do but style this out, so I swing my right arm forward, clamping my right knocker under it and move forward in Quasimodo-esque fashion.

From the hard stare the security guard at the BBC gives me, it's clearly not working. However, the show must go on. I do the usual rigmarole of signing in, getting a lanyard and being told someone will come and fetch me. Then who do I see, cooling his heels in the giant marble lobby? Only Dante. Not today! Not when I've just had a knocker emergency! And what the hell is up with the brothers Carlisle? Must they do *everything* together?

Dante's inspecting the ceiling, then checks his phone and then, with a sharp snap of his neck, spots me. Instantly he looks like an aggrieved whippet, as if *I'm* the one who shouldn't be there. Briskly, his heels clipping on the cold floor, he crosses to me. 'What's going on?'

'Hello to you too.'

He pauses, straightens the lapels of his suit jacket, then seems to gather himself. 'Sorry. Hello, Amy. But why the sudden need for action?'

Childishly, I don't want to tell him. 'Client confidentiality.'

He seems almost sad. 'I'm here to help.'

'Your help isn't needed. Seriously, Dante, I'm very good at my job.'

'Yes, you are.'

I receive this with a stiff nod.

'And I'd prefer if you called me Dan.'

'I know.'

He sighs audibly.

'Dan? Amy?' One of the thousands of people who work in television, indistinguishable with their clipboard, headset and trainers, has materialized.

We go up in a lift and the headset boy says, 'Matthew's in a meeting. He'll be out soon.'

On the third floor, Dante and I follow the minion down endless corridors and through clusters of workspaces. The underling is going at quite a lick and it's a hard job to keep my rogue knocker from jumping right out from the bra cup. Eventually, in a clearing outside a small office, the glass walls shielded with black venetian blinds, we stop. 'Wait here,' says the minion, who promptly disappears.

There's nowhere to sit. Dante gets out his phone, then so do I, but neither of us is giving them our full attention because we're waiting for Matthew to emerge and we both want to get to him first.

Finally he materializes from the glassy office, trailing a couple of other people. Dante and I hurry towards him – we're this close to actually shoving each other out of the way.

'Amy.' I get a cheek kiss from Matthew. 'Come in here.' Dante and I follow Matthew back into the office, which really is tiny, more of a cubicle. You'd think a man as important as him would have his own penthouse suite, but the BBC must be very egalitarian because there's barely room for the three of us around the tinchy desk.

'So?' Matthew's nervous.

'Okay. And it *is* okay.' I'm being Reassuring Amy. 'Ruthie's got a big interview coming in this weekend's *Sunday Times*.'

Matthew swallows. 'Saying what?'

'I haven't seen it. But I hear it's more of the same. Hints but nothing actionable. She's still getting flak for Ozzie Brown, which is why she's continuing to throw shade at you. We've no choice but to act now.'

'An interview!' Dante declares.

'Shush, Dante! I've told you why that's a bad idea and I'm not telling you again. We're doing a photo op.'

Matthew takes off his black-rimmed glasses and rubs his face. 'Okay. Let's hear it.'

'Paparazzi shots of you at the football with your kids. The picture we want to create is single dad, doing his best, while his wife has left him for another man.'

God, the pain on his face.

I give him a moment and say, 'The children must be warmly dressed and look cared for.'

'They *are.*' This, of course, from Dante.

'Do they have Fulham hats, scarves, all of that?' I ask Matthew. 'Good. The three of you will look like a mini-team of your own. Now this is important, Matthew. Be safety-conscious. Don't let the kids stand on the backs of the seats in front of them. Nothing that might make you look like a bad dad.' We could do without a Britney-driving-the-kids-with-no-seatbelts scenario.

He nods, chewing his bottom lip.

'Have lots of toys ready in case the kids start crying.' It would be potentially disastrous if photos of weeping Carlisle kids were taken on people's phones.

'And plenty of treats. But no chocolate or sweets.' That would also be Bad Dad stuff. 'Raisins, rice cakes, you know. Finally, look affectionate.'

'I don't need to be reminded to look affectionate with my own kids.' His mouth is mutinous.

'Of course, sorry, of course.' Such a delicate flower! 'But go big on it, Matthew. This isn't the time for subtlety. And I need your seat numbers to identify the optimum spot for the pap.'

'The idea of being spied on . . .'

To my surprise, tears start to roll down his face. I locate a tissue in my bag, then take his hand and close it around it. 'I'm sorry, Matthew, but it'll be worth it in the end.'

'Will you be there?' Matthew asks me, and no one could miss the alarm that lights up Dante's face.

'You can't be seen with another woman, remember?' I'm gentle. 'And this can't look staged – a PR person hanging around won't do your cause any favours.'

'But I can call you? From the match? If I need to?'

'I'd advise against it, Matthew. You're spending time with your kids. If you're caught on your phone, it's going to look like you're bored. So no checking emails or anything. Your phone doesn't exist for those two hours, right?'

'Matthew.' A young woman sticks her head around the door. 'I've got your shirt.'

'Greta?' Matthew wipes his face with his hands. 'Five minutes?'

She shakes her head and just about manages to squash into the tiny space, carrying a shirt and a handful of ties. 'Needs to be now. Time for make-up.'

Matthew stands up. 'Excuse me,' he says, in my general direction, then pulls his T-shirt over his head and tosses it to Greta. Sweet Jesus, the abs on him. Actual real-life abs. It's a long time since I've seen that sort of thing. And the chest! Dusted with dark hair, just the right amount, not too much, nothing gross.

Greta takes a vanilla-coloured shirt off a hanger and, in a rustle of freshly ironed cotton, Matthew shrugs it on and does it up. Before my astonished eyes, he quickly unbuttons the waistband of his trousers and unzips the zip, giving a shockingly enticing flash of navy Calvins and dark hair leading down to an evident bulge and – Oh! No! Way too quickly, the show is over: the shirt is tucked in, the thrilling stuff is covered with a bland white nothingness and I'm stunned with loss, as if I've been watching a gripping movie and suddenly, at the vital moment, the screen has gone blank. In under a second, everything is zipped back up and tidied away. Actually, my head is slightly reeling.

And what about Dante's face? Sour as you please. It must be hard to have a brother who's a demi-god. No wonder he's always cross.

'Well?' Matthew asks Greta.

'Good.'

He throws a dark tie around his neck, and Greta moves towards him. I see. Among Greta's duties is knotting Matthew Carlisle's tie.

'No one does it like Greta,' he says apologetically.

Greta says nothing while lifting his shirt collar, then methodically threading the tie over and under, her youthful face mere millimetres from Matthew's beautiful one. What a job! Mind you, she probably has a PhD in political science and hates every demeaning second of this.

When she's done, she silently holds out a little hand mirror to him, clearly part of a well-worn routine.

'Nice and fat.' Matthew shifts the knot a little and smiles. 'Thanks, Greta.'

Matthew is hustled away by Greta, then Dante and I and my rogue knocker make our way back downstairs into the outside world.

'Can I give you a lift?' he asks.

'You live in Islington. I'm going to Heathrow.'

'Can I do *anything* helpful?'

'No.' I'm abrupt. Then, 'Actually, would you be able to get me a map of Fulham's ground?'

He focuses on something in his head, his eyes flicking as he considers options, the same eyes as Matthew's, I notice, the only thing they have in common.

'How soon do you need it? ASAP, I know. Tomorrow morning do?'

I nod. What now? There's a spare hour before I should leave to catch the later flight. There's plenty to be done – nailing down a photographer, making contact with the picture editor at one of the nationals, probably *The Times*. But I'm tired and I need a new bra and the thought of buying something is attractive – the thought of buying something is *always* attractive. The bra wins.

60

'I've booked us a cubicle,' Matthew said.

'Okay.' I was breathless.

'In Marks & Spencer. You go there first. Pretend to be trying on bras. I'll see you in fifteen minutes. *For* fifteen minutes. That's all I've got, then I'm on the telly, shaming politicians.'

'Fifteen minutes is fine.'

Next thing I was in M&S. I'd picked up three bras and gone to a changing room. Just as I was wondering how Matthew would know which one I was in, the door barged open and he rushed in and was kissing me frantically. His glasses went skew-whiff and he took them off and flung them over the top of the cubicle door, and I said, 'Won't you need them?'

And he said, 'Wardrobe can get me another pair.'

'Did anyone see you come in?'

'Maybe.'

'No, but that's bad, Matthew, we might get caught.'

'That makes it even better. The chance of being found out. But we'd better be quick.'

He unbuttoned his trousers, took my hand and slid it inside – his erection was *huge*.

'Nice and fat,' he said.

'Like your tie knot!' I said.

'Nice and fat.' He laughed, and I thought, He's very different from the way I thought he was. Much more laddish.

I began pulling his trousers down and he protested, 'No, no, we can't take them all off. This is just a cheeky little shag.'

Somehow my knickers and tights were gone and he had his hands on my breasts because my dress wasn't a dress any longer

306

but a convenient top and skirt. He was standing up, I had my legs around his waist, he was inside me without any drama and it was all a lot easier than I'd anticipated.

He pounded himself in and out of me and we were looking at ourselves in the mirrors – we could see things from all angles.

'They're excellent,' he said. 'Aren't they?'

'The Marks & Spencer's mirrors? Yes, excellent.'

'You can see *everything*. You've a nice body,' he added. 'You shouldn't worry.'

I looked at myself and he was right: I had.

'I'm going to come now,' he said, 'because I'm late for make-up. So if you want to come, you'd better do it now.'

'Okay.' So I did. Then he did, and his face in the mirror reminded me of Richie's when I'd caught him with that girl all those years ago.

Next thing he was zipping himself back up. 'I'm leaving with Greta now,' he said. 'In five minutes you come out. Act natural.'

'Do I buy a bra?'

'Yes. I think I broke the one you've got on. And have you got the thing, the tag, with the number of items you took in?'

And then I woke up.

Jesus, that was quite a dream. I hadn't looked too bad in it . . . Then I realize that the body that had had sex with Matthew Carlisle was the one from twenty-five years ago.

I'm a little disturbed by it all – Matthew had been quite . . . *dislikeable*. Laddish, wolfish, even. And this morning I feel less compassionate and less protective of him than I had yesterday. Which is very unfair – it's hardly real-Matthew's fault how dream-Matthew behaves.

But something had happened yesterday in his little glass cubicle. A tiny moment so strange that I'd forced myself to file it away for consideration on some other occasion: when he was tucking his shirt into his trousers, it seemed like his hand, which was moving fast, slowed down infinitesimally when he reached his bulge. It seemed to pause for the briefest moment, cupping it – and while he was holding it, he had looked straight at me.

For way, *way* less than a second. This wasn't some lengthy, meaningful silent exchange, but something that was over as soon as it began. But our eyes had definitely met.

In fairness, though, was that even his doing? After all, the office was tiny and there was almost no place for his gaze to land. And, of course, it might have been an accident. Or perhaps he was touching himself as if his mickey was a talisman – I think lots of men do . . . to check that it's still there?

Then there was always the possibility that it was a look of apology: *I'm sorry you have to sit here and watch me partially undress myself.*

And maybe I'd just imagined the entire thing.

61

Friday, 4 November, day fifty-three

Mum has new hair! It's a blonde, bouffant bob, really glam. 'I got extensions!' she cries. 'Neeve organized it, got it done for free!'

'In exchange for a vlog, Granny. Nothing is ever free.'

'But that's no bother to me,' Mum says. 'I'm a natural at the vlogging, everyone says.'

Derry and I exchange a smirk.

'Well, you look *amazing*,' I say.

'I know! I'll tell you something, girls, all of those years when I was sick, I had no life, but it's never too late! I'm getting the two-week manicure on Monday, isn't that right, Neeve?'

'That's right, Granny.'

'And I'm thinking about an inking,' Mum says.

'Over my dead body!' Maura shouts from another room.

'In that case,' Joe says to Mum, 'please get it.'

To stop open warfare breaking out between Maura and Joe, Derry interrupts, 'I dumped my boyfriend.'

'Good for you,' Mum says. 'What would you want to be settling down for and you only forty-five? Play the field, love, play the field!'

I hoick Derry away for a private chat. 'What the actual? Is she on tablets or something?'

'You mean, anti-depressants? I don't think so. But it's all extremely fucking peculiar.'

'So what happened with your new man?'

'Nothing. His socks. They were the *worst*. Yeah, look, I know, I'm a commitment-phobe. We all have our thing.'

I'm just getting ready for bed when Neeve appears at my bedroom door. 'Mum?' The expression on her face worries me.

'What is it, sweetie? Come in.'

She sits on my bed but doesn't meet my eye.

'Tell me.' It's not like her to be reticent and my anxiety is growing.

Focusing on her hands, she says, 'Look, I don't know, I'm not sure . . .'

What's she done? Libelled someone in her vlog? Totalled Hugh's car? 'It can't be that bad.' Finally, she looks at me. 'Mum, I'm sorry. I wasn't spying, just like keeping an eye. On Hugh. On Facebook. And –'

Like a blow, I realize that whatever has gone wrong, it isn't about her. 'He's posted stuff?' It's a couple of days since I've checked.

'No. But he's tagged in someone's pic and –'

Automatically I'm reaching for my iPad. 'Mum, Mum, wait, wait a moment. Seriously, stop!'

So I stop.

She takes a breath. 'Mum, you need to prepare.'

That makes everything worse. My heart is racing, my mouth is dry. I need to see whatever it is and I need to see it *now*.

'It's okay.' My voice is high and unconvincing. 'I knew he'd be meeting other . . .' My fumbling fingers have opened Facebook. 'We agreed, it's all agreed –' Oh, shit.

It's Hugh. With a woman. Or a girl, really. Young. Pretty. Cute. Dark hair, shortish and tucked behind her ears, doe-like eyes, pointy chin. And Hugh, big and beardy, with a slightly ruddy tan. He's wearing his white linen shirt . . . and he's taken off his wedding ring. Well, of *course* he has. Why should that come as such a terrible shock?

They're on opposite sides of a rough, dark-wood table in what looks like a beach-bar at night – two identical bottles of sweating Thai beer stand on the wooden slats and a storm lantern flickers. Their heads are tilted towards each other – I mean, they would do for the photo – but everything fairly pulses with intimacy. Both of them, their far arms are stretched along the table, in two parallel arcs, almost but not quite touching.

I stare and stare while blood roars in my ears. The tips of my fingers are tingling and I feel as if I'm awake in a bad dream. I knew this would happen, knew it *was* happening, but to see it . . .

'Mum?' Neeve says, from far away.

Desperately, I try to get it together. 'Thanks, Neeve. Ah, thanks for showing me this, ah . . . You did the right – I mean, I'd have seen it myself soon. I look on his page most days.' I'm the adult here: she can't feel guilty about this and she can't see me fall apart.

'Mum.' Her voice is soft. 'It's okay. I know it hurts.'

The girl's name is Raffie Geras.

'Yes, but no, not really,' I babble at Neeve. 'Like I knew in *theory*, so it's all okay . . .' I'm clicking on Raffie Geras's page.

'Mum! Don't!'

She's Scottish, apparently, Edinburgh University, graduated in 2002, so she'd be thirty-five or -six, right? It's young but it's not shockingly so. Imagine if she'd been nineteen. That would have been much, much worse.

'Mum!'

She trained as a barrister – a barrister! How could I ever compete with *that*? I'm scrolling down her feed . . .

'Don't, Mum!'

There she is, snorkelling. There she is, on a boat. And – Oh, God. Oh, God, oh, God, oh, God . . . It's Hugh. In bed. Asleep. A white sheet covers him to his chest but it's obvious that he's wearing nothing. The bedroom is one of those simple South East Asian ones. A muslin mosquito net is gathered above the bed, slatted dark-wood shutters are on the window. Then I see the caption: 'Foxy Irish man in my bed.'

I'm going to puke. My feet hit the bedroom floor and Neeve scoots aside to give me a clear run at my bathroom. I barely make it. Everything in my stomach comes up in one go. I spend a minute or two slumped in place, waiting for my stomach to return to normal, then give my teeth a desultory brush and crawl back into bed.

'Christ,' I mutter, and close my eyes. The jealousy is hot and green in my veins and I start to shake, as if I've been injected with poison.

'Mum . . .' Neeve's voice is wheedling, apologetic. What is it now? 'Kiara and –'

'The girls!' I exclaim, sitting bolt upright. Kiara and Sofie can-*not* see the picture on Hugh's timeline. Because then they'll click on Raffie Geras's page and they'll see everything else.

'Exactly!' Neeve says. 'They can't see this. Hugh mustn't know that she's tagged him. You have to tell him.'

What should I do? Text him? Personal Message him? I could even ring him. This is a perfect opportunity. But I no longer want to talk to him – in fact, I don't think I could. A ball of toxic feel-ing has swollen inside me – a mix of grief, jealousy, betrayal and fury. I absolutely hate him.

'WhatsApp is the best way,' Neeve says. 'He reads his Whats-App.' Apologetically, she adds, 'It's what Kiara and Sofie have been using when they want to, you know, talk to him.'

This is so profoundly humiliating.

With trembling fingers I type, **Please get your girlfriend Raffie to untag you in the photo that's on your Facebook page. Make sure it doesn't happen again. You promised you'd protect the girls.**

'Show me,' Neeve orders. She reads it and nods. 'That's grand. Send it.'

'Is it bitchy to call her his girlfriend?' I ask.

'Who cares?'

I hit Send, then Neeve and I sit watching each other. 'You're not to feel guilty,' I say. 'Christ, I can't fucking breathe.' I heave air down into my reluctant lungs. 'I'm so sick of this.' Tears of grief and fury flood my eyes. 'But you're not to feel guilt–'

My phone beeps and my heartrate goes through the roof. My eyes can hardly focus on the words. **I'm sorry. It'll be gone asap. It won't happen again. Hugh xxx**

That's it? That's *all*? No enquiries as to how I'm doing? No denial that this woman is his girlfriend? Two months of silence and he sends *eleven words*? I didn't think I could feel more wounded or more angry, but apparently I can.

'Show me.' Neeve says. She reads in silence, then hands me a cushion. I shriek into it.

62

'Why are you watching a football match?' Neeve asks. 'Is it something to do with Dad?'

'Wh– Oh!' She means Richie Aldin. 'No. No. A work thing. A client is at the match. I'm just wondering how he's getting on.'

Every time they show the crowd, I search for Matthew and his kids but I don't spot them. In fairness, there are an awful lot of people there.

Last night, I literally didn't sleep for one second. I Facebook-stalked Raffie Geras for hours and hours. I stalked her friends, her family, her colleagues, and today I'm sleep-deprived, sick and stunned with shock.

I'd thought it was hard when Hugh first went away but that was nothing compared to this.

The photo had quickly disappeared from Hugh's timeline, but by scrolling through Raffie Geras's Facebook, this doesn't look like a casual sex-driven encounter. It seems more like an actual *romance*.

My worst fears are coming true: Hugh won't be coming back. It was delusional to think he ever would – once he got the newness and freshness he craved, the genie would be out of the bottle.

I'd sustained myself with the pathetic hope that, after plenty of empty sex, he'd start missing meaningful connection and decide he wanted me again. Now I'm watching the unfolding of a scenario I hadn't considered: Hugh meeting a new someone special on his travels and she's the one who'll provide the connection he may want.

He's going to fall in love with her – if it hasn't happened already, and it certainly looks like it has – divorce me and marry her.

And maybe that's what I deserve – maybe this is something I myself brought about, thanks to my carry-on with Josh Rowan.

I'm so grateful to have work to escape into. At around six o'clock, I get the images of Matthew with his kids at the match and they're golden. In every single one Matthew looks handsome, loving, kind and affectionate. There he is, crouching to tie Beata's shoelaces; speaking solemnly and lovingly into Edward's face; sitting with one child on each knee, his giant hands holding them steady; high-fiving Beata when Fulham score; squeezing Edward when Fulham eventually win; opening a mini-bag of raisins with earnestly fumbling fingers . . . Two or three shots have him laughing but mostly he sports this wonderful – and authentic – tragi-smile.

It's going to be a tough job narrowing these down to twenty or so for the newspaper. Out of the twenty, only three or four would make the printed version but they might run the rest online.

I already know that when the public see these pictures, their opinion of Matthew will improve. And they'll be *queuing* up to replace Ruthie – nothing as hot as a loving dad.

Of course, Matthew needn't for a second consider exploiting his hotness, he has to live like a monk for the foreseeable. But I'm slightly worried he might break out. He's done nothing wrong, but since that dream the other night, where we had sex in Marks & Spencer, I'm starting to think of him as a predatory cad. Which is mad.

'Sofie!' From her bedroom, Neeve is hollering. 'Come and sort my hair out NOW!'

There are the sounds of running feet and a sense of frenzy beyond my bedroom door because tonight's the night that Neeve is going to Richie Aldin's fecking charity ball. She's much more nervous than she's ever been about going on a mere date. *If he hurts her . . .*

Neeve has never had a long-term love. Well, of course she might have done – no doubt she has billions of secrets from me – but never a relationship where she brings the person over here to the house and we all lie around watching Drake videos together, the way we do with Sofie's Jackson.

Now and again she'd get uncharacteristically teary and fixated on someone but none of those – probably unsurprisingly – has developed into anything dull and ordinary. Recently – earning great approval from Kiara – she had a short thing with a girl but apparently 'I'm on the hetero-normative end of the spectrum and I feel, like, lame.' ('Hey, you *tried*,' Kiara consoled her.)

I used to worry that Neeve's apparent allergy to a steady love interest was Richie's fault. Had his serial abandonments damaged her ability to trust? Now I see I had it entirely wrong – what eejit would open themselves up to all that potential pain? Neeve is clearly far better off dedicating herself to her work and her friends, thereby keeping her heart safe.

I wish I'd had the sense to stick to the equilibrium I'd found after Richie had left me. It's wrong to say I regret meeting Hugh because Kiara is his great gift to me, but if I'd stayed as the self-reliant person I'd once been, I wouldn't feel the agony I'm currently in.

Kiara bursts into my room. 'Mum, come! With your sewing kit!'

It's like being a paramedic. Neeve's caught the heel of her shoe in the hem of her dress and torn a couple of stitches and she's as distraught as if there'd been a multiple car pile-up.

We fix her up, then she's good to go, groomed and cool. The dress, an asymmetrical black-and-white-lace affair by Self-Portrait is the fanciest thing she's ever blagged. The shoes, sequined black sandals are Dolce knock-offs and her black velvet choker is a copy of the Marc Jacobs one I'm currently lusting after. Her fabulous thick red-gold hair is piled on top of her head, adding about another four inches to her height.

'Mum, am I okay?' Her anxiety is tragic.

'You're stunning.' But the long and the short of it is, I don't trust Richie Aldin not to snap out of his hand-wringing guilt trip and revert to cruel, angst-free type. All I can do is hope he doesn't hurt her.

For the millionth time I hit Refresh. Still nothing. It's way after midnight and I'm waiting for Sunday's papers to come online. The thought of going upstairs and enduring a second sleepless night is so unbearable that pretending I'm working makes me feel a little less pathetic.

The worry is always that, despite their assurances, the *Sunday Times* won't run the Matthew shots. Until it's actually happened, you cannot trust any newspaper to fulfil their promises. Anything could scupper this – internal politicking, the whim of an editor or, of course, some disaster.

I take a swig of wine, then a swig of Gaviscon, hit Refresh once more and, finally, here are tomorrow's papers. Matthew is on page five, a great spot that guarantees maximum visibility. Sixteen of the twenty photos are up online, as well as a positive written piece, detailing the kids' warm clothing, Matthew's evident affection and how happy the three of them look together. Best of all, there's no mention of Sharmaine.

Then a quick scan of Ruthie's big interview: there are lots of allusions but no hard facts. I'm happy to declare this weekend's media a draw.

63

On Monday night Mum nabs me, yet again, for Pop-sitting. She looks radiant, really very beautiful. The new hair is wonderful and she's wearing a gorgeous pair of earrings. Well, gorgeous for *her*, some sort of blue stone surrounded by tiny diamonds. They wouldn't be for me in a billion years. 'Fancy earbobs,' I say.

'Some shop sent them to Neeve, for me! For free! All I have to do is Instagram them.'

'You're not on Instagram.'

'I am now. Neeve set me up. She does it all, takes the photos and that. But it's tremendous fun! I can't tell you how happy I am, Amy. In a way I feel like I've only just started living. Not just the hair and the vlog and my new red nails.' She flashes me her two-week manicure. 'But all of it. The new people and the gin-and-tonics and just everything.'

Something prickles in me, the same instinct that had stirred in the recent past. 'Tell me more about these new friends of yours. They all have spouses with Alzheimer's, you say? And would any of these new friends be men?'

She colours. She actually does. 'Of course there are men. The law of averages says that.'

'And how many of these men come along on a night out?'

She opens the front door and pokes her head into the cold night. 'Is that my taxi?'

I take a quick glance. There's nothing out there. 'So how many men come on these gin-and-tonic nights?'

'How did Neevy get on the other night with that waste of space Richie Aldin?'

She got on great. I suppose. She'd burst into my room at about three a.m., buzzing with happiness because she'd met loads of his friends and been introduced as his daughter.

'Mum, stop trying to distract me. So tell me, the gin-and-tonic men?'

'It's nothing like that, love. It's just a bit of fun. And gin-and-tonics, which are my new favourite thing.' Then, 'Amy.' She takes my wrist in a surprisingly strong grip and looks me in the eye. 'Pop, most of the time, he's in the land of the bewildered but there are moments when he's still all there. He's the man I married, and even though I find things hard going, I'd never hurt him.'

Instantly I'm sorry. Mum's life has been a sad one but finally she's having fun and, whatever she's up to with her ganky earrings and gin-and-tonics, it's her business.

64

Tuesday, 8 November, day fifty-seven

Today my tube from Heathrow on the Piccadilly line stops in a tunnel for twenty unexplained minutes, and I arrive late at Home House.

'Too much to hope that Matthew Carlisle isn't here yet?' I ask Mihaela, the receptionist.

'He's here,' she says. 'And looking lush. In the small meeting room on the third floor.'

I rush upstairs, all apologies, and Matthew Carlisle stands up, then leans down to kiss my cheek. He's smooth-jawed and smells like a mojito. Guerlain Homme, if I'm not mistaken. 'Um, hi.' This is the first time I've seen him since that unsettling sexy dream and it's an effort to deal with the real man instead of the cad who had seduced me in a Marks & Spencer's cubicle.

Lurking behind him is his brother. At this stage it no longer seems perplexing that he's always in attendance. No fear of Dante trying to kiss me, which suits me fine. Instead he gives a brusque nod and a terse 'Amy'.

'Dante,' I reply, and despite everything, it gives me a small squeeze of childish pleasure to see him wince. I will *never* call him Dan.

'So?' Matthew looks happy and hopeful. 'You think the photos worked?'

'There was no mention of Sharmaine,' I say. 'The shift has definitely started.'

'Safe to say we've turned a corner?' Matthew is bright-eyed.

Quickly I begin managing expectations. 'Those photos were a very good start, Matthew. But remember what I keep saying. This will be long and slow.'

'Long and slow?' He fixes me with his liquid eyes. And, honestly, I don't know if I'm still in the dream hangover, but that sounds suggestive. 'Okay.' He's suddenly mournful. 'So be it.'

I clear my throat and find my groove. 'Building on those photos, I've tickets for you and your kids for the preview of the new Disney film on Thursday evening. No need to organize paparazzi, they'll have official photographers. Also local news cameras, so say a few words. I've prepared some innocuous remarks. Don't deviate too far.'

'Okay.'

'How about a trip to Lapland early December? To meet Santa. You and the kids?'

'Um, sure.'

'*The One Show* will have you on to talk about it.' I run through various other proposals, all part of the mosaic that will eventually form the new, rebranded Matthew Carlisle.

'Fine, and now I really have to go to work,' Matthew said.

'Okay. See you both on Friday night in Brighton.'

65

'Deserted beach, Koh Samui' is the caption on the latest photo on Raffie Geras's timeline. Hugh and Raffie are sitting on soft white sands. She's snuggled between his legs, her back against his stomach, his arms tightly around her. They're both laughing – and why wouldn't they be, considering their proximity to crystal clear turquoise water and thickets of palm trees?

Mind you, their beach can't have been *that* deserted if they managed to get someone to take the photo. This gives me a sour satisfaction until I realize the camera probably just had a timer.

More tropical loved-up stuff is appearing daily. You can nearly *feel* the sultry, humid heat of Koh Samui coming off the photo. Here it's pissing down outside and already dark at four thirty.

A mad urge hits to send them a picture of me, sitting gloomily at my desk, titled, 'Deserted office, cold, rainy Dublin'.

Hey, to counteract the steady stream of carefree tropical languor she's posting, perhaps I should bombard the pair of them with pictures of my life!

How about 'Having a cold shower because something's up with the timer on the boiler and I haven't a notion how to fix it because that was my husband's job'. Then there's always, 'Watching *Inside the Minds of the World's Sickest Killers* with my Alzheimer-y dad who insists that I look like a dark-haired Myra Hindley'.

But it's imperative I don't drive myself mad with this. I've a duty to the girls to stay sane.

'What's going on?' Alastair walks into the office.

'Where were you?' I've been on my own in the office for over an hour and I don't like it.

'Getting man-scaped. Brighton tomorrow. Need to be ready for action.'

'Did it not work out with Sharmaine King?' Then, 'That's *the* single most naive question I've ever asked. When would that stop you?'

'I'm a serial monogomist, if you don't mind.' He's quite huffy. 'I'm not a cheater. And Sharmaine broke my heart.'

'Which is why you're all set for action tomorrow night?'

'Shur, lookit, life goes on. But, yeah, Sharmaine didn't want me.'

'Lifetime first?'

'Course not. I'm always falling in love with women who don't want me. Don't even notice me!' Suddenly he sees the picture on my screen. 'Oh, shit. Amy, stop stalking them.'

I wish I could. 'I'm thinking of sending them photos of my life. Like "Coming home after working an eleven-hour day to find there's nothing to eat, not even cheese, because my husband, who used to collect my monthly delivery from the cheese club, is now in Thailand banging some babe".'

'Oh, Amy.'

'Or "Me, my mind blown at the possibility that my mum is having an affair".'

'What? Lilian O'Connell, mother of five, having an affair?'

'Stay away from her, you dirty article.'

'Is there nothing left to believe in, in this empty, fucked-up world? She's not really, is she?'

'Probably just living life to the full, fair play to her. Is it five o'clock yet?'

'Twenty to.'

'Grand.' I grab my bag. 'I've had it for today. Getting my hair blow-dried, then meeting Derry for scoops.'

'Give her my best.'

I narrow my eyes. 'Stay away from my family.'

'See you tomorrow at the airport.'

'And I felt so guilty about Josh Rowan!' I rage at Derry. 'Now I'm fucking furious I didn't sleep with him.'

'So sleep with him now,' Derry says.

'How? I haven't seen him in more than a year. *And* he's married. But I'll tell you one thing, I totally get why Steevie wished for Hugh's dick to go green and fall off.'

My rage is epic. And underneath it is a loss so huge, so terrible, that I can't even look at it.

'Any word from her?'

'She unfriended me on Facebook. On any other week I'd be devastated, but all my devastation is used up.'

'You two will work it out.'

'I don't know, Derry. I don't even know if I want to. And another thing – I'm certain about this – I'm done with Hugh. Maybe if I hadn't seen those photos we could have got through this. But that hope was ridiculously naive.'

She shrugs. She'd always thought it was.

'Even if Hugh comes home and still wants me, which I doubt, I'll never get past it.'

'You're a survivor,' Derry says. 'And you'll meet someone else.'

'Absolutely not. I will *never* go through this again. Der, tell me how great it is to be single.'

'It's honestly the best. I get home and close the door on my little house and it's just *me*.'

'Don't you get lonely?'

'Never.'

There is more than one way to live. I tuck that thought away.

One of my many fears of being a single lady at my age and beyond is of becoming an unglamorous serene type. My hair would be shorn and free from colour so my head would look speckled with iron filings. I'd rise at six every morning and give thanks for blessings, and at Kiara's wedding I'd show up looking attractive-in-an-aged way, like yoga people do, with pretty wrinkles but no jowls. Those women usually have astonishingly taut jawlines and their skin is clear and bright, like they've been lashing on gallons of ascorbic acid, even though you know they haven't because they only use Dr Hauschka, which won't even let you have a night cream.

I don't want to be that woman. Far better to be a drunken Botoxed mutton. At least there'd be a bit of life in me.

And I see now I don't have to go the way of the yoga ladies – Derry is still glamorous.

'I don't think I could live with someone else now,' Derry says. 'I'm too used to pleasing myself.'

Derry has had long-term relationships, the equivalent of marriages. She knows what she's talking about.

'And if I do get lonely,' she says. 'I can always meet a man.'

'You're talking about sex,' I say. 'How could I do that with someone new? Like, look at the ancient old state of me.'

'If you fancy someone and they fancy you back, you get overtaken by passion and you don't care what you look like. I'm telling you, Amy, us peri-menopausal women, we're *crackling* with sexual energy.'

'I'm not. I'm more interested in having someone to watch telly and eat crisps with. Honestly, Derry, some of the happiest times of my life were lying on the couch with Hugh watching a boxset. Like, I didn't know at the time I was living the dream, but I was.'

'You're used to being married and you can get unused to it. One day you won't care about Hugh.'

'Despite all that he's done, that's a terrible thought.'

'It's a terrible thought *now*. But give it a chance. Don't be so co-dependent.'

'There's a difference between co-dependence and healthy mutual interdependence.'

She looks at me speculatively. '*Psychologies* again? You know what? This has happened. He's gone. And before that you were messing around. I know!' She stems my protests with a raised palm. 'You never slept with Josh Rowan. But, Amy, it was an emotional affair. Think about it – think about it *very hard*. You wanted something that you weren't getting from Hugh and your "healthy mutual interdependence".'

66

It's Alastair on the hotel phone. 'How's your room?' he asks.

I survey my mean-looking single bed and cramped shower-room. 'A shithole. You?'

'Same. Ideal if you were planning to blow your brains out. How's your "view"?'

'A dirty wall, about six inches away.'

'Still! It's good to be here.'

And, actually, it is. I've decided to work hard on being glass-half-full about my new normality, and being in Brighton for the Media Awards is good. I want to be around drunk people who are having fun. I want to dance and seize the day and stay up late and have a laugh. I want distraction, to connect with other humans, to know that I'm still alive.

'Come down for a drink,' Alastair says. 'Let's see who's around.'

'I've a quick meeting with Matthew Carlisle.'

'Oh, the pep-talk. Yeah, listen, this hotel is crawling with paps. He really needs to be on his best behaviour.'

Too right. But Matthew is *alarmingly* naive and needs constant reminders of the importance of optics.

My cupboard-like room is in a basement annex and there are two flights of stairs to be climbed before I reach the lobby and take the lift to Matthew's room on the top floor.

The hotel is teeming with people, several already swilling down the drink. After I've bumped into a few I haven't clapped eyes on in forever, I wonder, not for the first time, if Josh is here. Seeing him would be awkward, even thinking about him is painful.

The top floor is another world of light, air and wide corridors.

Matthew's room is right at the end. I knock on the pale oak door – and, oh, my God, there's a click and a flash of light from behind me! A photographer!

Whoever it is, they're holed up two rooms down from Matthew's. I scurry down the corridor, give the door a sharp rap, and when no one appears, I call, 'I'm Amy O'Connell, I'm Matthew's *publicist*.'

The door opens. It's a paparazzo I vaguely know and I start laughing because it's all so mad. 'Len . . . ah, Lenny? Right, Lenny. I'm his publicist, you fool. Amy O'Connell, you know me!'

Belligerently, Lenny says, 'He could be diddling you.'

'He's not.' I'm still laughing. I think it's the adrenalin. 'He's not diddling anyone.'

Lenny looks deflated.

'But everyone else will be diddling each other tonight,' I say. 'You won't go home empty-handed. Right. Bye.'

I give Matthew's door another good ra-ta-tat-tat and after ten seconds I hear the sound of hurried footsteps. Then the door is wrenched open.

'Sorry!' Matthew's shirt is crumpled and he looks stunned with tiredness. 'I fell asleep. Come in.'

'Oh, this is *lovely*.' His room is actually a suite. It has a living room with two sofas and armchairs, and the whole place is flooded with blue light.

'They upgraded me.' He stifles a yawn.

I rush to the window. 'A sea view!'

'You didn't get one?'

I laugh. 'I'm lucky I got a bed. So? Dante around?' I expect him to be hiding in the wardrobe.

He smiles. '*Dan*'s room is on another floor.'

Yeah, I can well believe it. Dante is probably billeted in the Shithole Annex along with me and all the other nobodies.

'Coffee?' Matthew asks. 'Or something else?' He gestures at a sideboard. 'Look. I've a bar with full bottles of alcohol.'

'God, no. Long night ahead. Coffee is fine.' He has an actual Nespresso machine!

He carries the two cups to the table by the sofa. 'Okay,' he says, fixing me with his brown eyes. 'So, tonight's instructions. No women?'

'You *have* been listening. Seriously, circumspection around all females.'

'No slow dancing at the disco? No grinding?'

'No disco at all.'

'What? It's a tradition.'

'Photos of you over-refreshed and enjoying yourself? No, Matthew.' Time to get brutal. 'There's a pap stationed in a room two doors down from here.'

He goes pale. '*Why?*'

'Because you're Ruthie Billingham's husband. Because Ruthie is still churning out cheating hints. The press, the public, they want incriminating photos.'

He puts his face into his hands. 'When is this nightmare going to end?'

'I don't know. All I can promise is that it will. Meanwhile you hold the line.'

He exhales, long and world-weary.

'Another thing, Matthew. Just say you don't win your award tonight?'

'You mean, "in the unlikely event"?' He tries an unconvincing twinkle.

'Exactly! You must smile. A lot. Clap enthusiastically.' In PR terms, it's almost better to lose graciously than to actually win.

'Got it.' Then, 'Do you think I won't win?'

'Of course you'll win.' He won't. Jeremy Paxman will win.

'Not Paxman?'

'Not Paxman.'

'I bet you a tenner.'

'You're on.' Shite. That's a tenner gone. 'Finally, what are you wearing tonight?' It's a black-tie do. 'Is it a hired suit?'

'It's mine.'

'Show it to me.'

It's from Zara Man. At least it's not a sharp-cut designer beauty from the likes of Gucci. All the same . . . 'Just try not to be too good-looking tonight, okay?'

'How do I do that?'

I'm not quite sure whether to laugh or not. 'See you later, Matthew.'

Downstairs in the bar, Alastair is waiting and Tim has joined us.

'How's Matthew?' Alastair asks.

I shake my head. 'If . . .' It's hard to find the exact words. 'If . . . yeah, if he had a sense of humour, he'd be the ridiest man on the planet.'

Something passes over Alastair's face and, in exasperation, I demand, 'What?'

'I've a sense of humour? *I'm* funny, right?'

I boggle my eyes at him. 'Funny *peculiar.*' I do a double-take. 'And needier than usual.'

Then, to my great surprise, Tim – Tim! – asks, 'Have you a crush on Matthew Carlisle?'

'Um, no.' I feel myself colour because *Tim* . . . I'm so uncomfortable talking emotions with him.

'I never feel right unless I have a work crush,' he says.

I'm speechless! The best I can manage is, 'But you and Mrs Staunton . . .'

Gravely he says, 'Mrs Staunton, I'm sure, has work crushes of her own.'

'But you don't actually do anything with these crushes of yours?'

He gives me a wry look, then twinkles – *twinkles*!

'You're messing with me,' I say, then beseech Alastair, 'He's messing, right?'

'You're asking me? I'm in worse shock than you.'

'Please, Tim, not this week of all weeks. I need something, someone, I can depend on. Please say you're joking.'

'I'm joking,' he deadpans. But I'm not sure I believe him.

67

'And here to present the award for Political Broadcaster of the Year is . . .'

This is Matthew's category and it's no surprise when Jeremy Paxman wins. Matthew jumps to his feet, claps wildly, wolf-whistles, then gives me a meaningful nod across the huge ballroom and mouths, 'You owe me a tenner.'

Dante Carlisle follows Matthew's gaze, and when he sees me, he looks cross. I blow him a kiss.

When the award-giving finally ends, the fun bit of the evening begins. I plan to table-hop, meet tons of people, go to the disco and dance till they throw me out.

But, first, I'd better commiserate with Matthew and give him his tenner.

He's sitting all alone at the big round table. Everyone else must have lunged towards the bar.

'Too bad,' I say.

'Told you Paxman had it.' Matthew attempts a smile but it wobbles off his face.

'Are you okay?' Did he want to win that much? Alarmed, I slide into the chair next to his. 'What is it?'

'Just . . . I miss my wife.' He twists his body away from the room and towards me. His gaze is fixed on the table-top. 'I still can't believe she's left me.'

Wide-eyed, I nod.

'Every morning when I wake up, there's a moment when I pretend it hasn't happened. Then I have to face it and the sense of loss . . . It's like being a kid again, when my dad left.'

All I can do is nod. This is agonizing.

'It's not just Ruthie I miss. It's our family, the four of us.'

Now I'm wishing he'd stop talking.

'Like Eden before the fall. It was perfect but it's gone.'

Hugh had adored me, he'd adored all of us – me, Neeve, Sofie and Kiara. We were a happy family. I haven't lost just him, I've lost every bit of it, our unique five-way dynamic.

A lump is swelling in my throat.

'People thought I took care of Ruthie,' Matthew says. 'But she took care of me, we took care of each other and . . . Are you okay? Amy? Are you okay?'

'Yep.' I nod, even though tears are spilling from my eyes.

'God! What did I say?'

'Nothing. Sorry. This is embarrassing.' I wipe my face with the back of my hand.

'Tell me. Please.' His brow is furrowed oh-so-handsomely. 'Please,' he repeats.

I know it's unprofessional, but I'm broken. 'Can I show you something?'

'Of course.'

I touch my phone a couple of times and scroll down through various stuff until I find Raffie's most recent photo, of herself and Hugh on a dock, wrapped around each other. 'See that man there? The man with that woman? That's my husband.'

'But he's –'

'Yeah. With another woman. They're in Thailand.'

'And . . . what? How do you know about it?'

'We're on a break. Well, he is. Six months. He'll be back in March. Except he won't be, will he? I mean, would you come back?'

Matthew's face is shocked concern. 'Amy, do you want to duck out of here? Knock tonight on the head? No one will notice. Come on, I'll see you back to your room safely.'

Suddenly I've run out of all steam, all strength, and I just want to escape. 'Okay.'

We stand up, and Dante appears out of nowhere, carrying drinks. 'What's going on?'

'Amy's calling it a night. I'm seeing her to her room.'

His eyes flick from my face to Matthew's, then back again. 'I'll do it,' he says. He puts the drinks on the table. 'You stay here, Matthew.'

'No.' I don't want Dante anywhere near me.

'Yeah, but –'

'I'll be back in five,' Matthew says. 'Stay here.'

As we walk away, I say to Matthew, 'What's up with your brother? Is he in love with you?'

He gives a short, dry laugh. 'Something like that.'

Oh, Jesus Christ. Jesus, Jesus Christ, it's Josh Rowan. Standing at the ballroom doorway, talking to someone. He's seen me, his eyes are locked on to mine. I thought I didn't want to meet him. I thought too much guilt was attached to the very notion of him. But now that I see him, it all comes back – the longing, the wanting, the wishing that things could have been different.

I see my own yearning written on his face. For a long moment, despite the jostling revellers, it's like there are only the two of us here. I can actually feel his emotion and I'm sure he can feel mine. Without speaking, we're communicating and it's as if the sixteen months since we've seen each other have telescoped down to nothing.

A drunk man, with a head like a blood-blister, throws an arm around Josh's neck, shouts jovially into his face, pulls him away and they disappear from view.

When Matthew and I push through the doorway, I scan the crowded lobby for Josh but he's nowhere to be seen. Matthew is all business, walking me down the back stairs, then sliding in the keycard and sticking his head around the door. 'Just checking there's no one hiding under the bed,' he says. Then, 'Oh, my God, it's like a cell!'

'It's fine.'

'It's appalling. I can't condemn you to this. Come up to my room for a while. We can have a drink.'

'No, no.' I haven't the bandwidth.

'One drink. I don't want to be on my own, not feeling like this. You'd be doing me a favour.'

'Ah, what the hell?' I say. 'All right.'

*

Matthew's suite has had a turn-down service, the lighting is ambient, and soft classical music is playing. I go to the window. It's too dark to see the sea now but I can still hear it, sucking and splashing. The sound is calming.

'Take a seat.' Matthew indicates the sofa, then surveys the line of bottles on his sideboard. 'What would you like to drink?'

'Vodka, I suppose. And Diet Coke.'

He pours a hefty measure into a heavy-bottomed glass, then joins me on the sofa. 'So tell me.'

I take a gulp of my drink, open my mouth and let my desolation unravel. My glass empties surprisingly quickly and Matthew refills it and encourages me to keep talking.

'Actually, no,' I say. 'I'd prefer to stop. This misery is exhausting and I'm sick of being sad.'

From outside comes the sound of music, the disco must have started and suddenly my mood changes. 'Hey, Matthew, there's no point wallowing! Let's go down to the disco, I want to go dancing.'

I'm a little drunk, but unexpectedly it's happy drunk, not maudlin.

'I can't go to the disco,' he says. 'You said.'

I clap my hand over my mouth. 'Oh, God, sorry!'

After an awkward pause, I exclaim, 'We could have our own disco here, stick on some songs. Really! It'll be great!' Guilt is firing my enthusiasm.

Matthew starts fiddling on the in-house sound system, and some dancy thing comes on that I half recognize. Kiara probably plays it, then I hear 'Groove Is In The Heart' and my mood soars. 'Oh, I LOVE this song!' I jump to my feet and kick off my shoes. 'Turn it up! Matthew, turn it up!'

Instantly the music is ten times louder and pulsing off the walls. The bassline is inside me and the melody is all around me and I feel *alive*. I twirl myself around the room and, briefly, all my worries lift away, there's just me and the music and I feel happy and free.

Then I notice him watching me dance, his face tense and still.

He's relaxed his body against the sofa, his arms spread along the top. His black tie has disappeared, his shirt collar is open three buttons – I don't remember that happening – and out of nowhere I'm super-aware of undercurrents. *It's like I'm giving him a lap-dance.* The thought makes me excited, uncomfortable, then a queasy mix of the two.

'Louder!' I say.

Moving only his arm, still watching me avidly, he reaches behind him and, without looking, twists the volume knob.

His silent gaze is too much. 'Come on, get up and dance.' I take his hands and pull him out of the seat.

He's on his feet, still watching me intently. 'Dance with me,' he says.

'I *am*.'

'Don't dance *at* me, dance *with* me.'

He tries to grab me around my waist and I twist away. But he comes after me, slides his hands around to my back and pulls me against him.

'No!' I don't want to slow down, I don't want to stop. But in a fluid motion, he sweeps my hair to one side, buries his face in my neck and gives it a small sharp bite. Suddenly he's got my attention. I'm not dancing any more. I whisper, 'What was that?' I want to move away but his arms are hard against my back and, caught in his force-field, all I can do is look at him.

His face is coming closer to mine, he's moved one hand to the back of my head and he's pulling me towards him. Then his mouth is on me, hard and probing, he means business, things aren't going to end at this –

I wrench myself free. 'We can't – I can't!'

I'm panting, he's panting, his shirt is crumpled and his eyes are wild.

He groans and I repeat, 'We can't.' I push myself away, creating distance.

'Why not?'

Because . . . because I don't want to.

I'm a bit drunk, I'm in shock, but I'm certain about this.

'I'm not sorry.' He steps towards me again. 'I've wanted to do that since forever.'

'You have?'

'Since the first time I saw you.'

They're good words, I should be flattered, but I'm not . . . 'What about Ruthie?'

'What about your husband? We could comfort each other.'

No. No way.

My phone rings, startling me. It's Alastair.

'Where are you?' he asks.

'Why?'

'Are you with Matthew Carlisle?'

'Yes.'

'Meet me in the lobby right now.' He sounds furious. 'If you don't come down, I'll be up to get you.'

I turn towards the door – and Matthew blocks me. 'Don't go.'

For a half-second I think it's more flattery, but he's suddenly a menacing figure.

'You've told me to stay away from all other women,' he says. 'So you've got to . . .'

Oh, God. Oh, my God, this is awful. And scary.

'If I don't go downstairs right now,' my voice is shaking, 'Alastair's coming up here.'

His face darkens with impotent fury. 'Go, then.' His mouth is a bitter twist.

Alastair is waiting, with Tim and Dante Carlisle, in the heaving lobby.

'Over here.' Alastair leads us to a sofa and the four of us sit.

'Have you?' Alastair asks. 'Did you?'

'Get with Matthew Carlisle? Would that not be my business?' I ask.

'No,' Alastair says. 'Number one, he's a client.'

God, he's a fine one to talk.

'Number two,' Dante says. 'He's having a thing with Sharmaine King.'

Oh.

'Sorry, Ames,' Alastair says. 'It's true.'

'How do you know?'

'She wouldn't, you know, sleep with me and wouldn't tell me why. But I suspected. When Dante here told me, I rang her. It's true.'

My head is trying to keep up. 'Is that why Ruthie left?'

'Last straw,' Dante says. 'He slept with all their nannies.'

'He can't keep it zipped.' Alastair sounds almost prim.

'There are other women too,' Dante says. 'Always.'

'But he loves Ruthie.' Well, he does a very good impression of it.

'He *does* love her,' Dante says. 'That's the tragedy.'

'Then why . . . ?'

'He's a sex-pest.' Alastair's tone is judgemental.

'Pot, kettle.' Tim speaks for the first time. His voice is croaky. Any trace of twinkly Tim has vanished.

'He's miles worse than me.' Alastair is earnest. 'Dante has stories.'

'Probably more politically correct to call him a sex-addict,' Tim says, 'than a sex-pest.'

I round on Dante. 'Why didn't you say?'

'He's my brother.' He makes a helpless gesture. 'But I tried to make sure you were never alone with him. I didn't want you working together, but he was adamant.'

Maybe that explains Dante's antipathy. 'I thought you just didn't like me?'

'I don't. I don't like you.'

Tim interjects: 'Why not?' He sounds angry.

'She's bossy. It's her way or the highway.'

'If she was a man, you'd call her efficient.'

I've a question. 'So was that all a line about Ruthie seeing Ozzie Brown for the past two and a half years?'

'No. That's true.'

'What about Greta?' I ask. 'Greta from Matthew's work? Is he – yes? Oh, God.' I knew it. The wolfish way he'd behaved in my dream. And despite all the weirdness of this evening, I have to say, fair play to me. Ten out of ten for intuition. 'So what happens now?' I ask.

'You stop working for him with immediate effect.' Tim's emphatic.

'Send a bill for the remaining hours.' Dante says. 'I'll sort it out. And I'm sorry for everything.'

'Hardly your fault your brother can't keep his lad in his pants.' Alastair has clearly never felt so far up the moral high ground.

Dante offers me his hand and says, 'Pleasure not to be working with you any longer.'

'Likewise,' I reply.

After he's been swallowed by the crowds, Alastair says, 'Sorry, Amy, if you thought you and Matthew had a thing going.'

'I didn't.' He's good-looking but, I don't know . . . Not sexy. Not to me, anyway. Something was warning me off him.

'By all accounts he'd get up on a cracked plate.' Alastair shakes his head sorrowfully.

'Oh, Alastair.' Tim's tone is bone-dry. 'This might be the happiest night of your life.'

'Well, I'm going to the disco to dance to the Killers,' I say. 'Are either of you coming?'

Josh might be there, he might not, but right now all I want to do is get drunk and dance.

68

Saturday, 12 November, day sixty-one

The heat wakes me. It's *roasting* in my tiny hotel room, like being buried alive in a furnace, and even though it's only just gone seven, I must get out.

I have a quick shower, pull a comb through my hair and lipstick across my mouth, throw on my coat and slip through the lobby, still peopled with randomers in last night's party threads, out into the day.

The sky is streaked mauve and royal blue – it'll be properly light soon – and the breeze is brisk and pleasantly chilly. I'm headed for the sea: I want to hear the waves and breathe in the salty air. The pebbles crunch under my too-high boots as I make for the water's edge. There's no one out here but me – the entire hotel is probably still deep in a drunken sleep. It's a wonder I'm awake myself. I'd danced like a mad thing with Alastair for hours and hours and it was nearly three when I'd tumbled into bed.

Mind you, I'm not fully with it. I've that disconnected thing hangovers give, where everything seems to be happening at one remove, almost as if I'm watching a movie of my life.

The small, polite waves aren't doing it for me. Huge, crashy breakers would be better at clearing my head.

I called it wrong with Matthew Carlisle, which is all kinds of disappointing. I've started the rehabilitation of a man who doesn't deserve any of it. And the loss of income is a bummer, especially coming up to Christmas. At least I didn't sleep with him. Small mercies and all that.

Along the beach, a person appears out of the dawn gloom, heading in my direction. Someone else who's woken early and is walking off a hangover. It's a tall man in a dark overcoat, his collar turned up against the chill. In my numbed, dreamy state, I almost convince myself that I've conjured him out of my imagination. It's Josh.

Our eyes meet, we walk directly towards each other, and when we're a few inches from touching, we stop. Neither of us smiles.

'So?' he says. 'How've you been?'

Although it's over a year since we've spoken, we've bypassed all social niceties and gone straight to the intimacy we shared during those lunches we shouldn't have had. And I don't know how he found out, but he knows about Hugh. 'Mmm, my marriage has gone a bit weird.'

His eyes are sympathetic. 'Aye.'

My lips clamp tightly together. I'm ashamed.

'I haven't been stalking you,' he says, 'but I still think about you, and now and again I . . . check Facebook. Sometimes I can't not.'

I shrug. 'How are things with you?'

'The same.'

'Your wife still doesn't understand you?'

'Don't.'

'Sorry.' Fervently I add, 'I *am* sorry. It's guilt.'

'You didn't do anything wrong.'

That's not true. 'I keep wondering if it was my fault that Hugh left. If he knew subconsciously that I'd been cheating. Because I *was* cheating, even if we never did anything, you and I.'

The breeze smacks a gust of chilly sea spray-speckled air against me, but I don't shift; it's a great relief to be face to face with Josh, to be talking about this.

'Can I ask you something?' he says. 'If you hadn't been married and I hadn't been married, would you have . . . ?'

I think about it, really consider it. 'I'm not sure we're temperamentally suited.' I could never have been so honest without the distancing effects of my hangover. 'But the physical thing, attraction, whatever you want to call it, that was, um, strong.'

Something flares in his eyes. 'Aye. It was.' Then he adds, 'Still is. At least in my case.'

338

Wearily, I admit it. 'Me too.'

'Right, ah . . .' He swallows hard. 'So what's stopping you?'

Very little. I've already lost my marriage. 'Your wife.'

'You want me to leave her?'

'Christ, no! The opposite.'

Perhaps it's disillusionment in the wake of the revelations about Matthew Carlisle. Finding out what he's really like, so soon after seeing the photos of Hugh, is making me think that monogamy is a lost cause. No one seems able for it. Not Hugh, not Matthew, not Josh, maybe not even Tim.

It's as if everything has turned to ashes and, right now, I feel there's very little left to lose. Well, except this notion I have of myself as a decent person. And that's probably no longer enough to stop me.

When I first started obsessing about Josh, my mad hope was for something magical to finesse away all awkward ethical considerations. But nothing is going to do that. If this is what I want, it's up to me, a grown-up, to make a grown-up decision.

'In every life we do stuff that isn't congruent with our moral core,' I say. 'Right?'

'Right.' He sounds wary.

'We do things we know we shouldn't because we're weak and want-y.'

His eyes have narrowed as he tries to follow my philosophy.

'Josh.' My tone is strict. 'You're never to talk about leaving her. You're *not* to leave her. And this needs to be time-limited. It's the only way I can okay it with my conscience. Until the end of the year, then it stops.'

'What do you . . . Amy, what are you saying?'

'Tuesday night, in London. Book a room.'

69

Monday, 14 November, day sixty-three

Not black satin. And *certainly* not red satin. No corsets, no basques, nothing remotely tacky. Nothing lace, nothing crotchless, nothing kinky.

In the end I buy plain black knickers and bra. Maybe they're not entirely plain, they have a sateen sheen, but there aren't any hidden surprises, like no back to the pants.

Reluctantly I also buy stockings and a suspender belt because I simply can't do tights to him, not on our first night. And I won't do hold-up stockings to myself, they can't be trusted not to detach themselves from my thighs and float down my legs just when I'm crossing a crowded bar.

And now it really is time to go back to work, my Monday lunch hour has lasted 128 minutes.

'How'd you get on?' Alastair asks, when I slink back into the office.

'Where's Tim?'

Alastair nods at the meeting room and its closed door. 'In there.'

Fine. I can speak freely. 'Sorry I was so long. But mission accomplished.'

'So you're all set?

'Nearly. I'm getting a spray-tan done this evening. The lightest shade. Just to take the pasty edge off my ancient body. And . . . I really shouldn't be telling you this, but what harm? I got waxed yesterday.'

'Oh? You mean . . . ?' He moves his eyebrows towards my groin.

'I usually work a nineteen-seventies vibe down there. Hugh likes – *liked* it. You probably think that's revolting.'

340

'No, I – Actually, let's not have this conversation. So you've made your peace with your repulsive body?'

'There's nothing I can do about it. I am the age I am, I've lived the life I've lived. And he's no nineteen-year-old either. He's forty-two. It's funny, Alastair, I don't want him to be like, you know, David Gandy, all abs and muscles. That would intimidate the daylights out of me. But I don't want him to be flabby and . . . you know. I want him to be the same level of decrepit that I am. Well, maybe not *quite* as bad as me.'

'So where's this thing going down?'

While I'd been out, Josh had texted: Sarah Hotel, meet at bar on top floor at 7.

'Sarah Hotel,' I say.

'Whoa!'

'I know. Fancy, right?'

'I've never stayed there but, yep, fancy. Spendy. He likes you, Amy!'

Anxiety spasms through me. 'Oh, fuck, now I've the fear. But what's the worst that can happen?'

'You tell me.'

'Well.' And these are thoughts that have tormented me since I threw out my invitation on Saturday morning. 'I might lose my nerve entirely, and develop vaginismus, thereby locking Josh Rowan out of my hidey-hole.'

'That would be grim.'

Grim is right. I lose myself in a picture of Josh slamming his blood-engorged penis up against me like a battering ram. I feel ExcitedHorrifiedScaredTurnedOn.

'Or Josh might find my forty-something body so slack and gross he won't be able to get it up.'

'That won't happen. No offence, Amy, but men, most men . . . Well, you've heard the saying that we have enough blood to run a brain and a penis, but not at the same time. Anyway, you're fine. You're cute. I'm sick telling you.'

'*Alternatively*,' I speak over him, 'it might be okay, by which I mean, *just* okay. Nothing special. Something neither of us could

341

be bothered to repeat, and that would also not be pleasant. I've spent a year and a half giving him a lot of space in my head. I'd be morto if there was no substance to it.'

'Then again, it might be amazing,' Alastair says.

'Word! Like Derry said, this isn't Josh Rowan's first rodeo. Surely he knows how to show a girl a good time.'

'It doesn't work like that,' Alastair says. 'You wouldn't believe the bad sex women put up with. The number of girls I've had to rehabilitate –'

'No, please, Alastair, shush now. Anyway, I'm not looking for hot monkey sex or – or – or nimble-fingered technique –'

'You want romance.'

'I need a *narrative*. And I need to believe there's a future for me, after Hugh.'

'With Josh Rowan?' Alastair sounds alarmed.

'No. Just a future. I don't know exactly what I mean, but I need to check that I still exist. And don't tell me that I do.'

'Wasn't going to. Like I said, Hugh leaving has fucked with your sense of self. It takes time to process that. You're flailing around, looking for other markers.'

'Is that what this is? And, morally, is that okay?'

'Not ideal. Josh Rowan is a human.'

'One I like.' My tone is heated. 'One I fancy.'

'Who has a wife.'

'Yeaaaaah.' There was no arguing away that shameful fact.

70

Tuesday, 15 November, day sixty-four

In the lift up to the top-floor bar, a gang of fabulous types pile in, looking like they've come straight from a yacht in Portofino.

I stare at my new shoes – black Rock-stud wannabes with needle-thin heels – and try to blind myself to the sun-kissed limbs, the gorgeous floaty dresses and the effortless glamour of my fellow lift-goers.

Nervy giddiness has propelled me through the flight from Dublin, a day of meetings, having my hair blow-dried into foxy waves, buying the shoes that were I-can't-think-about-it expensive, getting fake eyelashes done in Shu Uemura (the application was free; I had to pay for the lashes, but they're reusable so it was a bargain really, except it wasn't because any time I do fake lashes myself, they end up stuck so far from my lashline they look like rows of shark's teeth), haring back to Home House to dump my bags and change into a floaty cold-shoulder top and satin skirt, and getting a taxi to the Sarah Hotel.

The lift doors open to reveal a phalanx of hostesses, armed with iPads. They make me think of riot police. Over their shoulders, in the bar, everyone looks fabulous and I hope that with my gold-dusted collarbones, my tumbling hair, my glossy mouth and my too-high shoes, I'll fit in.

'Josh Rowan,' I tell the woman who blocks my path.

Oh, and here he is, making his way through the teeming revellers, looking a little Portofino-ish himself, in an inky-blue slubby sweatshirt and slouchy jeans that I suspect are new. We exchange a queasy complicity.

'I saw you,' he says. 'It's so busy in here I thought it best to come and get you.'

With an apprehensive smile, I let him lead me through the jostling crowds to a low booth, almost a pod, with two tapered, high-backed seats facing each other, like an almond sliced in two, across a narrow table.

I clamber into the cocoon-like chair and it's too squashy to sit upright in. But when I lean my elbows on the table, it tilts me far too close to him, so my face is about four inches from his.

An iPad with the drinks menu is slid in front of me. It's one long list of whiskies. 'God.' I'm grateful to have something to say. 'It's real.'

'What is?'

'A couple of weeks ago they said in Style that the modern drink is whisky, but this is the first time I've seen it for reals.'

Without much interest, he scans the list. 'What's it to be? A thirty-year-old Macallan?' His tone is a little mocking. 'A rarer-than-rare Laphroaig?'

'Water,' I say.

He's surprised. 'You sure?'

'I'm not getting drunk. I don't want to convince myself that this is anything other than what it is.'

'Which is?'

I don't know yet. 'Let's see.'

He flags a waiter and orders. Then he asks, 'Amy? How come we met on the beach on Friday morning? Sixth sense?'

'No such thing. It's just an amalgam of our other five senses. We know stuff, even if we're not aware we know it. A long time ago you told me you often wake early.' Then I realize another thing. 'And you'd told me you liked beaches, cold ones.'

'So did you come out *looking* for me?'

'I didn't know, not consciously anyway, that I was hoping to meet you. But lower down in my layers, I had all the information.'

'So there are no accidents?'

'I think . . .' I'm struggling to form my thoughts '. . . that we're responsible for our actions. We choose them. Even if we think we don't. Anyway, Josh, I brought condoms.'

He gives a bark of slightly scandalized laughter. 'So did I.'

344

I clamp my hand on to the back of his wrist. 'Josh . . .'

He waits.

'I'm . . . God, how do I say it? I'm traditional. In bed. I hate saying this but I don't want any unpleasant surprises. For either of us.'

'Okay.'

'Are you? Traditional?'

'I've never really . . . Yeah, I suppose I am.'

'Oh, Josh, that's a big relief.' I smile widely. 'Right, let's do this.'

He laughs. 'You had me at condoms.'

'Sorry. Not very romantic. It's nerves.'

He slides a plastic card across the table. 'Room 504. Fifth floor. Go ahead. I'll just sort things out here.'

I head for the lift, fizzing with a nervy paranoia. Can people guess what's going on? But even if they do – and why would they? – what would they care?

Something shifts in me, I've let go of an innocence about love, loyalty and fidelity. I'm different now, living a more louche life. I'm not sure I like myself, but perhaps I'll grow into it.

The card works in the lock, and I slip inside, shut the door quickly behind me and lean my back against it. The room's okay. Very male. Dark wood, angular mid-century furniture, statement lamps. You can see that it's tasteful – the cream angora throw, the tan leather design-classic chair.

I'm very sober and very grounded. There's no glitter or dazzle in me to make this easy. Every domestic detail stands out: the hum of the mini-bar; the weight of Josh's bag on the bed, wrinkling the snowy perfection of the duvet cover; the random shouts and yelps from people in the street below. And, oh, Christ, there's a bottle of something fizzy in an ice-bucket. Thoughtful? Or sleazy?

I move quickly, changing the lighting, creating pools of shadow, and circles of golden glow. As I'm wondering what music to put on, there's a quiet knock on the door. My heart almost jumps out of my mouth.

I twist the handle and Josh steps in and looks at me. 'Is this okay?' he asks. 'I mean, the room?'

'It's nice. I'm just nervous.'

'I'm nervous too.'

'What if you think I'm too old, too –'

'I won't. I swear. Is there a Do Not Disturb thing?' He locates it, quickly opens the door and slings the sign on the knob. Now there's no danger of us being interrupted.

We're standing facing each other, a little awkwardly. I'm waiting for some force to fling us together, to throw a bucket of passion over us and make this easier.

He steps towards me, places his hand on my waist. 'Don't look so scared.' He takes my right hand in his free one and moves in tighter. Our faces are so close they're almost touching and his breath is on my skin. 'I've wanted you for so long,' he says. 'I can't believe it's actually happening.'

It's time for him to kiss me, and when he doesn't, I plant my hands on his shoulders and tentatively move my mouth to his. My lips feel swollen and tender as they touch off his. He moves to take my face in both his hands and kisses me back with care and sweetness. It's unexpected – I'd thought he might be rougher, more macho – and it's lovely.

It's seventeen years since a man other than Hugh has kissed me – that craziness with Matthew Carlisle doesn't count – and everything is different with Josh. He tastes different, he smells different, there's no beard. Even his hand –

He breaks off the kiss – oh! – and half whispers, 'Stop thinking about him.'

There's a second of despair, I'm afraid I won't be able to, then I whisper back, sounding braver than I feel, 'Make me.'

There's a flash of his teeth as he gives a quick smile, then slowly he slides one hand around to the nape of my neck, lifting my hair and sending shivers of energy down my back. With his other hand, he strokes my cheek with his thumb, then kisses me again and this time it's deeper, more intimate.

He's really, really good at this.

'You have no idea,' he says, 'how much I want you.'

My hands move to the sides of his body, where they hold on, as

346

if he's a steering wheel. Gingerly, I force myself to move them around to his back. Again, all I can think of are the differences from Hugh – Josh is tougher, more muscled, and I have a flash of disloyalty.

The hand he's had on my neck slides all the way down to where my waist curves and becomes my bum, and he starts a sweeping cupping motion along the slippery satin, going lower and lower. 'You feel even more beautiful than I expected,' he breathes.

One of my hands slips into the back pocket of his jeans, pulling him against me and there he is, already swollen and erect. Instinctively, he lowers himself so I press him hard into my pubic bone and, yes, this is happening, my body wants this. It's a strange, sorrowful relief.

The hand that was on my face moves on to my stomach, then immediately starts inching upwards to my chest. His fingers advance, touch off the soft underside, then retreat again and both my nipples jump to attention. They're aching to be touched. It needs to happen so I take his hand and place it directly on my breast, which sends a charge of sensation straight to my hidey-hole.

'Slow down,' he whispers.

'No.' I can't endure hours of foreplay, not this, the first time. I want it to have happened, to already be in the future where I've been with a man who isn't Hugh.

'Our first time,' he says. 'Let's not rush it.'

'Seriously.' I look him in the eye – and it's a shock that he isn't Hugh. 'We'll have other times when it's slow but right now I just need it to happen.'

He looks pissed off, or maybe he's hurt, I don't know. But he slides his hands under my bum and, to my surprise, lifts me off the floor. Instinctively my legs wrap themselves around his hips as he carries me the few steps to the bed.

He lays me across the duvet, sweeps his bag to the floor and starts again with the swoony kisses while he unbuttons my top with impressive speed. I inch up his sweatshirt, so we're skin-to-skin. 'Oh, the touch of you,' he whispers.

With fumbling fingers I unbuckle his belt, unbutton his waistband, then he stops kissing me in order to watch as I slide down the zip. I part the denim and see the angry-looking tip straining from the top of his pants. I lay the palm of my hand against it and it twitches. Then I squeeze and he says, 'No.'

Oh?

'Unless you want this to be over right now.'

My top is open all the way down, his hands have moved to the clasp of my bra and there's a rush of release as he opens it. Efficiently he sits me up, removes my top and bra and pulls his sweatshirt over his head. 'I fantasized about this,' he says quietly. 'But the reality is so much better.'

Before he guides me back down to the bed, I get a quick look at his body, pale-skinned and dark-haired. He's not ripped, which is a relief because neither am I, but his chest is broad and his stomach is fairly flat.

We kiss again while the fingers of one of his hands tap my breast with little fluttery motions, sometimes brushing against my nipple, and when it does, I feel dangerously close.

His other hand explores under my skirt and when the tips of his fingers brush the line where my stocking ends and my thigh starts, he groans. 'Oh, *Jesus*.' With both hands, he pushes up my skirt, takes a look and groans again.

'How does this work?' He's unfastening and unzipping my skirt and pulling it off, and I use the time to slide my hands under his clothes and on to his bum, then peel the fabric all the way down until his dick bursts out, thrillingly purple, mesmerizing.

While his jeans and underpants are bunched mid-thigh, he slides down my knickers, and when he accidentally glances his thumb against my most sensitive part, a whimper comes from me.

'Oh?' There's a little smile from him. 'You like that?' He shifts himself to stare into my eyes, then with one hand he pinches my nipple and at the same time, he presses the other firmly against me, and it's too much, I pulse into his palm, my eyes startled with shock and pleasure, involuntary gasps coming from my chest. He laughs softly, almost mockingly.

'Put on a condom,' I whisper. Because if he enters me now, I can come again.

'You do it.'

My hands are shaking as I unfurl it and slide it along his length, while he watches, his expression agonized, his eyes almost all pupil. 'I need you on top of me.' I say. 'To start with.'

Propped on one elbow, he settles himself between my legs, and slides his way into me with astonishing ease, and I think, I've done it now, I've cheated on Hugh. Maybe it's only a technicality but there's no way back from this.

Josh moves in slow, deliberate circles, his pubic bone tight against mine, massaging the throbbing centre of me. 'Amy, is this what you want? Amy? Is this how you want it?'

God, he's a talker. I've never been with a talker before. Hugh and I, we just got on with it, we seemed to understand each other without the verbals.

But Josh is going too slow for me and digging my nails into his buttocks and speeding up my own hips isn't making any difference. 'Could you do it faster?' I'm embarrassed.

'Like this?'

'Um, yes, but . . .'

'Yes?'

'Harder.'

'You want me to fuck you harder?'

I whisper, 'Yes.'

'Tell me.'

Oh, Christ. 'Fuck me harder.'

'Josh.'

'Fuck me harder, Josh.'

'Like this?'

'Faster. Fuck me faster, Josh.'

'I'm going to fuck you faster, Amy. I'm going to fuck you harder.'

It's slightly silly. And, yet, sexy. Once more the thrills of pleasure build in me and Josh growls into my ear, 'I'm going to fuck you so hard, Amy, you're going to come.'

And then I do.

My centre explodes, my hips buck, my back arches, short gasps issue helplessly from my throat and I realize I've almost punctured his buttocks with the heels of my shoes.

While I'm limp with aftermath, he slides his way out of me, stands, takes off all his clothes, then rearranges himself to sit with his back against the headboard and pulls me to him. I lower myself on to him, place his hands on my hips and move up and down. We stare into each other's faces but I begin to feel strange, like I'm dreaming.

I close my eyes and hear his breath coming shorter and shorter, then he says, his voice hoarse, 'I'm sorry, Amy, I'm going to come. I'm going to – I'm coming, I'm coming, I'm coming.'

I open my eyes and watch his face as it contorts in ecstasy. It's so strange, this force that makes people betray the people they love.

We slide down the bed and lie together, my head on his chest, his heartbeat in my ear. One of his arms is around me, his fingers tangled in my hair. The other is stretched tightly across my body, the hand on my hipbone.

As everything settles in me, one emotion above all others rises to the surface and that emotion is grief.

Sleeping with Josh – with anyone other than Hugh – is a milestone, and even though I've gained a new life experience, so much has been lost.

I cry without moving or making a sound. A tear lands on his bare skin and, although he doesn't speak, the way he tightens his hold lets me know that he understands.

I wake up to find myself in bed. With Josh Rowan. We must have fallen asleep.

'What time is it?' I ask, anxiously.

'Just after one.'

'You can't stay the night. Neither of us can.'

His eyes cloud.

'Have a shower,' I say, 'and go home.'

'You can stay the night.'

'No.' I'm going to Druzie's.

'Amy, is this hotel a problem?'

'It's fine.'

'But?'

'Maybe I'd prefer somewhere less fashionable.'

'Yeah?'

I can't decide if he's being sarcastic or not. 'There's a small hotel near Marylebone we could book the next time?'

'Next time?'

'Next Tuesday.' In a rush, I add, 'If you want.'

'I want.'

A thrill fizzes my blood.

'I'll book a room,' he says.

I hesitate. I should pay for the hotel next week. We're equal partners in whatever this is.

'No.' He shakes his head. 'Leave that to me.'

71

Wednesday, 16 November, day sixty-five

The texts flood in on Wednesday: **Thank you for last night.**
  And
  I can't stop thinking about you.
  And
  You're amazing.
  And
  Next Tuesday is too far away.

When I arrive at the office on Thursday morning, Thamy greets me by saying, 'Someone's either really sorry or really grateful to you.'

'Oh?'

'Flowers. But not regular flowers. They came yesterday. On your desk.'

I hurry inside and – 'Oh, my *God*!' You can smell them before you see them and it's not just the size of the bundle, it's the nature of it – my desk looks like a meadow of wild flowers. Somehow, he'd got spring flowers: there are startlingly red poppies, their petals as thin as paper; graceful, lanky foxgloves in white and purple; yellow marsh-marigolds and stalks of bright blue speedwell.

The card says, 'You're a Goddess. Josh xxx.'

'Who're they from?' Tim asks.

My face flames and I don't know what to say. 'A man.'

'Hugh?'

I shake my head because I'm too uncomfortable to speak.

And here comes Alastair. 'Wow, Amy. Some flowers. All credit to Josh Rowan, those flowers are very you.'

'Josh Rowan sent them?' Tim asks. 'Why? Oh! Well!' He coughs and hurries away.

'I'd never heard of that florist,' Alastair says. 'Handy to know about them. So how'd it go?'

'Strange. Good. Sad. Lovely.'

'Excellent. Well, I've news of my own. I'm in love.'

'Are you now? Fast work.'

'I met her on Tuesday night at a salsa yoga workshop.'

'Of course.'

'She was the facilitator. Her name is Helmi and, Amy, the *connection*. It was instant and amazing. We stayed up most of the night talking and last night I went to a psychic –'

'Oh, Alastair, you're *such* a gobshite.'

'Seriously, Amy, I need to know if she's for me because I don't have any more time to waste. And the good news is that Helmi and I are soul-mates!' He flashes his dazzlers at me. 'We've met in countless past lives, the psychic said. Sometimes I was the mother and she was my son. It wasn't always like this manifestation.'

'Oh, Alastair.' I could weep for him and the utter shite he elects to believe in.

'Helmi and I are soul-mates,' he insists.

'There's no such thing,' I say. 'There are six billion people on the planet but how handy that most people meet their "soul-mate" within a few square miles of where they live and work.'

'No –'

'Cop on, Alastair! Seriously! This is how love works: you meet someone, you fancy them and that propels you to get to know them. Everyone has a checklist in their soul about what they want from their special someone, and this person won't tick all of the boxes, but they'll tick enough for you to decide, okay, I'm prepared to work to make this happen. But you have to learn to overlook the things about the other person that annoy and disappoint you, *and* you have to try to change the things about yourself that they can't stand.'

'No –'

'You learn to compromise. For example, you go, yet again, on a beach holiday to the Algarve instead of the road trip in Serbia to find your favourite artist.'

Alastair looks baffled but I'm not done.

'A soul-mate is like one of those seventy-nine-euro flights to New York – a lovely idea but they don't exist.'

'Wow, Amy.' Alastair shakes his head. 'That's dark. Harsh.'

'You need to be realistic, is all I'm saying.'

'You've been burnt first by Richie and then Hugh leaving you. But maybe you've met a new soul-mate.' He nods at the flowers.

'I haven't.'

'What do you think, Tim?' Alastair asks. 'Are you and, ah, Mrs Staunton soul-mates?'

'You'd have to ask her.'

'Do you feel she's the only one for you?'

'Like I say, you'd have to ask her.'

Thank God Tim has reverted to buttoned-up type. That other version of him scared the daylights out of me.

But, thanks to the lecture I've given to Alastair, my mood has sunk low.

'What's up?' he asks.

'I'm going to be twice-divorced. It's a bad track record. And it's no good trying to pass myself off as an innocent bystander. I've to own my part in it.'

'You were an innocent bystander with Richie "Think of the poor blind children" Aldin.'

'Maybe. We were too young, we shouldn't have got married. I didn't want to do it – I should have listened to my instincts.'

'And Hugh?'

'I'm culpable there, all right. But I don't want to think about it now.'

Something totally weird has happened. Raffie Geras is back in Edinburgh. Back at work, living her previous life. And without Hugh.

I'd just assumed she was a long-term traveller. Not for a moment did I consider she was just on a two-week sun holiday.

There's a photo of boots she bought in Dune in George's Street. (This sounds biased, I know, but they're not nice: the heel is a disappointment.) Another photo of her out on the piss with 'her girls' on Friday night, then one of her in bed – alone – on Sunday morning, drinking Berocca.

It's hard to know what to make of this. Except now I can't keep tabs on Hugh. I guess I'll have to wait until he pops up, tagged by some other woman. Unless he's planning to move to Edinburgh to be with Raffie.

It's possible – he'd be able to get work there. And maybe I should be happy because he'd be nearish, for Sofie and Kiara, but all I feel is sick.

72

Room 18, he'd said in the text. I've used this hotel a couple of times to house clients, but I've never been up here on the third floor, which is a warren. The corridor doglegs around a corner, leads through a fire door, up a half-flight of stairs and – oh! Right, here's room 18.

A quick moment to rearrange my hair, but before I've even knocked, the door is wrenched open and Josh pulls me inside. The door slams behind us and he's pushed me up against it. I can't believe I'd once thought his grey eyes were unremarkable when the promise they contain is probably the sexiest thing about him.

He takes my face in his hands and breathes, 'This has been the longest seven days of my life,' then kisses me with everything he's got.

My body is already alive, every nerve-ending hair-trigger sensitive. He's unbuttoning my dress, I'm fumbling to open his jeans, he takes one of my nipples into his mouth, I slide out his erection, he pulls down my knickers, I unpeel his jeans.

It's different this time, rougher, faster, everything happening very quickly, and it suits me.

In probably less than three minutes, both of us are half undressed, he produces a condom. 'I'll do it,' he says, and slides it along the hard length of himself. He lifts my legs, I wrap them around his waist, then he thrusts his way deep into me, pushing my back against the door.

It's so intensely sexy that I exclaim with pleasure.

'You like that?'

'I love it,' I gasp. 'Do it again. Do it faster.'

'Say —'

'Fuck me faster, Josh!'

His hands are on my bum, my hands are clawing his hair, his mouth is on my breasts, and my heels are pushing against his buttocks as he pistons into me.

'Amy.' He's panting into my ear. 'I'm going to come.'

I haven't yet and he knows. 'Please come, Amy,' he pleads. 'Please come.'

But it's too late: with a short, sharp howl, his body freezes and he pulses and twitches inside me. Eventually he whispers into my neck, 'Sorry.'

'But we've got all night.'

Tenderly, he carries – *carries* – me to the bed, and after a quick trip to the bathroom to dispose of the condom, he undresses himself, then me. Then, with his mouth, he delicately works me into a frenzy and keeps me poised on the edge for endless exquisite time, before eventually delivering me.

My head floats away and again and again I hear myself saying, 'Oh! Oh! Oh!'

When I open my eyes and return to the world, he's once more stiff and erect. 'Look at what you're doing to me,' he says. 'This week, Amy, I've been horny as fuck. I haven't wanked so much since I was a teenager.'

I cough with shock.

'What d'I say? What? Talking about wanking?'

'Mmm.'

He laughs. 'I can show you.'

'No!'

'No? So what should I do instead?'

'You know.'

'Say it.'

A long time later, he says, 'I've downloaded *The Grand Budapest Hotel* for you.'

I light up with pleasure at his thoughtfulness. He'd also ordered a cheese plate from room service for me.

'But what's with the sackcloth and ashes?' he asks. 'Wanting to come here, instead of the posh hotel.'

'This is fine,' I say. 'It's got everything we need, and we're less likely to run into anyone who might know you.'

'It's not just that, though?'

'I don't want money wasted that could be spent on your family.'

'And?'

'Mmm.' I try to find the words. 'It's not right to dress this up, to disguise it as something it's not.'

'So what isn't it?'

It's a struggle to express myself. 'It isn't a relationship. And it isn't okay. Your wife . . . I can't feel not guilty. And I don't want to.'

'So, as long as you don't enjoy yourself too much, you can do this?'

'No. It's as long as I don't lose sight of what's right and what's wrong.'

His expression is a mix of exasperation and affection. 'My little Sackcloth. You don't know the first thing about my wife. For all you know, she might hate me – she might be glad about this.'

It's hard to believe that. But who knows? People are endlessly surprising.

'What's she like?'

'You sure you want to know?'

'Yes.' Maybe.

'She's . . . confident. When I met her, I just knew that, yeah, I'd met my match. First woman I knew wouldn't take shit from me.'

'So why are you doing this? With me?'

He takes a while to speak. 'Things change, don't they? The kids. I love them, I'd kill anyone who tried to hurt them, but they're tough going.' He sighs. 'When you have kids, you live your life under a permanent shadow.'

I don't know what to say. The kids brought me and Hugh closer together. And yet Hugh is on the other side of the world and I'm in bed with Josh Rowan, so maybe I'm the very same as Josh.

As Josh drifts off to sleep, he turns over, snuggles into me and murmurs, 'My little Sackcloth.'

73

For *once* my flight home isn't delayed and the traffic isn't horrific, and when I arrive home on Wednesday evening, Neeve, Sofie and Kiara are clustered in a huddle on the couch. They're talking intently and, when they notice me, abruptly fall silent. Anxiety seizes my chest – something's up.

I'm not really superstitious, I don't believe in a vengeful God. But words flash through me – *punish, amoral, harlot.*

'What?' My breath won't come.

After a weighted hesitation, Neeve flicks her glinty eyes between Kiara and Sofie and says, 'She's pregnant.'

The internal condemnatory voices intensify: *bad woman, bad mother, bad example.*

'Who is?'

'Sofie.'

I drop my bag and go to her. 'How are you, sweetie?'

'Scared.' She begins to cry.

'Tell me.' I curl on the couch and gather her tiny, bony body to mine. While this isn't ideal it's not the worst thing that could have happened.

'It was an accident.' She sobs into my shoulder. 'I'd left my pill in Mum's but I was staying in Granny's.'

'She took the morning-after pill,' Kiara says. 'It cost sixty euro.'

'But it mustn't have worked,' Neeve says. 'She should get her money back.'

'What does Jackson say?' I ask.

'He's scared too.' Now she's really sobbing, the hard, out-of-control convulsing that comes from terrible fear. 'We're both so scared.'

'Shush, shush.' I stroke her head of soft bristles and let her cry. Already I'm in crisis-management mode. 'It'll all be okay.'

'Please can I have an abortion?' Sofie sounds piteous.

'If you're certain that's what you want?'

'You're kidding, right?' She pulls away from me. Paradoxically she's never seemed so grown-up. 'The state of me, I can't even take care of myself.'

I'll have to take her to London. Unless I can get my hands on some illegal pills and we do it here at home. But wouldn't that be dangerous, doing it without medical advice? How would you know the pills were the correct ones? How would I take care of her during it? And after? With sudden fierce force, I miss Hugh desperately – his kindness, his good sense, his reassuring presence.

I wouldn't be doing the right thing as Sofie's sort-of-mum if I didn't offer an alternative path. 'You know we'd all help you, if you decided to go ahead with the pregnancy.'

She stares in shock. 'Are you trying to make me have it?' Her voice gets high-pitched. 'Because I can't.'

'She's only seventeen!' Kiara is equally high-pitched.

'She's still at school!' This from Neeve.

'I'm shit-scared!'

'You can't make her have a baby!' Kiara says.

'I wish I hadn't told you now.'

'Sofie, sweetie, it's okay. It's okay, it's okay.' I make shushing, soothing noises. 'Just letting you know that, whatever you want, we'll help.'

I look over Sofie's shorn head at Neeve and Kiara. 'Maybe Sofie and I should have this conversation alone.'

'No.' Kiara grasps Sofie's hand in a we-shall-overcome gesture. 'We're in this together.'

'Yeah, what she says,' Neeve says.

I hesitate. It's hard to know whether to treat them as children or adults – and I wonder where Hugh is right now this minute, if he's on a beach, drinking a beer, utterly carefree.

'I just want to wake up tomorrow morning and not be

pregnant,' Sofie whispers. 'I wish I didn't have to decide this. I don't want to bring a person into the world who is like me. And to be brought up by a mum who can't be a mum, and a dad who isn't there. And I don't mean anything bad on you and Dad, Amy, you've been great. If it wasn't for you, I'd have no family.'

'You're not your mum.'

'But half of me is her. Maybe I can't love properly.'

'You can love. Of course you can.' This isn't the first time we've had this conversation. 'You love Kiara and Neeve.'

'And we love you,' Kiara says.

'And you love Jackson,' I say.

'I love him so much,' she says fiercely. 'And you, I love you, Amy, and Dad. And I love Granny. But I'm not ready to love a baby.'

'Not yet.'

'Maybe not ever.'

I let it go at that. 'So you're absolutely certain you're pregnant? You've done a test?'

She cry-laughs. 'I've done about a thousand.'

'Do you know how many weeks you are?'

'Six. Maybe seven.' She sounds uncertain.

'Six or seven weeks since you had a period?'

'No, since we had the unprotected, you know.'

'And you've been worried all that time?' I'm ashamed I hadn't noticed – and, quick as a flash, that mutates into rage at Hugh. If I hadn't been dealing with his absence I might have picked up that Sofie was worried.

'We need to get you to the doctor,' I say. To establish exactly how far along she is. An unexpected thought impacts: could the doctor report us for procuring an abortion? Our family practice is a busy one with lots of GPs, and while I trust the women, I'm not so sure about the older men.

I mean, I know abortion is illegal in Ireland but, until now, I'd never fully understood that I could actually be put in prison. Maybe that's the only time anyone knows anything – when it impacts them directly.

This is crazy. A civilized country, where I work and pay taxes, and yet I could be criminalized for helping my pregnant niece.

'Are you angry with me?' Sofie asks.

'Of course not.'

'Do I have to tell Joe?'

I sigh. 'Yeah.'

'Do I have to tell Mum . . . Urzula?'

I think about it. It's tricky being *in loco parentis* to someone else's child. 'Joe can tell her.'

'So do I have to go to England?'

'Unless we can get pills. We might be able to order them online.'

Neeve is scrolling away on her iPad. 'If she's under eight weeks, she can do the pills.'

If she's under eight weeks.

'Do Jackson's parents know?' I ask Sofie.

'Are you going to tell them?'

'We need to talk with Jackson.' Flickering in my head is some vague memory of a case where some man tried to sue his girl-friend retroactively for having an abortion, and Sofie needs to be protected from any such likelihood.

'But she's the one who's pregnant,' Kiara says. 'It's no one else's business.'

'Yeah, but he should pay half,' Neeve chips in. 'If we can even manage to get the pills.'

God, my head is melted. So many tricky questions and no one to offload on to.

74

'Amy, can I ask something else?' Sofie says. 'You know the people who say that abortion is killing a baby?'

'. . . yes?'

'Is that what I'm doing?'

Kiara and Neeve jump in, protesting, 'You're not! Not at this stage!'

I take a while to answer. I've always felt it's up to the individual woman to decide what's right for her, but opting to end a pregnancy is a choice no woman is ever happy to have to make. I know of three women who've had abortions – Derry, Jana and Druzie. All three were terrified at finding themselves pregnant, yes, even Druzie, and not once have they expressed regret for the choice they made.

But even when you're certain it's the best option, alternative scenarios inevitably present themselves. Like if Sofie had a baby, Joe would be a grandfather and Mum and Pop would be great-grandparents and Sofie might crack up and leg it, leaving the child to be brought up by someone else, just as she has been.

On the other hand, could having a baby be the making of her? I can't see it, but who knows? And that's the thing, we *can't* know. We can only make the best decision with the information we have at the time.

I settle for saying, '*I* think your body belongs to you so you should be entitled to make any choices you want about it, but it's much more important what you think.'

'I don't think I'm doing anything wrong either.'

'You're sure?'

'I'm sure.'

I want to believe her but there's a free-floating sense that I haven't done or said enough to give her all the options. I mean, I never feel I do *anything* right or fully, but I'm not sure what else I can say. Maybe the doctor will provide some advice. 'I'll investigate the pills.'

'And everything will be okay?' Sofie asks, her little voice plaintive.

'Yes, sweetie, everything will be okay.'

'See?' Neeve declared. 'Didn't we tell you Mum would make everything all right?'

Cripes, I'm not sure I'm worthy of being the receptacle for all their hopes.

'Mum.' Kiara is gentle. 'You need to go to bed, you look really tired.'

'Everyone go to bed.' I wrap my arms around Sofie. 'You like to sleep in with me, sweetie?'

'I'll sleep in with Kiara,' she says.

'I wish we could all sleep in the one bed,' Neeve says. 'Like when we were kids.'

And when Hugh was here.

'Oh!' Sofie breathes. 'They were lovely times.'

Memories stir of little bodies squirming and clambering over each other in the dark. Or waking to find one of the girls curled into me, deep in sleep, her sweet breath exhaling hotly into my face.

'Or the Saturday mornings,' Neeve says happily, 'when we'd all pile into the bed with you and Hugh.'

'You'd beg us to go down and watch telly.' Sofie is smiling at the memory. 'But we just squashed in with our toys.'

'And you and Dad were too tired to make us breakfast,' Kiara says. 'So we'd all share a big tub of ice cream in bed.'

'Or those mint and chocolate biscuits. With the shiny paper?'

'They were *yummy*!'

'But sometimes they were orange instead of mint. Those were *rotten*.'

'I liked the orange ones.'

'You're weird . . .'

Leaving them discussing the merits of mint versus orange

Viscounts, I trail up the stairs and wish, wish, *wish* someone would invent self-dissolving make-up. Micellar water was such a god-send, until I read some article saying you shouldn't rely on it incessantly, that you should double-cleanse at least every third night and, oh, Christ, isn't life hard enough?

I text Derry, asking her to call me. Suddenly I really miss Steevie, I wish I could talk to her, especially about Sofie. But – with a flash of wild paranoia – what if I told her our plans and she reports me to the law?

In bed my fingers are shaking as I start googling pills. Immediately I'm into a whole new set of worries: what if something medical goes wrong? What if Sofie starts haemor-rhaging? Every site advises that if she has to go to hospital to say she's having a miscarriage. If I tell the truth, I'm confessing to a crime.

But if I don't tell the truth, how can she get the correct medical care? What if she dies?

This is a strange, strange situation, the sort of thing I've only seen in movies. I'm not a natural criminal. Nor am I a natural nurse, I'm not good with pain, especially other people's.

What if I *do* get caught? What if I *am* sent to prison? Because it happens. A woman in Northern Ireland was sent to jail for three years for procuring pills for her daughter.

There might be a public outcry, but I don't want to be the poster-girl for a cause. I just want Sofie to be all right.

Then I remember the dream I'd had, where I'd been carrying all the babies. Most of them had been Sofie, and the baby I'd dropped and picked up by the ear had been a tiny, tiny version of her.

I must have suspected she was pregnant, subliminally catalogued that she was paler than usual, eating even less than normal, hadn't had a period in a while . . . My subconscious had been trying to break the surface when I wasn't ready to face the truth.

Well, I'm facing it now. I order the pills. The site is a friendly one but the whole business feels furtive and frightening.

75

Thursday, 24 November, day seventy-three

At four p.m. I stand up and say, 'Right, Tim, sorry to abandon ship.'

I'm taking Sofie to the doctor, I've stipulated a woman but I don't know which one we'll get. I really hope it's not Dr Frawley, the very young one, who'd told me I should reduce my stress and my weight, as if that could magically happen just because they're desirable. Back then she'd told me to take up walking.

'I *do* walk.'

She seemed surprised. 'Great. Where?'

'Aaaah . . . Glendalough.' Well, I did that one time. Was it New Year's Day? Or it might have been the previous New Year's Day . . .

'How many K would you typically do?'

'Up to the waterfall.'

'That's quite a climb.' Then she became suspicious. 'Unless you mean the first waterfall? The little one.'

Of course I'd meant the first waterfall. Which was about four minutes' stroll from the car park.

But who has time to exercise? In fairness, I did my best – on Tuesdays and Wednesdays I was in airports where I walked *miles* and every Sunday I cleaned my house.

'Get a Fitbit,' she'd said.

I'd kept my mouth shut. I had a Fitbit. I border-line hated it. I almost never reached the daily ten-thousand-step target. It was just one more way to feel like I'm failing life.

Mercifully, today it's Dr Conlon, who is probably in her forties and has always struck me as sensible.

Sofie is weeping, and wants me in the room as she submits to the examination. Even though she knows, when Dr Conlon says, 'You're pregnant all right,' she cries harder.

'How far along?' I ask.

'Without knowing when her last period was, I can't say for certain, but eight, maybe nine weeks.'

'Not that long.' Sofie is adamant.

'We count from the date of your last period,' Dr Conlon says. 'Not since conception.'

This throws me totally. Is it already too late for Sofie to do the pills? Shock makes me careless. 'Sofie isn't going ahead with the pregnancy. But is it too late for the pills?'

'Abortifacients can be used safely up to ten weeks.'

'You'd say she's definitely under ten weeks?'

'She needs an ultrasound to say for sure. But probably.'

I decide to take a chance. 'Is there any way you can prescribe the pills?'

She shakes her head. 'I'd lose my licence. Worst-case scenario, I'd go to jail.'

'Sorry!' I'm mortified for even asking.

'Why is it so illegal?' Sofie asks.

Dr Conlon sighs. 'Now there's a question.' She looks at us and there's definitely compassion there. 'Book the ultrasound as fast as possible.' She picks up some pages and gives them to me. 'Details of a few organizations who can give information, addresses in the UK, et cetera. A word of advice, if you use abortifacients bought online and someone reports it, you're liable for fourteen years in jail each.'

'That's crazy,' Sofie exclaims, all indignation and disbelief. 'They should mind their own beeswax! This is my thing, my decision.' This is what you get when a politically clueless seventeen-year-old finds her needs crashing against the limitations of the legal system.

'Also, Sofie,' the doctor says, 'see a counsellor. Talk things through. It's a decision you don't want to regret.'

'I won't regret it!' Sofie curls in on herself. 'I can't bring a person like me into the world. I'm so scared.' She collapses into a wild storm of sobs. 'I looked it up. Only two per cent of girls regret abortions and I won't be one of them.'

'Still.' Dr Conlon is firm. 'It can't do any harm.'

In the car, I phone for a scan, and the earliest appointment at the hospital is next Monday. This is a worry, time is tight, but what can I do? I dearly wish we'd sprung for the spendier health insurance that would have allowed us to waltz in any time of the day or night (or so the ads would have you believe) and get any procedure we wanted.

Then I square my shoulders. 'Sofie, you do know there are alternatives. Like you could have the baby and let it be adopted.'

'Amy!' She's shrill with fear. 'That would be *worse* than having it and keeping it, because I'd be worrying that it would be like me but I wouldn't know.' She begins to cry again. 'You don't know what it's like to be this scared.'

It's true that I've never been in her exact circumstances, but this sort of fear is familiar – the day-in-day-out dread when Richie left and there was no money to take care of Neeve. That was gruelling. Then the week-long attack of terror when I discovered I was pregnant with Kiara. Hugh and I had been together for such a short time, less than four months. Could you blame me for thinking, This is *way* too soon – it'll finish us?

But I'd been eleven years older than Sofie is now. I'd accumulated coping skills and was, fundamentally, a different kind of person, steadier.

I say, 'Why don't you wait until you've seen a counsellor before you decide for sure?'

'I won't change my mind, Amy, I want to go to college, I want to be a scientist and research cures for things, I want a future.'

This is the first time she's ever expressed any ambition. In other circumstances, I'd be thrilled.

'I'm sorry, Amy. For all of this. I shouldn't have been having sex.'

'You're a human. It's how we've survived this long.'

'But seventeen is a bit young.'

Is it, though? In the eyes of the law she's old enough. But my heart feels differently – my girls would always seem too young. If I could I'd coddle them in cotton wool for all time. Mind you . . . 'When I was your age, I couldn't get enough of it.'

'Serious? No!'

I'm mildly insulted by her horror and this close to telling her the story I'd told Alastair, about making Richie steal the boat from Greystones harbour. Only that she needs solid role models makes me keep my mouth shut.

But it really is true that every generation thinks they're the first to invent sex.

'At least Jackson and me used contraception,' Sofie says. 'Even if it didn't work. I mean, at least I'm not a total flake.'

'In my day,' I say, and then I pause. I can't believe I've just said, 'in my day'. I force myself to carry on. 'We'd no access to contraceptives, not even condoms, and we had to –'

'Use crisp bags. I know. It's barbaric.'

Sweet Jesus. *Crisp* bags? 'Not crisp bags. I was going to say we had to pull out in time.'

'That's nearly as barbaric.'

I sigh. 'Now we're going to tell your dad.'

'No. Please, Amy. Not today. Why don't we go for food?' Sofie is playing dirty – usually I'd be so happy to see her eat that I'd abandon all other plans, but this has to be done.

'Then we're going to talk to Jackson and his folks.'

'No, Amy!'

'Yes, Sofie.' I'm not exactly enjoying this either.

Joe does a disgracefully bad job of hiding his relief that I'm in control. 'Thanks, Amy. Appreciate it.'

I give him a look. I can't help it – and it's a mistake because then he feels he has to come the heavy. He glares at Sofie. 'Aren't you a bit young? You're only –'

'She's seventeen,' I jump in because there's a chance he's forgotten her age.

'Oh, are you? Well, that's grand, so.'

369

'Who's going to tell Urzula?' I ask.

'Does she have to know?' Sofie says.

I've back-and-forthed about this and part of me wants to punish Urzula – *and* Joe – for their neglect of Sofie. But Urzula is her biological mother.

'What if she says I must have the baby?' Sofie asks.

I can't see it.

'I can't tell her,' Joe says. 'I don't have a relationship with her.'

Well, neither do I. She's not right in the head, and maybe I should have more compassion, but there you are, I don't.

'You'll speak to her.' I'm firm with Joe. 'So, Joe, do you know anyone with medical skills? Who might, you know, be with Sofie while it's happening?'

He frowns. 'What do you mean? Won't it happen in a clinic?'

For eff's sake! 'Not in this country. It's illegal.'

'Even the pills?'

He is *such* a fool! 'Even the pills. Listen, don't tell Maura about this.'

'When would I be talking to Maura?' His scorn is withering.

'Good. Okay, Sofie, let's go.'

'Where now?' Joe asks.

'Jackson's parents.' At his clueless face, I say, 'Jackson's her boyfriend. He has been for the past year. Call Urzula. Bye.'

Jackson has already told his parents and they're suitably concerned. They're very nice people – it's obvious where Jackson gets his sweet, mannerly nature from.

Their relief that Sofie won't proceed with the pregnancy comes as no real surprise.

'We love Sofie,' Jackson's mum says over and over, 'but, you know . . .'

His dad keeps staring at Jackson as if he simply *can't believe* this wispy boy has impregnated a girl.

'Are you going to the UK?' Jackson's mother asks.

'We've ordered the pills.'

She nods. 'We'll share the costs.'

Which is more than Joe has offered to do. But I'd expected nothing from Joe – a long time ago, he'd absolved himself from any responsibility for Sofie. If I let myself, I could burn with fury at his – and Urzula's – neglect. But the only person who matters in this is Sofie, and so long as she doesn't mind, and she doesn't seem to, I can put up with it.

There's no point in my trying to make the world the way I'd ideally like it to be. It's better just to get on with things as they are.

76

Friday, 25 November, day seventy-four

None of the girls show up at Mum and Pop's for the Friday dinner. They didn't say they'd definitely be here, because no one ever does, but for all three to be missing is a sign of the cloud we're living under.

I leave half an hour earlier than usual, and at home, sitting on the stairs, looking like refugees, are the girls.

'Mum, when are the pills coming?' Kiara says. 'She's in bits.'

'If I have to have this baby, I'll kill myself,' Sofie whispers.

'Sssh, sssh, sssh, no one's having a baby, it'll be okay.' With my bum, I shunt Neeve and Kiara out of the way and wrap myself around Sofie. 'I've been tracking them,' I say, and show her the delivery details on my iPad.

'They arrived in the country this morning,' I say. 'They'll be here on Monday.' Hopefully.

'So we do it then?' Sofie asks faintly.

'After you've had the scan and seen the counsellor.' I'm adamant about this.

'What if the pills don't come?' Sofie asks. 'What if the Customs people won't let them through?'

This genuine possibility has been turning a flame-thrower on my stomach walls.

'Of course they'll come,' I say heartily, because we all need hope.

77

On Monday morning I knock on Neeve's door. Usually I'd be treated to a torrent of abuse for such a liberty but we've passed a sombre weekend.

'Neevey? Any chance you can stay home today?'

'Why – oh! In case the pills arrive? Sure.'

'Have you stuff on?'

'This is more important. I'll text you when they come.'

Sofie trips down sleepily from her attic room, still in her PJs.

'Sweetie,' I say. 'Clothes.'

'I can't go to school.'

I take her face between my two hands and plant kisses all over it. 'You must go to school. I promise you, everything will be okay.'

'Oh, Aaaaa-meee.'

'Dressed! Get! I'm going to make breakfast.'

'You *are*?' Kiara's bedroom door flies open. 'Wow.'

'Don't,' Sofie says. 'I'm not eating.'

'You have to eat, Sofie.'

'I won't eat until this is over.'

What should I do? If I cook food she won't eat it. But to do nothing feels irresponsible. Although I'm already late for work . . . Then I spot Kiara's hopeful little face. 'Hash browns?' she says.

And I can't help but laugh.

All morning I keep checking my phone, awaiting a joyous *They're here!* from Neeve. But nothing. And there's no notification on the courier site.

At lunchtime I ring. 'Neevey?'

'Not yet, Mum. I've a bad feeling about this.'

So do I.

She says, 'Maybe they'll come tomorrow.'

But I suspect they won't.

'I don't –' Alastair chokes – 'I don't fucking believe it.'

Tim and I whip around to look at him. 'What?!'

Alastair, still staring at his screen, swallows hard. 'Amy. It's Lilian O'Connell, mother of five. Again!'

It's Mum's second vlog, about her getting extensions and highlights. She's talking about her new look. 'I'd like to think I look like Mary Berry. Except . . .' she drops her eyes modestly, then raises them again in a flash of devilment '. . . younger!'

Tim gasps. 'Did she just diss Mary Berry?'

'Yeah.' Alastair shakes his head in admiration. 'And yet she didn't. There's respect in there, charm, a bit of pretender-to-the-throne. It's all going on with Lilian O'Connell, mother of five.'

'What's this on?' I ask Alastair, thinking he'll say Facebook or Twitter.

But he says, 'The *Independent*. They've done a link to it.'

The *Independent* is the biggest paper in Ireland.

'Serious shiz!' Thamy has materialized from Reception.

Neeve is the one I should ring, this is all her work, but Mum gets the call.

'Mum? Do you know about your vlog?'

'Yes! Neeve says I'm gaining traction. Amy, can I ask you a question – which is a stupid thing to say, because I'm already asking you one. Anyway, what exactly is traction? Neeve keeps saying I'm gaining it, but if I ask her to explain, she'll bite the head off me. Is it anything to do with weight?'

'Not weight. Listen, the *Independent* have done a link to your vlog!'

'The paper?' Her voice is hushed with awe. 'I'm in the paper?'

'Um, Neeve will explain it to you.'

'Amy, as I have you . . .'

Shite. I know what's coming.

'. . . any chance you'd do a couple of hours tonight? I'd love to have a few celebratory G-and-Ts.'

I'd rather set myself on fire, but then again, I'm feeling that way already.

'Nine weeks,' the ultrasound technician says to Sofie. 'You're nine weeks pregnant.'

'Do you mean nine weeks since her last period?' I ask. This is important.

'Yes.'

Okay, that's a relief.

78

Tuesday morning, I've landed at Heathrow, switched my phone back on and there's a text from Neeve: **Call me.**

My heart plummets but there's an odd relief. Now I know the worst.

'Neevey?'

'No pills, Mum. But a scary letter from the . . .' a rustle of paper '. . . the Customs people. Something about the Customs Consolidation Act. They say they've seized the pills. Someone from the Enforcement Unit at the Health Products Regulatory Authority will be in touch shortly. Will you be sent to prison, Mum?'

'Ah, no.'

'Isn't that fucking decent of them?' Then, 'I don't know why they have to be so fucking scary!' Her voice is trembling and she sounds tearful.

'It's fine, sweetie, it is.'

'Is it?' She sniffs. 'Time for plan B, I guess.'

But there's no point asking her what that is, I'm the one who's meant to know.

It's not until early afternoon that I get a long enough gap to make the necessary calls.

'Can I make an appointment for my daughter?' It's just easier to say Sofie is my daughter and, funnily enough, of the three girls, she's the only one who shares my surname. 'For the . . . um, pills version. For as soon as possible.'

'What was the date of her last period? She needs to come in for a scan. We have an appointment today at —'

'Um, no. She lives in Ireland. But she had a scan there yesterday.'

'We need our own scan. Which we can schedule for the same day as the procedure. But if she's more than ten weeks pregnant –' it's still profoundly shocking to hear little Sofie described as pregnant – 'the pills are no longer safe.'

'So can I book? For as soon as possible.'

There's a chance – admittedly tiny – that after seeing the counsellor Sofie will change her mind, but bird in the hand. I'll just have to risk losing the deposit.

'Let me look. Just to explain, we need to see her twice in twenty-four hours. We give her the first dose of pills, after which she'll leave. She returns the following day for the second dose. She stays with us until she has miscarried, which takes approximately three hours.'

'I see.'

'Our first appointment is next Monday, one p.m., returning the following day at two p.m. Your daughter needs to be picked up by another adult at five p.m. This is important. She can't leave on her own.'

Oh, no. The timing is atrocious. I've got the Tabitha Wilton/ Room press launch on Tuesday at five o'clock. It's far too late to change it. 'I may not get there until seven thirty,' I say.

'We close at six.'

'There's no chance of an earlier slot?' I ask desperately.

'We're fully committed.'

'If I tried another clinic?'

'Short notice but I can hold this appointment for twenty-four hours.'

The next hour and fifty minutes are spent talking with clinics in the London area and none of them can see Sofie within the week, so I end up calling back the first people and making the booking.

I'm given tons of information, and the woman says, 'Your daughter can't fly home on Tuesday night. Not with an afternoon

appointment. We can give you the names of local B-and-Bs.'
Then she stresses again, 'She must be picked up by another adult.'

But who?

Druzie's away for at least another month. I consider Jackson: he's sensible and kind and Sofie would appreciate him being there. But he's only seventeen and looks even younger. Bringing him along as an 'adult' is too much of a risk.

Maybe Derry could come. If she's not working in Ulan Bator or some other faraway locale. I could ask Joe, but I already know he'll invent some reason not to come.

Out of nowhere rage spurts up through me. *Fuck you, Hugh, fuck you for leaving me to deal with all of this on my own.*

He wasn't to know it would happen. But in fairness, leaving me in charge of two teenagers – *anything* could have happened. He couldn't have predicted these precise circumstances, but he must have known something would crop up because something *always* does.

79

In less than two hours I'm due to meet Josh, and it feels every kind of wrong.

After flip-flopping about what to do, I eventually text him: **When's a good time to call?**

Within ten seconds my phone rings. 'Sackcloth?'

'Josh, I can't see you tonight.'

After a long pause he says, 'Are you breaking up with us?'

'Something is going on at home and I don't feel . . . right about it, us, not tonight.'

'But you'll feel right about it on another night?'

'Yes.' Well, who knows?

'Is it your period?'

That elicits a surprise laugh from me.

'Because I don't mind,' he says. 'If you don't want to, you know, we don't have to. But we could still, like . . .'

'It's too complicated to explain on the phone.'

'We could have a drink? *Just* a drink.'

'Not tonight, Josh.'

'Next week?'

'Probably.'

'Okay, Amy.' His tone softens. 'I'll cross my fingers. And if you change your mind . . .'

'Okay, yes,' I say suddenly. 'Tonight, but just a drink. In the hotel bar.' Torn between sorrow and the need for comfort, I go for comfort.

He's waiting in a corner of the residents' bar in the small hotel in Marylebone. When he sees me he jumps up, his expression both wary and concerned. Solicitously he removes my coat and hands me a drink but I sense his anxiety. And maybe impatience.

'Are you okay?' he asks, when I'm settled.

'Fine. Like, there's nothing wrong with me, health-wise or anything.'

He's tense, waiting to hear.

'It's hard to put this into words . . . There's a situation. Not in my life. But with a young woman in my care and . . . I've already said too much.'

'A young woman in your care?' he prompts.

'Is pregnant. And she's not having the baby.'

'She's having an abortion?'

'It's the right thing for her. I'm pro-choice. Are you?'

He seems startled. 'Of course.'

'You Brits,' I say. 'You're so lucky to be free of all that guilt and shame.'

'Catholic upbringing?'

'Not really. Mum and Pop weren't big God-botherers. But living in Ireland, it's impossible to escape the shame. It hangs in the air.'

'You can't really blame the air for the shame. The shame is a by-product of Irish laws. Fourteen years in jail for taking a pill? That's quite a judgement.'

'Wow,' I say. 'I'd never thought of it like that. Anyway, I don't know exactly how to put this but it feels . . . unseemly for me, a married woman, to go to a hotel with you, a married man, when a young woman in my care is going to have an abortion. It feels all a bit, you know . . .' I pause '. . . Sodom and Gomorrah.'

His expression is impossible to decipher. All I know is that he isn't conflicted like I am.

'Amy.' He chooses his words carefully. 'I'm not being my best self. But you're doing nothing wrong. You're on time off.'

'Hugh might have given me time off, but I'm not sure I gave it to myself. This sounds mad but I don't approve of my behaviour with you. It's called cognitive dissonance –'

'You read about it in *Psychologies*?' A little smile.

'Yes. So there's that. I also feel sad. About lots of things. About the young woman. She's had a confusing life, in terms of whom she should love, and being pregnant is terrifying for her. And she's particularly close to my – to Hugh and I'm sad he's not here for her.'

Josh puts his hand over mine but I whip it away, he can't be touching me in public. Apologetically, I say, 'Sod's law, Marcia's best friend will walk in.' But I feel cold and shaky and I'd love him to hold me. 'I'm going to ask you a question,' I say. 'And you're not to read anything into it. Okay? Did you cancel the room, the hotel room, like?'

'No.'

'Please don't expect anything because I totally couldn't, but can we go up there?'

Fully clothed, we lie on the bed, curled into each other. He strokes my hair while I talk in fits and starts, relating inconsequential stuff, Mum's vlogging adventures, Kiara's idealism, the beauty of Jackson's long, dark hair. I lapse into silence for a while, then remember something else.

As time passes, calm steals over me and my sorrow lifts away. 'Tell me things about you, Josh. Do you write stuff? Film scripts?'

He pauses before he answers. 'Not any more.'

'You used to?' Almost absently, I begin playing with the front of his jeans, sliding my fingertips up and down the sharply creased fold of denim that covers his fly.

'Yeah, when I was – Amy, what are you doing?'

'I don't know.'

'Please stop.'

'Would you mind if I didn't?'

'But –'

'Can we just see what happens?' I whisper.

'No.' He catches my wrist and holds my hand away from him.

'Please. Please, Josh. I want to do this.'

'It doesn't feel right.'

'It does to me.'

This time is entirely different. It's tender, gentle and achingly lovely. When he enters me and begins his slow circles, silent tears spill from my eyes. Horrified, he freezes and I say, 'Please don't stop, Josh. I want this.'

He's rearing back and out. 'No.'

With my hands, with my legs, I clamp him to me. 'Please. Stay in me, stay with me.'

'But it's making you sad.'

'It's making me less sad.'

'It doesn't look that way.'

I manage a watery laugh.

'Are you sure?' he whispers.

I cry through it and he kisses my tears, and he says, 'Amy. Beautiful, beautiful, beautiful Amy.'

80

On Wednesday night when I get home from London, Sofie is even more peaky and pinched-looking than she was two days ago.

'I can't eat until it's all over,' she repeats.

Panicking, I make a rash threat. 'If you don't eat I won't let you go to England.'

'If you won't let me go, I'm never eating again.'

'Sofie!'

'You don't understand, Amy – I'd rather die than have a baby.'

'You're not having a baby. I swear to you on everyone I love that you're not.'

She shakes her head. 'The flight could be cancelled, the clinic could burn down, the anti-choice people might kidnap me –'

'Sofie, that's mad talk! How about if I made you some soup?'

'Soup is food.'

'Milkshake?'

'Food.'

'What about rehydration salts?'

'Oh-kay.'

Well, it was something.

Derry won't be in Ulan Bator next week, but she'll be in some other far-flung location so she won't be able to pick Sofie up from the clinic.

'Who do you trust?' she asks.

'Easy. Alastair. But he wouldn't be right for this.'

And as Steevie and Jana still aren't talking to me, and Petra never gets time away from the twins, my options are narrowing.

'What about Maura?' Derry suggests. 'Siena? Jackson?'

'No,' I say. 'No. No.'

'Jackson's mum?'

'She can't.' She has a special-needs kid, who needs a lot of care.

'Urzula?'

'No fucking way!' That makes both Derry and me laugh.

Doubtfully Derry says, 'Joe?'

I sigh. 'What do you think?'

'I think he'll lie through his teeth to get out of it. If he, by some unlikely chance, commits to it, he'll let you down on the day. You'd be a wreck, waiting for him to pull some stunt.'

She's absolutely right, on all counts.

'Derry,' I say. 'There might be another route. Sofie, she literally isn't eating. She says she won't until this is fixed. So could she be said to be suicidal? Because the law says that if a woman is suicidal, she can have an abortion.'

Derry shuts me down fast. 'They'd keep getting more and more opinions and by the time they'd decreed Sofie really *was* suicidal, the foetus would be starting university.'

'Or Sofie would have jumped off a bridge.'

'Or simply starved herself to death.'

'Right.' Well, it had been worth a try.

'It'll have to be Neeve,' Derry says. 'There's no one else.'

'She's too young.'

'She's twenty-two. And there's no other choice.'

She's right.

'And Kiara can stay with Joe,' Derry says. 'It's the least that useless fucker can do.'

'What's going on?' It's Thursday morning and Alastair has phoned me from London.

'What do you mean?'

'Thamy says you're out of the office on another mysterious skite this afternoon. And you're taking Monday off.'

'*Thamy* rang you? Rang you in London?'

384

'And you can't shout at her. I made her tell me. What the hell is going on, Amy? I mean, I know you're riding Josh Rowan's lights out. What can be more exciting than that?'

'You – you *fucking* nosy-poke!'

'I tell you everything!'

'But this isn't my secret to tell.'

'Oh!' He gets it now, that this isn't some jokey thing.

'But, lookit, I might have to tell you anyway. Sofie is pregnant.'

'Oh, shite.' Then, 'Why might you have had to tell me anyway?'

I almost laugh. 'She hasn't fingered you as the baby daddy, if that's what you're afraid of.'

'That's one thing I need never fear. I respect you so much that I'd *never* do any of your family.'

'Except maybe my hot sister.'

'Except maybe her. Yes. And Lilian O'Connell, mother of five, how is sh–'

'So my *skite* this afternoon,' I talk over him, 'is taking Sofie to a counsellor.'

'I am genuinely sorry, Amy, for calling it so wrong and for what you and Sofie are going through.'

'She's having an abortion in London on Tuesday.'

'Isn't that the day of your big Tabitha Wilton thing?'

'Yeah. So I might need you, Alastair.'

'I'm there,' he says. 'Just tell me when you need me.'

81

'Next stop is ours,' I say.

Sofie, Neeve and I stand up immediately, reaching for our wheely cases, trying to keep our balance on the wobbly train. We didn't need to get up for at least another three minutes but we're doing everything ahead of time. We're almost three hours too early for the appointment, but better to be early than late.

The clinic is in deepest Wimbledon and we kill time in a café that reminds me of the one the losing team in *The Apprentice* go to. It hurts my heart to see Sofie so young and lost. This wouldn't be easy, whatever country it was happening in, but it's worse that she had to get up at the crack of dawn to catch a flight and that she's having to make her way around a foreign city.

There's something I've back-and-forthed on: I don't want to load Sofie up with shame, but she needs to be protected.

I swallow. 'We should use a fake address. We don't want this to come back on Sofie.'

'This is *bullshit*,' Neeve says.

'Please, Neeve, not everyone in Ireland is like us. People judge.'

Her tone is placatory. 'It's okay, Mum, I get it. I'm just pissed off that it has to be this way.'

The clinic is in a big, ugly house on a busy road. The entrance is around the side. Sofie is visibly shaking and even Neeve looks fearful.

We say our hellos, and a quick glance around the room establishes that there are about eight other clusters of people, different ages and ethnicities. Maybe some of them are Irish, too. No one makes eye contact.

My 'address' is an amalgam of those of friends and family. Clues are everywhere and Derren Brown would crack the real one in thirty seconds flat. If only I'd had the foresight to use a fake surname when I made the booking. Medical records are supposed to be confidential, but if someone raided this clinic and published all the details to shame the women and . . .

God. My hands are sweaty.

'Y'okay?' Neeve asks.

'Yep, sure, yes, certainly!'

'Sofie?' A woman in a dress I recognize from Cos has poked her head around a door. 'Come through.'

'Can Amy, I mean my mum, come too?' Sofie asks.

'No, hon, we're going to have a chat. It needs to be private.'

Another counsellor. I'm glad. The more counsellors the better, as far as I'm concerned.

Sofie is gone for about an hour and no sooner is she back than a woman in scrubs takes her for her scan. This time I'm allowed to go with her.

'You're almost ten weeks, Sofie, just in time.' She gives Sofie two pills to swallow with a cup of water. 'If you vomit within an hour of taking these, you must come back.'

Seeing as Sofie hasn't eaten in days, what are the chances of her vomiting? Very low, I can only hope.

'You might start cramping tonight or tomorrow morning, but you might not. If you do, take ibuprofen, nothing else. Be back here tomorrow at two p.m. You'll be here for about three hours and you must have someone to take you home.'

I say, 'My daughter, er, my other daughter, Neeve, the one in the waiting room, will come with Sofie tomorrow and stay to take her home.' But I'm losing my nerve. Surely this is too frightening to burden Neeve with.

I know that other young women do this without the likes of me being involved. I know that when I was twenty-two I had a lot more responsibility than Neeve will have tomorrow. And yet I feel as if I'm abdicating my parental duties.

Should I ring Alastair and ask him to come to London tomorrow and cover Tabitha Wilton's launch?

Before we leave the clinic, it's time to cough up. Jackson's parents said they'll pay half the costs but we're waiting until I have a final figure. Meanwhile, I very much regret all the pointless dresses I've been buying and hope that my credit card doesn't explode.

But the amount is less than I'd expected. 'Is this only part of the cost?'

The woman says, 'We have a lower rate for those coming from Ireland. Because it's already costing you so much.'

'Thank you.' It's decent of them, extremely so. And yet I feel ashamed that a foreign country is helping us because our own country won't.

En route to Druzie's, Sofie perks up considerably.

'Please will you eat something this evening?' I ask her.

'Yes!' Then, 'You don't think that if I eat something I'm tempting Fate and something will go horribly wrong and –'

'Nothing will go wrong.'

We stop off at Tesco and buy doughnuts, fresh pineapple and other delicacies, and once the girls are installed in front of Netflix, I call Alastair.

'Hey,' he says. 'How's it going?'

'Good, fine, okay. I think. Just, I'm sort of losing my nerve about tomorrow. About leaving Neeve to deal with it all.'

Without even a breath, he says, 'I'll get the first flight to London in the morning. I can work just as easily from there as here.'

'Really? But where will you stay tomorrow night? We'll be here in Druzie's.'

'I'll get a hotel.'

'You could sleep on the couch?'

'I'll get a hotel.' Then, 'It's no problem, Amy. None. And it'll give you the choice about what to do.'

'You're a good man, Alastair Donovan.'

Sofie shares my bed and I skim the surface of sleep all night, never fully under in case something goes wrong and she needs me. But morning comes and all seems fine.

'No cramps?' I ask.

'No. I guess now they won't start until the second pills.'

I'm still undecided about what to do today. The notion of abandoning Tabitha Wilton and the charity to Alastair feels wrong, even though Alastair would have everyone charmed in four seconds flat.

However, I'm not sure how Sofie would feel about a man picking her up from the clinic. She knows Alastair vaguely, and seems well disposed to him, but she's at her most vulnerable. The best thing is to have him as back-up.

But now I'm anxious about undermining Neeve so I grab her while Sofie is in the shower. 'Neeve, you know Alastair I work with? He's in London today. If anything goes . . . happens, you're to call him.'

'Okay. You know, this . . . it's a bit scary.' Quickly she adds, 'Like, it's cool, I can do it, I'm totally down with it. But good to know that if anything . . . Yeah. Thanks, Mum.'

Grand. I ring Alastair and ask him to be standing by. It's a huge relief to know that Neeve and Sofie aren't doing this alone.

82

Tuesday, 6 December, day eighty-five

At twelve o'clock, the taxi arrives for Neeve and Sofie. Then I catch a tube to the Jade, a small, pretty, slightly shabby hotel near Goodge Street, more expensive than it looks. Finding the right venue for this event has been, frankly, a bloody nightmare. As it's being thrown by a charity, it can't look ostentatious, but because I need the media onside, it can't be too mingy either. This means there's wine but no Prosecco, Gruyère bites but no *kobe* mini-burgers.

The set-up has just begun when I arrive. Over the weekend, I had the brainwave of having a pick 'n' mix sweet stand – I thought it might send the subliminal message that Tabitha was sweet (which she so isn't). But now, looking at the big clear plastic bags of foamy bananas and fizzy cola bottles, I'm wondering if it looks frivolous, if everything has been disastrously misjudged.

The cloakroom is geared up for a hundred people – Tabitha Wilton is such a controversial figure, the media turnout will be high.

But the most important thing is that the food and drink comes thick and fast. 'Don't pace things,' I tell the staff. 'This isn't a civilized crowd. This is the *press*.'

The official start time is five o'clock, but at seventeen minutes to the hour, the first hack shows. Followed by three more right behind her.

'It's showtime,' I mutter in Tabitha's ear, and start steering her around the fast-filling function room, introducing her to journalist after journalist, keeping her on message, even as she's asked questions likely to rile.

For a while I actually forget about Sofie. Then I see a text from Neeve: **All good. On our way back now.** And I feel such a wave of emotion – relief and an odd sorrow – that I almost miss Tabitha giving an arsey answer to a man from the *Telegraph*.

At six thirty, when the event is meant to finish, the place is heaving and everyone is jarred. The waiters have stopped serving wine, which normally gets rid of people sharpish.

But we have a problem: the pick 'n' mix is a *massive* hit. There are crowds around the stand, stretching over each other, red-faced and happy, filling blue-and-white-striped paper bags with wine gums and jelly fried eggs. I wish to God they'd all just feck off home, instead of standing there, joyously recalling childhood memories.

'Cherry *lips*!'

'Apple *rings*!'

'How much are the penny sweets?'

'Ha-ha-ha-ha! We used to say that to the man in the shop! Did you say it too? Ha-ha-ha-ha!'

It's almost eight o'clock by the time I get rid of the last guest and haul myself into a taxi. I'm leaden with tiredness, my face hurts from smiling politely, and as I get closer to Druzie's, my stomach begins to burn with anxiety. Will everything be okay? Will Sofie ever recover from this?

Neeve lets me into the flat.

'Well?' I ask.

She nods. 'She's good.'

Sofie is in bed, curled into a ball. She's paler than I've ever seen her and it seems a struggle for her to sit up. 'How are you?' I ask.

'Relieved.' She bursts into tears. 'Oh, Amy, I'm so relieved. I'm not afraid any more. Thank you, Amy, thank you.'

'Does it hurt?'

'It's like bad period pains, but I don't care.' She sobs and sobs and sobs. 'I'm so glad, I'm so thankful. Now I'm just me again and I'm so happy, I'm so happy, I feel like I'll never be sad again. The relief, Amy. I couldn't bring another person like me into the world. And I'm never, ever having sex again.'

We'll see how long that lasts.

We lie on the bed and I wrap myself around her, holding the hot-water bottle to her stomach, drifting towards sleep.

Just before I tumble down into the delicious nothing, Sofie murmurs, 'I wish Dad was here.'

83

Wednesday, 7 December, day eighty-six

At Heathrow, we round the corner to queue for security – and oh, no! There are dozens and dozens of people, corralled into long, snaking lines, travelling off into the distance, then doubling back on themselves.

'Sofie?' I ask faintly.

She's so pale, she's almost green. She's doubled over with cramps and people are looking. Is there anywhere she can sit? A place I could stash her until I reach the security conveyor-belt? But there's nowhere.

What if she faints? What if she *collapses*? What if they don't let her on the plane?

'Mum,' Neeve mutters, 'give her more painkillers.'

It's too soon. I'm afraid that if I give her too many they'll thin her blood and increase the risk of her haemorrhaging. 'Can you hang on?' I ask Sofie. 'As soon as we're through here, we'll go to a lounge and you can lie down before we get on the plane.'

'Okay.'

It's an agonizing twenty-minute shuffle before we reach the conveyor-belt. 'What would it be like if Sofie had to do this on her own?' Neeve says quietly. 'This is such bullshit.'

As bad luck would have it, Sofie beeps on her way through the scanner and has to go into a Plexiglas cubicle to be done more thoroughly. The urge to howl rises up in me: will we ever make it home?

She passes the Plexiglas test, and once we're all through, I walk us towards the lounge. The distances in the airport seem vast today – I should have booked a motorized buggy. I'd always thought I'd be mortified to be seen in such a thing, but right now I'd kill to be sitting up in one, slowly beeping my way past people walking almost as quickly as I'm gliding.

'A trolley's what we need,' Neeve says. 'We'll stick Sofie on it. Keep an eye out for a spare.'

But before we've found one, we reach the lounge.

'Twenty-five quid each!' Neeve mutters, as I hand over my credit card. 'Another seventy-five pounds. It's utter bollocks, this whole business!'

'Shush,' I say. 'Get in.'

Sofie curls up on a two-person couch, her feet in my lap, my coat over her. Neeve takes off to get 'Twenty-five quid's worth of free stuff' while I catastrophize. What if Sofie isn't allowed on to the flight? Seriously, what will we do?

Oh, God, here's a high-heeled, bossy-arse lady to tell me off!

'Everything all right here?' She gestures at the little bundle of bones that is Sofie.

'Teenage daughter,' I say, with a confident smile. 'Bad period pains. Need to get her home to a hot-water bottle.'

'No shoes on the furniture.'

'They're not. They're in my lap.'

'Mum,' Neeve says. 'I've stolen enough biscuits to open a shop and the board says "Go to gate". C'mon.'

Outside the lounge, I spot an abandoned trolley. Neeve and I coax Sofie on to it, along with her case. I push, and Neeve wheels our bags.

'We'll laugh about this one day,' Neeve says.

Maybe.

At the gate, waiting to board, I feel as if holes are being burnt in my stomach lining. It probably looks like a piece of Belgian lace down there. I'm sweating with anxiety as I give our boarding passes for inspection. The steward gives Sofie a hard stare – but we're let on.

We stash her by the window and my body is as taut as a steel hawser while we taxi, then queue, then queue some more. Finally, mercifully, the wheels are up. None of us speaks while the plane ascends higher and higher, and it's only when the seatbelt signs ping off that Neeve and I both exhale long and loudly, then turn and give each other a tentative smile.

84

'Darker.' Mum is excited.

'It's not a good idea,' the beautician says.

'But why would I get my eyebrows tattooed if no one will notice?'

'They *will* notice them.'

'That poor beautician,' Alastair says. 'Lilian O'Connell, mother of five, has a will of iron.'

It's Monday morning and Neeve's latest vlog, starring my mother getting eyebrowdery, has just gone live.

'It's almost like a thriller,' Alastair says. 'Waiting to see whose will is going to prevail. My money's on Locmof.'

'Who?'

'LOCMOF – Lilian O'Connell, mother of five.'

The beautician – Elaine – calmly explains that as Mum's hair is blonde, her eyebrows have to match.

'But who says I'm staying blonde?' Mum asks. 'I could change it tomorrow to red. Or blue, even! So go a couple of shades darker on the brows. Please.'

The vlog takes us – speedily – through the hour-and-a-half process, and at the end Mum has beautiful well-defined mid-brown eyebrows and looks noticeably different.

'It completely changes my face!' she raves. 'I look *visible*. I'm a woman you'd notice. A woman you'd *respect*.'

'I respected you well before this, Locmof,' Alastair says. 'Amy, is there any way she'd adopt me?'

'You've a perfectly lovely mother of your own, you ingrate. Why do you always have to want the woman you can't have?' Then I see the time. 'Oh, God, Alastair, it's ten to one. Hurry!'

The Christmas madness is well under way – the lights, the crowds, the carrier bags, the catch-ups, the mulled wine, the hangovers. Work overlaps with pleasure, as I deliver gifts to favoured journalists and clients, then take them for lunch or drinks. Today we're having our office lunch, although, as Alastair says, 'It's a bit ice-to-the-Eskimos seeing as our job is one long piss-up.'

'Mine isn't,' Thamy mutters.

At home we've put up the decorations, although we've had to do without a few things, like strewing lights through the tree in the front garden, because we needed Hugh and a ladder.

In Hugh's absence, Kiara has requested a change to our usual Christmas Day. 'I don't want it to be just us four, I'd miss him too much and so would Sofie. Could we do something, maybe with Derry? Or Declyn?'

'We could go to a hotel?'

'Oh, no, Mum!' I should have known that Kiara would recoil at money being spent needlessly. 'That would be every kind of wrong. And I want us to cook together!'

Shite. A million times shite. Hugh always does our Christmas dinner and Kiara's idea of sharing the load is opening the oven door and shouting, 'What colour is "done" supposed to look like?'

Derry dislikes cooking even more than I do. It's going to be awful.

'Would it be okay if I bought Dad a gift?' Kiara asked. 'Even though he won't be here to open it.'

A bud of rage blooms in me: I hate him for doing this to her.

Next thing, Maura got involved in the Christmas Day arrangements and suddenly it was decided that the entire family was going to Mum and Pop's for the lunch.

Derry broke the news to me. 'But you've got off lightly, Amy, you're on trifle and cake duty.'

'Jackson and I will help,' Sofie says.

To my great relief, Sofie is doing well. Wonderfully, even. She's eating, she's engaging in things, and she and Jackson are as together as they ever were.

'We'll make a trifle,' I tell her. 'But I'm buying the cake. Life's too short.'

It's Mum on the phone.

'Amy. I got recognized from the vlog thing. In Cornelscourt. Some girls came up to me and asked, "Are you Neeve Aldin's granny?"'

'But that's great!'

'I know, right! They wanted to see my eyebrows up-close. Then they said I was a legend.'

'Mum. Mum.' Neeve comes into the kitchen, while I'm reluctantly cooking dinner. My heart contracts. What now?

'Mum.' Her voice is hoarse. Then tears begin to fall.

'What?'

'It's happened.'

For the love of God! 'What has?'

'Income. Money! Finally.' She's crying properly now. 'An agency want to advertise on my site. They'll pay me. The hits are high enough.'

'Oh, Neeve!' Things have been improving, I know. Her subscribers have increased sharply, the calibre of freebies has improved, and a few smallish companies have suggested a brand partnership. But this is in a different league.

'Mum, can you believe it?' Her voice is thick with tears. 'Actual real money. Earned by me, and not just the pennies they pay me in that effing nightclub. I'd been thinking of becoming a Deliveroo driver after Christmas and now I won't have to.'

'Oh, Neevey, well done! You've worked so bloody hard on this, you deserve it.'

'I have to thank Granny. Her first vlog changed something.'

It did. There are thousands of interchangeable YouTube style bloggers, all pushing a cross-section of the same stuff to the same demographic. For any to succeed, they need a USP: a cute doggie, a cute boyfriend or – as in Neeve's case – a cute granny.

'You had the idea to film her,' I say. 'You've got to take some credit.'

'Suddenly things have got better.' She's weeping again. 'Daddy is finally properly in my life and now this! I never thought I could be this happy!'

85

Tuesday, 13 December, day ninety-two

I bump awake. The world is in complete darkness and I'm wondering what's woken me – my head zips through my usual worries: Hugh, Sofie, money, Kiara, Neeve, Pop, Mum, Josh . . . Then I realize it's Marcia. Again. The guilt is acute. I'm not built for being the other woman.

I haven't seen Josh for nearly a fortnight – we didn't meet last week when Sofie was in London but I'll be with him tomorrow. Or – a quick look at the clock establishes – later today.

Josh and I have had three Tuesdays together in a hotel room, where all my sadness is put on hold. My complicated grief about Hugh disperses for those few hours and I lose myself in Josh, in how badly he wants me. During those hours, my guilt about Marcia lifts, but as soon as I'm on my own again – and that's most of the time, I see Josh for a mere six hours a week – it returns, often waking me in the middle of the night.

What I'm doing to Marcia is every kind of wrong.

Thinking of my devastation when I caught Richie or – far worse – seeing those photos of Raffie Geras with Hugh reminds me that I'm doing to Marcia what those women did to me.

In theory, Josh is the one who owes loyalty to Marcia – I owe her nothing – but life is not that simple. In fact, when men cheat, it's the women who get the blame: the wife for not being hot enough or the slutty adulteress for preying on a man who 'belongs' to someone else.

My plan had been to let things run until the end of the year. Tomorrow night – today, whenever – is the second last time I'll be in London before Christmas. So I've only two more nights left with Josh. And I don't want it to be over.

*

'Josh?'

'Sackcloth?'

'Next Tuesday will be the last Tuesday I'm in London before Christmas. I won't be here again until January the tenth.'

'What?' He scrambles to sit up in the bed.

'The Tuesday after next week is the twenty-seventh and the one after will be January the third. There's no point in me coming to London then – nobody will be around.'

Josh is doing calculations. 'So we won't see each other for three weeks?'

Now is the time to remind him of my end of year deadline, and I don't.

'I'm not happy,' he says. 'It's hard enough seeing you only once a week.'

I feel the same.

Suddenly he says, 'Come away with me. In the time between Christmas and New Year. For a couple of days.'

I don't instantly dismiss it. 'Where?'

'Where would you like?'

'Where would *you* like?' Because I'm curious.

'You love clothes,' he says. 'We could go to one of the fashion capitals? Milan?'

I'm surprisingly touched but I have to laugh. 'Milan would put the fear of God into me.'

'Paris?'

Sharply I shake my head, and he says, 'Too romantic for my little Sackcloth?'

'Too clichéd.'

An expression passes over his face . . . He looks pissed-off. Just slightly. But . . .

Quickly I say, 'Where would you like?'

'I like places with history. Berlin is cool. I've never been to Venice –'

'We're not going to Venice.'

'Cliché?'

'Cliché.'

'St Petersburg?'

'Absolutely not. Because Putin.'

'The Lake District?'

'Nowhere in the UK.' I'm certain about this. 'I feel shitty enough about your wife and we're not running the risk of anyone who knows her seeing us.'

'So where isn't too clichéd or too romantic or too in the UK?'

I can't think of anywhere.

'Is there a place you've always wanted to go? There must be somewhere.'

There is, actually. 'Serbia.'

He hoots with laughter, then stops abruptly. 'Oh, God, you're *serious*.'

86

My phone rings. I pick it up from the table and look at it — as expected, it's Josh. Again. The third time he's rung this morning. Usually our communication is via text, but I'm guessing he wants an actual conversation because we'd parted on very frosty terms last night. After he'd laughed at my mini-break location request, I'd got dressed in hot-cheeked silence and, even as he pleaded with me to stay, I left.

An incoming text beeps and, yep, it's from him: **Please talk to me. I'm sorry. I'm an idiot. Let me make things right.**

No. He can sweat a while longer.

Like, *obviously* I'm going to talk to him again. This — my pique, his contrition — is just a game, one I've played in the past. I genuinely was hurt but — gun to my head — this bit is enjoyable.

When he rings for the fourth time, I pick up and sigh, 'What?'

'Can I see you today?'

'No. Back-to-back meetings.'

'After work?'

'Airport. Then flying home.'

'What time is your flight? Meet me at the airport before you go?'

'Why?'

'Meet me and I'll tell you.'

He's hunched over his phone in a booth at the airport Prêt. His coat is off, his grey-blue shirt pulling against the broadness of his shoulders, and his sleeves are rolled up to reveal his forearms. Then he sees me and smiles, the real thing, the one he commits to. 'Amy.' Even how he says my name is pathetically thrilling.

'Hey.' I sit opposite him.

'I got you mint tea.'

'Thanks.'

Quietly, only his mouth moving, he says, 'I hate not being able to kiss you.'

'Who says I'd let you?'

He sighs. 'Will you forgive me?'

A sudden urge to cry nearly overwhelms me.

'I'm in pieces,' he says. 'I'm sorry I didn't take you seriously. I was surprised, is all. But, Sackcloth, that's you – you keep surprising me.' He shifts his hands across the table, and when he touches his knuckles off mine, a charge zips through me.

There are people all around us, but speedily I grab his hand, so I can feel the warmth of his palm against mine, then just as quickly relinquish it.

'So I've investigated,' he says, talking over the racket. 'Your Serbian museum is only an hour and a half from Belgrade. It's open for all of December because they don't do Christmas there until January the seventh.'

'You actually *spoke* to them?'

'A woman at work speaks some Serbian. She did the translating. So, early flight out of London on December the twenty-seventh, getting into Belgrade at one p.m. local time. Hire a car, head south, be in your museum by three. How's that sound?'

'Um, terrifying.'

He laughs. 'We can drive back to Belgrade that night and stay in a posh hotel for two nights. Or we can do a sackcloth-and-ashes special in your museum town – I've already looked, we'd be spoilt for choice – then one night in Belgrade. We fly back to London on the twenty-ninth.' He pauses for impact. 'Well?'

'What would you tell your wife?'

'Whatever you like. I can tell her the truth.'

'Don't!' That's the worst idea ever.

'What if I have to? What if I've fallen in love with you?'

I watch him. Is he even serious? 'Don't.'

'Should I book the flights?'

'Slow *down*. I don't know. Let me think about it. I've to go now.'

'I could come to Dublin for those nights instead?'

I definitely don't want that. Someone would see us and tell the girls. 'Seriously, it's time for my plane. I'll call you in the morning.'

'Amy,' he leans towards me and clamps his hand over my wrist, 'don't go.'

'I ha–'

'Get a later flight.' His face is hungry. 'Come to a hotel with me instead.'

I'm struck dumb. But my body has lit up, every nerve end wanting to feel his touch. It's so tempting . . .

'Go on,' he says. Then he mouths silently, 'I'm so hard for you.'

Under the table I slip off my shoe and slide my foot up along his leg until I reach his groin. I inch higher and he's quite right, he's rock hard – and the *heat* that's coming off it. With the sole of my foot placed along the length of him, I press down hard. He makes a choking noise.

Unable to hide my amusement, I wait for him to recover. 'You still good to go?' I ask. 'Or was that it?'

Huskily, he says, 'I'm still good to go.'

I grab my bag. 'Well, come on, then.'

87

Thursday, 15 December, day ninety-four

'Who's paying?' This is Derry's first question.

'Him.'

'Oh-*kay*.' She's impressed.

'Bad feminist?'

She sighs. 'People are still allowed to treat other people, right? Will you tell the girls?'

'Are you out of your effing *mind*? No! I'll tell them I'm going on a mini-break with someone I work with. But if they ask if it's a man, I *will* lie. Derry, what if he eats with his mouth open?'

'You've had lunch with him, you know he doesn't.'

'What if the car breaks down and he can't fix it and he loses his temper and flings his spanner on the ground and marches away in a fury?'

'That's most childhood car journeys with Pop you're thinking of there.'

God, she's right. 'Okay. What if it turns out he's disgusting?'

'What way?'

'Dunno. He's quite macho, more macho than Hugh. I don't want to think about it, but there's any number of ways for a man to be disgusting.'

Derry gets it. 'Maybe book two bathrooms?'

'How could I even do that? Oh, Derry, what if he says "lav" instead of "bathroom"? What if he says, "I need to use the lav"?'

'If that happens, just come straight home.'

Derry isn't the person to have this conversation with – after all, she's the one who ended a five-month relationship when the misfortunate bastard insisted 'kebab' was pronounced 'kebob'.

'What about me?' I ask. 'And *my* bladder? I've to go about every half-hour. The first thing I do in a new place is check where the facilities are. How will I survive a car journey in an underdeveloped country?'

Derry shakes her head helplessly.

'On long car journeys in this country,' I say, 'I've let myself become dehydrated rather than risk one of those dodgy loos round the back of a petrol station.' I shudder long and hard. 'And they'd be worse in Serbia, wouldn't they?'

'Christ, Amy!' Derry explodes. 'Why can't you do things like a normal person? Anyone else off on a sexy weekend, they go somewhere beautiful, like Barcelona, they stay in glitzy hotels with plentiful public bathrooms, instead of some B-and-B in the back-arse of nowhere, where you'll probably have to share an outhouse with an entire family, including the grandfather with no teeth and his ancient lad hanging out of his yellowing long johns. And they *certainly* don't embark on road trips with a man who's practically a stranger.'

What can I say? She has a point.

'Anyone would swear you don't actually want to enjoy yourself!'

'I don't. Well, I do. But not too much.'

She shakes her head again. 'Surely they'll have nice hotels in Belgrade?' She reaches for her tablet, clicks a few times and starts reading. 'This is from Lonely Planet. "Outspoken, adventurous, proud and audacious, Belgrade is by no means a pretty capital but its gritty exuberance makes it one of the most happening cities in Europe."'

'I don't know which word scares me more,' I say. '"Gritty" or "happening".'

Derry scrolls down. '"Surrounded by forest . . . baroque . . . beautiful riverside setting and half-ruined hilltop castle."'

'*Belgrade?*'

'Nope. Heidelberg. This is the mini-break you *could* have gone on. Or listen to this, "A saffron-and-spice vision from the storybooks, with one of Europe's most arresting historic hubs with imposing palaces and razor-thin cobblestone streets." That's

Stockholm,' she says. 'Just saying. But you'd prefer non-pretty grittiness.' Then she mutters, 'You effing oddball.'

'I'm offbeat,' I protest. 'I'm quirky.'

'Yeah,' she laughs, 'and riddled with guilt. So? Are you going to go?'

'I think I am.'

'Josh, will it be very cold in Serbia?'

Reluctantly he says, 'It'll probably be snowing.'

This is exactly what I was hoping to hear. I have visions of fur-lined hoods, wooden houses, embroidered tablecloths, boots with curly toes . . . 'I'll meet you there. In Belgrade airport, like.'

After a silence, he asks, 'Why's that?'

Because I'd have to fly to London the night before in order to catch the early flight. It's easier for me to fly from Dublin via Vienna. But there's another reason . . . 'We'd be stuck together on a three-hour plane journey. We don't know each other well enough for that.'

'But this is a chance.'

'No. It's really not a good idea.'

Sounding a little huffy, he asks, 'Do you trust me to book the hotels?'

'I don't think so, Josh.'

There's a long, wounded silence. You know, he's a leetle touchy . . .

'Sorry, Josh. But this is all so out of my comfort zone that I need some control.'

'Okay.' He sighs. 'But book a nice place in Belgrade, nothing too sackcloth. In Jagodina, only basic is available. So let's have two nights in Belgrade and really go for it. Let me give you my credit card details.'

And that's weird. I've had sex with this man. My most private parts have been in his mouth. But him giving me his credit card numbers feels shockingly intimate.

I've found *the* most fabulous hotel in Belgrade. It has every modern convenience but the rooms look as if they belong in a traditional Slavic home, like my dreams have come to life:

luscious rugs patterned with peacocks or spreading oak trees; wallpaper in exquisite flock; huge lengths of window with wavy frames, heavy falls of jacquard curtains; coloured crystal lamps; leather ottoman pouffes; free-standing stove-heaters with vibrant ceramic tiles; peculiar paintings of men who look like Cossacks; gorgeous-looking beds, with hand-painted headboards, layered up with numerous throws and pillows; embroidered cushion covers and – get this – actual antimacassars!

There's shameless clashing and crowding of patterns and colours and the whole effect is dazzlingly delightful. It's Bohemian, it's folksy, but it's *not* twee.

'It *is* twee,' Posh Petra says. 'I'm getting a migraine just from the photos. What's this Josh going to think?'

'I don't care. This is for me. Anyway, Josh won't mind what the room is like, so long as he gets to have lots of sex with me.'

Posh Petra's face is a picture. 'Amy?' She pauses. 'Is this, you and him, *serious*?'

'No. Well, I don't kn–, it's intense, which isn't the same. But there's no future in it.'

'Why do you say that?'

'Because, duh, he's married. We live in different countries. I've three kids, he's got two, we've no money, we know nothing about mundane day-to-day living with each other – the list is endless.'

'People make these things work. Men leave their wives –'

I think of Hugh at the same time as she does and she exclaims, 'Sorry! Honey, I'm sorry!'

'It's okay. Settle.' The pain abates to a dull ache.

'Marriages break up all the time – Josh and his wife might well be on the skids. And your girls are nearly grown, they'll be leaving home soon.'

'They fecking won't,' I say. 'The housing market being what it is, they'll be living at home for ever.'

'But *you* can leave.'

'Petra, stop. Please. Josh and me, it's just fun. At some stage I'll have to face my feelings about Hugh and that's going to be a bloodbath. Right now, I need to live in the moment.'

88

Saturday, 17 December, day ninety-six

'Mum! *Muuuuum!* MUM!' Shrieks of excitement are coming from upstairs so I abandon the washing-machine, I'm in the mood for something nice.

But the girls are racing down the stairs, Neeve waving her iPad.

'Look, Mum, look!'

It's some website and under 'Ones to Watch in 2017' is 'Neeve Aldin, Irish style vlogger. Charming, funny, tells it how it is. Watch out for occasional cameos from her granny, you will *die*.'

'I'm happening,' Neeve howls. She turns her face to the ceiling and yells, 'I. Am. Actually. HAPPENING!!!!'

'What's this on?'

'*Glamour*, their website. I know! It's real! I'm almost mainstreaming!'

'So, ah, is it cool with you girls if I go away for a few days after Christmas?' I'm striving for casual, but they have zero interest in my stuff. Neeve is off to some fancy hotel in Tipperary with Richie and his parents. All credit to him, he's making great efforts to enfold her into the extended family – even if I still don't fully trust him not to abruptly lose interest in her again in the future. Sofie and Jackson are off to a grungy-sounding house party in Connemara. And Kiara is going on a survival-style camping trip in Kerry with some other kids from her class.

Saying goodbye to Josh on 21 December is weird. 'See you in Serbia,' he says.

My stomach lurches. Am I making a terrible mistake?

'No.' He answers my unspoken question. 'It will all be cool.'

'But what if we don't get on? I might be starving and happy to put up with some shithole café but you might want us to walk around for hours in the cold until we find the perfect place. Or I might snore –'

'You do. I don't mind. But, Sackcloth, until then I'm going to miss you so bad. I'll be wanking for England. Can I call you? On Christmas Day?'

'No.'

His face darkens.

'Josh, no, seriously. It's disrespectful to your wife,' I say. 'Christmas Day is for families.'

'Which is why it's so fucking unendurable.'

'Stop it, Josh. Some things are sacred. Don't ring me on that day.'

89

'Mum! Get up!' Kiara's shaking me awake. 'We're opening the gifts! Happy Christmas!'

Neeve and Sofie appear at my bedroom door. 'Come *on*.'

The three of them thump and giggle their way down the stairs. I put on my snowman pyjamas and reindeer slippers and follow, watching fondly as the girls fling themselves on 'their' heaps and begin tearing off paper.

I've wrapped each of them a stocking full of trinkets – leopard-print socks, stuff from Claire's – and one 'real' gift.

'Oh, *Mum*!' Neeve shrieks. 'Tom Ford sunnies!'

The frame is caramel-coloured and the glass an unusual amber shade, which works beautifully with her red-gold hair.

'I totally, *totally* love them!' She puts them on and parades around in her onesie and fluffy slippers. 'How fabulous am I?' she demands. 'Totally? Or totally?'

'Totally!'

A tin of Roses has appeared and we all dive into it, even Sofie.

'Mum . . .' Kiara has opened her 'real' gift, a charity donation to buy shoes for four girls in the developing world, so they can walk to school and get an education. Her eyes fill with tears.

'Yeah, if I got that, I'd be crying too!' Neeve calls.

'Best gift ever!' Kiara flings herself at me and we tumble, laughing, to the floor.

Sofie's present is a new phone. 'You're great, Amy. You're super-great!'

They've bought me various bits and pieces – a massage voucher, earrings, 'And something good!'

They produce a bigger parcel from behind the couch and place it in my lap.

'What is it?' I ask.

'A fully grown Irish Wolfhound!' Neeve is in great form.

'Open it and see,' Sofie says.

And, you know, my hopes aren't high, because even though they're well-meaning, they don't entirely get me. Still, they've gone to some sort of trouble and that's touching in itself.

But, oh, my God, it's beautiful. It's a leather handbag, embroidered with a Slavic-looking peasant scene.

'Do you like it?' Kiara breathes.

'I *adore* it.'

This triggers a flood of information from them. 'It reminded us of those paintings you love.'

'We saw it on Etsy.'

'We were afraid it wouldn't get here in time!'

'But then it did!'

'And when we saw it for real, we *knew* you'd love it!'

'I LOVE Christmas,' Kiara says.

'Will we have a glass of Baileys?' I say.

'It's nine thirty,' Neeve says. 'In the Ay Ems! Ah, go on, so!'

As I rise to go to the kitchen, there's a noise from outside the front door. Visitors? But who? At this hour on Christmas Day?

The four of us exchange a quizzical look. Then, alarmingly, there's the rattle of a key being inserted in the lock. Who would be letting themselves in with a key?

With another rattle, then a clatter, the front door is shoved open – and oh, my God, it's . . . My eyes are seeing him, but my brain can't process it. Thinner, tanned, with longer hair and an unfamiliar jacket, it's Hugh.

The shock is disabling. I'm frozen in place as I watch him drag in a huge rucksack. Then the room erupts. Sofie and Kiara jump to their feet and run to him with cries of 'Dad!'

He stretches out his arms and gathers the three of them – even Neeve lets herself be included – into him.

413

He locks eyes with me, gestures to his enveloping arms and mouths, 'You?'

But I can't move.

Sofie turns to me. 'Did you know about this? Was it a secret surprise?'

Stiffly I move my head from side to side.

'Come in, come in.' They lead Hugh to the sofa. Kiara pushes me gently, so that I'm seated beside him, while they cluster on the floor.

'Why didn't you call?' Kiara asks him. 'Or text?'

'I wanted it to be a surprise.'

'It is! Best Christmas gift *ever*!'

'How long are you here for?' Neeve asks. 'When are you going back?'

He seems startled. 'No, no, I'm not. I'm home.'

'You are?'

'Oh, wow, like I was *hoping* . . .'

'Best gift ever!'

'It's Christmas *Day*,' Kiara tells him.

'I know.' He gives me a how-cute-is-she smile. He seems happy. I'm stunned and mute, feeling as if I'm dreaming.

The girls clamber all over him, demanding presents.

'I didn't have time to get you proper Christmas presents,' he says. 'But I got trinkets.'

He pulls his rucksack into the living room and produces vivid batik scarves, pretty beaded bracelets and small lacquered boxes.

I see it happen, as if I'm watching a movie.

'Hey!' Kiara checks the time on her phone. 'We'd better get going.'

We're due at Mum and Pop's for the exchange of presents. Only the grandchildren get gifts, but it'll be lots of fun. Well, it would be, if I wasn't in deep shock.

I hear my voice ask, 'Neeve, can you drive Sofie and Kiara?'

'Why can't you?'

'I need to stay and talk to Dad.'

'But you *are* coming?'

'In a while.'

They race upstairs, get dressed speedily, gather the bag of goodies, then depart, slamming the front door behind them.

Hugh and I are finally alone. I stare and stare at him. 'Are you really here?'

'Babe, I'm sorry.' He reaches for my lifeless hands. 'I should have texted or something. I thought it would be a surprise.'

'But it's a shock. You must have known it would be.'

He bites his lip in self-reproach. 'I was so happy about coming home that that was all I could think about. I'm sorry.' Gently, he says. 'Can I talk to you? Can we talk?'

'Mmm.'

'I shouldn't have gone. It was a bad, mad decision. It makes no sense to me now – I don't know how it ever did. I must have been crazy. Like properly, mentally not-right. I can't understand how it ever seemed justifiable.' His anguish looks real. 'Amy, I missed you so badly. I was lonely for almost every single second –'

No. 'I saw the pictures of you and Raffie Geras. You didn't look lonely then.'

He bows his head like a penitent. 'That was . . . It didn't last long. My heart was never in it. I'm so sorry about you seeing the picture.'

'There must be other girls I don't know about.'

He stays silent but looks sad. Then, 'It was a mistake,' he says. 'All of it, a mistake. I felt ridiculous. Always self-conscious. I'd tell myself to enjoy being in Paradise, but it was no use without you there. I'd have patches of feeling . . . in the flow, and I'd think, Okay, now I'm getting the hang of it. But it never lasted.

'Eventually I got clarity. About how much I love you. You and me, Amy, we love each other. I just, I don't know, I couldn't feel it for a while. But I appreciate it now, how connected we are, how lucky we are.'

But we're not lucky, not any longer.

'For about the last three weeks, the only way I could sleep was to pretend I was in bed with you. So I decided to come home. About thirty-six hours ago, I was in Burma, in a place in the mountains, and I realized that if I left immediately I might get home for Christmas Day. I felt like I'd walk if I had to. Once I'd made the decision, a huge burden lifted off me.'

I think he's expecting me to smile or be happy, but I can only stare.

'And now,' he says, 'I'm scared I've fucked things up for us.'

Mutely I look at him – what can I say?

'Have I?' he asks urgently. 'Fucked things up?'

I nod.

'Please, Amy. Give it a bit of time. I'm back now. It'll take a while for you to get used to me again and hopefully to forgive me and –'

'Hugh, it's not just that. I've . . . well, I think I've met someone else.'

He flinches. His face drains of colour. 'Oh.'

'You knew it might happen. You said it was okay.'

'Yeah, but . . . oh, Christ, Amy. Sorry, I just need a . . .' He rubs his hands over his face, then fixes his gaze on me. 'Is it serious?'

'I don't know. It might be. Like, not yet, but it might get that way.'

'Who is he?'

'A work person.'

'Known him long?'

Now it's my turn to flinch. 'A while.'

He chokes out, 'Is it Alastair?'

'No. Oh, no, Hugh.'

He looks relieved, but only for a moment. 'But there's someone else? So, would you like me to leave? This house?'

I can't send him packing on Christmas Day, but I don't know how to cope with being around him. 'Where have you been?' I ask abruptly. There's so much I don't know. 'I mean, which countries?'

'Oh, ah, Vietnam, Laos, Thailand and Burma.'

'Were they beautiful?' Before he can answer, I say, 'Look, Hugh, this is all messed up. I'd got used to thinking you were never coming back.'

He's perplexed. 'But I said I would.'

'I thought after . . . that girl that you wouldn't bother. That you'd go to Scotland to live with her.'

'I only knew her for ten days. It wasn't ever anything.'

'It *looked* like something.'

'I didn't think this through.' It's as if he's talking to himself. 'I got carried away. I've no right to show up here and expect things to be normal. I'll go.'

'Where?'

'Carl's?'

'You can't leave on Christmas Day. I can't send you out into the cold.' My heart feels like it's dying, like everything has turned to ashes. 'But it's fucked, Hugh. It's all fucked.'

'Don't cry, Amy, please don't cry. I'm so sorry, Amy, oh, please don't cry.'

'You're exhausted,' I say. 'Have a shower, then go to bed.'

'Where?'

'Our bed.' I mean, where else? 'I'm going out. To Mum and Pop's.'

'I could come.'

'No!' Then, more calmly, 'No, Hugh. That would be too weird for everybody.' Especially me. 'Get some sleep, I'll see you later.'

At Mum and Pop's all the talk is of Hugh's surprise return. The girls whine about him not having joined us for Christmas dinner but I mutter stuff about his jetlag, while wondering how they'll take it when I break it to them that his current presence under our roof is only temporary.

I get through the meal, but before the dessert, I have to go home. I need to check if this has actually happened.

Still feeling I'm dreaming, I climb the stairs and push open my bedroom door – and Hugh really is here. The weight of him in the bed, the heat coming from his body, this juxtaposing of extreme familiarity and shocking wrongness, it's beyond odd.

I tiptoe closer and realize he's still asleep. But he must have heard me because he wakes and sits up.

'Oh!' He reaches out and grasps me. 'Amy! I thought I'd dreamt it. I'm home!' He grabs me and plants kisses all over my face. Then the delight in his eyes disappears. 'Sorry, Amy.' He relinquishes his hold of me. 'I'm so sorry.' Furrowing his forehead, he asks, 'What would you like me to do?'

'I'm going away the day after tomorrow. For a few days.'

'Where?'

'On a sort of holiday.'

'With the man?'

I nod. 'Can we talk when I get back?'

He swallows hard. 'Yes. Yeah.' He swallows again. He looks wretchedly miserable. 'No more than I deserve, right?'

'It's not like that.' It's not about punishing him. 'Stay here while I'm gone, and when I get back, we'll talk properly.'

90

Tuesday, 27 December

As we come in to land, I wake up. I've slept almost continuously since Dublin. Belgrade airport looks like something you'd see in a post-war spy thriller: a grim grey block of a building, Cyrillic lettering and snow swirling in the air.

I'm fizzing with a mix of anticipation and anxiety.

Hugh's shock return went off like a bomb. I'm reeling. But I had a sharp word with myself: this trip is something I've wanted for a long time and I should try to enjoy it. Yes, the timing is terrible, but it is what it is.

A question that's bothered me for the past two days is, should Josh know that Hugh is back? Probably not. Strictly speaking, for the three days I'm with Josh, *I* need to not know that Hugh is back.

What's been really melting my head is where to put Hugh: he shouldn't sleep in our bed but the girls are so ecstatic he's home that despatching him to Carl's would cause untold distress. So for the last two nights Hugh has slept on our bedroom floor.

Like, it's crazy.

At three thirty this morning, leaving for the airport, I said to him, 'Get into the bed now.' But he just shook his head. 'I'm grand here.'

It's clearly some sort of self-flagellation.

'You look beautiful.' His voice was so sad.

That made me uncomfortable: the thing is, I've really gone to town on my look. It's the first time Josh and I will wake up together, and I refuse to be that woman who sleeps in her makeup. However, to take the edge off things, I've had eyelash extensions and pale fake tan done, and I shook Neeve down for a pearlescent day cream.

Yes, Josh has seen me naked and at my most vulnerable, but come on!

Time to get off the plane. I gather up my stuff. Neeve – though she doesn't know it – has loaned me her hat, gloves and scarf set, the ones with the flower embellishments. Derry's contribution to the cause is her Mr and Mrs Italy parka. It's navy but around the hood there is a ring of blue fur. Real fur. Look, I *know*. But I need to be warm, and I want to look good, and if I have to grapple with one more moral consideration right now, my head will explode.

My suitcase is mostly lingerie sets. In a reversal of most relationships, I'm only bringing out the big guns now. Asos were doing these fabulous fifties-style knickers, a homage to the Dolce & Gabbana delights, all high-waisted lace-and-silk with built-in suspender belts and matching bras, the type you put on just so they'll be removed and quickly.

I make my way through Passport Control – and there he is, his gaze narrowed, intently following the progress of everyone emerging. He sees me. He doesn't smile but trains the laser beam of his stare on me as I walk towards him.

Then I'm before him and I tilt my face to his.

He grabs my arm, hard enough to hurt. 'Sackcloth.' His voice is low and full of sauce.

'Hey.'

His hand slides to cradle the back of my head and he places a quick, tentative kiss on my mouth. Then, 'Fuck it.' And kisses me again, long, hard and passionate.

Now the movie I'm in is a Second World War classic, and I'm welcoming my sweetheart home from the front.

We break apart and stare into each other's faces. My heart is thudding and my fingertips are tingling.

'We should go,' he says. Then, practically growling, 'While I still can.'

He grabs my case of knickers, his own luggage is a black nylon holdall slung over his shoulder, and we step out into the swirling snow. And, oh, the astonishing cold, the clean pain of my breath. I adore it.

'Car's not far.' He's got no hat or gloves and his coat isn't a padded, insulated thing but simply a black wool Crombie.

'So it's true about Geordies, that you don't feel the cold,' I say.

'But I'm wearing a scarf, like. Been down south too long, gone
soft. Here's the car.'

We're guided out of the airport by his phone's Google Maps
and, in a head-spinningly short time, we're on the road south.

'According to this, we'll be in Jagodina at two thirty-three,' he
says. Then, 'You okay?'

'Mmm. Just, this is weird, right?'

'It's coming in waves.'

Okay. That meant there would be spells of normality.

'Have you eaten?'

'On the plane.'

'There's a bag of stuff, crisps and things. And garages on the
way. If you want to stop, just say.'

I smile. He's been warned about my faulty bladder.

He's made a mix tape of Serbian music, and as we drive, I stare
out of the window. This is proper winter and proper countryside:
silent fields under blankets of white; far-off farmhouses, their
roofs covered with snow; almost no advertising and what there is
is in Cyrillic.

I'm in yet another movie, this time an experimental European
one, perhaps about the disintegration of Yugoslavia.

From the outside the museum looks like a 'real' museum but
shrunken. It's small, pretty, pale yellow, and reminds me of a
beautiful cake. As Josh parks the car I'm frozen with how momen-
tous this is. 'I can't believe I'm here. Josh, I've looked at the photo
of this building for years and *yearned* to visit and now I'm actually
here.'

'But you've got to get out,' he chides gently. 'Won't do much
good if you're just sat looking at it.'

Josh's Serbian-speaking colleague had rung ahead so Marja, a
woman who speaks some English, is expecting us. I don't know
exactly what Josh's colleague said to her but it must have been

something good because a viewing room has been set aside for me. And, oh, the *beauty* of the paintings in real life!

'I wish I could climb inside and live in one.'

'What is it about them you love so much?' Josh asks.

'Partly the colour.' They're nearly all variations on blue. 'Posh Petra says that's *déclassé* but the heart wants what the heart wants, right?'

'Right.' His look is meaningful.

'I love the subject matter.' They're rural scenes, often with blue trees and blue flowers – there's a mild hallucinogenic feel to most of them. 'I dunno, Josh, it's about the way they make me feel.'

'And that is?'

'Happy and safe.' God, to own one . . . But maybe I can buy a print in the gift shop.

However, all the gift shop contains is a desultory collection of cards, none by my lady.

I don't know if this is an insulting question but I've come all this way and it would be lunacy not to enquire. 'Marja, is it possible . . . to buy one of Dušanka's paintings from the museum?'

A regretful shake of the head. 'Property of nation.'

Of course. *Shite.*

'But gallery in Belgrade have.'

Oh, sweet Jesus! The adrenalin rush! It's like being told that Selfridges is giving away all their Tom Ford products. 'Address? Do you have?' (To my shame, when I'm around people who not speak so good the English, I accidentally copy their syntax.) 'And the cost? Do you know?'

'Address, I know. The cost?' A sorrowful shrug. 'I do not know.'

But all the same! I turn to Josh, bursting with excitement. 'If they're for sale in a Belgrade gallery, maybe ordinary people can afford them. Not like the Van Goghs that cost more than a country and live in an underground vault in Japan.'

He laughs softly. 'Aye.' Then to Marja, 'Can you give us the address of the gallery?'

If I literally buy nothing else for all of next year and get three more clients on retainer . . . I'm already doing calculations, wondering how much I can let myself spend.

Gratefully I press a giant box of Butler's chocolates on Marja, then Josh and I leave for Belgrade.

91

It's only half four in the afternoon but the light is almost gone and it's different driving in the dark. There are no lights on the road north and I don't like the speed Josh is going at but I can't yelp, 'Slow down!' the way I would with Hugh. *Don't think about him. Don't think about him.*

'Josh, maybe a bit slower?'

He hits the brakes dramatically. But, within moments, the speed creeps up again and this time I say nothing.

And then we crest a hill and get our first sight of Belgrade, which strikes drear into my heart: grey, decrepit apartment blocks.

Josh reads my thoughts. 'They say the middle of town is attractive.'

As we approach the centre, the traffic becomes heavy and slow, not helped by rows of cars parked on both sides of the street. Trams run alongside the cars, spooking me.

Josh's phone is talking us towards the hotel, but something goes wrong and we're suddenly caught in a one-way system that the satnav lady knows nothing about.

'How do we get out of this?' Josh mutters, trying to look at his phone, as well as the road, which makes me really nervous.

'Maybe if you . . .' I'm downloading Google Maps, but it's only for form's sake – I'm useless with directions. 'Could you go right earlier?'

We go around again, which takes ages, about fifteen minutes and, despite taking a different turn, we end up being funnelled right back into the same one-way thing.

'The hell am I meant to do?' Josh asks.

I really don't know and we aren't helped by being unable to read the Cyrillic street signs.

'Why can't I take this turn?' Josh demands – and promptly takes it.

I'm not expected to know the answer, but realize I do. 'It's just for taxis and trams.'

He mutters, 'Oh, for fuck's . . .'

My stomach starts to hurt. This really *does* remind me of childhood journeys with Pop. Are we breaking the law? What if the police stop us? We're in an unfamiliar country, we can't speak the language, we know no one . . .

This is actual hell, isn't it? We're going to be stuck here, condemned to drive in the streets of Belgrade, for all eternity.

I look at Josh. *Who is this man? What am I doing here, in this alien place, with an angry stranger?* Momentarily I'm cold with fear. 'We could ask someone,' is my tentative suggestion.

'We can't speak Serbian!'

'Maybe they speak English.'

'Oh, go on, then!' Josh screeches to a halt, setting off a cacophony of beeping behind us. 'Ask him.'

Out of the window, I call to a young studenty-looking bloke and – thank you, God! – he speaks English. He knows the hotel and launches into detailed instructions. Then, because the beeping is still carrying on, he says, 'Is easier if I show,' and promptly gets into the back seat of the car.

Josh and I exchange a look. What have we unleashed?

But the man is perfectly lovely and gets us to the hotel in literally three minutes –

I'm astonished when he says, 'Is here. Hotel car park.'

'Already?'

'Yes. Near. I hope you have excellent time in Belgrade.'

'Thank you, but how will you get back to where you were?'

'Is near,' he says. 'More near walking than by driving.'

'Well, thank you.'

'Yeah, thanks, mate,' Josh says.

We park the car, get our bags from the boot and make our way to Reception. We're doing 'Wow, we're here' noises, but we're not making eye contact.

It'll be a while before the tension disperses.

Hotel Zaga is a pretty five-storey delight, with curlicued balconettes and embellished windows. Stepping over the threshold into the lobby is like stepping into a beautifully illustrated storybook. A bit happy-spendy, I'd booked a small suite, which had seemed sensible: not only has it a small sitting room but two bathrooms.

We're high up in the eaves, and when the hotel lady opens our door, the blue, violet, white and black colours of the sitting room explode out at us. Everything, the rugs, the paintings, the fabrics, the accessories, has been assembled with verve and care.

It's not girly and it's not twee. In my opinion, it's a work of art.

The lady leaves and I look at Josh. 'You hate it?' I'm so giddy with love I couldn't care what he thinks.

'No.' He seems bemused. 'It's, ah, authentic.' Then, from the bedroom, 'Hey. Nice bed.'

It *is* a nice bed – a striking headboard and a multitude of gloriously patterned throws and cushions. However, this isn't a comment on the décor.

'It'd be a lot nicer with a naked Amy in it.' He sweeps his arm around my waist, pulls me to him and tilts my head back into his other arm. His face is almost touching mine. 'I've had a hard-on since the airport,' he confides. 'Any idea how difficult it is to drive a car with a raging boner?'

But it's too soon, the rancour from the journey hasn't quite gone away.

He pulls my body closer, all the better to feel this raging boner, then with lightning speed, begins unpeeling my parka.

'Wait.' I step back.

'What?' He's surprised. And pissed off?

'Can we just . . . let things – us – settle? Take a moment?'

'Really?' He's definitely pissed off. 'We haven't seen each other for –' He stops abruptly. 'Hey, sorry, yeah. Yeah. Sorry. Of course.' Then, 'Amy, I *am* sorry. Moving too fast. Just, I've really missed you. You want to get a drink? Or a cup of tea? You think they do tea here?'

'You know, wine would be good. What would you like? I'll call the nice lady.'

But he's already lifted the phone. 'Red or white?'

Something isn't right . . .

Aaaah. Wrong man. It's Hugh who's terrified of ringing room service. *Don't think about him. Don't think about him.*

While we wait for the wine to arrive and smooth over the friction, we unpack, taking care not to collide with each other. The second bathroom is merely a 'lav' and hand-basin. 'This is yours,' I tell him. 'You can have your bath or shower in mine.'

He nods. There's a small smirk that he tries to hide.

'Yeah, well!' I say.

Here's the drink, thank Christ. A bottle of red wine and two crystal goblets appear on a small engraved silver tray and soon the alcohol starts to work its magic.

'What *is* it with cushions on beds?' Josh asks, in good-natured irritation. 'There's barely room for me to sit on it.' Then, 'What?'

'Nothing.' Looks like I'm still waiting to meet the man who'll love me for my bed cushions.

Josh starts flinging cushions on to the floor. 'I'm the Bishop of Southwark. It's what I do.'

Which is so unexpected and so funny that I'm afraid I might actually vomit from laughing.

When I've recovered, I say shyly, 'I got you a present. For Christmas, like.' It's a hefty hardback, which was described in the *Guardian* as the definitive guide to 1970s cinema.

Josh seems genuinely touched. 'You put so much thought into it and brought it all the way here. If I told you what my family gave me –'

'Don't!' Then, more gently, 'Let's just, you know, keep the real world at bay here.'

'I've something for you. Something small.'

I resist any remarks about how it couldn't possibly be his penis, in that case. 'Josh, no! You've taken me here, this is the best gift I could ever get.'

'It's no big deal,' he says.

I'm interested in what he thinks is 'me' and when I unwrap the paper and find underwear from Victoria's Secret, I'm totally wrong-footed. Feck's sake! That stuff is too young and *waaay* too tacky.

But all men are hopeless at buying gifts. I'd learnt that a long time ago.

'You could put them on,' Josh says hopefully.

'Maybe later.' Unless they met with an unfortunate accident – perhaps by getting too close to a naked flame and burning down half of Belgrade.

I stand at one of the windows and gaze out over night-time Belgrade. There are nothing like as many adverts or lights as I'm used to in a city. This is so very cool. All credit to me, the prospect of this scared me yet here I am.

'Josh, should we go for something to eat?' From our little eyrie, I see something I don't understand – then I do! 'Josh, come and look! There's a river and it's frozen!'

He leans over my shoulder and looks to where I'm pointing.

'First time to see a frozen river!' I say. 'It's *mad*-looking. Is it frozen all the way down?'

He's close behind me, and as he stretches for a better view, his erection grazes my bum, I catch a whiff of his neck and, all of a sudden, I'm wild with want. I whip around, snatch his face between my hands and kiss him in a frenzy. I pull at his jeans, his top, my own clothes. I can smell him and taste him, and if I don't have his skin against mine right now, I'll die.

'Help me.' Our clothes won't come off quickly enough – it's infuriating. Too many fucking buttons and belts and zips – and his *boots*! All that fumbling and unknotting. 'Let them stay on!'

His jeans and jocks are shoved to his knees, his torso is bare, his hard-on is huge, and I shove him on to the bed.

My skirt is off. 'The condoms!' Where are the fucking condoms?

'Leave them,' he says.

'No!'

'Bathroom.'

He moves and I yelp, 'No! Stay there.'

I'm back. I'm sliding it the length of him, his groan is long and helpless. 'Don't come!' I order. 'Not yet!'

I slide down on to him and he whimpers with pleasure.

'Take your top off,' he says.

'No, you'll come too soon.'

'Please.'

'No!'

'I'm begging.'

Still moving up and down on him, I leisurely unbutton my shirt. All that remains is my bra. 'Please,' he says.

'No.'

'Please.'

I reach my hands behind my back, unclasp it, then wait. Slowly I slide the straps down my arms as his eyes gleam avidly and one vigorous bounce is all it takes for it to fall. He comes immediately, howling the words, 'I love you. Amy, oh, I love you.'

Afterwards, flattened by exertion, we lie side by side. I speak into the silence: 'Don't say those words again.'

He tenses, but stays quiet.

92

Crooked stone steps lead down a steep, narrow alley towards the astonishing white river. Not many people are about. The snow has stopped, and old-fashioned black streetlamps cast pools of light that blaze but don't travel. The city is in black and white.

'It's like *The Third Man*,' Josh says.

'Is it?'

'You haven't seen it?' He stops short to display his shock. 'Sackcloth! A classic, a noir classic – Vienna, post-war thriller. Visually very stylish. I once wrote a remake of it.'

'You *did*?'

'Calm down. Nothing came of it.' He's suddenly clipped.

The steep descent ends and Josh consults the map the hotel gave us. 'So we go right, now.'

The buildings look middle-European, nineteenth-century types; handsome but crumbling. There's graffiti on the façades, elaborate double doors and fancy-framed windows tricked out with fussy crocheted or lace curtains.

There's no one other than us on the dark, slick street, and only an occasional car passes, the sound of its wheels almost sinister on the slushy road. It's gone ten and we're on our way to a restaurant on the riverfront.

'You'd never guess that Belgrade is a late-night city.' I'm a bit edgy.

'Aye. Or maybe we're too early.'

Through a high-off-the-ground window I see a young woman cooking dinner – these rundown fancy buildings must be apartments. I stare in avidly at the woman's Serbian jeans, her Serbian hair-bobble, her Serbian lampshade, her Serbian kitchen table. In awe, I breathe, 'What's it like being her?'

'Same as it is being anyone.'

'But living somewhere so atmospheric must be . . .'

'Not a great time to be a Serb – trouble getting visas to other countries, no foreign investment so not much employment . . .'

Okay, I was romanticizing my woman's life but Mr Cold Hard Facts has killed my mood.

'We go right here,' Josh says, then stops – there's a railway line between us and the waterfront. 'That's not on the bloody map.'

We look right, we look left. There are no obvious crossing points. I've no problem dashing across a track but a metal fence is barring our way. 'Um, we could try walking a bit and see what happens?'

But the cold suddenly makes itself known and as we trudge along in the shadows, my spirits are on the slide.

'They don't make it easy,' Josh mutters.

This isn't like other cities where everything is signposted and the sights are spoon-fed to you, where every avenue leads to something wonderful and all wandering is swiftly rewarded.

But there's some structure up ahead.

'Aye, aye,' Josh says – and I wince. 'Aye, aye' isn't as bad as 'lav' but it's not good either. We're at something that looks like a tiny metal hut, a bit like the Tardis but made of steel.

'I think it's a lift,' Josh says.

Ah, here. So now I'm in a science-fiction film? Or maybe an episode of *Lost*?

Josh presses a button, a door slides open and the light nearly blinds me. 'You think this will take us to the waterfront?' he asks.

But how the hell would I know?

'We give it a go?'

He can't be fecking serious. That feeling hits again. *Who is this man? What the hell am I doing here?* What if it's not a lift? What if it's a spaceship? Or a container to kidnap eejits? Or –

'It'll be okay.' His voice is soft. 'I understand now. This brings us down to the river.'

I don't want to but, feeling like I'm having an out-of-body experience, I get in. An eternity later, or maybe it's five seconds, the door opens and there it is, the frozen Sava.

'And here's our restaurant,' Josh says.

93

Wednesday, 28 December

The part of town where the gallery is looks nothing like last night's thriller-noir setting. 'It's all a bit touristy.' Josh looks around with distaste.

'But we *are* tourists!' I say happily.

It's like being in a prosperous rural village: the streets are cobbled and the restaurants and shops look like fairy-tale farmhouses. Christmas lights sparkle in the crystal-cold air. A small folk orchestra, huddled around a smoking brazier, plays a jaunty enough tune, undercut by pleasingly mournful Eastern-sounding strings. Misfortunate men, decked out in embroidered frockcoats and trousers, intercept us with menus, trying to lure us into their taverns.

'Maybe later.' Because I'm on a mission.

'Log fire,' the menu-man says. 'Pancakes with cream. Pork cooked in . . .'

In front of each tavern there are lots of tables and chairs, covered by pretty awnings.

'In the summer, everyone probably sits outside,' Josh says.

'We'll have to come back,' I quip, then really wish I hadn't because he pounces on it and demands, 'Do you mean that?'

I squeeze his hand and keep walking – and finally! My gallery! I am *shaking* with adrenalin.

The young man speaks good the English, but when I explain my quest, he gives an apologetic smile and says, 'None here in this moment.'

'No Dušanka Petrović paintings? Are you sure? Can I order one?'

'You give your details? I will email when next one comes.'

432

'When will that be?' My words are tumbling over each other.

'I cannot say. Artists . . .' He shrugs helplessly and, to win his friendship, I smile and make special eye contact. *Yes, indeed, artists! Unreliable crowd of unreliable feckers.*

We think the same, you and I.

'So she is still living,' I ask. 'Er, alive?'

'Yes. Still living.'

'Has she a website? I've tried so hard to find her and . . . No?' No, indeed. Why would he be giving me her details so I could contact her directly and cut him entirely out of the equation?

'How much are her paintings? Say –' I point to one at random – 'that size?'

My new friend quotes me a figure so low I want to vomit. Oh, why couldn't there have been one here for me to buy?

I extract a promise that he'll email me the very second a new painting arrives, then Josh and I return to the cold and, all of a sudden, I'm starving. A combination of acute disappointment and it actually being early afternoon – we'd stayed in bed all morning.

'Sorry, Amy.' Josh gathers me in his arms.

'Let's go back to the frockcoat man for pancakes.'

'Here? Are you sure? I'd rather see some of the real Belgrade.'

'The real Belgrade got into the back seat of our car yesterday to help with directions and we both nearly had a freaker,' I say. 'But if you're really desperate for authentic, we can go for another few laps of the one-way system?'

He's awestruck. 'You're amazing.'

Am I? Astonishing how a bout of hunger-rage can come across.

Soon we're inside, sitting next to a crackling open fire, and I order a shot of plum brandy. 'Staying local.' But I'm just looking for a quick fix for my disappointment.

I order the pancakes and Josh orders the pork thing the menu-man had been going on about.

'Sorry about your painting, Amy,' Josh says, again.

'No.' I'm fierce. 'I wouldn't be here if it wasn't for you. You're not to apologize. And just to see her work for reals yesterday was

433

amazing. And, you never know, the man might get a delivery. It's all good.'

'You sure?'

'Totally. Absolutely.' Christ, I want to have sex with him again. This is out-of-*control*.

'Are you thinking what I'm –'

'Oh. Yeah.' He bursts out laughing.

'No,' I say. 'We're not leaving. These nice people – Look, here's the food now. Stand down your weapon.'

My pancake looks lovely but Josh's pork, with apples and roast potatoes, is awe-inspiring. 'Wow,' I say. 'That's a good-looking plate of food.'

He gives me a funny look. Too late, I realize that's a *Hugh* in-joke – and the expression on Josh's face tells me he knows. 'Wrong man?' he asks.

'Um, yes.' No choice but to style this out. It would be worse to lie. 'Sorry. Josh, I'm sorry.'

''S okay.'

I'm the one in the wrong here, but there's a turn to Josh's mouth that leaves a bad feeling.

After

94

Thursday, 29 December

My luggage is lost. Of course it is, that's the kind of day it's been. Dublin airport is *a-swarm* with Christmas travellers and there are eleven people ahead of me at the lost-luggage desk.

Saying goodbye to Josh at Belgrade airport was sweetly romantic. We kept kissing until I had to say, 'I'm going to miss my flight.'

'Okay. Bye. See you on January the tenth.'

We kissed again. 'Enjoy the rest of your break,' he said. 'Can I call you on New Year's Eve?'

At that, I was hit by the realization I'd to face into the utter chaos of Hugh's return.

'What?' He was instantly wary. Then, when I hesitated, 'What is it?'

'Hugh, my husband. He's back.'

Josh twitched as if I'd slapped him. 'Back where?'

'Ireland. Dublin. Home.'

'For good?'

'Yes.'

'When did he arrive? Christmas *Day*? Where's he living?'

'I don't know. Well, ours, mine, but only for the – Look, I don't know, but probably his brother's.'

'Are you back together?'

'No! No, Josh, no.' I was certain about that. 'That's never going to happen. He knows about you. No details, but he knows I'm away with you.'

His eyes had darkened and his hand tightened on my shoulder. In a low voice, he bit out, 'Don't sleep with him.'

There was no *way* I'd sleep with Hugh, but I said, 'Josh, don't tell me what to do.'

'What?'

'I don't quiz you about Marcia.'

'I don't sleep with Marcia.'

Somehow I doubted that. And even if he did, I'd actually be glad. I don't understand why but obviously it's something to do with my guilt.

God, having an affair, it's all about extremes of emotion: the giddy highs, followed by painful soul-searching. Or downright depression – being back in Dublin after the glorious escape of the past three days, everything feels flat and sad.

The lost-luggage queue shuffles forward. My bag is probably stuck in Vienna, where I'd transferred. I just want to get this paperwork done, then go home – but Hugh will be there. We're going to have to address painful, painful stuff. It'll be borderline unbearable.

My phone rings, jangling my nerves. It's Josh. 'I'm sorry,' he blurts. 'I panicked. I just – It was a shock, hearing your husband was back. I feel I only got you because he went away.'

'Wait, Josh, no, *I*'m sorry. I should have told you. But I didn't want to make things weird. I wanted things to be perfect.'

'They were perfect.'

They weren't exactly perfect but not far off.

It's the weirdest thing, going away with one man and coming home to another. The three girls are all off on their various trips and Hugh is alone in the house. Even before my car is parked, he has the front door open.

'Where's your luggage?' he asks.

'Lost.'

'Oh, babe . . .'

His size, his maleness, in the house, there's so much of him.

'Can I get you something?' he asks. 'Tea? Wine?'

I don't want anything because I don't want us acting like normality has been restored.

'Did you have a nice time?' he asks.

'Hugh, we have to talk . . .'

'Where did you go?'

'Serbia.'

'Oh? . . . *Why?*'

'There's an artist I love and she's Serbian. I've joked about going on a road trip to find her?'

'Oh, right.' He remembers. Vaguely, by the look of things. Then, 'He took you? This new man? Wow. That's classy.' He doesn't sound sarcastic, more in awe. 'So, Amy, I've been talking to Carl and I can start back to work first thing in January. You can have the rest of Dad's money for whatever project you want. We can get our finances back on an even keel. Get everything back to normal.'

'Hugh?' He can't possibly be serious about this. 'No, really, we've gone way beyond that.'

'I don't understand.'

But I do: he's in denial. He'd thought he was coming back to the family he'd left behind. He's not ready to face what I've already accepted – that our family has gone for ever and we're facing into a totally different future, where we'll be living separately.

I go gently because I care about him. 'Hugh, you and I, everything has changed. You and I won't be living together.'

He persists in being confused and I don't know if it's real or not. 'It's that serious with this other man?'

'It's nothing to do with him. It's about you and me, Hugh. And we're . . .' I swallow '. . . done.'

'But I love you, Amy. Don't you love me any more?'

I hesitate and he looks stricken. Hurting him gives me no pleasure. It's just another sheet of pain to pile on to all of the others that have been building up since this started.

'Not the way I did, Hugh. I'll always love you. We'll always be connected, especially because of the girls. But it'll be a different sort of connection.'

His brow is furrowed. 'I was only gone three and a half months. How can that be long enough to change everything?'

'Seeing those photos –'

'I'm so, so sorry.'

'– had a weird effect on me. I nearly blew up with jealousy, and then it was like a blade came down.'

He's distraught. 'And did what?'

'It severed the love that linked me to you.'

'But love doesn't die that quickly.'

Unexpected rage erupts from my gut and emerges from my mouth in a toxic stream. 'Fuck you! Don't you fucking tell me how I should feel when I see my fucking husband in fucking Thailand with another fucking woman!' I'm yelling. 'I can feel whatever way I fucking well want!!' I'm on my feet and I hit his shoulder a clout with my elbow, then do it again. 'You try it for fucking size!'

He whispers, 'I am so desperately sorry.'

'This is how I am, Hugh.' I'm still yelling. 'This is how I fuck-ing well *roll*. I keep myself safe. That's what I do, Hugh. I'm keeping myself safe. I should *never* have trusted you. We were fine on our own, me and Neeve. "I'm loyal as a dog," you said. Well, you're fucking not, you know!'

'I am! And how could you stop loving me so quickly? You must never have loved me.'

'I did love you! You leaving me was the most painful thing that's ever happened.'

'And now I'm back!' Hugh starts to cry. He covers his face with his hands and cries and cries, and I look at him, my guts crushed with sorrow. There's nothing either of us can do for the other here.

'I'm going to bed.' I'm already longing for the sanctuary of my bedroom, then remember that Hugh will be sleeping there. 'I'll sleep in Kiara's room and you can sleep in mine, but tomorrow you leave.'

While I was away, in order to stay in my Josh bubble, I didn't look at Facebook. But it's time to re-engage and I'm dreading it because surely the news is out that Hugh is home. Yep, a quick glance at my timeline establishes that his return is causing a meltdown to rival the one his departure kicked off.

Take this post from one of my neighbours: **OMG, Amy, I saw Hugh heading off in the car, looking like a total HORN-DOG!!!!**

Pictures of aubergines and general phallic-ry abound. I even get a message from Jana, who has either forgotten that Steevie has banned her from talking to me or, in the general excitement of Hugh's return, is simply unable to follow orders: **Amy! Hugh looks so hot! Lock him in your bedroom and have your wicked way with him until Easter!**

This is far from enjoyable but not as humiliating as when he left. Thirty-one new private messages are sitting in my account. They'll remain unread until the end of time and it's probably a dead cert that voraciously curious texts and messages are zipping across Dublin, speculating on Hugh's status. Have I welcomed him home, or is he on the open market?

Well, they'll soon find out.

95

Friday, 30 December

In the morning, I wake in Kiara's room, sadder than I can ever remember feeling. Hugh is below in the kitchen, moving around, so, chastened and sorrowful, I go down to him.

When he sees me, his face crumples, he gathers me into a big bear-hug. I lean against his bulk and cry into his chest, holding him tight as he shudders with sobs. When the storm of tears has passed, I say, 'Hugh, last night, all the shouting and stuff, it's not good. Can we try, both of us, to behave like decent people? Because it's not just about you and me.'

With cups of coffee, we sit at the kitchen table and I say gently, 'You know you can't stay here, in this house, right?'

'Really? But —'

'It's confusing for the girls.'

During the long, mostly sleepless night, I'd considered living with him until Sofie and Kiara finish school, but this house is too small for us to live like flatmates. God knows how we'll manage the money — we were barely coping as things were — but we'll have to make it work.

'Can't you give me some time? Please, Amy. My regret . . . I'd do anything to go back and do things differently.'

His heartbreak is genuine. Mine is too. But the love I had for him has shut down. 'Sweetie, there's no going back.'

'You might change your mind.'

I won't. 'We're done, we're over, we're in the past.'

'How can you be so sure?'

It must be self-preservation. 'Something happened inside me. I didn't decide it, it happened by itself.'

He nods tentatively.

'I was sure you'd never come back.'

'But I did.'

'I was certain you wouldn't. But, Hugh, don't think I feel nothing. There's so much grief in me that I can only take tiny amounts at a time. It will take years to get over this, if I ever do. We've lost so much, not just you and me, but all of us.'

'But if you realize that, can't we just get back together?'

'We're over.'

'No. It's too quick.'

'You can snap the neck of a living thing and it dies instantly.'

Almost whispering, he says, 'Please don't say that.'

'Hugh, I'm a few months ahead of you on this, the . . . grieving. It feels horrific now, but I promise that even the worst stuff eventually becomes okay.'

'This will never be okay.'

He's probably right, but it'll become bearable.

'Amy?' His voice is soft, but something about it unnerves me. 'What happened?'

'What do you mean?'

'The summer before last.' He pauses and icy fingers seize my heart. He looks at me for a long, silent time.

'I . . .'

'You slept with someone else?'

Colour floods into my face. 'No, no, Hugh, I didn't.'

'Amy. I knew something was going on.'

'How?' Who would have told him?

He half laughs. 'Because I know you.'

Carefully I choose my words. 'I met a man. I got a crush. But nothing happened.'

'The man you're seeing now?'

I bow my head. 'Yes.' Hotly I add, 'But I'd never have slept with him if you hadn't run away.'

And maybe he'd never have run away if I hadn't . . .

Defensively, I demand, 'So, are you saying this is all *my* fault?'

'No, of cour–'

I feel ashamed and conflicted and I don't like it. 'Grand.' I'm snippy. 'So long as we're clear that this is entirely your fault.'

He nods.

'So. You wanted six months off?'

'I don't any more.'

'Shush. Here's the plan. We tell the girls you're taking your full six months, which is another ten weeks. You'll live with Carl and Chizo, so we can all adjust to the new normal. The girls will get used to us living in the same city, but not together. When the ten weeks are up, we'll tell them it's permanent.'

He winces.

'Meanwhile we look for solutions to our finances.'

'Amy –'

No. This is the only thing that will work. 'Above all, you and I, Hugh, we speak to each other with respect. Sofie is in her last year at school, Kiara's only a year behind her. They need stability so we provide a united front. Right?'

'Right.'

'There's something you should know. While you were away, Sofie got pregnant –'

'I know. She, I . . . We spoke to each other regularly. It was always the plan they could contact me if they needed.'

Right. I'd known that. I'd got that their needs were more important than mine. But, still, it hurts.

I wait until the mix of pain and fury passes, then say, 'Can I ask one favour? If you're putting it about, could you steer clear of Genevieve Payne?'

'Are you insane? I love you, I won't be putting it about. And Genevieve is married.'

Married makes no difference to anything, as we've both discovered.

He reads my thoughts. 'Okay, I'll steer clear. And if you and your . . . man split up, there's someone I'd like you to stay away from.'

'Who?'

'Alastair.'

That's the second time he's mentioned Alastair in this context. 'What's the fixation with that eejit? Hugh, he'd be literally the last man in the world, apart from Richie Aldin.'

'I dunno. You're so close. He likes you such a lot. And he's so . . . good-looking.'

It's hard to know where to start. 'He's not my type.' I like my men more dishevelled. 'But if you don't sleep with Genevieve Payne, I won't sleep with Alastair.'

We share a tremulous smile.

96

I go upstairs to Kiara's room and stay there until I hear the front door click closed behind Hugh, then the sound of his car driving away, leaving me in a house howling with absence.

Emotional pain can't kill a person, I know that. Unbearable as this is, I *will* survive. Time will heal me. But, second by second, I must live through this.

I want to climb into bed and sleep for a week, but in my own bedroom all I can smell is Hugh, so I change the bedlinen and put on a wash. In the fresh bed, I close my eyes and await merciful escape but my head won't stop flashing pictures of Hugh. Again and again I see him coming through the front door with his ruck-sack, collapsing into tears, pleading with me . . . My elbow hurts from where I hit him.

The pictures in my head won't stop. It's a little like being in a scary movie.

Too much has happened too quickly, I've overdosed on bad adrenalin – perhaps I'm in some sort of shock.

My phone vibrates with a text. It's Derry – for about the twentieth time. She's agitating for a massive debrief but I can't inhabit my reality any longer.

I text her back: **Have you any sleeping tablets?**

Her reply is almost instantaneous: **Is Barack Obama a woke bae? On my way.**

She's with me in minutes, hoping that the price of the sleeping tablets is a full account of everything.

'No, Derry, I'm in a state. I barely slept last night –'

'But Hugh is ba–'

'I know. But, Derry, please . . .' Tears spill on to my hands. 'Not now. Gimme the tablets. I need oblivion.'

'Oblivion? What sort of oblivion?'

'Temporary.'

'I dunno . . .' She's eyeing me with concern. 'I'm only giving you two.'

There's no chance of me taking an overdose, but I haven't the energy to argue. Two will have to do.

I take one, and it's as if I've been hit on the head: instant darkness. In the middle of the night I lurch back into consciousness so I take the second tablet. When I next come to, it's ten past two on New Year's Eve.

Twenty-five hours gone. Twenty-five hours nearer to me feeling okay again. There'll be an unholy number of twenty-five-hour parcels to live through but it's a start.

My phone is full of invitations to New Year's Eve bashes – a night I've always hated. Now that I'm trending again, it's even less attractive. The thought of all those avidly curious people glomming on to me, trying to extract information about the status of my marriage, under the guise of congratulations, is giving me the horrors.

I stay in and, other than a call from Josh, speak to no one.

New Year's Day I spend doing stuff around the house, dreading the dawning of 2 January, the day Hugh and I are telling the girls that he won't be moving back in 'just yet'.

97

It's around noon when Hugh shows up. I let him in and we nod awkwardly at each other.

'How's Carl's?' I ask.

'Fine,' he says. 'Good. Grand.'

I'm sure it's anything but, but it'll have to do. Carl is the flashiest, richest Durrant brother, and even though his fancy home has three spare bedrooms (they've only one child, Noah, the Boy Wonder), I sense Chizo won't be keen on Hugh sticking around for too long. Runs a tight ship, does Chizo. Never misses a chance to tell me that my set-up is appallingly chaotic. I like her a lot, but she scares me sideways.

'Kiara should be home in about half an hour. Go on into the living room.'

As soon as Hugh and I explain the plan to Kiara, she's suspicious. Her eyes flick from Hugh to me, then back again. 'But you came home because you wanted to be with us, right?' she demands of Hugh.

'Yes.'

She turns her stare on me. 'And you missed Dad really badly?'

'Of course, bu–'

'So why can't you just be together like now? Why do you have to wait until the six months are over?'

'Leaving you all was a huge thing to do.' Hugh is hoarse. 'I didn't take the decision lightly and –'

'– he needs to be sure it's all out of his system,' I say.

Emotions scud across Kiara's face, like fast-moving clouds. 'No, Dad.'

'What, hon?'

'No, you know, with other ladies. Women. People who might know us. Whatever you did while you were away, well . . . I can't even go there. But here, where it would throw shade on Mum –'

'I won't. That's not what this is about!'

The cold look Kiara gives him tells us that a lot has changed since he left. I have to wonder if she's seen that picture on his timeline. Well, something has happened, even if it's just that she's grown up a bit.

'Sweetie,' I say. 'You're allowed to be angry or disappointed or worried.'

'I don't need your permission to feel my feelings.' She stalks from the room.

I'm shaking with distress. Hugh and I exchange an oh-shite look. Our sweet Kiara, is this going to ruin her, turn her sour and suspicious?

'Should I go after her?' Hugh asks.

'Do.'

I'd hoped I'd feel less unsettled when the three girls had been told that Hugh won't be living here, but seeing how badly Kiara has taken it, the worry is that Sofie will be even worse.

Unexpectedly, she isn't.

'On Christmas Day,' she says to Hugh, 'I thought you were just home for a few days and I was okay with that. I know it hurt you to leave us back in September, and you only did it because you had to, so I guess it's important enough to do it right.'

'Thanks, hon.'

'You're a person too,' she says. 'You've got feelings and stuff. I get it now. I love you, Dad.' She gives him a quick kiss and goes, leaving both of us flustered.

'She'll be in bits when she finds out you're not coming back at all,' I say.

'Yep.'

'One thing at a time.'

'Just Neeve to go.'

But Neeve will be glad Hugh won't be living with us just yet. And when she finds out it's for ever, she'll be overjoyed.

She isn't due home for another couple of hours. In the living room I sit politely with Hugh but quickly it becomes too uncomfortable and I make noises about having to 'get organized' and scoot from the room.

Upstairs, I lie flat on my back, staring at the bedroom ceiling. I just want all of this to be over and for it not to hurt any more. I close my eyes for a moment . . .

. . . I'm woken by the roar of a car engine outside, followed by the sounds of our front door being shoved open and feet thundering through the hall.

Neeve's voice shouts, 'Mum! Kiara! Sofie!'

What the actual . . . ? It's ten past three in the afternoon. I must have fallen asleep.

'What?' Kiara yells.

'Come outside!'

More thundering of feet, followed by shrieks of excitement out in the road. Someone races up the stairs and shouts, 'Mum! Mum! Where are you?' It's Kiara, and she bursts in. 'Come, you've got to come!'

What's up? But she seems wildly excited rather than panicked.

A shiny silver car is parked outside the house, an Audi, the cute round one.

'It's Neevey's!' Sofie exclaims. 'Brand new, look!' She points out the '17' registration plate.

Oh, my God, Richie Aldin has bought Neeve a car. He is such a colossal arse. He could be helping her with a down-payment on a flat, giving her some independence, but instead he buys her a flashy toy.

'Mum!' Neeve's eyes are manic and she crushes my hands between hers. 'It cost sixty-five grand.'

Sweet mother of Jesus, I barely earn that in a good year.

'You know *he's* got an Audi too?' She's so proud. 'We parked them beside each other and they look like the daddy one and the baby one.'

'Wow, Neevey, that's amazing.'

'I know, right! I told him Hugh was home and that I had to give him back his car and he said he'd buy me one and I thought it would be some second-hand yoke. But he called a man and we just walked into the showroom place and Dad said, "That's the one," and he paid, like, *there*, and the man did the plates and I, like, *drove* it home!'

If Richie Aldin had paid decent maintenance for the first eighteen years of Neeve's life, it would have come to a lot more than sixty-five grand, but no way would I ever say that.

'Each of my sisters has one too.'

Who? Oh, she means Richie's other daughters.

'But mine's the newest!'

'When you come down to earth, can Hugh and I have a little chat with you?'

'About what?' She's instantly suspicious.

'Hugh won't be properly back until his six months are up,' Sofie supplies.

'Oh, yeah?' Neeve's eyes are narrowed. Twirling her car-key fob around her index finger, she says, 'Now is good.'

Hugh is waiting in the living room. 'Cool car, Neevey.'

'Whatevs. So? Story?'

'The plan was that I stay away six months. So I'm sticking to that.'

'But where will you be? Living, like?'

'Uncle Carl's.'

'You mean, here in Dublin?' She sounds furious. 'No fucking way.'

'But, Neeve –' I try.

'Don't embarrass my mum,' she says. 'Bad enough that in Thailand you were knobbing girls young enough to be your daughter. But don't do it here. And stay away from that skeevy-ass Genevieve Payne.'

'I wasn't –'

'And all of Mum's friends. Stay away from them. You've no idea what you put Mum through.'

'Neevey,' I say. 'Stop.'

'I saw her. You wouldn't let a dog suffer like that.'

98

Tuesday, 10 January

The hotel-room door flies open, Josh hoicks me inside, slams it shut and presses me against it. Into my ear he rasps, 'Did you sleep with him?'

'You know I didn't.'

'Sackcloth?'

'I didn't sleep with him.'

'I kept thinking about him fucking you. It's driving me mental.'

During our twelve days apart, this possessive thing, which began in Belgrade airport, has become a sort of game. And I don't like it. But to be here with him, *actual* him, overwhelms all rational thought. I pull his face to mine and, God, the heat of his mouth, the swoony pleasure of kissing him, of being kissed. When we break apart, I sigh, 'I've missed you.'

The relief of being with him, to hear his voice, to smell him, that special secret place at the side of his neck, to touch his skin, to slide the pads of my fingers up his back.

I'm pulling off his sweatshirt and he's unbuttoning my dress, his fingers fumbling. 'I want you too badly,' he says. 'I can't do this properly.'

He lifts me and I pull my legs around his waist, pressing his hardness right against the part of me that wants him most. The relief and longing makes me groan.

'The bed,' I order.

He lays me down and lifts my dress to take off my knickers. 'Lie on me,' I say. 'I need to feel the weight of you on top of me.'

He slides himself along me, pressing his erection against my pubic bone, making me groan again.

'Has he moved out?' He means Hugh.

'You know he has.' Josh and I have talked almost every day since Serbia.

'Has he been back to the house since?'

'You know he has.' I'm opening his jeans and taking him in my hands, such soft, delicate skin covering such promising hardness. 'I have to smell you.' I roll him off me and bury my face in his musky heat – but there's something else, a faint scent of lemon. 'Hey, Josh, on Tuesdays, don't have a shower.'

'Why?'

'Because you smell so good and I don't want shower gel in the mix.'

'Stop changing the subject – how often has Hugh been over?'

Most days. Picking up his clothes, seeing Kiara and Sofie, there are a hundred legitimate reasons he needs to drop by. 'Josh, don't talk about him.'

'Why? Got something to hide?'

'Please, Josh. My time with you is so precious, please let's just . . .'

'You're serious.' He's pleased.

I am. This night with Josh has been the only bright spot on the horizon for the past twelve days. Being at home has been tough going: Hugh showing up, looking stunned with grief; Kiara angry and tearful; Neeve seething with suspicion; Sofie blithely – bizarrely – upbeat.

As for me, I can't contain my sorrow. I keep trying to box it away but it persists in leaking out and, in moments of horrible pain, breaking the surface.

The trigger is the frequency of Hugh's visits. Carl and Chizo's house is only a fifteen-minute drive from ours. In addition, Chizo hasn't let Hugh move all his stuff into theirs, so he often has to call into mine to get things.

In his defence he's doing nothing wrong. Like, he swung an unexpected meeting with the bank to discuss remortgaging the studio he co-owned with Carl and needed to call in to pick up his lone suit. Or Sofie wanted his insight into a physics conundrum for school.

Even *I*'ve been complicit. On Saturday night a fuse blew, plunging us into darkness. Flicking countless switches while holding a wobbling torch didn't restore power. So when Sofie said, 'We could always call Dad,' I didn't take much persuading.

He was over in a quarter of an hour, and after he'd found the right fuse, I offered him a beer.

'I'll get it,' he said.

As soon as he opened the fridge, there was a time-slip in my head and, for a split second, I forgot that this was now. I thought I was back *then*, when life was settled and comfortable and a little dull, when Hugh was my husband and we all lived together, mostly happily, even if that happiness was rarely noticed.

For a sliver of time, that safety-net feeling filled me and shifted my entire sense of myself on this earth: I was secure, I was safe, I belonged and I was carried. Then I remembered and all was confusion until I crash-landed into hard, cold reality. These time-slips and the consequent feelings of loss, like falling into an abyss, keep happening – they're probably happening to all five of us.

Clean breaks suit me better. Constant contact with Hugh is keeping the ground beneath my feet perpetually shifting, and if it wasn't for the girls, I'd make it my business never to see him.

But the girls are the most important people in this.

All I can do is ask myself to live through it, one day at a time, and at some stage it will become easier. The weirdest, most painful situations eventually become normal.

'So,' Josh asks, with a smirk, 'how did you like our FaceTime sex?'

I swallow. 'Oh, my God, the hottest . . .'

It was probably the most thrilling, exciting sex I've ever had in my entire life. We'd done it on New Year's Eve – Josh was alone in his house, I was alone in mine, and I saw in the new year watching Josh do . . . *that* to himself. Even thinking about it starts my blood pounding in my veins, and sets off a throbbing in me that needs immediate attention.

'We could do it again,' he says. 'You know, during the week . . .'

'No. And you know why not. I won't do it with Marcia in your house.'

'I could ask her to leave.'

I roll over and face him. 'Don't *ever* do any such thing.' I'm fierce. 'I can just about cope with my guilt the way things are. Don't push it.'

99

I fly home from London. Thursday passes, as does Friday, then the weekend and next thing it's Monday again. The time is passing. Yes, agonizingly slowly. But we're more than halfway through January. It *is* happening.

In the office on Monday afternoon, Alastair keeps hitting Refresh, hoping for Neeve's latest vlog because he has 'a feeling' that it features Mum.

And, sure enough, it does!

'How did you know?' I'm suspicious.

'Intuition.' He shrugs, then freezes in the act. 'Jesus Christ, I think she's getting inked!'

'*What?*'

'A tattoo!'

'My *mother*?' I hurry to Alastair's screen, as do Tim and Thamy. It looks like Alastair is right.

Mum reclines in a chair and a woman – riddled with piercings and inkings – is poised over her, holding a needle.

'So you're ready for the pain, Lilian?' the tattooist – her name is Micki – asks.

'How sore can it be?' Mum asks.

'Yeeeesh,' Neeve says, off camera.

'Try childbirth if you want to talk to me about pain.' Then Mum adds anxiously, 'I don't mean *actually* try it. Never have children, Neevey. They ruin your life.' Mum looks directly at the camera. 'No offence to my own five.'

Alastair, Tim and Thamy crease up laughing.

'I'm not having kids.' Neeve sounds scornful. 'But seriously, Granny, being inked can really hurt.'

'But you're giving me the anaesthetic spray? And we can take breaks?'

'Wow,' Alastair says. 'Locmof is my hero. Inkings are torture.'

'What have you?' Thamy asks.

'Let me guess,' I interrupt. 'Some Sanskrit shite across your lower back that you think means, "The greatest generosity is non-attachment", but actually says, "2 for 1 on the family bags of marshmallows".'

'Feck off,' he says, while I howl laughing.

'Shut it.' Tim is serious. 'We're watching this!'

'Sorry.' I make my face solemn but quickly I mouth, 'Marsh-mallows,' at Alastair and he mouths back, 'I hate you.'

On screen, Micki is asking, 'Why do you want a Lapras?'

'I was playing Pokémon Go with my grandsons over Christmas –'

'*Was* she?' Tim asks.

Actually, I haven't a clue. I was so deep in Hugh's shock return, then off on my jaunt to Serbia, that Mum playing Pokémon Go with my nephews entirely passed me by.

'I got a bit addicted,' Mum says.

'Wow. Like, wow.' Micki is having her ageist assumptions challenged. 'So Lapras is your favourite?'

'No, Lapras is super-rare –'

'Super-rare!' Alastair yelps. 'She's too cute!'

'Would you shush!' Tim says.

'We never managed to catch one.'

'And you want a tattoo so your grandsons can "catch" it?'

'I do not! I want it to annoy them! To rub their noses in their failure.'

At this, everyone – Micki, Neeve, me, Alastair, Tim and Thamy – erupts into mirth.

'They treated me like some – some moron but I caught more than them. Wait, can I say that bit again, Neeve? Edit out the first line. I *totally* caught more than them.'

More convulsions from me and my colleagues.

'She didn't edit it out,' Thamy says.

That's because Neeve is no fool and knows what appeals to people.

'Oh-*kaaay*,' Micki says. 'And you're totally sure you want it just above your wrist? Because if you, like, change your mind, it's gonna be hard to cover.'

'I'm certain,' Mum says. 'The blue part of the Lapras is the same colour as my favourite cardigan and it'll save me wearing a bracelet.'

The rest of the video doesn't dwell on the nitty-gritty. Now and again, a sweaty-with-pain Mum takes a break and speaks to the camera. 'It hurts but it's not as bad as labour, and at least at the end I'll have something I actually want and not a baby.'

She winks and Alastair murmurs, 'I'm in love.'

They fast-forward to the finish and a big plaster covers the inked area, then jump ten days to the big reveal, when the plaster is removed. And there's *my mum*, with a tattoo of a Pokémon Go character on her arm.

'No matter what anyone says,' she says, with a wicked smile, 'if you want to do something, it's never too late.'

And there it ends.

'Don't be over,' Alastair says sadly.

'That's her best vlog yet,' Tim says, as we all drift reluctantly back to our desks.

'Did you know about this?' Thamy asks.

'There's a lot going on for me right now.' I feel defensive.

Last Friday, at the weekly dinner, Mum probably had the plaster covered with her sleeve. But even if she hadn't, like I say, I probably wouldn't have noticed.

I try to resume work, but my concentration is patchy. It has been since the start of the year. I really want to get a handle on it – everything in my life is so uncertain that I must retain control over my income. But it's hard, the connections in my head just won't happen, the ideas won't come . . .

'Amy!' Alastair yelps, startling me from my introspection. 'Come and look!'

'What the hell? You scared me!'

'You'll like this.'

It's guardian.com, the caption is 'InstaGranny' and there's a fuzzy shot of Mum from the video.

An Irish grandmother, who's been making guest appearances on her granddaughter's YouTube channel *Bitch, Please*, has become the latest unlikely YouTube star. Lilian O'Connell's most recent post, where she gets inked with a Pokémon Go figure, has been viewed forty thousand times since it went live earlier today.

'Jesus Christ,' I say and look at Alastair. 'This is ... It's mental!'

'I told you she was special,' he says.

'I feel bad for Neeve. She's been slogging away at *Bitch, Please* for more than a year, then her granny pops in a couple of times and the whole thing takes off.'

'But it was Neeve's idea to include Locmof. Props for that. And traffic is traffic. Either way, Neeve will benefit from this. More ad revenue, more product placement ...'

'Alastair!' I clutch his arm. 'Imagine if she could afford a place of her own to live!'

'Wouldn't you miss her?'

'Yes ... yes. But she can't keep living with me for ever.'

100

On the way home I buy a bottle of Prosecco – dry January be damned – to celebrate Neeve's vlog going viral. But Neeve doesn't come home, and both Sofie and Kiara are in swotty mode and don't want any. For a moment I contemplate opening the bottle anyway, but there's a danger I might drink it all by myself. So I summon the willpower from the soles of my feet and manage to stick it at the back of the fridge. It'll do for another time.

I'm upstairs, desultorily flinging things into my wheely case, when the doorbell rings. I flinch. Please, God, don't let it be Hugh.

Down I go and, to my great surprise, it's Steevie who's standing on my doorstep. I goggle at her. She looks exactly as she always does: same little pixie face, same excellent haircut, same wantable coat. She's the last person I expect to see on this miserable sleety Monday evening.

'Oh!' I'm stunned almost into silence. '. . . hi.'

'Amy, I'm sorry.' She sounds close to tears.

'Aaah.' I'm not sure I'm able for her. I feel exhausted. I seem to be tired all the time. 'Um . . . come in.'

We go to the kitchen where I open a bottle of wine. Not the Prosecco, she doesn't deserve that. But tea won't do either, not for this.

She slides her coat on to the back of her chair, then squares her shoulders. 'I'm sorry, Amy,' she repeats.

In the absence of knowing what to do, I take a hefty swig from my glass. Christ, that's *nice*.

'When Hugh went away.' Steevie sounds like she's rehearsed this. I have to admit I'm touched. She swallows about half of her wine and starts again. 'When Hugh went, the way I'd felt when

Lee first left, those feelings came flooding back, and it sent me a bit mental.'

I nod.

'It felt good not being the only one to be humiliated. But when you wouldn't bitch about him, I felt . . . I'm sorry, Amy, I felt betrayed.'

I remember now how I'd wanted Hugh's dick to turn green and drop off after I'd seen those photos on Facebook. But all that rage had dissipated – right around the time I starting doing the sexing with Josh. I don't want to tell Steevie any of this. Not yet. We've been friends for a long time and I hate being on the outs with her. It took a lot of guts for her to show up here without advance warning but I can't forget that she ghosted me for two months, defriended me and turned Jana against me.

'So he's back?' she says.

'We're not together.'

'But, like, what are you *planning*?'

I'm confused. 'How do you mean?'

'Key his car? Cut one leg off all his trousers?'

'Ah . . .' Is this a joke?

'I heard a really good one!' She's suddenly animated. 'This woman caught her husband cheating and threw every left shoe he owned into the Thames. And he, like, *loved* his shoes – he collected Nikes. So he was left with dozens of single trainers that were no good to him.'

I have a think. 'I could do something with his music collection, maybe snap all of his vinyl records in half.'

'He's so precious about his vinyl, right?' Now she's laughing. 'He'd hate that. And you need to YouTube it.'

'Of course!'

'We could have a party.' She leans towards me, her eyes sparkling. God, I've missed this – I've missed *her*, she's so much fun. 'We could get Jana over. Not Tasha or Mo. I'm so sorry about that lunch. But good women. Petra. Derry. How about it? Friday? This coming Friday night?'

I can't quite get a handle on her tone, but she's got her phone out and starts texting.

'What time should I tell them?' she asks.

'Are you, like, *serious*, Steevie?'

'Yes.' She's surprised, and disappointment slides from my heart.

Steevie realizes that we've misunderstood each other. 'But, Amy,' she sounds almost angry, 'you can't do nothing. You've to punish Hugh.'

That's not what I want. I just want never to see him again. But because Steevie and I have been friends for so long, I offer, 'Well, I hit him a few times. Would that do?'

With a short laugh, she says, 'Got to be lots worse than that. He cheated, so you punish. Then you can take him back with your self-respect intact.'

'That's not happening.'

'Stop, Amy. You can be honest with me. I hear he wants you back.'

I bump over the discomfort of knowing people are talking about my marriage. 'Me and Hugh are done.'

She goes white with surprise.

After a few moments, I try to lighten the mood. 'Do people *really* do that stuff to cheating men? Cutting off their bollocks and nailing them to a lamppost? Planting prawns in the curtain poles of their new bachelor shag-pad?'

She makes a cute-funny face. 'Ladies be *cray* when their man stray.'

'I'm not cray.'

'Why not?' She's confused.

'Sad is what I feel.'

After a long, long pause, she says, 'You're too passive.'

'I will never get back with him. That's hardly passive.'

We eye each other warily. Neither of us knows what to say – which feels strange and tragic.

'So, listen.' She stands up and puts her coat on. 'It's good to see you. But Monday night, you know, work tomorrow, better head, loads to do, see you soon, yeah?'

'Um . . . Soon. For sure.'

We give each other an uncomfortable half-hug and Steevie darts out into the cold dark night.

I'm not sure what happened there except that, once again, she thinks I've let her down.

Her unexpected arrival had given me hope that I wouldn't be quite as alone as I have been. Now, as she scoots off as fast as she can, I understand that Steevie won't be plugging any gaps in me, and I feel bereft.

Instantly I flick through everything good I can think of – KiaraWineDerryFoodSofieNeeveNewShoes – to try to make the loneliness go away and nothing works. Then I think of Josh and it's like the sun has come out. I'll see him tomorrow night. I give thanks for Tuesday nights. As long as I have them, I can keep going.

101

Tuesday, 17 January

'Josh, tell me about your movie scripts.'

We're lying in bed, wrapped tightly around each other, and I feel him tense up. He pauses before he answers. 'That's all in the past.'

I've tried a couple of times in the previous weeks and he's shut me down, but I know it's an important part of him. 'Tell me anyway.'

After another taut silence, he mumbles, 'It was a long time ago.'

'I want to know about you. Everything.'

'I hate talking about it.'

'Why?'

Another stretch of nothing. Then, 'At twenty-one, I thought I was so talented and, you know, original, that it was all mine for the taking. I didn't realize that everyone is arrogant and clueless at that age. But my talent was nothing like as big as my self-belief.'

'And what happened?'

He shrugs. 'I wrote movie scripts, lots of them. I even got an agent. But nothing ever came of any of it.'

'Nothing?'

He sighs. 'Producers took meetings with me. They'd ask for changes to my script and I'd do them. Then they'd ask for more changes. Or something else would get made that was too similar to my stuff. Or they just lost interest.'

I tighten my hold on him.

'The ten years between twenty-one and thirty-one were just one knockback after another. In the early days I was surprised that not everyone got my genius but I was young and thought I was God so I rolled with the punches. But it kind of all caught up with me eventually and collapsed the whole stupid dream, and I saw that I'd never be good enough.'

I don't know what to say that doesn't sound patronizing.

'And now I'm middle-aged and it's a hard thing, knowing that my glittering future is far behind me. That it never actually happened.'

'You're not middle-aged. That concept doesn't really exist any longer, does it?'

He gives me a look. 'Oh, believe me, it does.'

'But . . .' And there's nothing I can actually say.

'I had to make peace with none of my dreams coming true. That wasn't easy.'

'But you have good things in your life. Your –' I'd been about to say 'wife and kids' but stop myself in time. 'You've a great job at the *Herald*. Being features editor.'

'Jesus Christ,' he mutters.

'Wha-at? You get pride, satisfaction from it? Don't you?'

'I hate it.'

Christ. Everyone complains about their job, me included, but I thought a fair bit of Josh's sense of self was tied up in his.

'I hate the internal politicking,' Josh says. 'I hate the shite we publish. I hate the damage we do with our post-truth facts.'

Oh, my God . . .

'And the worst thing is that I can't complain – I'm one of the lucky ones with a job that pays okay.'

'So that's good.' My voice is small.

'I'm trapped. I've two kids, a mortgage, the usual.' He sighs heavily. 'I'm a mediocre middle-aged man. Look, Sackcloth, I'm not complaining. I'm no different to anyone else. Everyone slams up against these truths sooner or later.'

I don't know what to say. I'd known he wasn't ecstatic about his life choices but that he carries so much disillusionment is a shock to me.

'I look at the rest of my life,' he says. 'I'm forty-two, and there's nothing good ahead. I'll just keep trudging through, being medio-cre, fighting with Marcia, wishing the kids would leave home and be financially independent, but they won't be, not the way that twenty-first-century capitalism works. Everything will go on being exactly the same until I get Alzheimer's, like my dad, then die.'

I swallow hard.

'All we can do,' he says, 'is take our hope and happiness where we can.'

I'm guessing that's what I am to him.

'What about you, Sackcloth?'

'I'm probably the same.' Although nothing like as depressed as he so clearly is.

'What was your big dream?'

It's hard to rally but I make myself, because this has to be res-cued before we both drown in the brutally cold waters of reality. 'I wanted to do something arty. Like design clothes or work in interiors. But I never did anything about it and now it's never going to happen.'

'I'm not even going to bullshit you and say, "It's never too late,"' he says. 'Because nothing happens for people our age. It happens young or it doesn't happen at all.'

But not everyone can be Angela Merkel or Malala or Beyoncé, most of us have to be ordinary. If there weren't so many ordinary people, the extraordinary ones wouldn't stand out. And that's okay with me, it's not painful, or nothing like as painful as it clearly is for him.

'Valentine's Day is coming up.' Abruptly he changes the sub-ject. 'Let's go away for a couple of days.'

I'd read some article in *Grazia* about a woman who lived in Manchester having an affair with a man from Düsseldorf. Every month they'd meet in some city – Amsterdam, Prague, Madrid – stay in a fancy hotel, shag each other's brains out, eat strawberries, drink Champagne and do some light luxury shopping, before returning home, sated and happy, to their clueless spouses. For a moment I wonder if I could emulate her. Mind you, I'd need bet-ter luggage . . .

Then sanity prevails. 'Josh, get a hold of yourself. There isn't money.' Then, more gently, 'It's your *wife* you should be taking away for Valentine's Day.'

'I want to go with you, Sackcloth.' He's narky.

'You can't.'

'It'd be hard to find a location grim enough to accommodate you and your guilt,' he says. 'Won't stop me trying.'

'I'm not going,' I say. 'And don't ask me again.'

'Why? Planning to go away with Hugh?'

'Stop it.' Now I'm genuinely upset. 'Hugh and I are over.'

'You're sure about that?'

'Entirely. And please stop asking me about it, Josh. I don't like it.'

'Oh. Okay.' Then, 'I've been thinking. To save money, instead of coming here every Tuesday we could go to your friend's house? Druzie?'

No. Absolutely not. It's Druzie's home he's talking about. Okay, she's not always there, but sometimes she is. Me and Josh going at it hammer and tongs in the spare room, while Druzie does her laundry and cooks dinner, a few feet away? No. Wrong, every bit of it. I'd feel ill-mannered, ashamed, and like all boundaries were shot to hell.

102

Tuesday, 24 January

A week passes – another seven grim, gruelling January days – during which a grit of worry snags its rough way into my heart: I'm fretting about Josh.

The last thing I want is another mention of us moving our Tuesday nights to Druzie's flat. There's a world of difference between a night in a hotel and a night in a friend's spare bedroom. One feels acceptable, but the other feels . . . *sordid*. This week we've just rolled away from each other, panting and gasping, when he says, 'How often is your mate Druzie in London?'

My heart plummets, like a stone off a cliff.

'Did you hear me?' he asks.

'Josh. It can't happen. It would be wrong.' He doesn't speak, so I add, 'I can't do it.'

After a lengthy spell of silence he says bullishly, 'Will you come away with me for Valentine's Day?'

'Josh.'

'What?'

'No. The answer is no. Please don't do this. Our time together is so short.'

He sighs, lifts his pillow from behind his head, punches it into shape, slings it back on the bed and flops down on to it. He sighs again, and I start wondering if I should leave. What's to be gained by lying here with my stomach on fire with dread?

'Hey,' he says, and I jump. 'Is that your *mum* who was in today's *Mail*? The one who got inked? Is that your daughter's site?'

'Oh. Yes. Right. It is.' God, Josh knows about it!

'I recognized her name.' He's smiling now. 'You must be really proud.'

'Ah, yeah.' In the eight days since the *Guardian* first picked up on the vlog, Neeve and Mum have got a lot of attention. 'It's been lovely. Neeve has worked so hard. And now she's gone viral – well viral-*ish*. Zoella has no immediate cause for worry. It's great.'

'Maybe I should have a word with my team.' He gives me a sly smile. 'We could pull off a juicy exclusive, seeing as I have unparalleled access to a member of the family.'

'You'd want to be quick about it.' I'm glad his mood has improved. 'They're going on *This Morning* on Friday, and after that, maybe even I'll have to make an appointment to speak to them.'

Friday, 27 January

'So you spent a lot of your life in hospital?' Holly Willoughby gently questions Mum.

It's Friday morning and Alastair, Tim, Thamy and I have the telly on in the office to see Mum and Neeve being interviewed on *This Morning*.

'Locmof looks fantastic,' Alastair says.

Locmof *does* look fantastic – blonde and pretty in a shirt-and-skirt combo that is an outrageous Gucci copy.

'All told,' Mum says, 'I probably wasn't in hospital that long, but whenever I was discharged, I knew it was just a matter of time before I was readmitted.'

'How did that affect you?' Phillip Schofield chips in.

'I suppose . . . it made me into a bit of a scaredy-cat,' Mum says.

'Scaredy-cat!' Alastair yelps. 'Love that word.'

'What was life like as a scaredy-cat?' Phillip asks.

'I never took part in anything,' Mum says. 'There were things I wanted to do but I thought there was no point.'

'Look at her,' Alastair says, with huge admiration. 'Sitting there, chatting away, not a bother on her.'

'And what were some of those things you'd wanted to do?' Phillip had clearly been primed for a researched 'funny moment'.

'I wanted to be a drummer in a band,' Mum admitted, with a delightful little blush. 'Girl drummers are cool.'

'And all around the British Isles,' Alastair says, 'millions of people have just fallen in love.'

For some reason I'm finding him wildly annoying.

'And you, Neeve?' Holly says. 'Your dad is none other than Richie Aldin.' Quickly she adds for those who wouldn't know, and that would be just about everyone, 'He played for Rotherham United in the nineties. So you're no stranger to fame?'

'*Weeell*...' poor Neevey has to dissemble madly '... Dad always stayed beneath the radar.'

'He certainly stayed beneath our radar, Neevey,' I yell at the telly. 'The giant colossal *arse*.'

'So!' Phillip takes over, when they realize there's no point mining the 'famous connection' seam. 'Your YouTube channel, I can't say the name, because it contains a naughty word!' A little light-hearted finger-wagging. 'Let's just say it rhymes with "itch". We've a couple of clips here.'

'This is great for Neeve,' Tim says, and suddenly I'm furious with him too. I *know* it's great for Neeve, I under*stand* how publicity works.

The segment finishes with Mum rolling up the sleeve of her Gucci-knock-off shirt and displaying her inking.

'No regrets?' Holly asks her.

'None!' Mum is passionate. 'Life is for living. Never let anyone tell you you're too old. If you want to do something, do it now because you might not get your chance again.'

'Wise words indeed.' Phillip is pulling the piece to a close. 'And now over to our kitchen where ...'

'She's an effing star,' is Alastair's conclusion. 'An inspiration and a star.'

'Who represents her?' Mrs EverDry demands. At our blank faces she increases the volume. 'Who? Is? Her? Agent?'

When Alastair, Tim and I remain flummoxed, Mrs EverDry narrows her eyes. 'You mean she isn't with a talent agency?'

'She's just my mum,' I say, with a little too much attitude.

Slowly, and with contempt, Mrs EverDry spells it out. 'Lilian O'Connell is a. Phen. Om. En. On.'

Mum? She's a five-minute wonder that could only have happened in January.

'Call yourselves a PR agency? Jesus Christ, as soon as I've the money I'm going elsewhere. You three gligeens couldn't organize a piss-up in a drinks cabinet.'

'Mrs Mullen –' Alastair makes an ameliorative move towards her.

'How continent is she?' Mrs EverDry barks at me.

'You mean is she *in*continent? How the hell would I know?'

'She could pretend,' Tim says.

'Is she short of money?' Mrs EverDry demands. 'Everyone could do with a few bob, right?'

I don't reply and Alastair throws me a confused look. 'I think,' he says cautiously, 'Lilian just wants to have fun.'

'And we have our strap-line right there. "Girls just wanna have fun." Swear to God!' Mrs EverDry is in a fury, perhaps even worse than mine, but at least hers is justified. 'Why the hell am I paying ye when I'm pulling this entire campaign together all by myself?'

'What about men?' Tim asks. 'The incontinent *men*? Men won't buy things marketed at women.'

'Most men don't buy anything. It's their misfortunate wives who have to go to the shops. Anyway, I'm thinking of doing specific male-friendly packaging, a nice dark grey shade to soak up all those manly wees. Then there's always Pierce Brosnan.'

'P-Pierce Brosnan?'

'I'm still holding out hope that he'll fall on hard times and finally answer my emails.'

'Alastair,' I say, through gritted teeth. 'We're not a talent agency.'

'We could be, though,' he says. 'I don't mean full-time, but we can manage Locmof while she's the face of EverDry. Should I say face or bladder?'

'For the love of Christ! Are these lights ever going to change?' We're in my car, en route to Mum and Pop's house. Mrs EverDry's visit put a rocket under us and Alastair begged for the chance to work with Mum so he's gatecrashing the O'Connell Friday dinner.

'Amy, are you okay?'

'Grand,' I snap.

'You know anger is one of the phases of grief?'

'Oh, shut up, would you? I'm just tired!'

'Okay. Tired. Fine. So who's going to be there this evening?'

'Derry's night, so everyone.'

'Jesus ... Locmof, your hot sister, the saucy sister-in-law, Siena – is that her name?'

'You behave yourself out there.'

'Course I will.' He flips down the sun visor, opens the mirror and tweaks his hair. I itch to slap him.

Neeve has the front door open before we've even got out of the car. 'Whooah!' she exclaims, at the sight of Alastair. 'Silver fox!'

'Hey there, Neevey.' He struts – yes, actually *struts* – into the hall and treats her to The Smile. 'You were awesome on the telly-box this morning.'

'I'm made of awesome.'

She colours and I think, *Oh, get a grip, he's just a preening man-boy.*

Now he's moved on to Mum. 'Lilian O'Connell, mother of five,' he murmurs. 'It's an honour.' He kisses her hand.

'Wh-who are you?' Mum seems overwhelmed. 'Amy's new boyfriend?'

'Hardly!' I bark.

'No need to take my head off!' Mum says. 'You could do worse.'

'I'm Alastair Donovan. I work with Amy.'

'Your suit is nice.'

'Alastair!' Maura's got wind of his presence and rounds on me, Mum and Neeve. 'Don't keep him standing in the hall! Come in, Alastair, come in!'

Alastair is dragged into the jam-packed sitting room, where his glamorous presence electrifies all present. Pip and Finn are frozen with awe, Dominik assumes a suspicious crouching aspect, as though he might have to tackle someone, and Pop yells, 'WHO THE HELL IS THE FILLUM STAR?'

'This is Alastair,' Maura introduces him to the room. 'He's Amy's boss.'

'He's not my boss!'

Then something unimaginable happens – The Poor Bastard speaks. 'Hello.' His voice is scratchy, as though it hasn't been used in some time, but he's definitely made a noise.

Only Derry hangs back, wearing a cool, not-exactly-pleasant smile. Well, well, well. She's going to cop off with Alastair ...

If Neeve doesn't get there first.

They're welcome to each other. All of them. Whatever I mean.

Without pleasantries, I hoosh Neeve, Mum and Alastair up to the bedroom and the Floods' Wi-Fi, then listen with a sour expression as Alastair lovebombs Mum, telling her how great she is at everything and how much money she'd make. But Mum isn't keen on being the EverDry ambassador. 'I like doing the vlogs with Neevey. We have fun.'

'You can still do Neeve's vlogs, Lilian. The EverDry campaign wouldn't be a full-time job.'

'But incontinence . . . It's embarrassing. And wouldn't I be a bit young?'

'I take your point, Lilian,' Alastair says. 'Absolutely, of course, but all ads use younger models to sell to their older target market.'

'I can't imagine that people often say no to you,' Mum says. 'But I think I have to.'

Once again, for the billionth time in my life, she breaks my heart. 'Okay, Alastair.' I stand up. 'We're done here.'

'Are you leaving?' Mum asks. 'But it's Derry's night.'

'Yep. Leaving.'

'But your special bread?'

'Fuck the bread. Come on, Alastair.'

'He can stay and have your dinner,' Neeve says.

'Yeah,' I say unpleasantly. 'Fill your boots, Alastair. But I'm off.'

'Amy?' Mum sounds anxious. 'Would it help you, profession-ally, like, if I did the incontinent thing?'

'Oh, don't worry your pretty little head about that.'

'Ehhhhh, on second thoughts,' she stumbles over the words, 'I've decided to do it. You got a raw deal from me when you were growing up, you all did.' She watches me intently, hoping I'll play nice. 'And maybe with the extra money coming in, we could ask Dominik if he'd be exclusive with us.'

'Exclusive.' Neeve nudges Mum and they topple around the place, laughing at the thought of being exclusive with Dominik.

Christ, they're pathetic.

104

Saturday, 28 January

I'm way down in the bliss of sleep when the doorbell rings. *I'll ignore it.* Even though it's Saturday, I'd spent the morning working on the paperwork to fast-track Mum's ambassadorship and then I hit a wall, suddenly so knackered that I got into bed and fell asleep.

These days, I'm always exhausted. Everything is a monumental effort and there are days when it literally feels as if lead weights are strapped to my legs. The only time I feel positive about life is when I'm with Josh – or thinking about being with him.

Go away, Mystery Caller. I need this sleep so badly.

But the doorbell *brrrrings* again and suddenly I'm energized with fury. Who the hell is it? Some pestery feck, no doubt! Looking for sponsorship for some shite or other. Or maybe one of the girls has lost her key. Clueless eejits.

I'm in the mood for a fight so I thump down the stairs, wrench the front door open and demand, 'What?'

Hugh is standing there. Seeing him shocks me. Seeing him always shocks me: we were once so close and now we're strangers.

I will *never* get over this if I keep meeting him.

'Amy, sorry,' he says. 'I texted you to ask if it was okay . . . You didn't get my text?'

'My phone was on silent. Because I was having a sleep!'

'Sorry to wake you. I just need to pick up my –'

'Why did you ring the doorbell?' My voice gets louder. 'You've got a key to this house – the locks haven't been changed!'

'It feels wrong to just let myself in. I mean, I would have, if you hadn't answered, but this is no longer my home.'

'And don't you forget it! For the love of Christ.' I thump back up the stairs. 'Not only have you ruined my marriage, you've ruined my power-nap.'

He looks chastened and sad and I pause on the stairs. 'Why are you here anyway?'

'Picking up my sleeping bag.'

'What? Chizo's kicking you out? Are you *homeless*?'

'I'm staying in Nugent's garage for a few weeks. There's an airbed but no spare duvet.'

'Oh, for God's sake! Don't try to make me feel sorry for you.'

'I'm not.'

'Chizo has three spare bedrooms, she's kicking you out, and *I'm* the one who has to worry.'

'She's got family coming from Nigeria. I'm only in Nugent's for a couple of weeks, then I can go back.'

Wrong-footed, I accuse, 'Next you're going to tell me we need to talk money.'

'Now doesn't look like the best time.'

'You mean because I'm so narky? I'm only narky because . . .' Yes, why *was* I so narky?

'Because you're so tired.'

'Grand. Well, I'm only narky because I'm so tired.' And I'm only so tired because I'm so . . . so something else. Perhaps sad. But it's nicer being narky.

'Can I do anything to help?' he asks.

I glare at him. 'Actually, you can.'

His face becomes radiant with hope.

'You can rewind the clock to last September and stay here with me, instead of fucking off to Thailand to fuck a hundred other fucking women.'

'Amy,' he whispers, 'I'm so sorry.'

'Whatevs.'

'Listen to me, Amy. I'm begging you to hear what I'm saying. I'm not a cheater. Until . . . this, I never even looked at another woman. Genuinely. Truly. And I never will again.'

'You might want to rethink that,' I say. 'Because you and me are done. *Beyond* done.'

After a hesitation, he says, in a strangled voice, 'I'll just go to the shed to get the sleeping bag, then I'll be out of your way.'

'Your beloved shed.' My voice is bitter. 'Where you hatched your Great Escape.' I thump up the rest of the stairs and slam my bedroom door behind me. I climb into the bed again and, out of nowhere, I wonder how Hugh had felt the year before last when I'd been flirting with Josh.

He'd said he'd known something was going on. That must have been hard for him. Really hard.

I don't want to think about this. It's making me feel uncomfortable and ashamed. Anyway, he was probably fine about it. And even if he wasn't, it's all in the past, and so much has happened since then that it's irrelevant.

But something in me needs to check. I jump from my bed, hurry down the stairs and catch Hugh just as he's about to leave. 'Hey!' I call. 'I want to talk to you.'

He looks wary. 'Okay.'

I sit on the stairs and he takes a step a couple below mine.

'The summer before last,' I say, 'when I had an innocent thing, a crush, on Josh . . .' How do I voice this without making it sound as if I was in the wrong? 'How did you know?'

He stares at me. 'You want to talk about this now?'

'Aaah, yeah.'

'Oh-kay. You were different. Absent. I'd be talking to you and you'd be miles away. You removed yourself emotionally.'

Well, that wasn't so bad. That sort of thing happens in all marriages.

'And you looked different.'

I did?

'You bought new clothes —'

'I'm always buying new clothes.'

'These were different. The shoes were higher, the skirts were tighter . . . And your hair. You started getting it blow-dried every Monday evening.'

I hadn't realized I was that obvious. But, looking back, I admit that he's right.

'You were always in good form on Monday evenings. And in bad form when you came back from London on Wednesdays.'

'Because I was tired! I'm still in bad form every Wednesday night.'

'You asked how I knew,' he says levelly. 'I'm telling you.'

'Okay.'

'You wanted to have sex more often.'

'That's a good thing!'

He presses his lips together and shakes his head. 'You know something? It wasn't.'

My skin flames. I don't like this but, in fairness, I *did* ask. 'How did you feel, though, that time?'

'How d'you think I felt?' He touches my knee and his voice is soft. 'Amy? I was scared. Shit-scared. Terrified. I love you, *loved* you, you're my life, the idea of losing you –'

'So why didn't you say anything?'

'It would have made it real. I didn't want it to be real. So I hoped it would run its course.'

'Which it did.'

'Which it *didn't.*' He sounds unexpectedly angry.

'It did. I stopped seeing him.'

'You're with him now.'

'Only because you went away.'

For a moment I think Hugh is going to lose it. His eyes darken and he swallows the hot words he visibly wishes he could unleash.

'That's not why you left, is it?' I ask. 'Because of Josh? It was because of your dad? Then Gavin?'

'Yes, but –'

That's all I need to know. Stiffly I say, 'I appreciate you talking to me about this. Let yourself out.'

I go back to bed. That conversation with Hugh hadn't gone exactly the way I'd have liked. It hasn't dispersed my guilt, not entirely, and I don't like being saddled with it.

But everything ebbs and flows – something I've learnt over the years. No emotion stays constant. Anything that increases eventually decreases. At some point, this niggly flame of shame will be snuffed out.

I squeeze my eyes shut and desperately try to resume my slumber but my phone rings: Maura.

'What?'

'Are you and Hugh getting back together?'

'No.'

'I was afraid of that.'

'It's none of your business.'

'Sorry.' She sounds humble. 'I know I'm controlling. I'm trying to stop.'

There's a danger she'll launch into her well-worn speech about her painful childhood and I'm too irritable to hear it. 'Good luck with that,' I say.

No sooner have I ended the call than the front door opens and slams shut and someone thunders up the stairs. 'Mum? Mum?'

It's Neeve. She bursts into my bedroom and declares, 'My advertisers have offered me a new package. More money!'

'That's great.' My voice is flat.

'You okay? Was Hugh here?'

'How did you know?'

'Because you're always narky after he calls round.'

'I was narky before he called round.'

'Oh, God, it's spreading. You're going to be narky all the time now. You over at Granny's yesterday, *eeeesh*.'

'Only because Alastair was being a clown. And Granny a selfish –' I stop.

'So how about that Alastair?' she says, with a sly smile. 'Would he be open to a hook-up? Asking for a friend?'

'You don't have any friends.' This isn't even true.

She creases with mirth. 'So funny to see you pissed! Anyway, I could be talking about Derry. Too cute how she totally blanked him.'

Oh, whatever. Neeve and Alastair, Derry and Alastair, Neeve and Derry – the three of them can become a thrupple for all I care.

'About your new offer, Neevey. Don't sign anything until a lawyer has looked at it.'

She should go to the firm that Hatch uses, they'd take good care of her.

She sounds surprised. 'I've got a lawyer. Daddy set me up with him.'

Oh. 'Well, that's brilliant.' Simply fucking brilliant.

105

Tuesday, 31 January

Josh says slowly, 'Marcia found the book . . . The one you gave me for Christmas.'

I'm waiting. I didn't do anything stupid like inscribe it, there's nothing incriminating, no story here.

'She had a go at me for spending money.'

Okay. Not the worst outcome.

'But I told her it was a gift.'

What?

'From a woman.'

Oh, my God, he's a total asshole.

'She went apeshit.'

'Of *course* she did! Josh, where was it when she found it?'

'On my bedside locker. Hiding in plain sight, like.'

'Or right in Marcia's face. *Like.*'

'What're you saying?'

'You're . . .' I'm trying to formulate my thoughts. 'You want to bring something to a head with Marcia? What did she say to you?'

'She told me to end it with whoever the woman is. I said I'd think about it. But, Sackcloth, no way am I going to.'

'Josh. What are you *thinking*?'

'Marriages run their course. I think mine is done.'

This has suddenly got too big, too serious, too life-changing, and I don't want to be part of it.

And there's something else: I'm not convinced that Josh is sincere. Something is telling me this is a well-worn pattern with him and his wife. 'Josh? Be honest. Am I part of some game you're playing with Marcia?'

'*What?* How can you even – ? No, I'm *serious* about this. About you.'

I don't know what to think. I'm confused, suspicious and very afraid. If he's not playing games with Marcia, then the alternative is actually worse.

Sulkily Josh says, 'I want to tell her about you –'

'No!'

'– how sweet you are, how different you are to her.'

'Josh! Stop! Please! What would be the point? Our lives are in separate countries.'

'They don't have to be.'

I feel as if I've fallen into a deep, narrow well.

'Seriously, Amy,' he says. 'You could live in London. With me. I've been thinking about nothing else. You could get a job here.'

It's hard to know which objection to mention first. 'I have three kids.'

'They're nearly adults. And they all have dads. Klara could live with Hugh.'

'Do you mean Kiara?'

'Yeah, Kiara. I meant, sorry, *Kiara*. And Sofie too.'

'And Neeve?'

'She's twenty-six. She's not your responsibility.'

'She's only twenty-two.'

'Same difference.' He's exasperated.

This is whirling way out of control.

'Anyway, what about you?' Suddenly I need to hear about his future 'plans'.

'Marcia and I split up, sell the house. The kids stay with her –'

'What if she doesn't want that?' Because I wouldn't want to end up living with two traumatized pre-pubescent boys.

'Okay, we can share their care, fifty-fifty.'

'What about Yvonne and Buddy?' The dogs.

'I want the dogs.' He's emphatic about that.

I've never had a dog, they seem lovely, people get so much happiness from them, but aren't they a lot of work? 'And where would we live, you and I?' My questions are purely theoretical, there's no way this is actually happening.

'We'd buy a place. Marcia and I would split whatever we'd get for the house, and you'd put in your share from your house.'

'We hardly know each other, Josh. This is madness. All of this talk is madness.'

'I know what I want. And I want you.'

But I don't want you. This hits me like a blow to the heart, and I think I'm the most terrible person alive. I wanted him when it was passion and fun, and when I thought that was all he wanted from me. 'Josh, please . . .' I say haltingly. 'This is insane. I don't want to move to London.'

'Okay, I'll get a job in Dublin.'

My surge of horror shocks me. 'Josh, you don't want to split up with Marcia.'

'Aye, I do. I've wanted to for a long time. We make each other miserable.'

That may be true. But . . . 'If you and Marcia split up, don't do it to be with me.'

His exasperation vanishes and he's icy. 'What the fuck does that mean? You're bailing?'

'I mean . . .' Christ, I'm nervous. 'You and your wife, you need to sort your stuff out. Just between the two of you.'

'Are you breaking up with me?'

Am I? It hadn't been my plan. But the sudden swerve into life-altering territory has scared me rigid. Certainly scared the lust out of me. Fabulous secret sex once every seven days is a totally different thing from moving home, moving job, moving country . . . I fancy him. But not enough to do those things.

'Josh . . .' I pick my words carefully '. . . this is big stuff. Huge. We'll see each other next Tuesday. Let's use that week to think about what we really want from each other.'

'Are you breaking up with me?' he repeats.

'I'm not, I'm truly not.' I don't want this to end. But I have to admit that it's veered *way* off course from what it originally was.

'It's because your husband is back. I knew it, I fucking knew it.'

483

I can hardly speak for exasperation. 'I miss the family that Hugh and I made, but me and Hugh, it's gone for ever.'

He stares me down. 'You are so cold.'

Christ, you can't win. 'Look.' My tone is placatory. 'Let's both have a think about what this means to us and we'll talk about it next week. Okay?'

'I don't need to think. I know what I want. And I want you.'

106

Steevie and I haven't had any contact since the night of her surprise visit – our friendship is probably over. After thirty years, that's a weird one.

The ending feels ragged and unpleasant, and I know if I bump into her, it'll be awkward as hell. Our stumbling block was that we didn't – couldn't – see eye to eye on the issue of cheating husbands. Steevie has her set of rules: after inflicting some pain, she'd have taken back Lee, if he was keen. But my rule – which I didn't even know I had until I was in the situation – is that I can't give Hugh another chance. I didn't 'decide' to be this way, it's just the way I seem to be.

I wish Steevie could have accepted that. I'm hurt and resentful that she didn't. But at least I'm sticking to my guns. There's a certain comfort in that.

Although I'm down a second important relationship – first Hugh, then Steevie – I have no belief whatsoever in astrology: I wouldn't even glance at my horoscope but might there be something in my planetary chart that indicates this is a time of endings?

Speaking of endings, my phone beeps with a text. One word. **Kabul?**

Since Tuesday night, Josh has been texting me mini-break location suggestions, each appropriately grim for my sackcloth sensibilities. He's probably trying to be funny, but his tone is more passive-aggressive than good-humoured.

Alastair looks up from his screen. 'You okay?'

'Another suggestion from Josh for the Valentine weekend that's not going to happen.'

'Let me guess? Aleppo?'

'Close. Kabul.'

'Christ, he's gas. Today's, what, February the third? He'd want to get on to lastminute.com fairly sharpish. I booked my mini-break to Nice weeks ago and I don't even have a girlfriend.'

'Please shut up,' I murmur. Then, 'Sorry.'

'No need to apologize,' he says cheerily. 'You're in the anger phase of your grief.'

I wish he'd stop telling me this.

'You've done denial and bargaining. All you need now is to get through depression, then you'll be into acceptance.'

'That's not how it works and everyone knows it. You hop from phase to phase at random. I'll be hopping for years. I can't imagine feeling okay ever again.'

'You will. Grief is a process.'

At the moment it's hard to have faith. 'The only thing that made me happy was Josh,' I admit. 'And now even that's gone weird. Him talking about leaving Marcia and me living in London. It's insane.'

'But what did you think was going to happen? Was it just going to continue like this, every Tuesday, for years and years?'

'No. Sooner or later we were going to run out of road.'

'Maybe,' he suggests, 'this is just the end of the beginning.'

I can't see it. 'All that upheaval, it would be horrible for everyone.'

I'd told Josh that we should use this week to think about what we really want from each other. But I'd only meant that he should get his head straight. I already know what *I* want: nothing serious or soul-searching. Just fun. And, yes, hot sex.

Other people having affairs might be different, their connections are genuine and go way beyond incendiary sex. They are actually in love, and they change their lives for each other — leaving jobs, moving cities, breaking up families.

But I don't love Josh, and Josh — despite whatever he might be telling himself — doesn't love me. I suspect I'm being played and in ways I don't understand. All I know for sure is that I don't want it to be over because without Josh I have nothing. Actually, that's not true and I feel guilty for even thinking it – I have Neeve, Sofie, Kiara, Mum, Pop, Derry, even Alastair . . .

I look at my phone. It's ten to five. 'I'm calling it a day,' I say. 'It's Friday after all.' I switch off my computer, put on my coat, then squint at Alastair. 'What will you do if you don't have a girl-friend by Valentine's Day?' I'm curious.

He shrugs. 'She may not be the woman of my dreams but I could probably scare up somebody.'

With undeniable affection, I say, 'I despise you.'

'And I *love* you. Although not in that way. Have a nice weekend.'

Well, that would be wonderful. I can but hope.

However, when I get to Mum and Pop's, I discover that Sofie, Jackson and Kiara have hatched plans to go to the cinema club on Sunday night – with Hugh!

'Why don't you come too, Mum?' Kiara says. (Kiara, after her initial suspicion that a freshly returned Hugh was going to be making overtures to every woman in Dublin, has warmed to him again.)

'Do, Amy.' Jackson is all smiles.

'Ah, do,' Sofie says.

Goggle-eyed, I stare at them. Are they *insane*? I don't want to spend any time with Hugh. Like, never. Every time our paths cross – when he picks the girls up or delivers them home again – I can hardly breathe from the assault of my emotions. All that out-of-control sorrow, jealousy, rage, guilt . . .

But to go to the cinema club – I can't think of anything worse! I haven't been there in ages, not since before Hugh came back, and I've no plans ever to go again. It's the place where I feel most exposed and most judged. Too many 'friends' of mine go there. And to show up with Hugh, to masquerade as a happy family, to know that everyone is speculating about us would be too shaming.

All these thoughts explode in my head as Sofie, Kiara and Jackson smile encouragingly at me.

'No,' I say. 'Um. No. It's okay. I don't want to. No.'

Such a clamour of objections breaks out – 'Ah, Mu-um!' And 'Oh, Aaa-mee!' – that I have to leave the room, go upstairs and wait for the high water of feelings to abate.

As a result, every second of Saturday and Sunday is infused with a type of angry dread. I don't want all those bitches – Genevieve Payne and her ilk – checking out Hugh.

Maybe it won't happen, though. Maybe Hugh will realize what a bad idea it is.

But at four thirty on the dot on Sunday, he arrives to pick up Sofie, Kiara and Jackson. It hurts terribly to see how handsome he's looking. He'd always been burly, which I'd loved, but every time I see him these days he's slightly thinner. He's now at the stage where his clothes are noticeably looser; any woman's nurturing instincts would be alerted. It's even happening to me. I want to hold his body and comfort him, sit him down in my kitchen and feed him.

'Sure we can't persuade you?' His tone is gentle.

'Quite sure,' I mutter.

Sofie, Kiara and Jackson troop down the stairs and out of the house. I close the front door behind them. But as soon as the car has gone, I open it again and slam it with all my might, then sit on the stairs and sob hot, angry tears. They mutate into howls of sorrow because the stupid, mortifyingly middle-class cinema club had represented something rare and precious. It was the one part of my life where the people I love the most came together harmoniously – Hugh, me, the three girls, even Jackson.

If I look back over my life I can honestly say I've never been as happy as I have been in *Pizza Express* on some random Sunday evening after seeing a very odd Iranian film.

Separation, then divorce . . . It really is one of the hardest things any person will ever go through. Well, maybe not everyone. Other people fall out of love gradually and in perfect synchronicity, so by the time they realize it's all over, both of their landings are super-soft and they're able to be friends.

Hugh and I, though, it's different. We were so tightly bonded and our sundering has been shocking and brutal. His departure was too sudden; the wrench was ragged and rough. We've been pulled apart as carelessly as someone tearing off a piece of baguette. The destruction couldn't have been cruder and I am *raw*.

But one day I won't be, I remind myself. Even if it doesn't feel like it, I'm already healing because every second that passes is bringing me closer to a new normality. One day I'll be in the middle of something and I'll suddenly see that I'm happy and everything will be okay.

It will come. I just need to be patient.

107

Tuesday, 7 February

'Fuck me, Josh, harder!'

He duly slams into me with more force. I moan and thrash about a bit on the hotel bed . . . but something's wrong.

I don't want to be doing this. I actually hadn't wanted any of it – being yanked into the room, discovering Josh already undressed and naked, having my knickers whipped off, lowering myself on to him, moving with deliberate calculation on top of him, listening to him plead for me to remove my shirt and dispassionately watching his face as he disappeared inside his climax.

It's just what we always do, he hoicks me inside and we start tearing into each other, but if it hadn't been so habitual, I wouldn't have done any of it, not today.

Instead we should have talked. Too many serious considerations erupted last week and it was a mistake to think we could sex our way past them.

I'm not going to come. I just want it to stop. He's behind me, going for it hammer and tongs, and I wonder if I should fake it.

But faking it is the worst, it's a violation of intimacy and I haven't done it in literally decades, not since I was with the nice-but-dull single dad from Neeve's crèche, back in the day.

Also, I haven't the energy to fake it.

However, if I don't come, it's a line in the sand. Josh will take it personally.

But something worse seems to be happening . . . For a moment I think I've imagined it, then I feel it again, the floppiness, the lack of control, he keeps thrusting but he's slowing and I'm not stupid enough to rub it in with another yelp of *Fuck me harder.*

Then he exclaims in frustration and my heart sinks like a stone.

It's gone. It's over. His weight lifts off me and angrily he disappears into the bathroom. When he comes back and climbs under the covers, he won't meet my eyes.

I say nothing. Josh is not a man you discuss that kind of masculinity fail with.

'Do you want me to . . . ?'

'No!' Whatever he's offering, to help me come, I don't want it.

More silence ensues while lines run through my head. *There's no shame in it. It happens to every man at some stage. Anyway, he came already. Even if normally he comes two or three times with me.* None of them seems suitable.

'Yeah, you know, I'm going to go,' he says.

'Okay.'

With short, angry movements, he's dressed and gone within seconds. I wait ten minutes until I'm certain that he's really gone, then I leave too.

The following day is just as bad – an emotional hangover from the previous night. It feels as if everything's dying.

I fly back to Dublin, go home, and I'm wearily removing the remnants of my make-up when Neeve sidles into my bedroom. Instantly I know that another ending is happening. 'Mum,' she says. 'Promise me you won't cry.'

'You're moving out?'

She nods, almost as if she's afraid she'll burst with happiness.

I fake excitement. 'Oh! Neeve! That's great! Well, I'm heartbroken, but tell me.'

'It's Daddy,' she confides gleefully. 'He owns an apartment.'

All of a sudden Richie seems to be a *lot* more involved in Neeve's stuff. It would be nice if it isn't connected to her recent change in profile but that's delusional thinking.

'Wait till you hear where it is.' She pauses dramatically. 'Riverside Quarter.'

'Wow.'

Riverside Quarter is a development of luxury apartments on

the Liffey. It's very high spec, has its own gym and viewing room, and is right in the city centre.

'Well, he actually owns four apartments there. He bought them just after the crash for, like, *nothing* and now he lets them out.'

Oh, Christ, I absolutely hate him. Rents in Dublin are at an all-time high, and people are crippled with the payments. There are no properties available for first-time buyers because vultures like Richie Aldin swoop in and take advantage of the insolvency of others. His own daughter – Neeve – is a victim of this: can't afford to rent and can't afford to buy. Sofie and Kiara will be too. Even Hugh.

'So he's letting you live in one of them?'

'Yep.'

It's hard to ask the next bit but I must. 'For free?'

'Not free! Mu-um! Like, he has to cover the mortgage payment on it.'

But interest rates are low, his mortgage payments must be fuck-all.

'He's only charging me half the market rate.'

'Well. Great.'

'And he's going to help me find a place to buy. We're going to go scouting together. He says he can't actually come into the places because as soon as the estate agent sees him the price automatically goes up by twenty per cent. It's a Richie Aldin tax!' Her tone is upbeat.

Okay, so this is capitalism. But he is *loathsome*. Worse, Neeve admires it.

'So he'll check out the area, see if the neighbours are scumbags, all that.'

Scumbags! If Kiara heard her, she'd literally cry.

'When are you going?'

'Saturday.'

'This Saturday? Three-days-away Saturday?'

'That's the one. Daddy's hired me a van.'

No, no, no, no, no. It's too soon.

108

Saturday, 11 February

At nine thirty a.m., Neeve's removal van parks outside and I feel as if my heart has been smashed, as fragile as an empty eggshell.

I've wanted Neeve to be independent and to live a fun, single life. Not like this, though. Not having crossed over to the dark side under the sway of Richie Aldin. I've no right to dislike her choices, and I can't wish for her independence but only on my terms. My head is well aware of the facts, but no one has told my heart.

All day long, the girls and I are up and down the stairs, carrying boxes of Neeve's clothes, moving her equipment, emptying her room. It feels almost as if I'm experiencing her death. Finally everything is in the truck.

'Right!' Neeve is super-cheery. 'Well, I'm off!'

'You won't forget about us, will you?' I've managed not to cry all day, but now my face is wet with tears.

'Oh, Mum, you giant douche! I'm only four miles away.'

How can I tell her that I'm afraid her move is more than merely geographical? As I stand and wave her off, I have a ridiculous fear that none of us will ever see her again.

Sunday I spend in bed crying, mourning Neeve's absence, and Monday morning is a disaster – it takes me ages to get up and I'm thirty-five minutes late for work. I put in a half-baked performance and it's a relief when the day ends so I can leave Tim's gimlet-eyed stares. Monday night won't be any better, though – Hugh is coming over for a grown-up talk. He's been back in Ireland for six weeks, it's time to grapple with our problematic finances and formulate a plan so that we all have a place to live.

Life feels like one ordeal after another after another. My only relief was Josh and I'm ominously aware that we're about to sputter into an ignominious ending. I really hope that Hugh will cancel but, exactly at the agreed time, the doorbell rings. *Shite*. There's a very real chance this conversation might get ugly, so I've sent Sofie and Kiara over to Derry for a couple of hours.

I open the door, and there he is, looking forlorn and even thinner. He's starting to become gaunt.

'Come in,' I say. 'We could probably do with wine to help us get through this, but we need to have our wits about us so we're having tea. Okay?'

'Okay.'

The box file of documents is waiting on the kitchen table. Face to face, we take our seats, warily watching each other. We've only been alone with each other a couple of times since he came back.

I *hate* having to do this. Being with him, even just catching a glimpse of him every time he drops the girls home, makes me tired to my bones.

'Before we start crunching numbers,' he says, 'can I say something else?'

'What?' My stomach shrinks. What is it?

'It's less than a month before my six months is up. You and I, we need to talk about telling the girls.'

'Oh, God.' It's going to be so difficult. Neeve won't care but Sofie and Kiara will be devastated. I'm too beaten down to come up with any great plan, so I say, 'I think we have to be honest with them.'

'Me too.'

The biggest worry is Sofie, she's sitting her Leaving Cert at the end of May. Yes, the timing is bad but Hugh can't move back in with us, I simply couldn't endure it. Nor can we string the girls along for another three months.

'They're young women,' he says. 'Not kids any more.'

'They *are* young women, but it won't be easy for them. We've got to be really there for them.'

'Especially Sofie.'

'How do you think she is?' I'm interested in his opinion, it's been difficult carrying the worry all by myself.

'Good. Maybe better than she used to be. Less anxious.'

'Does she speak to you about the abortion?'

'Sometimes. She seems at peace with herself.'

'And why wouldn't she be?' My tone is sharp.

He looks surprised. 'I wasn't saying anything.'

But a ball of rage that I didn't even know was there is bursting out of me, like the thing in *Alien*. 'You left me alone!' I blurt. 'Sofie was pregnant! I had to take her to London.'

'I know. I'm sorry.'

My face is hot and suddenly tears of fury are spilling from my eyes. 'While you were shagging your way around South East Asia, I was handling a medical crisis!' I'm almost spitting with emotion. 'One that could have had me arrested!'

'I'm sorry,' he whispers.

I'm worried I might hit him again, the way I did the night I got back from Serbia, so instead I thump my fist hard against the table. 'You fucking bastard!'

'Amy . . .' He stands up.

'Don't fucking *touch* me. Sit down!'

He obeys, watching me cagily.

Angry sobs erupt from my gut and I cry and cry and cry. I cry until my eyes feel swollen and my face is sore with salt.

Long minutes pass. Now and again, he makes a move to come to me and I shriek, 'Don't come fucking *near* me!

'You're selfish,' I hurl at him, needing to hurt him, insult him, shame him. 'You're weak. And pathetic!'

'I know.'

'The sex I have with Josh, it's *waaaay* better than anything I ever had with you.'

He blanches.

'It's fucking fantastic!'

That Josh and I are going to finish tomorrow night suddenly becomes clear. But I'm not telling Hugh.

A fresh bout of bitter tears heaves up from my gut. 'I only slept with one person, while you slept with hundreds.'

'You can sleep with more people,' Hugh says. 'As many as you want.'

'*Were* there hundreds?' I ask thickly.

'Two and a half.'

'What's the half?'

'We didn't have sex. I just wanted to sleep in the bed with her and pretend she was you.'

'How was the sex you *did* have?'

He hesitates, and before I yell at him again, he says quickly, 'Terrifying. Different. New.'

'Say it was great. Because of course it *was* great.'

'It was great.'

I thought it was what I wanted to hear but it isn't.

'But they weren't you,' he says.

'*They!*' I'm racked with jealousy and fury at the thought of all the steps Hugh would have gone through in order to slide his mickey into those other vaginas – the eye-meet on the beach, the smile, the offer of a drink, the grazing of hands against each other, the promise in his eyes, the kissing, the touching, the undressing, the intimacy, all of it. 'You were meant to be mine!'

And I was meant to be his, but I don't care about that right now.

'This is healthy,' he suggests tentatively. 'You've a right to be angry.'

'Just shut up with your fucking platitudes! You and Alastair!' I really can't bear this. Jerkily, I stand up, stomp to the fridge, pour some wine, head into the living room with the glass and the bottle and thump myself down on to the sofa. A few moments later, Hugh follows, keeping his distance.

We sit in thick silence for a long, long time, me slugging the wine, him staring at his hands.

Eventually I say, 'Steevie said I should break all your vinyl.'

'Would it make you feel better?'

'No.'

'Is there anything that would make you feel better?'

'No.' Then, 'Except maybe if you died.' After a moment I say, 'I didn't mean that.'

'And maybe you did.'

'Oh, stop being so fucking reasonable!'

A noise from the hall startles me. It can only be Kiara or Sofie – they weren't expected back until later. But a quick glance at my phone establishes that it *is* later – Hugh and I have been locked in this bitter exchange for two and a half hours.

'Dad! Dad!' They're both delighted. 'We thought you'd be gone.'

'No, I . . . ah . . .'

Sofie's face changes: she's picked up on the loaded atmosphere and now so has Kiara. Nervously, they look from Hugh to me, then delicately back out of the room. 'Just going to . . .' Kiara says.

'Me too.' Sofie calls, moving up the stairs. 'See you Saturday.'

When I hear their bedroom doors close, Hugh exhales and says, 'I'll go.'

'Do that. You've a real talent for it.'

109

Tuesday, 14 February

Josh asks to meet me in the bar of the hotel, instead of our usual bedroom. I'm guessing he hasn't actually booked the room, which means he knows what's coming – he *must* do. Why would he shell out eighty pounds if there was going to be no sex? So here we are in the little bar in the hotel.

What an irony that today is Valentine's Day.

We mumble our hellos and I sit down.

'Go on, then,' Josh says.

Shite. I have to do it?

'Go on,' he repeats.

I settle my elbows on the table and try to form the words.

'I thought you'd have a speech prepared,' he says.

Well, I had, several speeches, and now none of them seems right. Instead I surprise myself by asking, 'Josh, has this happened to you before?'

'Someone like you breaking up with me?' He nods. For a moment there's a suspicious shininess in his eyes.

'I'm sorry.' Gently I take his hand. 'But I'm not your answer.'

'To what?'

'You think the hole inside you will be filled if you set up a sparkling new life with me. But it won't.'

'And what's your excuse?'

'The same – I really fancied you and I wanted to escape from my life.'

'You used me.'

Now I'm ashamed. 'I guess we used each other.'

In the last week I've come to see our set-up as tawdry and tragic, as two flawed people trying to transcend their disappointing

498

ordinariness. I'd always known there was no future in this but I didn't think it would be over so abruptly. And it *is* over.

'People who do crazy stuff in mid-life,' I say, 'and that's nearly the entire human race, from what I can see, apparently they're trying to defy death. But for both of us, I think we were mourning youthful promise that was never realized.'

'If we lived in the same place,' he says, 'and there weren't other people, like, if we weren't married, do you think we'd . . . ?'

'I don't know.'

'You do know.'

I sigh. 'Okay. I don't think so, Josh. We're different kinds of people. I'm not wildly upbeat but after a while my chirpiness would irritate you.'

'And how would you feel about me?'

'I think I'd find you too . . . pessimistic. And that's not a judgement,' I add, very quickly. 'People are the way they are. You don't have to change. You just have to find someone who's happy with your pessimism.'

He half smiles at this.

'Like, you and Marcia. I don't know the ins and outs of your marriage, but she seems well able for you.'

He nods. 'Maybe. And you? Getting back with your husband?'

'No.'

'Aw, Sackcloth, come *on*. As soon as he came home, I knew we were done for.'

Trying not to raise my voice, I say, 'Two weeks ago you said I was cold. Maybe I am. Because it's never going to happen. I miss him, the way we were, and I don't want anything bad to happen to him, but we're done, me and him.'

'Okay.' Is he convinced? Who knows, and does it matter?

'So what are you going to use next to fill up the hole inside you?' he asks.

'Nothing. There's nothing.' And that's a hard truth to face. I'll just have to live alongside the unfillable hole. 'Josh, thank you. For everything, all of it.' More than anything I mean the sex, but

I'm not naming it because I want nothing to be misconstrued as flirting. 'It was . . . *lovely*.'

'It was lovely,' he says.

And now I want to cry. I get to my feet. 'I hope you'll be happy. Bye, Josh.'

Every bubble in the galaxy has burst. The million shards of sparkle suspended in the air have turned to wet ash. All the colour has leached away and the world is just grey, grey, grey.

110

Monday, 27 February

In the days that follow, I feel as if I've slammed hard against unforgiving granite. During my time with Josh it was like dancing through a luminous universe where paths of stars formed themselves under my glittering feet. Now the magical music has stopped, and all I'm left with is me and my feelings.

A week passes, without my hearing anything from him – not an email, a text, not even a like on Facebook. Another week commences and still there's no communication. As I head towards the two-week mark, I begin to relax.

It's looking like it really is over – my relief is huge. Not entirely unalloyed, though: I'm ashamed about what I did to his wife. I broke my own rules and that's a fairly shitty feeling. And I'm ashamed about using him. It wasn't deliberate or cynical but it still happened. Unless all relationships are transactional? Whatever, it's over and I won't do it again. Not with a married man and, actually, not with any man. I don't want one. I don't need one. I can manage grand on my own.

Admittedly, though, life doesn't feel in any way pleasurable or joyous.

Work is particularly tough because I'm spending most of my time on the EverDry account – working with *my own mother*. From someone who didn't want to be the ambassador in the first place, she's surprisingly opinionated about her role: she didn't like the cosy clothes we bundled her into for the photoshoot ('They make me look ancient'), she doesn't want any of the bus-shelters in her neighbourhood to feature the ads ('In case anyone I know sees me'), she won't do any interviews with the *Guardian* ('Badly dressed') and so on. This, coupled with Mrs EverDry's conflicting but equally implacable will of iron, has meant that going to work, these days, feels more like going into battle.

I haven't seen Neeve since the Saturday she drove off behind her removal van. I text her a lot, probably too much, and though I keep things light, she still won't commit to a visit.

Nor have Hugh and I had another meeting about our finances – not after the last one got so ugly. God knows that conversation needs to happen – apparently he's still living in Nugent's garage. We've crossed paths only once since the ding-dong when we exchanged an awkward nod as he dropped Sofie and Kiara home. Right now the issue is on ice. In fact, there's a sense that everything is suspended in perpetual winter.

Then, one Monday morning, Alastair brings an armful of vibrant orange tulips into work. They glow with life and light.

'It's like you've declared spring open!' I say.

'I thought we needed something.'

'I know February is the shortest month of the year,' I say, 'but this one feels like it's gone on for years.'

'First of March, day after tomorrow,' Alastair says. 'Reasons to be cheerful!'

'I had another horrible dream last night,' I announce to the office.

'*Nooooo*,' Alastair whimpers softly.

I've been having vivid dreams in the past week, then relating them to my colleagues.

'Don't tell us,' Alastair begs. 'It's as bad as having to admire someone's baby photos.'

But I don't care. 'There was a man,' I say. 'He was homeless and it was really cold and he needed new boots. So I took out a hundred euro but before I could give it to him, I woke up.' Tears leak down my face. 'It made me so sad.'

'She crying again?' Thamy calls in from the outer office.

'Yep,' Alastair says.

'Your feet were probably cold,' Tim says. 'Our body creates stories to keep us asleep.'

Alastair shakes his head, like he knows better.

'What?' I demand of him.

'Nothing.'

'You think I'm thinking about Hugh sleeping in Nugent's garage, don't you? You think I feel sorry for him.'

'You do.'

'He deserves it. But I'm allowed to be sad about it.'

'The crying is hard to take,' Tim says, 'but at least you're not still biting everyone's head off.'

'I never bit your head off. Only Alastair's.'

'And mine,' Thamy calls.

'Because you booked the wrong flight.'

'She didn't!' Tim and Alastair yell. 'You got it wrong.'

Well, maybe I had, but it's nicer to blame someone else.

'It's up!' Tim calls. He's talking about Neeve's vlog and I hurry for a look because this is literally the only time I see her, these days.

This week she's showing us her fancy new crib.

'Whoa!' Alastair recoils. 'It's all a bit . . .'

'Flash?'

'Yeah.'

'She's gone over to the dark side.' The tears start again. 'She's been seduced by that asshat's money and connections.'

'Amy,' Tim says, and there's a note of warning in his voice, 'why don't you go on home? Cry it all out.'

And start afresh tomorrow, restored to mannered professionalism – that's his implication.

'Hugh's coming over this evening,' I say. 'We need to decide how we tell the girls he's not coming back.'

Tim and I stare each other down. 'That's right,' I say. 'The crying goes on for a while longer.'

'If you're that sad,' he's exasperated, 'why don't you just get back with him?'

For the love of God, why do people *persist* in un-nuanced thinking? 'I don't want to be with him. But I'm allowed to be sad.'

*

Hugh and I sit at the kitchen table and I say, 'Next Monday, that's the sixth of March, a week before the deadline, that's when we tell them.'

'Okay.'

'So we start by telling them how much we both love them,' I say.

'Which of us should say it?'

'Can't we just wing it?'

'We need to present a confident front. We can't display doubt because it'll make them feel insecure.'

'Okay, you say the first bit, and I'll nod and smile, like I'm agreeing. Then I'll say that even though you and I aren't together any more, we'll always be a family.'

'And I'll nod and smile through that bit?'

'Yes.' Oh, Christ, I just want it to have already happened. 'But, Hugh, they might be angry. Or cry.'

'We let them do what they need to do.'

'They might be very angry with you,' I say.

'I deserve it. I can take it.'

Guilt twangs in me. Maybe Hugh isn't entirely responsible for the failure of our marriage. 'Where should we tell them?' I ask. 'Which room?'

'I think the living room. Sitting at this table would be too formal.'

'Should you and I sit next to each other? Or should I be on the couch and you on the chair?'

'Optics is your speciality.'

'Grand. We'll sit together on the couch. Should we hold hands?'

'No.'

'To demonstrate a united front?'

'It would only confuse them. You think Neevey will come?'

I doubt it. She never comes here now – she doesn't even text except when she wants something. The last time was because she needed a baby photo of her with Richie. Apparently they've done the 'Relative Values' interview for the *Sunday Times*. 'Let's not depend on it,' I say.

His tone is wry. 'It'll be a shame to miss her happy face.'

He's right. She'll be delighted. Or maybe she won't even care.

'Right,' I say. 'Let's have a practice. You start.'

'You mean say the words? Now? Hold on, gimme a minute. Right.' He takes a breath and stares at nothing. 'Sofie, Kiara,' his voice is hoarse, 'Amy and I both love you very, very much.'

I nod and try to smile, but my mouth is wobbly.

'Now your turn,' he says.

'Hugh and I aren't together . . . or should I say "won't be getting back together"?' I look at him for confirmation, then wipe away tears with my sleeve. 'I think "aren't getting back together" is the best thing to say.'

'Amy . . .'

'It's so sad, Hugh. It's just so sad.'

'I know, baby. C'mere . . .

'C'mere,' he repeats. And even though I know it's probably a bad idea, I get up, go to the other side of the table and sit myself on his lap. It's what I always used to do when I was upset. This will probably come back to bite me, but for a few blissful moments I let myself settle into the comfort of his arms, the heat of his body, the scent of his skin . . . His arms tighten around me – then, with a huge effort of will, I murmur, 'Boundaries.' I sit up straight and look into his face and there he is, Hugh. *My* Hugh. One of those time-slips happens.

'Oh, God.' I clutch my head and slide off his lap.

'What?'

'Nothing. Just a time-slip. Sometimes I forget. I think things are the way they used to be.'

'I know, babe, me too.'

'You do?'

'Of course.'

Back safely on my side of the table, I ask, 'But it'll pass. It'll feel more and more normal as time goes on.'

'Will it?' He looks miserable.

'Of course. It's how life works.' I'm in my chair again. 'Okay. Let's get back to things . . . Next I think we should say that we'll always be there for each other. All of us.' I stop. 'Oh, Hugh!' Another bout of crying overtakes me.

'What is it, honey?'

'You're so *thin*.'

'I'm fine.'

Tonight I'll probably dream about a hungry man, and just before I feed him, I'll wake up. 'Can you not eat?' I ask.

'Ah, you know . . .'

'I'm sorry.' I'm sincere. 'I'm sorry I can't mend my heart. I'm sorry I can't feel the way I felt before I saw those photos. But I can't help the way I am.'

'It's why I love you.'

'Don't, Hugh, please don't. Listen, we'll be okay, both of us. We'll be fine in the end.'

'And if we're not fine –'

'No!'

The *Marigold Hotel* quote is one that neither of us can stand. Him attempting it lightens the mood.

'Maybe we'll knock it on the head for tonight.' He looks exhausted. 'See you next Monday.'

'Next Monday.'

III

Monday, 6 March

The week I spend waiting to have that conversation is the toughest so far. I'm fairly certain I feel worse now than I did in the beginning, after he first left, and that's weird.

But back then I was in shock. That's obvious now. Stunned and reeling. The full depth and breadth of his departure hadn't revealed itself to me. That's how humans bear the unbearable: we expose ourselves to just as much pain as we can take in a day or an instant. Only when we've processed that can we absorb some more.

It might explain why life's big losses take so long to metabolize.

However, I *am* moving through this. At times my progress can be measured – the initial disbelief has gone and the out-of-control shopping has calmed to normal levels. I've stopped trying to behave as if nothing is wrong so when I meet people, such as Bronagh Kingston, I don't slap on an exhausting veneer of fake cheer. Instead, without weeping all over everyone I meet, I indicate that my circumstances are still a struggle.

Even my incendiary rage has abated – at least for now. At the moment my overwhelming emotion is sorrow, and that will eventually pass too. The end of my marriage will never not be sad, but the grief won't cripple me the way it does now.

Sometimes I look back and wonder how this all happened. From the outside, you'd never have thought that Hugh and I were likely to split up. We never exchanged a cross word, like, not *really*, we weren't that kind of shouty couple. But I suppose things don't have to end with a bang, they can also expire with a whimper.

Other times it seems entirely inevitable that Hugh and I

wouldn't last. Not just the double-whammy of Gavin dying so soon after Hugh's dad and the existential impact it had on Hugh. But I had to look at my caper with Josh the summer before last. Like, what was that all about?

I still can't make sense of it. The best I can come up with is that I'd felt like I had nothing, ever, to look forward to. But billions of people have hard lives – mine was hardly tough – and they don't start flirting with someone they shouldn't be flirting with.

I had loved Hugh, I had loved the family we'd created, and still I had wanted extra.

We're meant to learn from our mistakes, but if I don't understand *why*, there's nothing to stop me doing it again.

'So.' I try smiling at Kiara and Sofie. 'We need to have a talk.'

'Shouldn't we wait until Neeve gets here?' Sofie asks.

'Neeve isn't coming.'

'Oh,' Kiara says. 'Anyway, we know what you're going to tell us.'

Both Hugh and I tense.

'Dad won't be moving back in with us, will he?'

'No, honey,' I choke out.

'It's okay,' Sofie says softly.

But this is all wrong. Hugh and I were supposed to do our reassuring two-hander.

'I kinda guessed,' Kiara says. 'We all did. We understand. We're sorry you're both so sad.'

'Don't.'

'We've had time to get used to living without you,' Sofie says.

Well, that's good. That had been the idea, after all.

'But we're totally going to see you all the time, right?' she asks.

'Totally,' Hugh answers. 'Of course, honey, any time you like.'

'But we want to see you and Mum together,' Kiara says. 'Not just us with you, then us with Mum. All of us together.'

'Ah . . .' Hugh glances at me for the right answer.

'Um, sure.' My tone is horribly jovial. 'For birthdays and those things.'

Sofie and Kiara exchange a look – it seems Hugh and I weren't the only ones to have prepared for this.

'Not just those,' Sofie says. 'We want us to do regular family stuff.'

'Like, watching *Crazy Ex-Girlfriend* together on Mondays,' Kiara says. 'The way we used to.'

'But –'

'We've been chill about this,' Kiara reminds us. 'Really chill. But there are conditions.'

Helplessly, I look at Hugh. He seems as flummoxed as I am. 'Okay,' I say, because it seems there's no choice.

But it'll be strange and exhausting.

'Where will you live?' Kiara asks Hugh. 'With Carl and Chizo?'

'Um, no. I'm looking for a flat.'

Is he? Well, what had I expected?

'Good luck with that,' Sofie says. 'Maybe Richie Aldin will rent you one of his.'

'I know, right!' Kiara says. 'From his "property portfolio".'

'And he'll only charge you half the market rate!'

'*Such* a cool guy.'

'*To*tally such a cool guy.'

Sofie and Kiara laugh and bump fists and, I must say, it lifts my heart to hear them bitch about Richie.

'So, don't worry about us,' Kiara says. 'So long as we act like a family a lot of the time, then we're good.'

'Oh-kay.'

'I love you both to the moon and back,' Kiara declares.

'Me too,' Sofie says. 'I love you to the sun and back.'

'Well, I love them to, like, *Venus* and back.'

'Venus is nearer than the sun, you dumbass.'

'Is it? No!'

'It totally is! So are we done here?' Sofie asks. 'Because I've got to study. And so do you, Kiara. Like, you *really* do – "Venus and back"!'

'Sure, yes, fine, absolutely.' Poor Hugh is trying to gather himself.

'See you tomorrow,' Sofie says.

'Yep. Tomorrow. That's right. Physics tutorial,' he reminds me.

Sofie and Kiara make for their rooms, and Hugh and I look at each other.

'That went well,' I say.

'Yeah.' He's stunned.

'They're so mature,' I say. 'And calm.'

'More calm than me,' he says.

'Me too. I suppose they're adults now.'

'Even though they'll always be our little girls.'

'Oh, Jesus Christ, Hugh, stop!' The high of it having gone smoothly has suddenly disappeared and now I want to die from sorrow.

'I hate to do this, Amy . . . We need to talk money.'

Mutely, I gaze at him. Then, 'This never stops, does it? The separation that keeps on giving. Okay, when? The weekend, it'll have to be. I'm too busy at work.'

'Saturday?'

'Grand. Saturday.'

112

Friday, 10 March

Four days later, Mum's EverDry ads are rolled out. Suddenly her smiling, slightly airbrushed face appears on bus-shelters and in railway stations across (some of) Ireland and Britain, with the immortal tagline 'Still Having Fun'.

I see one when I race out at lunchtime to buy a new blur serum and the shock almost ends me. I'd known it was coming – after all, it had been me who'd negotiated with Adshel – but it's beyond weird when your elderly mother crosses over into being public property.

It's only two months since she became the ambassador, but as it's a quiet time of year in advertising, it was easy to fast-track the whole business.

I text Neeve to make sure she knows. To be honest, I'm just using it as a lame excuse to contact her. Too many times now I've left pathetic messages, where I laugh weakly and say, 'Are we ever going to see you again? Ha-ha-ha. Your sisters miss you.'

So it's nice to have something concrete to convey.

Mostly she ignores my missives. Sometimes she shoots back a couple of kisses or hearts. The only time I've had actual words from her since she left was after I told her that Hugh wouldn't be moving home. **Good**, she'd texted. Then, **Watch Crazy Ex-Girlfriend with him every Monday? Prefer to eat glass.**

Well, I wasn't wild about the idea myself. In fact, I was so unhappy about it that on Monday evening, waiting for him to show up and play happy families, I'm unable to eat my dinner.

I can't do this, I thought. *I really can't do this.*

But I had to. That was the long and the short of it. I would get used to it. People eventually become inured to the most appalling circumstances. Like, sometimes I think about what it would be like working in an abattoir or chopping the heads off chickens – jobs no one *yearns* to do. But if you have no other option, you get on with it. And your revulsion couldn't stay at its original sky-high level, could it?

I'm watching a giant bowl of popcorn rotating in the micro-wave when Kiara says, 'Here's Dad.'

And, yes, indeed, here is Hugh, letting himself in with his own key, as instructed.

'Hello again,' he says to me.

'God.' I'm striving for humour. 'You might as well be living back here, I see you so often!' This is in reference to the meet we'd had on Saturday afternoon to straighten out our finances.

He indicates his key. 'Was that cool? To use it.'

'It's what we agreed!' Once again my tone is slightly too breezy. Well, it's a process. We'll get there. Soon we'll be one of those divorced couples who are in and out of each other's lives and the very best of friends.

Well, maybe not soon. But sometime.

'Hey!' Hugh exclaims. 'I saw one of your mum's ads! On a bus-shelter. I nearly crashed the car with shock.' He's laughing. 'She looks fantastic.'

'I know!' Kiara cries. 'It's mad, right? Like, *Granny*.'

'Good for her.'

It *is* good for her. It's also good for me because Mrs EverDry has paid Hatch a bonus, a lovely lump of cash that went straight into the yawning hole of my joint account with Hugh. It's bought us a bit of wriggle room.

'C'mon, Mum, c'mon, Dad.' Kiara sweeps us into the front room.

'There's beer in the fridge,' I say to Hugh.

'Oh. Ah. Thanks.'

He looks slightly stunned and I say, 'Time-slip?'

'Yep. Time-slip.'

Awkwardly I pat his arm. 'It's shit, I know, but it'll eventually pass.'

'Sofie!' Kiara calls up the stairs. 'Come on!'

Sofie scampers down and into the living room, and we all clamber on to the couch. Hugh and I park ourselves at each end, as far away from each other as we can get. None of us mentions Neeve, even though her absence feels huge.

We pass the popcorn back and forth, Hugh and I drink beers, and we all watch *Crazy Ex-Girlfriend*.

This was a habit for us every Monday night but we're unable to replicate the true experience. It's like eating chocolate brownies made with artificial sweeteners – they might look the same but something is definitely off.

When the episode ends, my mood is low but Hugh and I have been pleasant to each other and I'm willing to declare the evening a qualified success. A little too quickly the girls hug Hugh good-bye and disappear off to bed, leaving me standing alone in the hall with him.

'While I remember,' he says, 'there's a date for scattering my dad's ashes. Easter Saturday.'

'Oh? You mean . . . Am I invited?'

His face darkens. 'Of course! You're part of the family, you and the girls.'

'Still?'

'Yes! Nothing changes that.'

'Christ, it's so weird, all this new etiquette to cover separated couples. You know, who's invited to funerals and who isn't.'

He nods, looking very sad. 'I still can't believe it's happened. I never thought we'd split up. I never thought we'd be that couple.'

'Me either. I thought we were different.'

'But I suppose everyone thinks they're different.'

'So.' My throat aches with the onset of tears. 'Tell me about the ashes.'

'Like I said, Easter Saturday morning, that's five weeks away. Howth Hill, then a fancy lunch in Maldive –'

'Maldive! Fancy!' I actually mean, 'Over the top.'

'Fancy is right.' His expression is wry. 'Chizo's gig.'

'Ah, suddenly it all makes sense.'

'She's been tasting menus in Ireland's finest for the past ages.'

'And who's coming?'

'Everyone. John, Rolf and Krister from Uppsala, Brendan, Nita and their kids from Manchester, Carl, Chizo and Noah, the Boy Wonder, from Foxrock, and you, me, Neeve, Sofie and Kiara from Dundrum.' He flushes. 'I mean . . . what I meant . . . I know I don't live in Dundrum.'

'Stop.'

We exchange one of those looks, a stoic acceptance.

'And Neeve?' I ask. 'You're sure you want her there?'

'Dad was fond of her.'

'God alone knows why!'

'Ah, she's fine. So, yes, of course Neeve.'

Unexpectedly I think to ask, 'How are you, Hugh? You know, with your dad? And Gavin?' In all my resentment over him having left me, I had no interest in the – doubtless ongoing – grief of his double bereavement.

'Ah, I'm okay.'

'Hugh. Give me a real answer.'

He squirms. 'I don't know, Amy. I miss them both. I think about Dad a lot, about when we were all kids. He was such a good man.'

'So you're lonely?'

'Yes, but –' He cuts himself off. I'm sure he'd been about to say that he was lonely for me and the girls, as well as for his dad and Gavin, and he doesn't want to sound like he's blaming.

'You're sad?' I ask.

Thoughtfully, he says, 'It's more accurate to say I feel scared.' He sighs. 'I dunno, Amy. I don't know the names for most of my emotions. All I really know is I'm not insane, the way I was last year, when it seemed like I had to rush out and seize the day and live fully and all that.'

113

Friday, 17 March

On Friday evening, on the drive out to Mum and Pop's, the sky is still light. It's the first time in months that it hasn't been dark at six thirty. I do a quick calculation – the clocks will be going forward in two weeks. Spring is definitely here.

I should be glad at this visible marker that time is passing: every second is taking me closer to that magical place when my pain will have healed. Today, though, it hurts me. Every new event, every turn of the seasons, every dawning of a fresh month, is another milestone, taking me further away from when Hugh and I were a family.

When I turn into Mum's driveway, there are two kids playing in the front garden. Then I see it's actually Sofie and Jackson, doing handstands. Their peals of laughter fill the evening air.

'Hi, Aaa-mee!' they call across to me, when I get out of the car.

I stand and watch them.

'Spot me,' Sofie orders Jackson.

'What does that even mean?' he asks.

'I dunno, but spot me!' She manages a passable handstand and he holds her legs. 'Okay, let go now.' But as soon as he steps away, she collapses on to the grass, where she lies on her back, laughing and laughing.

'Now my go,' he says. 'Spot me!'

They're so very sweet. Both of them are starting their Leaving Certs in less than three months. They've been diligent about studying and it's heartening to see them having such innocent fun.

I'd wondered how they'd survive the trauma of Sofie's pregnancy – my suspicion had been that they'd split up. But they seem as close as ever.

'Amy!'

515

I look around. Derry has the front door open. 'C'mere!' she shouts.

'What?' I hurry towards her. 'What is it?'

'Mum.'

'What?'

But I can hear her talking loudly, so she mustn't be dead.

Instinctively I hasten towards the source of all the nervy energy in the house: the living room. Mum has the floor.

'. . . me,' she's saying. 'Yep, little old *me*! Less of the "old", though, mind you.'

Joe is there with Siena, and Finn, Pip and Kit, as are Maura, The Poor Bastard, Declyn, Baby Maisey and Kiara. And poor Pop, of course, looking utterly bamboozled.

'Amy!' Mum notices me. '*Wait* till you hear. Tonight's *Late Late Show*! They've bumped Ed Sheeran for ME!'

Christ. Well, this is news. Mum is due to start the media part of her ambassadorship on Monday, but *The Late Late Show* had resisted all my pleas for an interview.

'I'm amazing?' Mum asks. 'I'm amazing, right?'

'You're, ah, wow . . .' Joe's voice trails off.

'Unbearable,' Derry butts in. 'That's the word you're looking for. Or insufferable, if you'd prefer.'

'Insufferable is good,' Joe says.

'WILL SOMEONE TELL ME WHAT IS GOING ON?' Pop beseeches.

'Kiara,' Mum commands. 'Call Neevey. Tell her she needs to style me. Tell her it's *urgent*.'

My heartrate speeds up. How will Neeve respond? Is she going to hare out here at a moment's notice to help her granny, when she hasn't made even ten minutes for me since the day she left?

'AS THE HEAD OF THIS HOUSEHOLD I INSIST THAT I BE TOLD WHAT'S GOING ON.'

'Shut up, Pop,' Kit says.

'I'LL SHUT YOU UP, YOU LITTLE SCUT.'

Sofie has appeared at my elbow, she plucks at my sleeve. 'So, Amy? Can I talk to you?'

My stomach lurches.

'It's okay.' She collapses into giggles. 'I'm not pregnant again. So listen, in the Easter holidays, there's an intensive revision course at the Institute. Can I do the physics and chemistry modules?'

My hopes for Sofie have always been modest, I only ever wanted her to be happy. Suddenly, though, she actually has ambitions. She's applied to do physical chemistry in university and she's really going for it.

'But it costs money.' She winces. 'Lots.'

'Let me talk to Hugh,' I say. 'But don't worry, we'll find it.'

Anxiously I return to the action. Is Neeve really coming?

'Yes,' Kiara confirms.

And, sure enough, she materializes not half an hour later, looking shiny and expensive.

'WHAT HAPPENED TO YOU?' Pop looks alarmed. 'YOU'VE GONE ALL SPARKLY.'

I lunge at her and hug her so hard she says, 'Ow! Mum, for the love of God.'

'My little girl.' I cover her face with kisses.

'Would you get fecking *off* me!' But she's grinning.

'I've missed you, honey.'

'There's no need to drench me.'

'Can I have a quick word? In private?'

'Oh, shite.' She flicks a look at Sofie and Kiara.

'Nothing bad. Just . . . come upstairs.'

In the bedroom that functions as the overflow room, I say, 'Easter Saturday. Keep it free. We're scattering Robert's ashes.'

'Robert?'

'Hugh's dad. Sweetie, you *know* who Robert is. Was.'

Her face hardens. '*I'm* not going.'

'But –'

'I'm not going. He wasn't my real granddad. I don't have to go.'

'But –' Robert was always so nice to Neeve.

'Not. Going. Now I have to style Granny. Excuse me.'

Suddenly I'm furious. 'Hey! Have some respect. Robert loved you. And you know what? You owe it to Hugh!'

'Hugh?' she splutters. 'Joking, right? He's not my dad –'

'He took care of you for years, collected you from parties and –'

'I've got a dad! And I don't even know why *you*'re going. You and Hugh are over.'

'I want you to come.' I'm adamant.

'*Why?*'

'For *Hugh*.' Our faces are very close and we're almost hissing at each other. This is exactly how it was all through her teenage years.

'Why do you care? He fucked off! He publicly humiliated you. He deserves nothing from you. He. Is. An. Asshole.'

He isn't. He's a man who made a mistake. A big, huge mistake, admittedly. But he wasn't cruel to me, not deliberately. He was very good to us all for a very long time and he deserves our support as he says this last goodbye to his beloved dad.

'I'm going.' I grip her arm. 'And so are you. And that is the end of the fucking matter.'

114

Monday, 20 March

Mum's interview on *The Late Late Show* is a bit of a bust. All the adulation has gone to her head and she doesn't remember that she's only there to promote a product. She barely mentions Ever-Dry, which means that Mrs Mullen has been sending me furious emails all weekend.

Also, Ed Sheeran was *not* bumped to make way for Mum. No one knows where she came up with that piece of nonsense.

On Monday morning, Tim, Alastair and I have to hold an emergency meeting about getting Mum back on track.

'Someone needs to set her straight.' Tim is grim.

'I beg you, don't let it be me,' I say.

'Grand.' Even Alastair seems daunted. 'I'll do it.'

The relief!

My energy is always in such scant supply, these days, and Petra has offered an explanation that sits comfortably with me: 'Those in constant physical pain are exhausted. Enduring the unendurable saps one's strength. I conclude it must be the same for emotional pain.'

It's having to see Hugh that is so bloody draining. Chronic dread is eroding the lining of my stomach, the burning sensation waking me up during the night.

But Sofie and Kiara are adamant about our happy-family TV-watching every Monday night.

Tonight, after the show has ended, and Sofie and Kiara have scampered away to leave me alone with Hugh, we discuss Sofie's request for extra tuition. It's a lot of money, a sum we don't have lying around.

'Extend our overdraft?' I suggest.

He grimaces. 'Not sure the bank would go for that.'

'A loan?'

'Maybe. The most obvious thing is the deposit for my flat.'

As I'd suspected, Chizo hasn't let Hugh move back into her fancy gaff. I'm not even sure I believe her story about family coming from Nigeria. So he's still living in Nugent's garage. But we've just about assembled enough to pay for a deposit and the first month's rent for a small flat for him. 'But, Hugh, you're borderline homeless.'

He rolls his eyes. 'I've a roof over my head, Wi-Fi, access to a bathroom. What more does anyone need?'

'You're living in a garage. Oh, Hugh, it's too fucking sad!'

'Stop, Amy, it's cosier than it sounds. And we're only deferring things for a few weeks. In a month's time, I'll be in my own place.'

If some other unexpected financial demand doesn't land on top of us.

'C'mon, Amy. Be brave. It's fine. Sofie can go on the course and I'll have a flat in a month.'

'Okay.' Almost in admiration, I say, 'Look at us, Hugh. Talking about our kids. Being adult and civil. We're getting there.'

'Yep.' He swallows hard. 'We are.'

We look at each other a little desperately.

'Hugh . . . I want to ask you something.'

'Mmm?' He looks wary.

'When we were together, before your dad was diagnosed, were you happy? Before you automatically say yes, please think about it. What would you have changed about us? I'm not talking about more money or any external stuff. What would you have changed in our relationship? And don't say, "Nothing". Be honest.'

He goes quiet. He's acting like he's thinking, but I'm certain he knows his answer. He's just too shy to say it.

'Sex.' I put it out there. 'You'd have liked better sex. Different sex?'

'I'd have liked more of it. With you,' he adds. 'Just with you.'

'But you'd have liked me to send you saucy Snapchats, or sexts?'

'I wouldn't have said no to them. But mostly I would have liked it to happen more often. It's not nice, feeling like some horny beast pawing you when you'd no interest.'

'I was always tired,' I say defensively.

'I *know*.' Now he's defensive. 'I know how hard you work. But you asked me to be honest. It was difficult fancying you, wanting you, and knowing there wasn't a hope of getting near you. And before you dismiss me as just some horny man,' he adds hotly, 'it was the intimacy I missed as much as the physical stuff.'

I'm not liking what he's saying. I feel stung by criticism. But I'd asked for this, it's no more than I'd suspected, and I know he's right.

'Once we were actually doing it,' I say, 'I was glad. Getting me from vertical to horizontal was the part I found . . .' Disruptive, irritating, a waste of my time when there was always a meal to be cooked, laundry to be sorted, online clothes to be looked at. 'But once my body was switched on, it was . . .' Actually, now that I remember, fabulous.

Hugh took charge in bed. He was big and confident and knew what he wanted – in sharp contrast to his easy-going, gentle, everyday demeanour. He didn't have a sex-god body, he'd never had abs in all the years I'd known him, but he was self-assured and unapologetic.

'I felt like I was last on your list,' he says.

And he was right. Having sex with him was just another item on my to-do list, way down at the bottom.

'It's difficult,' I say. 'Making the sudden jump from being housemates and . . . colleagues, almost, to seeing each other as smouldering sex objects.'

'Not for me.'

But it was for me. Nobody sets out to become a cliché but it's what happens.

'How do other people do their sex lives?' I wonder out loud. Because sex is the one thing people don't talk about. 'I used to think everyone else was at it non-stop. Far more than you and me. Then I decided they were just saving face. It's hard to know what normal is.'

'So what would you have changed?' he asks. 'And don't say, "Nothing".'

'I felt like I was last on everyone's list. But I don't know if that could have been avoided – we didn't have enough money to do everything that all of us wanted.'

'I'm sorry.' He looks woebegone. 'Is that what you liked about Josh? Him taking you to Serbia and all?'

'He treated me like I was special. If you gave me the special treatment, I'd have just thought it was to persuade me to have sex with you.'

But then again, when Josh had given me the special treatment, it was for the same reason, wasn't it? If we'd been deluded enough to try to build an actual life together, the incendiary sexual she-nanigans would have died a speedy death.

'Maybe if we'd had these conversations a couple of years ago, things wouldn't be the way they are today.'

'But we didn't. And they are.'

115

Friday, 14 April

All the time I move in lockstep with my predictable routine – *Crazy Ex-Girlfriend* with Hugh on Monday nights, London on Tuesdays and Wednesday, Dublin the rest of the week, Derry or Petra on the weekends.

Work stays marginally too frantic to be coped with and generates income that's just slightly too modest to quieten my chronic financial anxiety.

Mum's EverDry campaign keeps me busy right up to Easter. After Alastair got her head back in the game, she's been on message. For a couple of weeks in late March and early April, she seemed to be everywhere – in every paper, on every light-entertainment show. Admittedly much of the coverage was slightly patronizing, but who cares? Publicity is publicity.

As we finish up work on Good Friday, there's an air of completion: a successful campaign coming to a satisfying close.

Mrs EverDry drops in and gives Tim, Alastair, Thamy and me Maltesers Easter eggs. In a giddy holiday mood, I wrestle mine out of the box, peel off the tinfoil, hit it a sharp crack with my phone and eat a giant chunk.

'I'll have what she's having,' Alastair says, and attacks his own. Moments later, Thamy does the same.

Tim stares disdainfully.

'Go on,' Alastair mocks. 'Eat yours.'

'It's not Easter Sunday yet.'

'Go crazy,' Thamy says.

'At least try,' I say.

High from sugar, we keep at him until he succumbs. Frankly,

I've never seen him so unwound: his tie loosened, his hair mussed, chocolate around his mouth.

Alastair and I are in fits. 'Tim, you look like the nun from the chocolate helpline on *Father Ted*!'

The worry is that this will snap Tim out of his relaxed state. Instead he tells us to knock off work.

'You're not our boss,' Alastair says.

'But he is mine.' Thamy is scarpering before Tim rescinds his order. 'Man says I can leave. Happy Easter, y'all.'

'Go,' Tim says. 'Amy, Alastair, go. Have a nice Easter. Get some rest.'

My plan is to sleep an unholy amount. But first Robert's ashes have to be scattered.

Easter Saturday is a blue, blustery day, as we tramp up Howth Head. It's where Robert walked his dog every morning and evening. He loved it here. The urn is carried by John, the eldest of the Durrants, who has come from Sweden with his husband Rolf and their son Krister.

Clustered behind that photogenic trio are Brendan, Nita and their three girls.

Next is me, flanked by Kiara and Sofie. And behind us, Hugh is walking with Carl, Noah, the Boy Wonder, and Chizo, who's yelling instructions at all of us.

Neeve didn't show and right now I hate her.

The worst part was down in the car park when, as time ticked on without any sign of her zippy little Audi, it became obvious that she wasn't coming.

'No Neevey?' Hugh asked me.

'Doesn't look like it.'

'Ah, well . . .' He looked unbearably bleak.

'Hugh.' My throat felt swollen and sore. 'I'm sorry.'

'It's okay,' he said.

But it wasn't okay. It was a rejection of Robert, who'd filled her biological grandfather's empty shoes, and an even bigger kick in the face to Hugh, who'd loved her and cared for her for so many years.

'Stop walking,' Chizo yells. 'This is a good spot.'

Obediently the cavalcade comes to a halt.

'So line up,' she instructs. 'Take a scoop of ashes, have your moment, and just before you scatter, look at me. Photo op.'

Anxiously I turn to Hugh. 'Should I?'

'Of course.' He's fierce. 'You're part of this family!'

John goes first, he scoops a small amount of the ashes. 'Thanks, Dad, for being a great dad. I'm glad you're out of pain.' Then he releases the specks into the wind.

Nita goes next. 'Thanks, Robert,' she says. 'For raising four great sons and for welcoming me into the Durrants.'

One by one, we all say our goodbyes.

'Thanks, Granddad,' Sofie says, 'for showing me how to drill a hole and for making Dad so kind.'

Now it's my turn. In my head I say, *Thank you, Robert, you were such a nice man. Thank you for being so good to all three of my girls, and even though it's over, thank you for Hugh. He's kind because you showed him how to be.* And I let the ashes blow into the breeze.

'Okay!' Chizo claps her hands. 'Let's go!'

The private dining room at Maldive is suspended on stilts over the sea. The long table is covered with snowy-white linen, glinting silverware and light-reflecting crystal. Beautiful – unfuneral – flower arrangements are distributed throughout the room.

Chizo, a master at these things, discreetly disposes of Neeve's place-card and commandeers a handy waiter to vanish her cutlery. 'Lil bitch has fucked with my seating plan,' she whispers hoarsely into my ear.

We take our seats and I'm between Chizo and Kiara. Opposite me is Rolf, and beside him is Hugh. I wish he wasn't. Looking directly at him still hurts me.

I turn my attention to the set menu, there are vegetarian and vegan options, the meat is all organic and locally sourced, the vegetables direct from the garden here.

'This looks wonderful.' Rolf surveys the menu. Very polite, the Swedes.

'Mmm, yes, delicious.' To my distress, tears start to trickle down my face.

'Amy?' Hugh sounds concerned. 'Are you okay?'

'Fine.' Except I seem to be crying. Crying quite a lot.

'But –'

'You heard her. She's fine.' Chizo presses a tissue into my hand. This is an order to cease and desist with all tears.

But it's way beyond my control.

'Why are you crying?' Chizo whispers.

Because Robert is dead. Because I loved Hugh and he loved me but it's all ruined. Because this was my family and now it isn't. Because something went wrong and maybe I made it happen. Because everything is losable. Because pain is inevitable. Because being human is unbearable.

'I'm pre-menstrual,' I manage.

'Not today you're not. Cop on, Amy.'

A lot of work has gone into this lunch, I know that, and it's costing plenty. It's been styled to perfection and people are expected to display grief but only in a dignified way: some sad smiles, and if there really *must* be tears, they must be discreet and quiet, none of this ugly, heaving, gaspy stuff.

'Stop crying,' Chizo hisses.

And I try so hard because I am shit-scared of her. 'I can't.'

'So go to the Ladies room.'

'Okay,' I choke. 'Scuse me.'

Once the door of the Ladies has shut behind me, my crying really gathers force. Oh, Christ, and here's Chizo.

'Get a hold of yourself! Today isn't about you. Leave. Go home. Get a taxi. Don't drive.'

''Kay.'

Hugh is hovering outside the Ladies. 'Oh, Hugh!' I fling myself against him and he wraps himself around me and I convulse into his chest.

'I know, babe, I know.'

I look up at him. 'You do, don't you?'

'Of course.' He's crying too, and our tears are being shed for a lot more than the loss of Robert.

'I'll drive you home,' he says.

Gratitude makes me weak.

'What?' Chizo says. 'No way. You can't leave.'

She's right.

'Stay,' I tell him. 'Please. I'm fine.'

'You're not fine.'

'You have to stay.' Chizo snaps her fingers and, as if she's conjured her from the air, Kiara materializes, followed by Sofie.

'Take your mother home,' Chizo commands.

'I need my bag,' I manage. 'And I should say goodbye.'

I dart in before Chizo can stop me, but she catches up, grabs my bag and hustles me back out of the room, muttering, 'Very fond of Robert. She was very fond of Robert. Overcome. But carry on enjoying yourselves. *Amuse-bouches* arriving in five.'

116

Monday, 1 May

Days pass and I hear nothing from Neeve. It hurts terribly. Then a week has gone by, another starts, and I have to wonder if she and I will ever talk to each other again.

But there are other things to worry about: the calendar clicks into May, which means that Sofie's exams start in just over a month. She – we – have only five weeks for her to learn everything she needs to know. I'm not alone in my anxiety; every parent in the country with a kid doing the Leaving Cert is feeling it.

Sofie needs proper nutrition to survive this route march, so I buy twenty energy bars, hoping she'll eat them. Then, miracle of miracles, she comes to me with a shopping list: avocados, eggs, salmon, berries, almonds and pumpkin seeds.

'Of course!' I'm thrilled. 'I'll go right now and get them.'

'Calm down.' She's laughing. 'Listen, I've been thinking. I need a job for the summer. I need to save money for when I start college in September.'

Hopefully when she starts college. *If* she gets the right grades. Her stumbling block is physics and, much as I'd like to help, I'd be more use if she needed to be tutored in Martian. Hugh, however, can do science and has been working with her. (I sometimes wonder if Sofie decided she would focus on science subjects just to show how alike she and Hugh are.)

'Could Derry help me find a job?' she asks.

Christ, I don't know. Probably. 'What sort of thing were you thinking of?'

'Maybe in a hotel. Waitressing? Preferably in Europe, because the pay is better than it is in Ireland.'

Well, she's thought this through very carefully. 'Just for you. Or for you and Jackson?'

'Just for me. And maybe Kiara.'

'Not Jackson? What's going on?'

'He's working for his dad this summer. We're not breaking up, if that's what you were thinking.'

Well, good. Just . . . This needs to be said. 'Honeybun, you'd be apart for three months, you and Jackson. You're both at an age when people change a lot.'

She looks surprisingly wise and twinkly. 'We both know that. But we're together, me and him. We've talked about it. We've decided.'

Yes, but what if she meets someone else and gets torn in two with guilt? 'You'll be coming into contact with all kinds of other people. It's not inconceivable that you might fancy another –'

'I'm with Jackson. I belong to him, he belongs to me.'

'All I'm saying, sweetheart, is that going away for three months is risky.'

'Everything's risky, Amy. There are no guarantees, not when you love someone. But we want to stay together so we've decided we're giving it our best shot.'

'Um, very good, then.' I feel I should say more but nothing comes to mind.

Luckily, my phone rings. 'Mum?'

'Amy, will there be any more work for me? In my role as ambassador?'

'No, Mum. Didn't Alastair tell you all of this?'

'Well, he did, but I thought there might still be interest in me.'

'I'm sure there's lots of interest in you.' Jesus, the fragile ego! 'But Mrs EverDry is satisfied with all that you've achieved so there's no need to do more.'

'I don't mind, though. She doesn't even have to pay me.'

But she'd have to pay me and the lads and that's not going to happen. 'Mum, the campaign is over. It's been a huge success so you should be proud.'

'I'm finding it hard, though, settling back into ordinary life, stuck here in the house with Pop.'

'Dominik's around, though? You can go out whenever you like?'

'*Yeeees*. I know. It's just . . .'

I've seen this before, the comedown from fame. It's brutal.

On the second Tuesday in May, the Press Awards are on in London. It was at this same do, two years ago, that I propositioned Josh and invited him up to my hotel room. It's very hard to believe that I – *me* – behaved so recklessly. He may be here tonight and I fear I'll bump into him. But things go well. All the speeches and awards take place without me clapping eyes on him.

Then, just after the formal part of the night ends and the throng have started circulating, I spot him, standing with a crowd of about six people, all of them talking animatedly.

My mouth goes dry. It's the first time in nearly three months since I've seen him. He's not looking my way and I'm able to study him covertly. To my surprise, he's almost nothing like I remember.

I'd thought he was so hot, so sexy, but here in this hotel ballroom, among all of these people, he looks, well, *ordinary*. I must have projected a huge amount of wishful thinking onto him because all through that time I'd thought he was *extra*ordinary.

Images of that night two years ago rush at me. It was only the third time I'd ever met Josh and I'd invited him up to my bedroom. What the hell? Like, seriously, *what the hell*?

Worse still, the following day I went home to Hugh, sat in our kitchen and tantalized him with murky allusions.

Subsequently Hugh told me he'd known something was up and I'd believed him. But astonishingly, in a visceral way, I can now *feel* it. It's as if every one of my cells have lit up with guilt: my body is alive with it.

Of *course* Hugh had known! My giddiness, my arch hints, my insistence on having sex the night I got home – all the signs were there that something had happened with another man.

And Hugh had been correct when he'd said I was different throughout the entire flirtation: I was moody – frequently irritable. Occasionally I overcompensated by being gushingly nice for very short bursts of time.

I bought sexier clothes, higher shoes – even my underwear was saucier. I've memories of sitting opposite Josh in that restaurant we used to go to for lunch, turned on by the knowledge that my knickers and bra were made of sexy black lace.

In the crowded ballroom, I turn away from him. I don't want him to see me. More importantly, *I* don't want to see *him*. Because I'm ashamed. I'm terribly, terribly ashamed.

Worse, I'm sad. Hugh must have been so lonely during that time – which lasted about three months. Until then I'd been his best friend, his shared-brain and, abruptly, I was replaced by a callous stranger. As a result of selfishness, rather than cold-blooded cruelty, but all the same.

117

Wednesday, 17 May

When I wake in Druzie's spare room, last night's shame is still with me and stays with me all day long. I need to talk to Hugh. I have to apologize.

At the airport, waiting for my flight home, Derry emails to say she's got summer jobs for Sofie and Kiara. Impulsively I ring her, I want to offload to someone.

'Right!' She launches into the news. 'They'll be chambermaiding in a glitzy health-spa in Switzerland. Very decent money. They'd better not let me down.'

'They won't, they won't.' Obviously I hope they'll behave and, all credit to the pair of them, at least they know how to clean.

'Ames, are you okay?'

'Aaah.' I squirm. 'I saw Josh last night.'

'*What?*'

'No, not like that, he didn't see me. But I've got an awful bout of the guilts. About Hugh, I mean. All those weeks I was meeting Josh for lunch, Hugh knew something was up, and I know it's two years ago but, Der, I feel shitty. I feel so guilty.'

'Then Hugh ran away to Thailand. Get over yourself. The scorebook is even.'

'Derry, there's no scorebook. There are two wrongs here. It's hard to face this but I was cruel to Hugh.'

'So what are you going to do?'

'I want to make it right. I want to take his hurt away.'

'It's probably long gone.'

That doesn't make me feel better so I say my goodbyes and call Hugh. He answers after two rings.

'Amy?' He sounds worried. 'Everything okay?'

'Grand. Except. Can you come round to my – our, ah, *the* house later? Just for a quick chat. I'm about to get on a plane. I'll be home in about two hours.'

When I let myself in, Hugh is already there. Sofie and Kiara are flitting around. They look apprehensive – I suppose any unexpected meetings between Hugh and me are cause for anxiety. Broken marriages are truly horrible things.

Hugh stands up when he sees me.

'We'll just, ah . . .' Sofie and Kiara disappear.

'Would you like something?' Hugh asks me. 'To drink? Eat?'

His solicitude serves as a forceful reminder of this night two years ago: he'd just collected my cheese from the sorting office and fed me some when I got in.

'Nothing, thanks,' I mutter. 'Let's go to the living room.' We have to leave the kitchen, I can't take these memories.

Once we're seated, I start: 'Hugh, I want to say sorry.'

'For . . . ?'

'The summer before last, when I was, ah, flirting with Josh, and you knew. I'm sorry for hurting you, for worrying you. I did feel guilty at the time, but it's worse now.'

'It's okay.'

'It's not. I did something terrible, you can't just . . . let it go.'

'I understand your reasons,' he says. 'The grind, the stress, the constant worry about money. Josh was an escape. Some people drink too much, or take up running, something to give endorphins.'

'No.' I don't deserve absolution. 'My life was lovely. But I wanted more. Something to look forward to. I don't understand why.'

'But –'

'When you left, it was because you wanted two lives – to be a family man and a single man. I didn't like your reasons but I get them now, better than I get my own.'

'Look.' He sounds weary. Maybe he's just sad. 'What's done is done.'

'I wish it wasn't. Everything's a big mess, and a lot of the time I just don't understand how it all got so . . . bad.'

'Amy, if you could go back to when you first met Josh, would you do things differently? Knowing how everything has played out?'

'Yes.' I'm certain about this. 'You and I, we've lost something very . . .' my throat hurts '. . . very beautiful. But it's too late.'

He nods. 'Listen, I've found a flat.'

This qualifies as good news, but it's another turn of the blade that's unpeeling our life together into two separate strands.

'It's in Tallaght.'

Tallaght is way out on the western edge of Dublin. Poor Hugh, all on his own out there, so far away from his family. But we're not his family any more – well, I'm not.

'Is it . . . nice?' I ask.

'It's fine. Small, but fine.'

'I feel sad for you.'

'Don't. I deserve it.'

'Stop. Let's not talk that way any longer. Hugh?' I ask. 'Will we still buy each other birthday presents?'

'Aaaah?' He's nonplussed by the change of subject. 'How d'you mean?'

'What happens when my cheese club runs out in July? Will there be no more cheese every month?'

He laughs. 'A world without cheese, what a thought!' He places his hand over his heart. 'Baby, I promise you that, for as long as I'm alive, you'll get your delivery of cheese every month.'

Then it happens – my chest fills with warm feeling. It's love. Love for Hugh. It must be the final stage of the grieving process.

Obviously this isn't the *end* end – two steps forward and one step back. There isn't a full stop here so that everything stays on an even keel from here on in. I'll probably regress to bitterness and sorrow and fury from time to time. But I've known the peace of acceptance, so there's proof that it's possible.

118

Thursday, 1 June

'People joke about it.' I step into my kitchen on a Thursday evening to find Hugh standing there. 'But, I swear to God, the parents of children doing exams have a tougher time of it than the pupils.' I dump a load of shopping bags on the table. 'To what do I owe the pleasure?' I ask. 'Physics?'

'Physics.' He looks very, very tired.

Because the Leaving Cert is kicking off in less than a week, a fierce heatwave is building. It happens every year at exam time.

'What have you here?' Hugh helps me unpack.

'Multi-vitamins for all-round good health, B6 and B12 for her nerves, kava-kava to keep her calm, ginkgo biloba to keep her alert. Rescue Remedy, but that might be for me. And those bottles of wine, they're for me – and I suppose for you. Here.' I open the bottle of multi-vitamins and give him one. 'Take that. We've got to last the pace too.' Sofie's exams run until 20 June.

'It's going to be an intense couple of weeks.'

'The health-food shop's shelves were almost empty,' I say. 'It was like they'd had a riot. Every parent in the country must be at this lark.'

I decide to open a bottle of wine and let Hugh unpack the rest.

'What?' He's looking at bags of spinach and boxes of eggs. 'Are they for her?'

'Rich in B vitamins,' I say, feeling like Smug Mummy. Two mouthfuls of wine and I'm already giddy.

'Percy Pigs!' he says.

'Hands off! They're hers, for when she's doing the actual exams.'

'I thought sugar was the instrument of the devil.'

535

'But it gives short bursts of mental energy.' Then I add doubt-fully, 'Apparently. God, it's so hard to know what the right thing is.' I give him a glass of wine. 'There are times when I want to volunteer to sit the exams myself. But what do I know of physics and chemistry? You could do it.'

'I'd hardly pass for Sofie.'

'No.' He's too big, too hairy. 'You need a haircut.' Then I blurt, 'Sorry. God, sorry. Time-slip! They're not happening so often now, though.'

'No, they're not.'

'And eventually they'll stop entirely.'

'I'm looking forward to it.' He smiles. And, after a moment, I smile too.

'Okay!' Sofie bounds into the kitchen. 'Let's get to it. Is that *wine*? Dad, no! I need your head in the game.'

They sit at the kitchen table and embark on some horrendous-looking equation. In a burst of sympathy, I quietly place the bag of Percy Pigs beside him.

The night is so hot that Kiara and I sit outside in our postage stamp of a back garden. I drink a bit too much wine, lie on the grass and enjoy the sensation of stopping for rest in the midst of exhaustion. Enduring Sofie's gruelling schedule is so taxing that my body actually aches. My lower back is enjoying the sensation of being pressed flat to the ground. When Kiara shoves me and says, 'Mum, you're snoring,' I realize I've fallen asleep.

In the kitchen Sofie and Hugh are still grappling with the phys-ics conundrum.

'Night,' I say, 'I'm going to bed.'

'Me too.' Kiara yawns.

Sofie and Hugh raise their heads, their eyes red-rimmed.

'Dad,' Sofie says. 'Maybe we should stop now, get some sleep, and do another couple of hours in the morning.'

'Okay.' Hugh stands and stretches, his T-shirt lifting to expose his belly. For a moment I want to lay my hand on it. Our eyes meet and my face goes hot.

'Don't go home,' Kiara says.

'Yeah,' Sofie agrees. 'Stay on the couch, and we'll both get up at six. Mum, have we a spare duvet?'

'He can have Neeve's.' Kiara takes the stairs two at a time, reappearing with sheets, pillows and a duvet. She and Sofie do up a bed for him in the living room and make a big fuss of him as they tuck him in.

'Sleep tight, Dad,' Kiara says, and gives him a kiss.

'Yes, sleep tight.' Sofie also kisses him. 'Mum, kiss Dad goodnight.'

'Kiss *him*? You never know where that mouth's been.' I'd meant it as a joke but I sound bitter.

'Mum!' Kiara is shocked.

'Well, sorry.'

I look at Hugh. 'Sorry. Okay?'

'Okay.' He's got his mild voice on but I'm guessing that's not how he's feeling.

As soon as Sofie and Kiara have disappeared to bed, I look down at him lying on the couch and say coldly, 'I can be sore for as long as I like. There's no time limit on it.' I'm furious, as furious as I was the night I got back from Serbia.

Just when I think the end is in sight, all the rage and sorrow kick off again. Will it ever end?

The heat of his body was how I knew he was in my bedroom. He moved stealthily to the bed and I rose to meet him, taking his face in my hands, moving my palms over the roughness of his beard. My sigh was one of relief, then I put my mouth to his. He moved his lips to fit against mine and, oh, the shock of the beloved familiar. *Hello. I've missed you.*

Everything, how he tasted, how he felt, it was all so right.

This is the one, this is the right one.

It was just like it always was – his size, his certainty, the confidence with which he played my body. We moved together in perfect synchronicity. Hugh had always been very good at knowing what I liked. No clumsiness, no clunkiness, just a fluid blend of sexiness and familiarity.

After it had come to a thrillingly passionate close, I was left feeling – maybe an odd descriptor for sex – profoundly comforted.

What rule said that sex could only be great if it was wild and frantic? Well-worn sex could be just as good as stranger sex.

When I wake up, it takes several seconds for me to understand that it was only a dream. It had felt so graphic, so intense that I'm convinced I can still smell Hugh in the room.

Why had I dreamt that dream? Maybe it's a warning that Hugh and I are getting a little too close for comfort and I need to be careful.

Or, more likely, it's just one more part of my grieving. I'd been letting go of the sex part of our shared life. Soon every last thing will be gone and I'll be free.

119

Thursday, 22 June

Sofie did her final on Wednesday, and as soon as it was over, she and Jackson went out on the rip. She's still MIA when I get home from work on Thursday evening.

In fact, there's nobody in the house – Kiara is babysitting Joe's boys.

This is something I'll have to get used to because, in a week's time, Sofie and Kiara are going to Switzerland. For the first time in forever, I'll be living alone.

I've known this for ages but because all my energy was in exam-mode I haven't had time to feel it. It'll be strange. The house will feel achingly empty. But I'll get used to it. Painful as it was, I've got used to living without Hugh.

All in all, he and I are doing pretty well. Okay, my occasional bursts of bile aren't pretty, but things could be a lot worse.

I rattle around the house, unable to settle to anything. After the gruelling route march of Sofie's exams, this sudden nothingness feels like falling off a cliff. Hugh, having been my comrade-in-arms these last few weeks, seems the right person to ring. 'What are you up to?' I ask.

'Nothing much. It's weird. Suddenly I don't know what to do with myself.'

'Me too! I was thinking,' I say, 'we deserve an end-of-exams celebration too. We worked as hard as Sofie – well, you did any-way. Will we go for a drink?'

'Okay.'

'The Willows. It has a garden. How soon can you be there?'

'Depends on the Luas.'

'I'm leaving now. Hurry.'

I change into high sandals and a proper 1950s dress in periwinkle cotton and call a taxi, in which I have to work hard to neutralize the driver's wrath when he discovers he's ferrying me less than two miles. 'You could have walked,' he grouses.

'Not in these shoes. I'll give you a decent tip. Shush now, I'm in good form, I want to stay that way.'

'Meeting a man?' He eyes me in the mirror.

'No. Well, yes.'

Astonishingly, when I arrive Hugh is already in the beer garden and has bagged a table.

'How?' I demand.

'You told me to hurry. You look nice,' he says. 'One of Bronagh's finds?'

'Yep. Never worn before. At least, not by me. You look nice too.'

'That dress makes your eyes look very blue.'

'That shirt makes *your* eyes look very blue.' It's a black-and-blue check thing, one of my favourites of his.

'Make up your own compliments,' he says. 'Stop stealing mine.'

A glass of white wine is being put on the table, with a bottle of beer for Hugh.

'What'll we drink to?' I ask.

'To Sofie getting As in everything?'

'We're not being too ambitious for her?' I ask anxiously. 'Maybe we should just drink to her happiness.'

'How about "To Sofie being happy, and if that happiness includes getting As in everything, then we don't mind".'

'Excellent!' We clink drinks.

'I feel like we've spent the last month living underground, never washing, eating crap ... I'm wrecked,' I say. 'Are you wrecked?'

'Yeah.'

He doesn't look it. He looks great. Still too thin, but clear-eyed and groomed. His shirt is ironed, his beard is neat and his longish hair is – 'Oh! You got your hair cut.'

'You told me to.'

'And you do everything I tell you to?' At the start of the sentence my tone was light and teasing, but by the end, I'm inexplicably tearful.

'Babe? Are you okay?'

Accusingly I say, 'Now her exams are over, there's no reason for you to be round all the time.'

His face is stricken.

'I've got used to it,' I say. 'And I'll have to start detaching all over again.'

'I'm sorry.'

'You shouldn't have gone away.'

'I wish I hadn't.'

'Don't ever fucking do it again.'

'I won't.'

'Hey, do what you like. You're your own man now.'

'I'm not. I'll always be your man.'

I stare at him in silence, then quickly gather my stuff. 'I'd better go home,' I say. 'Sorry. I thought I was able for this. But –'

When I get back, Sofie has reappeared. She's flanked by Kiara and, astonishingly, Neeve. To the best of my knowledge Sofie and Kiara have barely spoken to Neeve since her no-show at Robert's memorial over two months ago.

'Mum,' Neeve says, without preamble. 'There's something you need to see.'

'Oh?' I'm instantly anxious.

'I'm not asking for your permission. This is simply a courtesy.'

What on earth? 'Go on.'

She hits play on her iPad and something starts running. A home-made video by the way it's wobbling all over the shop. It's in black-and-white and someone – a woman, from the look of her shoes – is walking through a busy space, which at first I think is a shopping centre but then, with creeping dread, recognize as Dublin airport.

Then Neeve's voice issues from the speaker, 'During their lifetime one in three women worldwide will have an abortion.'

My heart drops like a stone.

'Ireland's abortion rate is the same as the global average,' Neeve's iPad says. 'But in Ireland abortion is illegal, so women have to travel outside the state to access the service.'

I whip round to her. 'Neeve, no! You can't do this to Sofie!'

'There's nothing to identify Sofie,' Real Neeve says, at the same time as Sofie says, 'Amy, I want Neeve to tell my story.'

iPad Neeve says, 'My friend missed a pill, and even though she took the morning after, she got pregnant. She's young, has no money, and emotionally wasn't ready to be a mother. I went to the UK with her.'

The film is all movement, you don't see any faces, but you do see Dublin airport, the departures board, the inside of the plane, the tube – Neeve must have had her phone on the entire time. But when she shows Druzie's spare room I lose the head. 'Does Druzie know her flat is in your –'

'She's cool with it.'

Making clear that 'the pregnant friend' is being played by an actor, a silhouetted woman describes everything that happened to Sofie, as if it had happened to her: the terror; the shame; the physical discomfort; the appalling financial cost.

'Why does our country do this to our women and girls?' iPad Neeve asks, as we see Sofie (pixellated out) being put on the luggage trolley, too weak to walk.

'Our abortion rate is the same as everywhere else in the developed world. Can we please stop pretending it doesn't happen?'

In every vlog Neeve does, she links to the items she's showcased so people can buy them. This week, she has links to Aer Lingus, London black cabs, London tourism, the Marie Stopes site, etc, and the combined sums come to over two thousand euro.

'This happened six months ago,' iPad Neeve says. 'My friend is getting on with her life. She does not regret her decision.'

I don't know what to say. I'm worried about Neeve, about Sofie, even – to my shame – about Mum: with her connections to Neeve's site she might be seen as an endorser of abortion.

'I can't not do this,' Neeve says. 'I have strongly held views, I have a platform . . .'

'Neeve, not everyone will agree with you.'

'You're right. I'll lose subscribers. I might gain new ones. But that's not why I'm doing this.'

'What about your advertisers?' What if she loses her income due to this?

'I've talked with them. They're good with it.'

'What does your dad say?'

'He's chill.'

'What about Granny?'

'Granny knows. All of it. About Sofie. Granny is on our side.'

'You'd get a lot of hate. The trolls. All this goodwill you've built up . . .'

'I'm shifting my position, reaching out to those who think the way I do. I'm finding my tribe. It goes live on Monday afternoon.'

120

Monday, 26 June

'It's up,' Tim announces.

Shite. Alastair, Thamy and I gather round his screen to watch Neeve's abortion vlog. All day Monday I've been a wreck. In silence, we watch the four minutes forty seconds of it.

'Brave.' Tim sounds like he thinks she's certifiable.

'You should be proud of her,' Alastair says to me. 'She's a hero.'

But not everyone will agree.

There's no way I'll get any more work done this afternoon. I monitor online news-sites, Twitter, those horrible boards, and a trickle of comments begins. I follow the feed on YouTube and mercifully every single post is supportive. I keep watching. More than two hours has passed and maybe this is all going to be okay. And then . . .

'Oh, God, it's . . . Some man says he's going to stab her.'

Alastair hurries to my side and stares at the screen. 'He thinks Neeve's "the friend".'

'What should I do?' I ask him.

'Might be just a one-off.'

But a few minutes later another person has a go, this time calling Neeve a baby-murderer who will burn in Hell.

'Par for the course,' Alastair mutters.

A new message pops up from a man saying he knows where Neeve lives and that he plans to rape her with a broken bottle. I start to shake. 'These people,' I say. 'These threats. Can they be stopped?'

'Maybe.' Alastair does some clicking and it's as I suspected. 'Sock puppet accounts. Untraceable. The police might be able to do something more sophisticated with their technology.'

I switch back to Twitter: 'Neeve Aldin' is trending in Ireland.

Then, to my absolute horror, I see that an anonymous head has tweeted Neeve's home address in Riverside Quarter. It's up there for all the world to see and before my very eyes it's being retweeted.

'Call her,' Alastair hisses.

I'm already on it. 'Neeve.' My voice is shaking. 'Are you at home? You need to get out of there.'

'It's cool, Mum.'

'No, your address has just been put on Twitter.'

'Oh. Shit . . . How?'

Easily – Neeve has done vlogs from her fancy pad. She's said publicly she's living in her dad's apartment. Ireland is a small place.

'There's a concierge here,' she says. 'Fingerpad entry. Electronic surveillance. I'm safe.'

'Promise me you'll stay inside.'

'This will all calm down in a couple of hours,' she says.

'Until it does, stay inside. Don't answer the door to anyone. Maybe you should call the guards.'

She laughs. 'Mu-um, please!'

I hang up and ask Alastair, 'Am I overreacting? These are just strange, lonely men wanking at their keyboards?'

'Ah. Probably.'

But all you need is one evil person determined to remake the world according to his liking.

Paralysed, I watch the thread of comments. I'm afraid to stop monitoring it in case something even worse happens. There's a lot of love for Neeve, but even the people on her side assume she is 'the friend', and the stream of positivity is more than matched by the hate.

'Oh, God,' I say. 'Now Richie's getting some of the flak.'

Many of the keyboard warriors reference the recent article in the *Sunday Times* in which Neeve and Richie boasted about how close they are.

'Did Richie Aldin fund this for his daughter? Soz! For his daughter's "friend", I mean.'

And 'Richie Aldin aborted his own grandchild.'

*

545

At home, Sofie and Kiara are pretending to be calm but they hadn't expected Neeve would get so much hate.

'It was – *is* the right thing to do,' Kiara insists.

There's the sound of a key in the front door, then Hugh steps into the hall.

Oh, right, it's Monday night, *Crazy Ex-Girlfriend* night. It had slipped my mind.

'Y'okay?' Hugh asks me.

'You know about it?'

He nods. 'It'll be okay,' he says. 'She'll be fine.'

'I wish she was here.'

'She's probably safer where she is.'

'Hugh, do you mind if we cancel tonight?'

'Ah, no,' Sofie says. 'We want him to stay.'

'Please,' Kiara says. 'Let him stay.'

'Okay. But I'm not watching it.' I need to sit at the kitchen table and monitor social media, to see if the situation escalates.

But when the show starts, Hugh comes to the kitchen door and says, 'Why don't you try and watch it? You need a break from the worry.' He moves closer and everything about him is reassuring.

'Will she be okay?' I ask him.

'She'll be okay.'

We sit beside each other on the couch, he holds my hand and I let him.

After Hugh leaves, I decide I can't go to London in the morning. This might all amount to nothing, but then again it might not, and I want to be here for Neeve.

I sit up in bed and send a dozen emails cancelling my meetings, then try to sleep.

121

Tuesday, 27 June

I wake at a godawful early hour and immediately google Neeve. The important thing is how the mainstream media are reporting this.

There's a robustly supportive article in the *Irish Times*, and another nice one in the *Examiner*. But the *Independent* has a well-known columnist who really lays into Neeve, calling her 'stunt' shrill, immature, attention-seeking and all-round pathetic. There's an even more damning piece in the *Mail*. No surprises there.

One journalist has a go at Richie. He was barely in Neeve's life back in December when the trip took place but the fact that they've been as thick as thieves for the last few months is impacting badly on him. They were at a film premiere together last week, and there's even a photo from the 'poor blind children's ball'. Facts connecting them are trotted out – that Neeve lives in his apartment, that Richie had done a couple of guest vlogs for her, even how alike they look.

So long as Neeve is okay, that's all that matters. I want to ring her but it's too early, so I settle for a text and get no reply. Immediately I'm thinking she's been butchered and is lying in her gaudy apartment in a pool of blood.

But what can I do, except behave as normal?

I'm not long in the office when she rings me. 'Dad's kicked me out.'

'What?'

'He's kicked me out of the flat and taken back the car.'

'But didn't you say he was cool with all of this?'

'He's getting hated on and he wasn't expecting it. He's pissed, Mum. Can I come home?'

'Of course! I'll pick you up.'

'Mu-um.' For a moment she sounds as if she's smiling. 'I'll get a taxi.'

'But – Look, be careful, will you? Are there people, you know, protesters, outside?'

'Ah, Mum.' Now she really is smiling. 'Yeah, there's a big dirty mob out there, waving placards.'

'Make sure you're not followed. I'll meet you at home, and get you settled.' I hang up and say to Tim and Alastair, 'Sorry, lads, I have to go.'

When I arrive home, exactly one hour after I'd left for work, Neeve has let herself in. She looks pale and stunned.

There's only one canvas bag in the hall so I conclude that Richie hasn't actually evicted her, he's just throwing a tantrum.

'No, Mum.' She reads my mind. 'He wanted me out immediately. He's getting all my stuff boxed up and sent on in a van.'

Christ. Just when I'd thought he couldn't get any more heinous. This is going to be the heartbreak of Neeve's life.

'Dad said it was all good with him, me taking a stand. I don't understand.' She's getting tearful.

But *I* understand. He's an unprincipled prick. He'd thought being pro-choice would play well, but all the negative publicity has scared him. Who knows how this will unfold in the medium term, if Neeve will be declared a winner or loser? Richie doesn't have the guts to hold his nerve, even for his daughter.

As always, though, my mouth stays shut.

The sound of my phone ringing makes us both jump. It's Hugh.

'Amy?' He sounds frantic. 'Where are you?'

'At home. What's up?'

'Is Neeve with you?'

'Yes, wh–'

'Your address is up on one of those boards. People know Neeve is with you, or they're guessing. Either way, it's –'

With shaking hands, I go online. Oh, fuck, this can't be real, this can't be happening – Hugh is right. There's our address.

It was hard enough knowing threats of rape and painful death were aimed at Neeve while she was secured inside a state-of-the-art apartment. But here? In this small suburban house?

At lightning speed a scenario plays out in my head – a brick through the window, the angry men inside the living room in twenty seconds, and up the stairs in another ten. Us all in our beds with nothing to protect ourselves and no one to help us. *Which one of you is Neeve?* If the house alarm goes off, it takes about fifteen minutes for the monitors to ring to see if everything is okay. By then we'd all be butchered.

If this was happening to someone else, I'd think, Yes, it's bound to be unpleasant, but no actual harm will come to anyone, these keyboard cowards are just throwing shapes to scare people.

But now that it's actually in play, I'm terrified. I look out of the kitchen window, half expecting to see men bumbling along the windowsill or for a gloved hand to try the handle on the back door.

'I'm on my way over now,' Hugh says. 'But ring the police.'

I phone the local station, feeling foolish, petrified and embarrassed all at once. 'My daughter's received some death threats.'

Within twenty minutes, a pair of guards have arrived, a woman and a man, who insist the threats have to be taken seriously. The man goes off to see how vulnerable we are to home invasion and the woman starts taking down all the details. Then she spots something in the hall. Fearfully she jumps to her feet and shouts, 'What is your business here?'

It's Hugh. Oh, thank God, it's only Hugh, who must have let himself in with his key.

'It's okay, Officer – Sergeant.' I have *no* idea of police hierarchy. 'This is my husband, ex . . . Neeve's step-dad.'

'He lives here?'

'Not any more but it's fine, we know him.'

The male guard is back and he says to Neeve, 'You can't stay here. Is there a friend you can go to for a few days? Till things calm down?'

'Um, yeah, I'll just make a call.' Neeve hits a button and

launches into a high-pitched exchange, lots of 'Totally!' and 'I know, right!' as if getting death threats was the most exciting thing ever. But when she makes her request for accommodation, the entire tenor changes. All energy drains from her. 'Right. I get it. Totally. Yeah. Later.'

She rings someone else and has a near-identical conversation. When she hangs up, Hugh asks, 'What's going on?'

'They're too scared to let me stay with them.'

'What about a hotel?' I suggest.

But it wouldn't be the guards' preferred option: too many opportunities to be spotted.

Tentatively Hugh says, 'What about my place? There's very little to connect Neeve and me. I haven't lived here for nine months. Neeve and I have different surnames.'

The guards are interested, and after they've established that Hugh lives alone, without any pesky flatmates to dob Neeve in, they seem happy to let her go there.

'How long for?' Neeve is tearful.

'Impossible to say. Would you also stay there, Mr Durrant?'

Hugh looks at Neeve. 'I don't have to. I can stay at Nugent's.'

'Is there room for both of us at your place?' Neeve asks. 'I'd feel safer if you stayed.'

The guards break the news that they have to take Neeve's laptop and for the first time I think she really *is* going to faint.

'It's inadvisable for you and the other occupants of this house to remain here either,' the lady guard says. 'For a few days anyway.'

'I'll just call my mum.'

Mercifully Mum is home and not out gin-and-tonicking. I launch into an explanation and she gets it immediately.

'So can Sofie, Kiara and I stay for a few days?'

'What about Neeve?'

'She'll stay with Hugh.'

'With Hugh? And him not even her real daddy?' Mum's laugh is grim. 'Isn't she lucky he's never held that against her?'

*

Mum and Pop are sitting in their overgrown garden, drinking tea.

'EXCELLENT TIMING,' Pop greets me with. 'THIS WOMAN HAS JUST AGREED TO MARRY ME!'

'Humour him,' Mum says.

'Congratulations, Pop.'

'SHE'S THE WOMAN OF MY DREAMS. I COULDN'T BE HAPPIER.'

'That's lovely news.' In a way I mean it.

Soon Pop needs to return to his serial killers. Mum and I remain outside.

'Poor Mum.' My sympathy is profound. 'Do you still see your gin-and-tonic friends?' It's a genuine question, asked without judgement.

A long pause follows in which she stares at her lap. Eventually she looks up. 'It's hard, Amy, sharing a house with a headcase.'

'I know.'

'You don't. You have no idea. But my gin-and-tonic friends, that was nothing. Just some light relief.' She grasps my wrist and forces me to look at her. 'I'd never do anything to hurt your father. For better, for worse, it's what I signed up for when I married him.'

'You could never have anticipated this, though?'

'But that's the point, Amy. It's easy to love someone when they're on their best behaviour – you can do that in your sleep. The real test is when they're – to use Neeve's expression – a pain in the hole. That's what love *actually* means.'

'Does that not just make you a walkover?'

'There's a difference,' she's uncharacteristically grim, 'between being a doormat and forgiving someone for being human.'

'Grand. Well.' I'm keen to escape from her and her odd mood. 'I'd better find the sheets and stuff, get myself and the girls organized.'

'Do that.' She calls after me. 'Make your bed, Amy. Make your bed.'

122

Friday, 30 June

The social media firestorm continued to blaze with promises of a variety of slow, lingering deaths for Neeve; the mainstream papers and chat shows call her silly, shrill and strident.

But by Thursday morning I could almost feel the interest ebbing, like the tide going out. The posts on Twitter, Facebook and YouTube dried to a trickle and by Thursday afternoon it was over.

Neeve was allowed to come home, and now that it's safe, I'm sheepishly wondering if we all overreacted.

On Friday morning Sofie and Kiara leave for Switzerland. Hugh and I meet at the airport to see them off. After countless hugs and checks, some friendly advice and more hugs, it's finally time to let them go. Kiara is the first to disappear around a screen to security. But just before Sofie also vanishes from sight, she turns and looks directly at me and Hugh. Very deliberately she pats her heart, and mouths, 'Thank you.' She's smiling, but even from a distance it's clear that she has tears in her eyes.

Instantly so do I.

I whip round to Hugh. 'Do you remember –'

'– when she first came from Latvia?' His eyes are also shiny.

'– and she was so scared? You were the only one she'd trust.'

'– and remember the day we bought her bed?'

'– and painted it pink?'

'– and you made her those magical curtains?

'Look at her now, Hugh.'

'We did good, didn't we, babe?'

'We really did.' My mouth is wobbling.

'We can be proud of that.' He gives me a big, reassuring smile and I want to press myself against him. 'Okay, I'd better go,' he says. 'See you soon.'

'When?'

He seems surprised.

'September,' I answer myself.

There's no reason for us to see each other until the girls return.

'Well, we could –' he says.

No, September will do fine. I'd wanted time away from him to recover properly. Now is my chance.

It's eleven thirty when I get in to work.

'Did you cry?' Alastair asks.

'Not really. Not until the end.'

'Heartless mare.'

'Alastair? I won't see Hugh until September.'

'But that's good. The plaster's finally been torn off and you can spend the summer forgetting all about him.' Then, 'What? What's up?'

'It's just I can't bear the thought of being me in a year's time or five years' time or twenty years' time without Hugh.'

'Oh.' He blinks. 'That's . . . that's quite a statement, Amy.'

'I thought those sorts of feelings for him were, like, *severed* . . .'

'Aaaah, you might want to revisit that.'

'I don't understand what's going on with me.'

'You're the one who's always saying that a love thing is a relationship just like any other, that you can be really close, then fall out terribly, then make it up again. Practise what you preach.'

'I've got some thinking to do.'

'You could go on a silent retreat.' He's animated. 'Glenstal Abbey? I'll give them a shout. They'd do me a favour, get you in quickly.'

'No abbeys, none of that lark. My own house will be as empty as the grave this weekend. I'll do a . . .' I feel foolish even saying the word '. . . "retreat" there.'

At two o'clock, I shut up shop.

'What's going on?' Tim asks.

'Got to go. Sorry. I'll work from home. Neeve is calling round to collect her belongings. Richie's van delivered them last night.'

'She has a new flat already?!'

'Unlike the rest of us, she has plenty of money.' I feel I should add something. 'Tim, after this weekend everything goes back to normal. There'll be no more missing days.'

'Good. Glad to hear it.'

'Leave her alone,' Alastair cries. 'She's had a shit time of it!'

'It's fine. Stop. It's grand. Goodbye.'

I make for the door and Alastair calls after me, 'Good luck with your silent retreat!'

Neeve seems unfazed by her Trial by Public. 'In a crisis you find out who your friends are.' She sounds philosophical. 'Or, should I say, you find out who your friends *aren't*?'

I'm not sure if she's talking about the friends who wouldn't let her stay with them or if she's referring to Richie. Then it becomes clear.

'Was Dad always like this? Selfish? All-about-him?'

I waver before I lay into Richie. He's Neeve's flesh-and-blood – she gets half of her DNA from him. What can I say that doesn't invalidate the shitty way he treated her *or* make her fear that she might turn out just like him?

'He was different when I first knew him,' I say. 'He was great then. Very loving.'

'So what happened?'

'I think . . . perhaps too much success too young?' I genuinely don't know, but this is the best I can produce.

'I've been a total bitch lately,' she says. 'And it's coincided with me having a lot of success.'

My instinct is to flim-flam her, but she *has* been horrible.

'I'm sorry, Mum. And I'm sorry about Robert's ashes-scattering.'

I make myself say it: 'Hugh was more upset than I was. You should apologize to him.'

'Okay. Hey, have you been to Hugh's flat?' she asks. 'Oh, *Mum*. Like, he cleans it and that, but it's so small and there are these cork tiles on the ceiling and they're falling off and, yeah, it's bad. He doesn't deserve to live like that.'

We sit in silence, then she says, 'I always had a thing about Hugh, about him not being good enough for you.'

'Really? I don't think I noticed.'

Playfully, she pushes me. 'I was wrong, Mum. He's really kind. I used to think he was nice just so I'd like him but I think it's for real.'

'Oh.' It's immaterial now.

'Richie only wanted me when I made him look good, and he ditched me at the first sign of trouble. But Hugh, who isn't even like my real dad, gave me his bed. He slept on the kitchen floor. He bought me doughnuts and he cooked stuff. He lent me his laptop and his car.'

'I'm sorry about Richie,' I say.

'It sucks.' She sighs and wipes away a tear. 'I don't know why but he's never going to love me.'

Oh, Christ. 'Neeve!'

'It's okay. It's not my fault. Just because he doesn't love me, it doesn't make me unlovable.'

'I don't think he loves anyone but himself,' I say. 'I love you. We all love you.'

'Thanks, Ma, love you too. So! You think you and Hugh will get back together? Because you totally should.'

'C'mon. You saw the pictures of him with that girl from Scotland.'

Her face becomes troubled. 'Yeah. Everyone would think you were a total sapsucker if you took back a cheater. Sorry, Mum. I should just butt out of stuff that's not my shit. See you later at Granny and Pop's.'

As soon as I arrive in Mum's, Derry yells across the kitchen at me, 'By Christ, have I got plans for you for this summer!'

Maura's head jerks up.

No! After months of freedom from her interfering in my affairs, I really don't want a resurgence of it.

People are milling about the place – Dominik, Siena, Joe's thuggish little boys, Declyn, Mum . . .

'You and Hugh have been broken up for nine months. It's time for you to meet a new man!' Derry declares.

'No. Like, no *way*. I don't want any man, ever again. I'm done.' I move right up next to her. 'Derry, let's not have this conversation, not here.'

'Sit down, so.' She pulls two chairs into a corner.

But Mum takes one of them. 'I'm your mother,' she says. 'I might have wisdom.'

If she has, it'll be a rarity.

'Go on,' Mum says to Derry. 'Tell her.'

'Amy, you're only forty-four,' Derry says.

'I'll be forty-five next month.'

'You've got the rest of your life to live, you'll be lonely.'

'But a man wouldn't make me less lonely.'

'You're kinda missing the point. If you loved him, he would.'

'*You*'re kinda missing the point: I wouldn't love him. I'm done. I've loved enough men. I've no love left to give.'

'What you mean is, you still love Hugh.'

Carefully I say, 'I *do* still love Hugh. In a way.'

'In *what* way?'

'In a "friends" way.' After some prompting, I tell Mum and Derry about the night when Hugh said he'd always get me the cheese club membership. 'I felt so much love for him when he said it.'

'A "friends" kind of love?' Derry's look is suspicious. 'You sure that's all it was?'

'It was definitely love.'

'*Yeeeeeah.* Hey, Neevey, what do you think?'

Neeve has just arrived and bursts into our little circle. 'Mum.' She seems anxious. 'I feel bad. Something I said earlier. About you being a sapsucker if you got back with Hugh.'

'It's okay, Neevey. It's what everyone would think.'

'Who are all these people you think are judging you?' Mum interjects. She's been listening quietly until now.

'Well, Steevie and Jana and them.'

'Who cares what they think?' Derry says. 'Anyway, you cheated too. Technically before Hugh did. Amy wins cheating! You could issue a press release, telling everyone you went first. Then no one would judge you for being a sappy wifey.'

'Did you really cheat?' Neeve is agog.

'Not now, Neevey, *please.*'

'Okay. The important thing is, if you got back with Hugh, would *you* think you were a sap?'

'Yes.' I have to be honest. Then, 'But I'm not sure I care.'

'Remember what I said,' Mum says. 'About loving people when they're at their worst.'

'That's just a recipe for abuse!'

'Nothing is ever black and white!' Mum is suddenly animated. 'Life is all about the grey. If Hugh was the type who made a habit of dirty dealings, I wouldn't advise you to give him another go. But Hugh is lovely.'

'It's like you all want me to get back with him!'

'We do!'

123

Saturday, 1 July

I wake with a thought: This is my life. I've only got one. I should live it the way I want to.

Just as I'm trying to establish exactly how that would be, my phone rings: Alastair. I shouldn't answer but I do. 'What?'

'And hello to you too, Amy.'

'You know I'm doing my silent retreat.'

'I know, but listen!' His voice is fizzing with excitement. 'I'm on a course right now and I've just heard something that will *definitely* help you. You *need* to hear this! Ask yourself one question. What would I do if I wasn't afraid?'

'Afraid of what?'

'I don't know. Afraid of being hurt again? Afraid of the judgement of others? Afraid of being alone?'

'I'm not afraid of being alone.'

'So what are you afraid of?'

'I need to talk to someone about this.'

'You are.'

'I mean a friend.'

'I *am* your friend.'

'Yes, but . . .' What *had* I meant?

I'd meant that there's only one person who really understands me. And my greatest fear right now is of being seventy and it being twenty-five years since I broke up with Hugh.

'Ring him, Amy, for pity's sake.' Alastair hangs up.

We take a beer into the garden and we sit cross-legged, facing each other.

'I need to talk to you,' I say. 'I'm tying myself into knots about what the right thing to do is.'

'About what?'

'I need some wise person – someone like Oprah – to tell me, "This is your life, Amy. You're the only one living it. Do what makes you happiest." I need someone to give me permission.'

'You can give yourself permission.'

'Should I get back with you? Without breaking all your records?'

'Please break them,' he says. 'You can destroy everything I own if you'll just take me back.'

'Then it defeats the purpose. I need to hurt you.'

'You *are* hurting me. Every second without you is agony.' Tears come to his eyes.

'I don't want to hurt you,' I say. 'Except sometimes I do. I get these bursts of rage, and I want to be mean to you.'

'So be mean. I'm willing to take it.'

'But what if you decide you don't want to. And you leave again?'

'I won't.'

'In the six months you've been back, have you . . . you know . . . slept with anyone else?'

'No.'

'You could be lying.'

He rummages in his jeans pocket. 'Here's my phone. You know the code. Check texts, calls, anything you like. Go on.' He presses it on me.

'You could have deleted stuff.'

'So check in "trash".'

'You could have a second phone.'

'I haven't. But feel free to search me.'

'You're not going to wait for ever,' I say. 'Life doesn't work like that.'

'It did in *Love in the Time of Cholera*.'

'That's South Americans for you. You're Irish.'

'I will wait for ever,' he says. 'You're the best. The sweetest, the sexiest, the prettiest, the most interesting. I promise I'll never hurt you again.'

'You can't promise that. No one can.'

'Babe, I'm not one of those guys. Some people are natural cheaters. They can do it, no bother. I'm not like that. When I was away, you were the one I wanted. Even when I was with those other girls, I was lonely for you.'

'See? Now I want to thump you for reminding me of them.'

'So thump me.'

No. I wait it out and eventually the rage passes.

'What do I mean to you?' he asks. 'Forget for a moment about how "good" I am for "taking in" Neeve and Sofie. What do I mean to *you*?'

'You're the person I most want to watch telly with. You're my best friend and I love you. And,' I add, 'you're a man. A really sexy one.' I pause. Because he *is* really sexy. 'I thought my love for you ended when I saw that photograph. But it's come back.'

'Oh, wow.' His voice is hushed and his face is aglow.

'But, Hugh, I haven't learnt from my mistakes. I still don't know why I started . . . messing, you know, flirting . . . with Josh.'

'Course you've learnt. You say that if you could go back in time you wouldn't have started seeing him.'

'But what if I get a crush on someone else? Like, I don't want to. But what if I do?'

He shrugs. 'Don't.'

'As simple as that?'

'Life is unpredictable. Everything carries risks. But you can intend not to act on it if it happens.'

'That's very wise. What if you decide you want to run away again?'

'I won't.'

'How can you be so sure?'

'Because I can.'

'Okay.' Cautiously, I say, 'So I won't get a crush on anyone else and you won't run away. Have I got things correct?'

'You have.'

'Okay. Okay?'

He looks amused. 'Okay.'

'Is that it?'

'Is what what?'

'Just, I thought if we got back together it would be more dramatic than this.'

He doesn't move but his eyes darken. 'If you want drama, I can give you drama.'

Epilogue

Neeve fiddled with the white rose in Hugh's button-hole. 'Stand fecking still, would you?'

'I *am*.'

But he wasn't. Hugh was way out of his comfort zone dressed in a morning suit – any sort of suit, really – even though he looked handsome and impressive.

'Check you out,' I said. 'The paterfamilias.'

'Check *you* out,' he said. 'Hot wife.'

'Vom.' Neeve rolled her eyes.

'She's coming down now,' Kiara called from upstairs.

Mum, Derry and Maura were among the people who dashed to the foot of the stairs to see Sofie start her careful descent. Her dress was a simple satin column and she had nothing in her long, tangled, white-blonde hair but fresh flowers. She looked like a creature from a fairy tale.

I clutched Hugh's hand and squeezed it hard.

'Not too late to change your mind,' Neeve called up to her.

'Shush.'

'Seriously,' Derry said. 'Twenty-six is far too young to get married.'

'Quiet, you.' Maura was aghast. Sofie was the first of the new generation to get married. She'd have liked every single one of them boxed away safely – nothing could be permitted to jeopardize this.

'Just because Alastair won't put a ring on it,' Mum retorted.

'Hah.' Derry was blithely unaffected. 'He'd marry me in a heartbeat.'

'I don't believe a word of it.'

'Just because you wish he was *your* boyfriend.'

Mum put her hand to her chest and gasped. 'Poor Pop barely dead three years, how very dare you?'

'I wish he was here today,' Sofie said.

Cantankerous as he'd been, we all missed Pop dreadfully.

'But he wouldn't have known where he was,' Mum said. 'He's better off where he is.'

By the time Pop had passed peacefully in his sleep, he'd been entirely gone in the head. He'd no longer recognized any of us, and that had been hard. But it meant that a lot of our grieving had been done while he was still alive.

The photographer, who'd been fussing around, getting in everyone's way, called, 'If we could have the bride and her brides-maids.' He gathered them on the front step, where they made a comically mismatched trio: Sofie, a luminous wisp, Kiara, grave and unadorned, and Neeve unnaturally glossy – almost laminated-looking, the way media stars tend to be.

'State of you.' Neeve flicked a finger at Kiara's bare face.

'State of *you*.' Kiara shoved Neeve's hand away and they both laughed.

Kiara had spurned the hair and make-up services that Neeve had procured for free. The only thing about her appearance that Neeve approved of was her tan. Despite my suspicions that she'd outgrow her do-goodery tendencies, as soon as Kiara had left school, an NGO had given her a job. She had moved speedily up the ranks and about eighteen months ago had been seconded to their Ugandan office.

A phone on the hall table beeped.

'It's Jackson,' Derry called to Sofie. 'He's begging you to give him another chance.'

Good-humoured laughter greeted this. Sofie and Jackson had broken up about three years after they'd left school but had man-aged to stay the best of friends.

Sofie's soon-to-be-husband David was a researcher in the hospital lab where she worked. He understood her in the way Jackson had.

(Nevertheless, I thought, they were *ridiculously* young to get married. But we all had to live our own lives. No one else could do it for us.)

'We should go,' Maura said.

'Go on, then,' Mum replied. 'No one's stopping you.'

'You're coming with me,' Maura said.

'I am fecking not. I'm going in Derry's convertible. Can we put the roof down, Der?'

'Ma, *no*. Our *hair*.'

'I don't want to go on my own.' Unexpectedly Maura's voice wobbled.

'The Poor Bastard will see you at the venue, right?'

'But I want company for the drive!'

Hugh stepped closer to me. 'Soon,' he muttered, 'they'll all be gone and we'll have the house to ourselves again.' He gave me a wink.

'Oh, yeah?'

'Oh, *yeah*.'

Suddenly I was reminded of that summer, all those years ago, when Hugh had come home again.

It had been the most extraordinary time – the empty house, all that freedom, the never-ending thrill of rediscovery. It had felt almost as if we'd just met and were in the throes of the giddy early days of a love affair. We felt – and acted – *young*. We ducked out of work early to see each other, we went out and got drunk together, and spent entire weekends in bed.

Everything went to hell.

We stopped cooking – if we ate at all, it was impromptu dinners at ridiculously fancy restaurants or, just as enjoyable, late-night drunken kebabs. All housework was abandoned, and so was any semblance of a budget. Hugh took me shopping in Brown Thomas, plucking things from the rails and insisting I try them on. There was a Sandro dress I loved but wouldn't let him buy. The next day, when I got home from work, a Brown Thomas bag was waiting for me.

The entire two months were like that, a phase of our relationship that somehow we'd missed out first time round.

'We're making up for lost time,' he said, often.

And it wasn't just about sex – although there was plenty of

that – it was the novelty of having each other's undivided attention. We talked so much during those two months, rarely deep-and-meaningfuls but instead lots of light-hearted fun and the occasional nugget that surprised one of us. I mean, how had I been with him for eighteen years without knowing that, for three months during his teens, he'd been a motorbike courier? Or how had he not known that I'd once milked a cow? After all, it was one of the things I was most proud of!

Now and again the old fury would erupt in me and I'd rage at Hugh for half a day. But he took it without complaint and never reminded me of my flirtation with Josh, which had preceded his shenanigans.

I didn't smash his record collection – I didn't subject him to any dramatic punishment. I'd no heart for it. We'd been through enough – both of us – and the idea of piling on more pain repelled me.

I could have hazarded a guess at what Steevie thought of me, but I could live with it.

All that I knew for sure is, I wanted to be as happy as possible for as long as I'd got, and my every second was so much better with Hugh than without him.

At the end of that summer, Sofie and Kiara came home from Switzerland. In some ways, life was easier: there were fewer people thronging the house now that Neeve had her own place. For the same reason, we had more money. In addition, Sofie had matured so there was less drama, less worry.

But it was as if Hugh and I had embarked on a new marriage. Our expectations of each other were more realistic and the previous innocence was gone. It felt somewhat sad.

And then, you know, it didn't. Then we just got on with things.

Eventually, my anger storms dispersed. (Probably around the same time as our sex life reverted to normal levels.)

'We need to go.' Kiara brought me back to the present. 'Sofie and Dad can't leave until we've all left.'

Everyone ran for their cars and the front lawn cleared with remarkable speed, until only Hugh, Sofie and I were left.

'See you there.' I kissed Hugh.

'Mum!' Neeve yelled from her car. She was driving Kiara and me. 'Come *on*.'

'Can't you come with me?' Hugh asked.

'In the wedding car with you and Sofie? No, you big eejit.'

'I don't want to be without you.'

'You'll see me in forty minutes.' But I knew what he meant. As we'd got older, we'd become more dependent on each other.

'What if I make a show of her, walking her up the aisle? If I cry? If I trip and take her down with me?'

That made me laugh. 'You won't.'

'Mum!'

'Coming!'

As Neeve drove, she revisited the matter of Sofie's wedding being held outdoors.

'An open-air ceremony in *Ireland*, even in August, is risk-taking that borders on psychopathy.' Despite countless people 'having a quiet word' no one had been able to dissuade Sofie from having her wedding at Apple Blossom Farm.

'But the weather today is lovely,' Kiara said.

'For now,' Neeve said darkly. 'It could change at the drop of a hat, right? What kills me is that Sofie pretends to be such a push-over, but she's the most stubborn person I've ever met.'

'Maybe everything will turn out grand,' I said.

And maybe it would.

'Where the hell is this place?' Neeve asked.

We'd turned off the motorway on to a narrow road, made even narrower by the lush vegetation of late summer crowding over walls and fences into our path.

'It's menacing, isn't it? The way those bushes are?'

'It's here!' I cried. 'In here.' We turned off the road and bumped along a track, past a whitewashed farmhouse. 'Here they all are!'

Suddenly lots of people were milling around in the sunshine, their fancy duds fitting in unexpectedly well with all the verdant beauty. I spotted Joe and Siena, Declyn and Hayden, and the groom, looking somewhat grey around the gills. Close by were his mother and two sisters, rocking some serious hat action. I caught a glimpse of Mum's face: she seemed extremely put out.

And there was Urzula, looking haggard and as thin as ever. I was glad to see her: it would have hurt Sofie if she hadn't come.

Joe's sons, Finn, Pip and Kit – each more lanky and awkward-looking than the next – were acting as ushers. Kit, his Adam's apple the size of a small car, said, 'Amy, would you like to be ushered?'

'Right so.'

'That way.' He pointed at a path through gnarled trees, their branches heavy with fruit.

At least there was a wooden walkway so that my heels didn't sink into the soft earth.

The clearing opened up to reveal a hundred white chairs, organized on two sides of a makeshift aisle, which led to a delicate pergola threaded with flowers and small apples.

The chairs were garlanded with lustrous ribbons blowing in the light breeze. I could actually smell the apples from the orchard – then, right into my ear, Neeve said, 'One heavy shower, and those chairs and the pergola, the whole lot'll be swept away!'

'Stop it, you killjoy. This is lovely.'

'She's here,' someone called. 'Seats. Positions!'

David darted to the pergola, followed by his best man and the celebrant. The guests filed hurriedly into seats, then the music started.

First up the aisle, walking at the speed of a tortoise, as instructed, came Maisey the ring-bearer, then Kiara, followed by Neeve, smirking away good-oh. Finally, Sofie and Hugh stood where the red carpet began. Sofie looked extraordinarily happy and beautiful. I knew I couldn't shed a single tear because if I started I might find it hard to stop.

Hugh said something to Sofie, she patted him reassuringly, tucked her hand inside his arm and they began their walk.

Swallowing the painful lump in my throat, I watched them. In his unfamiliar suit Hugh looked like a handsome stranger. There was so much love in my heart for him and for Sofie and for Neeve and for Kiara that it pained me.

Hugh was smiling and smiling, and his eyes were shiny, as if he might burst with pride. When he and Sofie reached the pergola, he gently released her hand and 'gave' her to David, then stepped out of the aisle into the spot I'd been keeping for him. He slid his hand into mine.

'Yes,' I whispered, answering his unspoken question. 'You were great. You couldn't have been better.'

Acknowledgements

Thank you to everyone at Michael Joseph for publishing me with such enthusiasm, flair and attention to detail, with particular gratitude to the renowned Liz Smith.

Thank you to Jonathan Lloyd, king of the agents, and all at Curtis Brown for taking such lovely care of me and my books.

Thank you to Annabel Robinson and all at FMcM for keeping my books in the public eye.

Thank you to my foreign language publishers around the world, I'm very grateful for the chance to connect with so many readers.

Several people read this book as I wrote it and gave invaluable feedback – sincere thanks to Suzanne Benson, Jenny Boland, Roisin Ingle, Cathy Kelly, Caitriona Keyes, Mammy Keyes, Rita-Anne Keyes, Colm O'Gorman and Louise O'Neill.

Especial and heartfelt gratitude to Kate Thompson, who read countless drafts of this book and kept the faith when I'd none left myself.

Thanks to Betsey Martian from Twitter for the word 'Scandilusts'.

Thank you to Bronagh Kingston, who donated to Carol Hunt, to have a character named after her.

Thank you to Caroline Snowdon who donated to Highgate Has Heart (who help refugees), to have a character named after her.

Thank you to Himself, who is forever in my corner. His belief in my writing is unwavering, his support is constant and his criticism is kind and constructive. None of it would be possible without him.

Thank you to you, my beloved readers, for sticking with me all these years and in particular for your patience for this book. I hope it won't be as long for the next one . . .

Some information on the Serbian trip that Amy makes: Dušanka Petrović is real, she lives in Jagodina, an hour and a half's drive from Belgrade. I love her paintings but could find almost no information about her. However, in November 2016, connections were made and I went to Serbia to meet her.

Thank you Ljiljana Keyes for making the phone calls which eventually tracked Dusanka down. Thank you to Marica Vračević, Nina Krstić and all the wonderful staff at the Museum of Naïve and Marginal Art in Jagodina who faciliated the introduction. Thank you to my beloved nieceling, Ema Keyes, who came with myself and Himself and translated admirably in the museum, the hotel and with Dušanka herself.

Sadly, Hotel Zaga in Belgrade is imaginary. Instead I stayed in a hotel called Square Nine – it's fabaliss, but instead of the folk art décor of the imaginary hotel, it's sleek and mid-century modern.

Finally, Louise Moore has been my editor, publisher and beloved friend for the past twenty years. From the word go, she championed my writing and galvanised entire teams of people to go to bat for me. She is visionary, passionate, fierce and unstinting on behalf of my books. She has made my career and as an expression of my gratitude, this book is dedicated to her.